A FIGHT FOR LIFE

"I am your bloodmaster, Simon. You *will* obey me!"

Eyes glittering with rage, Franz stalked toward his brother. The force of his will spread through the room, causing the other vampires to drop to their knees and the humans to stumble back. Simon's eyes were sick with pain, but he still stood proudly.

"No."

Franz's fist crashed down on Simon's face and sent him reeling to the floor. He spun away, then charged back as a wolf, slashing at his brother's throat. Simon hit the furry chest just before the sharp fangs clicked shut, then bounded up, on four feet. The two wolves circled, then leapt to the attack. Simon slashed at Franz's suddenly exposed head, but realized too late that it was a trap. Franz's jaws twisted upward, under his brother's chin, and Simon felt the cruel fangs in his flesh . . .

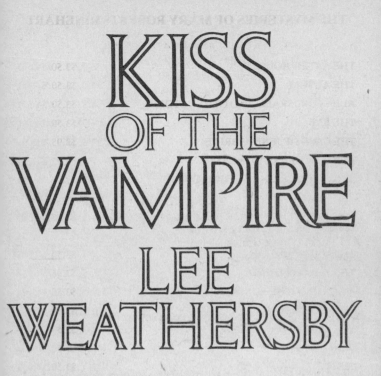

KISS
OF THE
VAMPIRE
LEE WEATHERSBY

ZEBRA BOOKS
KENSINGTON PUBLISHING CORP.

This book is dedicated to my parents,
Pete and Myrna Weathersby,
in gratitude for their unfailing example of
courage, honesty, generosity, and love.

ZEBRA BOOKS

are published by

Kensington Publishing Corp.
475 Park Avenue South
New York, NY 10016

First printing: March, 1992

Printed in the United States of America

Prologue

They pushed the heavy crate carefully, as if handling unstable explosives. As the three men shoved from the side and ends, a fourth stood back and supervised, holding a Bible and a large cross in front of him. He alternately cursed their efforts and recited the Lord's Prayer as they carefully, fearfully, pushed the ebony crate. It slid slowly on the deck, sticking every few inches as it approached the side of the freighter. A foot from the edge, it stopped.

"It won't go no further, Cap'n." One of the men panted with exertion and fear. He looked up, squinting against the bright sun, to see the bulky figure of the ship's master outlined against the stark blue sky.

The captain roared at them angrily, "Make it go!" He took a step closer and stopped. Close to the box it felt like winter, cold and dark; from this distance he could feel waves of frigid anger that chilled his blood and wrenched at his stomach. He stepped back hastily.

"Get Conners up here." He pushed the nearest sailor toward the hold and stepped back into the heat of a summer's day.

"Aye, sir." The boy ran off quickly, grateful for even a short reprieve.

The captain could feel their eyes on him, watching, always watching for any sign of weakness. They were desperate now. If he faltered and allowed his voice, expression, or demeanor to show the slightest hint of doubt or fear, the crew would break. They would run and hide until it was too late — for

5

them and for him. He raised his Bible, opened it at random and held it as a shield, reading loudly:

"For the morning is to them even as the shadow of death: if one knows them, they are in the terrors of the shadow of death."

He slammed it shut on Job 24, wondering how in hell he had turned to that particular passage.

The boy returned slowly, his footsteps dragging. He raked his fingers through his sunbleached blond hair and his eyes slid reluctantly to the casket. "Conners won't come, sir."

"It wasn't a request, Wilkins." The captain's growl became a furious whisper. "You tell that cowardly son of a bitch that if he doesn't get his black ass up here right now, I'll throw him off next."

The first mate's head popped into view from below decks. It was a toss-up as to which he feared more, the captain or the crate. He swallowed audibly as the captain glared at him, then he climbed reluctantly up the ladder.

"We only need a little push." The captain lowered his voice persuasively, watching as six feet four inches of muscle sidled crabwise across the deck. "Just one little push and it will go over."

Conners's eyes rolled fearfully until the whites gleamed in the bright sunlight. The bitter stink of fear drifted toward the captain and he choked back the sharp words he wanted to scream. Instead, he walked over and put a consoling hand on the first mate's arm. Now was not the time to bully and bluster.

"C'mon, mate. With all of us pushing it will be over in a second." He coaxed the big man forward, toward the gap in the rail. The others closed in behind them. They faced the big box and the day darkened. A small cloud scudded in from the north.

"We can't do this, Cap'n. He'll get us for this. He'll kill us!" Conners backed up a step and bumped into one of the crewmen. He jerked around violently.

"Shut up and push that damned box over, you stupid coward. If you're scared now, think how you'll feel once it gets dark," the captain snapped, his fist clenched. The deck rocked under them, but no one noticed.

Larger, darker clouds, as if in reminder of the darkness to come, moved unnaturally fast to join the first. The wind cooled and freshened noticeably. A soft creak jerked their attention back to the deck.

"It moved!" Conners shrieked wildly and led the rush toward the hatch. The captain was a step behind them. He used the heavy Bible in his hand to swing ferociously at the nearest back. It connected solidly and sent the crewman reeling into Conners, who tripped and started a chain reaction.

"Stop!" The captain roared. The habit of obedience was strong. They turned back reluctantly. As he continued, his eyes and voice had a soft, hypnotic intensity. "A squall's comin' in. We got no radio, no help, and the sun is going down. We can't make Mobile by nightfall. If he has anything to say about it, we won't make port at all. He'll kill us all tonight. We'll just be another ghost ship, driftin' into port. He'll kill us just like he killed the others, Sid and Tom and Johnny-boy. Look around! Ain't but half of us left. We got to get him now before he can stop us."

Conners moved first. He was not known as the bravest member of the crew. His size and strength had protected him from all but the most foolhardy of brawlers, and his willingness and good humor had protected him from the sneers that would have followed a smaller coward. His massive shoulders squared, and his dark eyes were cold as he moved reluctantly toward the ominous black coffin. His feet scuffed the deck and he almost tripped, but he kept moving. He scrubbed his wet palms on his jeans and panted with fear as the captain and crew stared after him with awe and terror. He took a deep breath and held it, squatted down and pushed his shoulder against the crate.

Lightning cracked from the sea, so close that the ozone fouled the air. The captain roused himself with a start.

"You goin' to let him do it on his own?" He moved the crew with cuffs and curses, forcing them to the edge of the deck. They shoved tentatively at the box.

7

It moved slowly at first, rasping across the deck like a file across teeth. Conners gasped for breath and the stench turned his face yellow.

"I'm gonna be sick." Tears ran down his face as he gasped out the words.

"Then puke on the box," the captain snarled back.

They struggled to push it overboard. The gloom increased as the squall spattered the first raindrops onto the pitching deck.

The crate gave way unexpectedly as the deck lurched with a sudden wave. The wind blew the sour, acrid smell of death into their faces. Conners gasped and leaned over the box as it teetered unsteadily on the edge. He retched violently, tears leaking from under his tightly closed lids. His hand, groping blindly for support, brushed the slick, cold coffin and stuck. Unbalanced, it toppled over as if in slow motion. His flesh stretched where it touched the ornate box, as if it had suddenly been fastened with some quick setting glue. He took one step forward, then another, a look of disbelief on his face.

Conners screamed horribly as his hand and arm were pulled forward. His body leaned over the side and his feet did a macabre dance as he fought frantically to stop his fall. His free arm waved wildly. His companions grabbed for him, reaching through the railing as he was pulled over the side. The captain managed to catch his hand, but it was wrenched from his grip as the huge sailor fell, still attached by his skin to the shiny casket. His scream ended suddenly as he hit the water, then started again as both man and crate bobbed to the surface.

"Help me! God! Please! Help me!" His words were interrupted as waves splashed and broke over his head. One arm waved desperately. His body swung around and he kicked at the wood.

"Let go. Let go my hand. Sweet Mary, Mother of God, it's got my hand! Dear Jesus, help me!" He choked as a wave broke over his head.

The captain screamed impotently as the coffin drifted away. "Lower the boat. Burt, Jim, go get him!"

No one moved.

8

He took one step toward the lifeboat, then glanced back, over the water. He was the first to see the triangular fin cutting through the choppy water.

"Shark!" The word ripped through his throat and burst into the air.

"Shark!" Three voices screamed discordantly as the horrible spell was broken. Fear battled with relief, and lost. This was a natural creature, something that could be fought. One man rushed to the nearest life ring and flung it over the rail. The captain bellowed orders as he watched the fin close in on the screaming man. Only Conners seemed unaware of this new danger. He still beat wildly on the coffin with his free hand while the other twitched and writhed against the dark wood, black on black. The captain screamed at him again.

"Shaaaarrrrk!"

The fin was only a yard away when Conners's hand came free. He flailed at the water and backstroked into the ragged jaws of the shark.

He sank suddenly, and came up screaming. One arm ended at the elbow and blood gushed from the stump.

"Lower that boat. Faster," the captain yelled.

Conners was jerked under again. This time his screams were weaker as he bobbed to the surface. The boat hit the water and the captain realized for the first time that no one had been brave enough to go down in it. He watched the small boat toss aimlessly in the waves. Even through the rough water, the captain's practiced eye could make out a spreading red stain.

Conners screamed one more time, weakly, hopelessly, a final protest against death. His body surfaced a yard from the boat, face down and inert. A wave washed over him and he turned slowly, almost weightlessly. His head was pulled under suddenly, and they watched in horror as what was left of his body turned upward.

One leg was gone. Shreds of flesh hung from the empty, gleaming white hip joint. The other leg ended at mid-thigh. A shaft of splintered bone poked out from torn, bloody flesh.

The captain turned away. He tried to control his nausea, but it was a losing battle. As he vomited over the side, the eerie

9

storm broke around them. The ship pitched violently. Rain stung his eyes as he searched the sea for that awful black box. He found it and watched, entranced. Sounds of sea, storm, and men faded as realization hit him.

There was one clear patch of blue water, untouched by rain or gray foaming waves. In it, the coffin drifted tranquilly south, driven by the storm, but not touched by it.

The hair on his arms writhed as the captain turned resignedly back to his ship. He knew what was to come. He flinched as lightning leapt from the lifeboat to the sky and thunder crashed through his ears. Choking billows of smoke brought tears to his eyes.

He was dimly aware of the bustle around him as the word was passed that *it* had been thrown off the ship and the crew came up from below. They were still scared but they were ready to take their posts against the storm. Only half the men he had left shore with still survived. Someone asked for orders and he shook his head wearily. There was no use.

His eyes turned back to the sea. It had been a good life, mostly. Maybe a little lonely, but he had few regrets. His wife was long gone. His only son was an accountant for a tax firm; a job the captain could neither understand nor approve. He shrugged, regretting briefly that he hadn't tried harder. They had hated and feared the sea. Now he wished he had not been so contemptuous of their fear. He tried to remember their faces, but nothing came.

His eyes closed sadly as the lightning struck again. The ship shook as the fuel tanks blew. There was one instant of searing heat and anguish before he died. The storm raged on as the ship sank.

The lone survivor chuckled softly from the safety of his earth-filled coffin.

Now to get himself out of this mess. Luckily, they weren't far from land when they had tossed him over. His bed rocked gently, almost comfortingly, but he knew the deadly threat that moving water represented to him. At least he didn't have to worry about bad weather. He chuckled again at the thought.

First, transportation. He would have to locate a sympathetic mind, control it, and arrange a rescue before. . . . For the first time he realized his mistake. The small rain clouds had been over land when he had called them. He had brought them down from the north and prodded them into becoming a storm. Now it was driving him south into the Gulf of Mexico.

Away from land. Away from help.

His mind reached out, as it had for the cloud, but this time he was searching for a human mind. He had to find one before he was out of range. His thoughts flew north to Pensacola, only fifty miles away. He searched desperately, but the few susceptible minds would take too long to control. He found one candidate, but when he investigated further it was unacceptable. It would take too long to break it out of the asylum. He moved east along the coast, found one that might work, then hesitated, torn with indecision. Should he put all his effort and the little remaining time into trying to subdue one that might work, or should he move on to find a better one?

Something drove him on. If he had to come back, there might still be time.

He found what he needed in Ft. Walton Beach, Florida. His mind leapt with joy as he recognized the mind as he would have recognized his own signature.

"Simon!" His mind screamed joyously. "Brother, I am here. I need you. Come to me." He commanded powerfully.

Chapter One

Casey's Book Stop was Cassandra Lane Brighton's pride and joy. Six rooms of mystery and excitement, information and imagination, romance and history. Over one hundred thousand books, each with its own story, each with something different to say and a unique way of saying it. It didn't matter that they were used and sometimes worn; someone, somewhere, would enjoy them again.

The double glass doors led from the outside into the main room, which was dedicated to best sellers and historical romances. A doorway to the right led into Casey's office, with the counter parallel to the back wall so that she could see anyone who came in. Her desk faced the far wall and was usually covered inches deep in papers, bills, catalogues, advertising posters, and pamphlets. The children's section filled the rest of the room with books and comics. On the floor were boxes labelled Goodwill and Vet's Hosp, and occasionally, boxes of unfiled books.

Left of the main room was a short hall that led to a room filled with modern romances. Straight through the main room was another hallway with three rooms leading from it. The rooms and hall held stacks and racks of horror and occult, science fiction and westerns, mysteries, adventure, and nonfiction.

These six rooms comprised half of Casey's life. Sometimes she thought it was the best half.

Business often picked up in the late afternoon. This time of day customers would stop by on their way home from work to pick up a book for the evening or the weekend. Friends would drop in for a minute and stay for an hour chatting with Casey and each other and choosing books while she waited on customers. It made for a congenial atmosphere, although waiting on customers and chatting with friends at the same time created a certain amount of confusion.

"Did you find what you wanted, Mrs. Wiltz?" Casey turned from her desk to the counter and smiled at the slender, middle-aged woman.

"Oh, yes, Casey, but if you get in any new Harlequins, especially about nurses, will you hold them for me? I may not be able to pick them up right away, but . . ."

"I'm glad you reminded me. A woman called this morning and she's bringing in six old ones that she wants to trade. I know they're old, but there may be some that you haven't read. Would you like for me to hold them for you? I'll give you first refusal on them if you'd like."

"I better not. Thanks, but I could never take that many at one time." The woman looked almost guilty as she refused the offer. "Jerry wouldn't like that."

The man by the window shifted impatiently and asked, "Is it a date then?"

Casey ignored the question and looked at the woman sympathetically, wishing that there were some way she could ease her discomfort. She had never met "Jerry," but she knew the situation as well as an outsider could. Estelle Wiltz was obviously terrified of her husband, and it showed all the more for what she never said. Now her big brown eyes, almost hidden by plain brown glasses, seemed to waver and blur behind the thick lenses. The secondhand paperback books that were Casey's specialty usually ran in price from seventy-five cents to $3.50, but Casey had never known her to choose one that cost over $2.50. Those were getting harder and harder to find nowadays. Even used books were expensive, and Estelle had read and returned for credit most of the cheaper ones.

"You may still have some credit. Let me check." Casey

14

made a show of going through her account cards and came up with one triumphantly. Fifteen cents. "That's right, you have $1.50. Remember, you brought in several books last week, didn't you?"

"It was only two books, and they were just some that the kids had lying around. I don't think it could be that much." She looked suspicious of the sudden windfall, so Casey put on her most bored expression.

"That explains it then. That boy of yours just loves science fiction and we give top prices for those. Most people don't seem to want to trade them in. Are these the only ones you want today?"

"Yes, I guess so. And if you would hold one or two of the ones coming in, I'd love to at least look at them." Her initial suspicion trailed off into vague pleasure. Casey suppressed a flutter of irritation. The poor woman really shouldn't be let out alone. She needed someone around to protect her. It would have been just as easy for someone to take advantage of her as to help her. Why was she so damn humble anyway? There was a woman who should have had a lot of pride. She had brought her children in more than once, and a nicer, more well-behaved bunch of kids would be hard to find. They had trooped in behind their mother, the oldest carefully carrying the youngest. Neat clean kids in clean old clothes, they ranged in age from less than a year old to fourteen. They didn't play hide and seek between the racks, or run through the store yelling and screaming. They treated books with respect. They even agreed almost quietly on two books among the five of them, and watched with shy eyes as their mother dug deep into her purse to pay for them.

"Casey? Would you like to go sailing after dinner tonight?" Eric broke in again. His fingers beat a rapid tattoo on the window.

Casey thought about those quiet children with their big, haunted eyes, about the youngest girl who had a hunger for words in her face, and about the children's books and the comics that hadn't been selling well lately.

"Mrs. Wiltz, would you mind doing me a favor?" Casey

15

drawled the words with Southern sugar on them. "It's just a small thing really. I have some comic books and some fairy tales that I need to get rid of to make space for more that are coming in. They aren't really appropriate for the Veteran's Hospital." She moved over to the children's section and sorted rapidly through the racks. "Would you mind dropping them in the trash on your way out? Or maybe your kids could give them away at school. Kids might enjoy reading even these old things." Casey watched as Estelle left with a dazed smile on her face.

"If you keep that up, you'll wind up giving away the whole store."

Reluctantly, she turned back to Eric Tyler, her friend and neighbor. He was leaning against the window frame, outlined in a splash of sunlight. The right side of his profile was a study in planes and angles, the left was in shadow. He was a little above medium height, with brown hair and hazel eyes, and the scowl on his face looked permanently engraved. She stared at him accusingly.

He tried once more. "We can talk over dinner."

"Talk? About what? *My* land, *my* beach, *my* home?"

"I just want another two acres, Casey. It's not that much and—"

"Beachfront. You want two acres of my beach and you can forget it. It's not for sale." Casey watched his eyes light up.

"That's what you said three years ago," he countered, "about the land my house is built on."

"I'm beginning to think I should have stuck to it," she muttered. He was enjoying this, the bastard. He had probably been one of those rotten brats who would hit a beehive with a stick at the church picnic, just to see what would happen. There was just something in him that liked stirring things up.

"How much beach can one person use? Besides, you'll always have access, just like now, you know that. What's the big deal anyway?"

"It's my land, that's the big deal. My grandfather's land

16

that he left to me in his will. I already sold you almost half of it. You've got plenty of beachfront. Build your dock on that." She shook her head firmly and settled her considerable bulk on the stool behind the counter.

"I told you I had the contractor out. That little piece of land is just perfect for a dock. The deep water comes in close and there's a ridge of rock just under the sand. It's just perfect." He leaned forward urgently as he spoke.

"It's just perfectly mine and it's going to stay mine and that's all there is to it." She stated flatly.

"C'mon, Casey. You can use the boats any time you want."

"Boats? How many are you going to have? And how big is this monstrosity supposed to be?"

"Just big enough for a few tiny little boats. You know how you love to sail. You can take the sailboat out any time you like. We can take moonlight sails from our own dock. Maybe a little champagne, swimming off the boat. You'll love it." His voice lowered intimately.

"No." She swiveled the stool around, still shaking her head. He walked over to the counter and circled it to face her.

"Why not?" The tone was reasonable, but she could see a muscle jumping in his cheek.

"I don't want to look out my window and see a dock and six boats instead of beach. I don't want the gas scum fouling my water, and I don't want to borrow your damn boats!" She smiled at him sweetly and contrarily swiveled the chair away. He circled the counter the other way.

"Three boats. Just three. One sailboat, I figure about a thirty footer; one small power boat, something fast; and one for deep-sea fishing." His hazel eyes gazed deeply into hers and his voice was soft and intimate.

"No." She matched his tone perfectly.

"I'll give you more than it's worth. Whatever you ask." He had given up on that approach and now he was all business.

"Don't you dare start flashing your money at me! I don't need it."

17

"You didn't seem to mind my money three years ago. I paid you a fair price for that land. You couldn't have started this bookstore without it." He fired back at her.

"Which is the only reason I sold it to you. I didn't know you'd try to take the rest. What will you want next? My house?"

"Casey." He stopped suddenly and took a deep breath. "We'll talk about it later, at dinner, okay?"

"I told you," she replied sullenly. "I'm on a diet."

"You're always on a diet. What is it this time, carrots and celery?" His amusement showed with the quirk of an eyebrow. He had the naturally slim figure that she would have done anything to get. *Anything but diet,* she thought.

"Nope. It's supposed to be a health diet. Vitamins, minerals, and herbs. I think the real idea is to fill you so full of pills that there's no room for real food."

"How long have you been on it?"

"About a week."

"Then you need a break. Have you lost any weight yet?"

"If you have to ask." Casey sighed, thinking of all the hungry hours ahead. They stretched into days and weeks and months of diets, exercise, and starvation. Was this any way to live? What would one good meal hurt?

"So why do you always seem to start a new diet the week before I ask you out to dinner?" He noticed her start of surprise and wondered idly which nerve he had struck this time. Casey was so touchy about her weight and diets that it was almost impossible to avoid hurting her.

"Where did you want to go?" she asked, ignoring his question. She knew very well why it was that she started a new diet a week or so before he asked her out. Maybe one day he would figure it out too, but until then, she would enjoy his company.

"There's a new Italian place on the Strip," he replied, referring to the Miracle Strip Parkway that ran along the Florida coast of the Gulf of Mexico. "I thought we might try it out. Antipasto, veal parmesan, maybe linguini with clam sauce?" He watched the hunger hit her eyes and smiled. He

18

would have interesting company tonight for dinner, and so what if no one's head turned to watch her walk by? Casey's good-natured humor and wit would more than make up for her double chin. "What time do you close up shop tonight?"

"Seven. I'll have to go home and change." She thought wistfully of the new dress in her closet. It was a size smaller than she was. She had bought it for inspiration. Could she have lost enough in one week to squeeze into it? Not bloody likely, but she would try it on just to make sure. There was always her old navy blue standby, if worse came to worst.

"Seven-thirty, your place. And we'll talk about the land." He opened the door for a young man in uniform with an armful of books, then kept it open as an attractive black woman came in behind him. Casey kept a wary eye on Eric and the woman as they stopped to chat. Beverly Watkins was a good friend, as was Eric, but just because Casey liked them both didn't mean that they liked each other.

The customer had brought in books to sell and Casey divided them absently into two piles, one larger than the other, but her eyes kept wandering to the door. Even at this distance, she could see the bulge of muscle in Eric's arm as he propped the door open, and the way the yellow shirt he wore was pulled tight across his chest.

"I only buy the ones I think I can sell." She reluctantly turned her attention back to the airman, then watched with relief as Eric and Bev said goodbye to each other, apparently on good terms. Beverly strode to the desk, casually pushed some papers aside, and perched on the edge. She waited impatiently, one foot tapping the air, while Casey chatted with the customer.

"I'll give you $7.50 cash. Or, if you'd like credit, that'll be $4.15 in science fiction and five dollars even in everything else."

"What about the rest of them?" he asked without much hope.

"I can't use them. Some of them are good sellers, but I already have several copies. You could take them to another store. There's one in Mary Esther. Do you know where the cutoff is?"

"Uh, I don't think so. I'm still pretty new here."

"Where are you from?"

"Minnesota. It's beautiful there, but this is incredible. Like something in a movie. I've never seen water so clear or sand so white."

"We call it sugar sand. Did you know that it's so different from other sand that geologists gave it a special name? Pensacola white. It's the only place in the world you can find it. I'm Casey Brighton, by the way."

"Mike Boyd. I go to the beach every chance I get. I hear the fishing is good, too. I've never been surf-casting before, though."

"The fishing's great, but if you go out surf-casting, keep a sharp eye out for sharks." The shiver caught her by surprise. She glanced at the air conditioner vent, then smiled and nodded as he looked at her doubtfully. "No big deal, just be careful." Before he left, Casey gave him directions to the other bookstore.

She turned back to see Bev swing her long legs moodily from the desk and begin to pace, ignoring Casey's annoyance as she straightened the papers Bev had pushed aside.

Beverly Watkins was one of the top real estate agents in the area. Her clothes were tailored to make that tall, slat-thin figure look stylish instead of skinny. Her white blouse was blindingly bright and complimented her glinting teeth and the blue-white corneas of her dark brown eyes. Her tan skirt and jacket set off her chocolate brown skin and black fuzzy hair. If she hadn't chosen to stay in the Florida Panhandle area and be a real estate agent, she might have made it as a model, but it was her keen intelligence and sly sense of humor that Casey liked best about her.

"I was going to ask if you wanted to share a pizza tonight." Bev's voice was rich and deep.

Casey didn't answer for a moment, then asked, "What's the matter?"

"Matter? Why does anything have to be the matter? I just felt like a pizza."

20

"C'mon, Bev. It's Friday night. Are you and Doug having problems again?"

"We don't have problems. I have problems. He thinks everything's great." She leaned against the window where Eric had been earlier. "He just doesn't understand how hard I worked to get where I am."

"And you don't understand how he could be happy working at a gas station the rest of his life."

"Well, I don't! He could be anything he wanted to, if he would just shut up with that 'down-trodden Black' routine. But he just keeps pumping gas and complaining how unfair the world is, and how hard he has to work."

"But you keep going out with him," Casey commented.

"He's such a hunk! How can I help it? And he's not stupid, he's just . . ."

"Lazy?"

"No! You know how hard he works . . ." Her voice trailed off as she noticed the teasing note in Casey's voice. "Okay, maybe he is, in a way. And I know you've heard it all before. Anyway, I'm going to back off for awhile. Maybe I'll even find someone else." Her generous lips pouted as she stepped back into the shadows, away from the hot sunlight streaming through the glass.

"You know, Bev, Doug isn't going to change, and neither are you. When it comes to ambition, you have more than your share and from what I've seen, Doug has none at all. If you don't find someone else right away, maybe the break will be good for you." Her voice caught as she shivered again. She stared at her friend intently and blinked, squinting against the glare.

"What's wrong? Do I have a smudge on my nose?"

"No, it's nothing."

"C'mon, Casey. You look like you've seen a ghost." The light softened suddenly as dark clouds rolled in.

"Nothing. It was just a trick of the light. For a minute there, it looked like I could see straight through your skin to the bones. It . . . I . . ." She took a deep breath and tried again. "The light and shadows made your

21

face look like a skull."

"Hey, kid, you've been on that diet too long. Your eyes are playing tricks on you."

"Yeah, that must be it." Casey shrugged, "Maybe you're right about the diet."

"Speaking of diets, you decided to go out with Eric tonight. Don't tell me, let me guess. You started a new diet a week ago, so Eric is probably getting tired of his latest little cutie, right?" Her voice was sarcastically sympathetic.

"Is it that obvious?"

"Only to those who really care about you. Don't worry, Eric will never notice."

"Ouch. That's hitting below the belt," Casey complained.

"This from someone who just gave me a lecture on incompatibility and the virtues of being alone?"

"Yeah, well. Maybe I was talking to myself."

"If you weren't you should have been. And I could add a few things, like, if he doesn't like you the way you are, then losing weight won't help."

"I'm not losing weight for him," she protested loudly. "I'm doing it for myself. He just serves as inspiration. And I need a lot of inspiration."

"Don't we all." Bev's lewd smile gave the words double meaning. "And Doug is mine."

"Then why don't you call him and get inspired tonight?" Casey grinned back.

"I will if you will."

"Forget it then. Eric and I are pals." The last word came out with more force and bitterness than she had intended. "He thinks I'm just one of the 'guys.' "

"Eric Tyler thinks anyone over a size ten is 'just one of the guys.' "

"Oh, Bev, I don't even know if it's Eric that I really want. I don't think we could ever make anything permanent out of it. And maybe that's okay, too. Not everything has to be permanent. But I don't know if it's me he really cares about, or just entertainment for an evening."

"Case, I've been out with men like that. And to them sex

is about as important as a sneeze; it's just more fun. You deserve more than that."

"Damn right I do! But until I get it, I guess I'll go out with Eric. And I'll worry about sneezing if I catch cold."

"Just don't run a fever over him unless his temperature is up, too."

After Bev went into the back rooms to browse, Casey sat for a few minutes, watching the storm build and listening to the occasional rumble of thunder. Afternoon thundershowers were an almost daily occurrence in spring and early summer, and she enjoyed the brief, violent flashes of nature. The strong, cooling winds seemed to blow away the heat and dust and leave an illusion of tranquility in their wake.

She couldn't see the Gulf from here, but she knew that the water would be gray and rough, the sand patterned with miniature volcanic craters from the force of the raindrops. Her office window faced north, and she noticed that instead of coming out of the south or west, as such storms usually did, these dark clouds were rushing straight for her, driving the wind and rain before them.

Fire and ice. That was her first impression.

She hadn't heard the bell on the doorjamb ring, much less the outer door open, but she looked away from the window and he was there, standing in the doorway. He was tall with wavy gold hair that formed a crown above icy blue eyes. His broad shoulders were outlined in a silvery gray raincape against the dark storm clouds, and his flared red collar was pulled up now to shield his neck against the storm.

"May I come in?" His voice was deep and calm. It vibrated softly inside her head, or maybe it was just an echo of thunder. His foot hesitated on the sill.

"Please do," she replied. Still under the calm spell of the storm, his presence did not intrude on her peace of mind. She smiled up at him and watched him smile in return. She watched in fascination as he shook the rain from the gray cape, revealing a dark red lining, and hung it on one of the hooks near the door. His long sleeved black shirt and black

23

jeans must have been uncomfortably warm on such a hot summer evening. He was certainly one of the most handsome men to come into the shop in a long time. Perhaps a trifle over six feet tall, slim and elegant even in jeans, he had a deep chest and strong shoulders. He moved with the unconscious grace of a natural athlete.

As he turned to face her, she noticed long strong hands, held as if poised to caress some valuable, delicate piece of crystal. On the index finger of his right hand was a carved ruby ring. Her eyes did not follow the detail, but moved to his face.

His face was chiseled rather than carved. A high, broad forehead with eyebrows that were three shades darker than his hair emphasized deep-set blue eyes and a fair complexion. A nose like a ridge, strong and proud, set off by high, flat cheekbones. It was a face that could have been cruel, but was softened by an expressive mouth and sensitive, finely molded lips.

Her cursory inspection had turned into such a detailed examination that it would have embarrassed her if she hadn't moved her eyes up to meet his level gaze. That act took her mind off small matters of embarrassment and focused it on light blue eyes with just a hint of sea-gray, like the waters of the Gulf after a storm. They held a mocking glint that said he was perfectly aware of the impression he created. And he enjoyed it.

That telltale glint brought her back to earth with a resounding thud. She knew from hard experience that such good-looking men with thick blond hair and intelligent bright eyes rarely had time or inclination for a second look at overweight, behind-the-counter bookstore girls, even if they did own the shop. She took a deep breath and tried to retain her hold on reality.

"Is there something special I can help you find, sir?" she asked politely. Meanwhile a traitorous voice inside her head cried, "Me! Me!"

"Do you have any books on psychic phenomena? I'm especially interested in anything concerning re-

24

incarnation or past lives."

"Of course. Check the occult, horror and mystery room down the hall and to your left. It seems to me I bought something like that a few weeks ago, though I can't remember why. Try the second shelf." She had noticed a trace of an accent. British? Perhaps. It was too faint to identify. She led the way down the hall.

He had returned her gaze curiously. Her hair was a black so glossy that it caught the light and held it. Long and wavy, it hung past her shoulders and curled just above her full breasts. He felt the first, faint stirrings of hunger and wondered if she were busy tonight.

Her midnight blue eyes were startling under unusually heavy eyebrows and lashes. He noticed that her left eyebrow arched naturally into a peak that gave her expression an inquisitive look. Her eyes were wide-spaced, and a demanding intelligence looked boldly out at the world. Her skin glowed with a healthy rosiness under her tan, and she wore just enough makeup to minimize the roundness of her face. She carried a lot of excess weight, but she carried it like a queen. She would make a good companion for dinner, or even a night or two. He watched her walk down the hall ahead of him, and her movements were graceful and sure. He had felt her withdrawal, but he ignored it. It was not her choice to make.

"Are you the owner?" he asked.

"Owner, manager, clerk, and janitor. I'm Cassandra Lane Brighton. Casey."

"I have passed this way many times, but usually at night, when the store is closed. I am Simon Tepes Drake." The name was said with a certain unconscious arrogance, and Casey suffered an immediate urge to burst his bubble.

"Tepes? That's an odd name. Any relation to Vlad?" The words just seemed to pop out and she could have bitten her tongue. When you met a man whose middle name was Arnold, did you ask if he were related to Benedict? she silently chastised herself.

"I beg your pardon?" His gaze sharpened on her until she

25

was sure that he had understood exactly what she had said. The force of his eyes was a shock to her system, stimulating and smothering her at the same time, making it difficult to breathe. She forced out the words, "Never mind." She stumbled as she turned to go, suddenly needing more air than was available in this formerly bright, spacious room.

He turned to watch her leave. Where had that question come from? Out of the thousands of people in this area, out of the very select few to whom he would have offered his full name, what incredible mischance would cause her mental leap to connect Tepes to Vlad Tepes the Impaler, Vladimir Dracul of the Castle Dracula? If she knew that, what else did she know? His ears followed her light steps back to the office.

She is certainly full of surprises, he mused to himself. First dear old Uncle Vlad, then leaving of her own free will. Of course, he had not tried to hold her, but very few women voluntarily left while he was looking at them. He made his decision. She would be his for the evening, and for as long as he chose. It should be interesting.

As he turned back to browse, he heard the tinkle of the bell above the entrance door. Another customer, but that was no problem. He was in no hurry. It was dusk, and the sky had not cleared. She would be closing the shop soon. He would wait.

Fifty-five miles south, in the Gulf of Mexico, the crate tossed and whirled with the action of the water. Inside, the man was realizing the enormity of his mistake. He screamed his brother's name, over and over, as if sheer volume and intensity could carry over the distance between them. A particularly rough wave tumbled the box and he clawed at the sides, suddenly unsure of even his most basic refuge. The box steadied as he controlled himself and his emotions. The unnatural calm spot reappeared in the storm.

He sought his brother's mind again, projecting over the

26

water, calling for help. He found him readily, but again, there was no answer. He tried harder, willing him to respond, trying to control his desperation. He called with his childhood name, then the family name, then with the power of their shared blood, but there was nothing.

"You can hear me. I know you can hear me. I need help. Come to me." His desperation grew with the force of the waves. For the first time in centuries, fear crept into his heart.

"Please." He begged out loud, setting aside his pride. "Please, Brother, help me. I will never ask another thing of you. I will free you from your bondage to me. I will grant you any favor, just don't ignore me. Come and get me."

Convinced at last that there would be no response, anger grew in him. "You'll pay, Little Brother. Little Bastard! Don't pretend you don't hear me!" He yelled until the wind screamed with his fury and he feared that the towering waves would crush his ancient coffin like a rotten shell. When he gave up, his brow was beaded with bloody sweat.

He stared dully at the ebony wood, so close above him. Even in this absolutely lightless space, his eyes could make out the fine grain of each individual fiber.

"You'll pay for this," he muttered. "I'll make you pay." His bed gave a sudden lurch, and he swallowed dryly. His hatred for his brother focused his thoughts. His mind was so close to his brother's now that he could sense what was happening around him. He focused on the environment, trying to see with other eyes. It worked. He could read the interest surrounding a woman. Her mind glistened and shimmered, like oil over deep water, and he tried to break into it, to pick up some hint of weakness or vulnerability. He could find none. At this distance, her thoughts were closed to him, even when he tried to force her. Was this why his brother was interested? Or was it just hunger for a night's pleasure? He couldn't tell, but either way, the bastard would be disappointed.

He had no choice. He would have to wait for a suitable time and a suitable mind. He needed one that was warped

27

or crippled, handicapped in some basic way; one that he could take over, even if only for a short while. It didn't matter that his victim would never recover from the effects of having his mind taken over and used, forced into some action over which he had no control.

He would wait. And watch. And plan.

Casey walked slowly back to her office, thinking of the man she had just met. He was an odd one. Striking as well as handsome, and there was definitely something compelling about those blue eyes.

She sat at her desk and shuffled through a stack of papers. Bills, advertisements, letters, and more bills. She wrote one check, then stared out the window into the dusk. The rain was moving on now, and there was a streak of blue sky in the north, but the air still had the charged, expectant feeling of the storm.

She shrugged off a feeling of unease and opened a letter. The headache hit without warning. The center of her forehead felt as if a hot needle had been plunged into it. She scrubbed her brow with her fingers and they came away damp. Then it was gone. As suddenly as it had come, the needle disappeared, leaving only a slight ringing in her ears and a churning in her stomach. She put down the paper without reading it and walked to the window, staring out blindly. What was happening? Was she coming down with something? She had that uneasy, slightly out-of-focus feeling that sometimes presaged the flu.

She jumped as the doorbell jangled, then smiled as one of her favorite people made his way through the stacks into her office.

"Paul, it's good to see you. How's Clarise?"

"You mean you don't know? I'd figured you'd have talked to her at least twice today."

"She called once," Casey admitted, grinning, "but I had three customers waiting. Anything special going on?"

"I'm meeting her for dinner in town tonight. I was a little

28

early so I thought I'd pick up a book."

"Knowing your wife and my cousin, I'd say you've got plenty of time. The last time I was supposed to meet her, she was an hour late."

"She promised she'd be on time for once."

"And you believe her? Dreamer!" She grinned as Lieutenant Paul Bellecourt moved a stack of books from a chair and sat down. He leaned back comfortably and his feet barely touched the floor. He was the shortest cop on the force, but she had never heard of him having a problem because of it. Compact, well-built, with small hands and feet that were always precisely where they should be, he gave an impression of purpose and self-confidence. She had never seen him stumble, or fidget, or make any move that was less than precise and graceful. His face was sharp and sensitive. The bones showed clearly under the skin, making a ridge of his brow line and small hills of his cheekbones. His mouth was wide and generous, but half hidden under a thick mustache. His Cajun ancestry showed in his dark hair and eyes, but only came through occasionally in his speech. When he was excited, he had a tendency to slip into a dialect that sounded as if he had just swum out of the swamp. He had married Cascy's cousin Clarise eight years before.

"How's business?" he asked.

"Doing good. Of course it usually picks up this time of year. The tourists who tried to get all their summer tan in one day are burnt to a crisp and they usually pick up a book to read while they stay in their rooms and suffer."

Paul grinned knowingly. Tourists who got sunburned were fair game for jokes. You could always tell a tourist by the color: fish-belly white on the first day and lobster red for a week. The second week they were both, depending on which areas peeled first. Locals ranged from light to dark tan, depending on whether they stayed out of the sun completely, in which case reflected glare was enough to give even the most careful ones a healthy color, or whether they courted the sun and turned a deep, nut brown. Paul's face was the color of an old pecan shell.

29

"Many locals stop by?"

"A few. Mrs. Wiltz came by today. You know her, don't you?"

"Know her husband better. Bad one there. We've never been able to prove anything, but I'd say he's pretty rough on the wife and kids."

"Shame," Casey commented. "I've never met him, but she walks around like she was scared of her own shadow."

"My Daddy used to have a saying about people like him: he's breathin' air that could be put to better use."

"Speaking of such," she glanced through the glass doors and watched a man park a huge old Chevrolet next to Simon's Jaguar. "Look what crawled out from under a rock."

Paul looked up in time to see the door open carelessly into the side of the Jaguar and he winced. "I didn't know he could read."

"I'm not sure he can. He drags his wife in here about once a month, like he was trying to show her just how low she's sunk. They pick a fight and usually leave screaming at each other." She watched them walk up the steps. "But it's worse when he comes in alone."

Paul glanced at her sharply. "It's almost closing time," he suggested mildly.

She shook her head. "If I don't let them in this time, it'll be worse the next. He's harmless. Just kind of slimy." She broke off abruptly and forced a smile as they came through the door.

" 'Lo, Casey. Got anything good for me?"

"The comic book section is behind you."

Even his smile is disgusting, Casey thought as she looked at Billy Bazzel. He stood about six feet two, but his slump took off three inches. His beer belly looked out of place on his slat thin frame, like a small pouch hanging over a scarecrow's belt. His green shirt had dime-sized yellow patches of egg yolk dribbled down the front and his jeans were so stiff with filth that it made her skin crawl. As he leaned toward her, Casey moved unobtrusively back. Did the man really think that deodorant and cologne were a substitute for bathing?

"Hello, Laura, how are you?" She looked with compassion on what had once been a beautiful woman, but was now a female counterpoint to her common-law husband. Her hair was long and stringy, and her bright red lipstick had smeared onto one front tooth. As for the yellow dress she wore, Casey wouldn't have used it as a cleaning rag. There was little left to show that Laura was from a once proud family.

"I'm fine," she said huskily, sliding one hand down to pat her hip. "Have you been gaining weight again, Cassandra? I swear, I think your face gets rounder every time I see you." She smiled maliciously and moved toward the front room, ignoring Paul pointedly as he stepped out of her path. "Ah just came in for one of those trashy little romance novels. You must have hundreds of them and sweet ole Billy-boy won't have them in the shop."

"That's because they don't have pictures," Paul drawled as Laura sidled past him. Then she backed up unexpectedly as Beverly came through the other way.

"Hello, Laura." Bev's crisp voice held none of the casual drawl it did when she was talking to friends. She turned to Casey. "Case, you going to the Boardwalk tomorrow night? What about a swim? And a pizza later?"

"Oh, hello." Laura stepped further back into the room to avoid contact. "Ah didn't know y'all could read."

Casey began to burn. The use of the word "y'all" was a deliberate racial slur. A Yankee might not know the difference, but when a Southerner used the plural form to an individual, he meant more than just the person he was talking to.

But Bev could take care of herself. "Of course you wouldn't know, Laura-Sue," she said, almost kindly. "You dropped out of school before I graduated."

"Valedictorian," Casey added. "Of course, you probably don't know that word either. It has more than two syllables. I'd love a swim, Bev. Meet you at eight?"

"Fine."

"A nigger on the beach," Billy laughed. "You tryin' to improve your tan?" He turned to Casey and smirked. "Y'all be careful now. Sharks like dark meat."

Bev turned away disgustedly and set her books on the counter. Casey gritted her teeth and totalled up the prices.

"Wha' d'you keep in here that brangs 'em in?" Billy snickered, glancing sideways at his wife to see her grin.

"Intelligent conversation," Casey snapped, and turned to Bev. "I'll put it on your account. You sure you'll be free tomorrow night?"

"Free? She may be cheap, but I nevah heard of none of 'em givin' it away." Billy's snicker turned into a guffaw of laughter as Casey whirled on him.

"Shut up, Billy-boy!" Paul snapped. "Just because you pimp for your wife and sister doesn't mean you can come in here and insult a lady."

"A lady?" he said incredulously. "I ain't nevah met no nigger lady before."

"I don't like that word, Bazzel." Paul straightened up to his full height of five feet five inches. His brown eyes narrowed and turned dark. "And that's twice you've used it."

"Well, I'm right sorry 'bout that, Bellecourt," he drawled sarcastically.

"What did you come in here for, Billy?" Casey interrupted quickly.

"I told you. I want some of those trashy li'l romances and Billy won't keep them in the shop." Laura moved languidly to the door, still enjoying the disturbance.

"Why don't you wait in the car, Billy?" Paul suggested quietly.

"I got as much right here as any ni . . . as she does." Bazzel moved to the vacant chair and sat down firmly. "There're a lotta people who'd be int'rested to know you favor *them* over your own race, Casey."

"You aren't my race, Bazzel. You're not even the same species," Casey shot back.

Bev grinned at her friend, and left with a thumbs up gesture. "I'll call you," she said as she went out the door.

32

Paul hesitated, looking at Billy, then at Casey, who shook her head. "I close in ten minutes anyway. Let him stay. I'll have the chair disinfected tomorrow."

"I don't think the stink will clean out. Better burn it," Paul added as he left. "I'll check the windows to make sure they're locked."

"You mean that nigger set here? I thought I smelt somethin'." Billy propped his feet casually on the counter, blocking her in. Casey ignored him and started totalling up her receipts, wondering if they would cover this month's bills. Some people just never knew the joys of owning their own business.

In a moment, she was trying to keep from fidgeting. She could feel his eyes on her, and when she finally glanced at him, he licked his lips suggestively. His eyes glittered and he stared at her until she couldn't miss his meaning. "What about you, Casey? You take off a few pounds here an' there an' I reckon a man could fin' somethin' to int'rest him. 'Course he'd still have to look mighty hard."

It was particularly humiliating to be told to lose weight by such a slug. "Why do you come in here, Billy? Just to nauseate me and my friends?"

"I like it here. You got class, baby. It's all a mattah of class. Laura-Sue used to have it, but all she does now is sit aroun' reading tha' trash she buys here, an' drinkin' my whiskey. Fat an' all, you got real class. All you need is a real man to show you what to do with it."

She struck at his ankles and he let his feet slide to the floor. "If you don't want any books, wait in the car, Billy. I don't want you in my store." She was working to control her voice, but her anger had evaporated with the blow. If she weren't careful, she would laugh in his face.

"I'll jest wait right here an' talk to you." He stood up and walked toward her. She had never realized how tall he was. He seemed to tower over her and suddenly it wasn't at all funny. There was something scary about him. It had hit her when she struck him, and clung to her like an odor. She told herself she was being absurd. She turned her head to

33

avoid the rancid smell of his breath and he misunderstood the motion. "Now I jest cain't unnerstan' why a pretty girl like you ain't nevah been married. Why d'you s'pose that is, Casey?" His hand reached toward her.

She moved suddenly, startling him by whipping the side of her hand up to knock his arm away from her face. She moved toward him and faced him squarely, trying not to breathe in. Her anger was back.

"I reckon it's cause I'm so mean, Billy-*boy*," she drawled, and the venom dripped from her words. "So you better get your dirty ass out of my store, an' don't you ever come back!" She saw the hesitation in his eyes.

"Ain't polite to crowd a lady." Paul strode casually back into the office and surveyed the scene. "That store of yours clean, Billy? Or are you still selling whips and chains?"

"Sex aids ain't against th' law, Bellecourt." He moved back slightly, and Casey realized she had been holding her breath.

"You oughta be 'gainst de law. 'Sides, what d'you bet dat I can't find some violations if I just walk myself by dat shack o' yours a couple times a night? I see you in here ever again, an' I'll pull your license . . . permanently." Paul smiled again and Casey felt herself relax. Her legs were suddenly weak and she leaned back casually against the counter as Paul continued, "You go ahead on out, now, boy, 'fore I done get mad."

She had seen Paul like this once before, but it had been so long ago that she had forgotten how dangerous he could be. His trim body seemed to settle into itself, like a spring coiling. He gained solidity. His brown eyes narrowed and darkened to black. Even his moustache seemed to bristle. Casey could see the hard line of muscle in his jaw.

Laura Susan Harrington Bazzel, once of the proud Pensacola Harringtons, but disowned long ago, walked into the office to see her common-law husband cowed and sweating. She giggled unexpectedly.

"Why, honey, what's going on here? Is that itty-bitty poleece man too much for you?" Her glee at seeing her mate disconcerted was undisguised. He whirled on her bitterly.

"You stupid bitch! I tol' you we oughtn'ta come in here. This high class, uppity—"

Paul's hand moved slightly, warningly, and Billy's words chopped off abruptly.

"You told me?" She screeched at him. "You spineless, no-good whore's son. I warned you 'bout coming here. I tol' you to let her alone. Those goddamned Brightons have always been too uppity for messin' 'round with. That bitch'll cut your balls off if you look at her wrong." They all missed the astonishment on Casey's face. Did they believe that? She felt obscurely pleased.

"I don't know why you drag me down here. Won't she let you in when I'm not along?" Laura's tirade continued as they moved from the office to the main room. "You could get the same books for me if you tried and I'd never have to set foot in this dump."

Furious, Billy whirled on her, then noticed the books she still clutched. He struck her hand viciously, sending them hurtling into a rack and starting a small avalanche. Paul and Casey moved uneasily to the inner doorway, watching them leave. Billy picked up a book from a rack and drew back his hand, ready to heave it through the glass door.

"Bazzel." Paul took one step into the front room and Billy dropped the book as if stung. Casey touched Paul's shoulder in restraint as Billy shoved Laura toward the door.

"Let them go, Paul," she muttered quietly.

"Fuckin' cop. I waren't doin' nothin'. Casey's a friend of mine. She knew I was jest foolin'." He said sullenly.

"Let them go," Casey repeated as the door closed behind them. "I'd rather clean up the mess than have them in the store any longer than necessary." Paul glanced through the window just as he and Casey finished picking up the books. The argument was continuing in the car as the couple drove off.

"What got into him?" Paul sounded as bewildered as she felt.

"I don't know. Thanks for the help." As they walked back

35

into the office, she clenched her hands into fists to keep him from seeing that they were trembling.

"Does he do this often?"

"Not like this. Never like this. He's sleazy, sure, but this time he acted downright crazy. I've handled it a hundred times before, but this time was different, wasn't it? I always thought he was harmless, you know?" She couldn't get the look in his eyes out of her mind. He had wanted trouble.

"I can't figure it, Casey. But I'll be on watch for him from now on. And I'll tell Bev to be careful, too. You keep a gun in the shop, don't you?"

"Yeah, but," Casey looked at him in disbelief. "You don't think it would have gone that far, do you? The gun never even crossed my mind."

"Well, just keep it where you won't forget it next time. When was the last time you took it out for practice?"

"Weeks." She replied, then thought again. "Months, probably."

"I'm off Monday, and the shop is closed, right?" Paul was not one to put things off. She nodded resignedly, and he continued, "Okay, we'll go over to the practice range."

"As long as we're doing that, why don't you and Clarise come for barbecue Monday night?" she asked.

"Sounds good. We'll bring the beer. You going to invite Eric?"

She shrugged nonchalantly. "If he doesn't have a date. Maybe."

Paul nodded, satisfied with the arrangements. "I didn't finish checking the windows. Why don't I do that now, and you get ready to lock up? I'll follow you home."

"Aw, come on, Paul, that's a little extreme, isn't it? I only live ten minutes from here, and Eric will be next door. In fact, if I know him, he's already at the house waiting for me, thinking that he's pulling a fast one. Besides, you're late already. You get the windows and go meet Clarise. I'll be okay. I have to wait for my last customer anyway. It wouldn't look good if Clarise beat you to the restaurant. You wouldn't have anything to tease her about."

The storm had almost subsided and the coffin rocked gently in the waves. The man inside was free to concentrate all his powers on the one he had chosen. He thought his wait was almost over.

It was only beginning.

Paul grinned as he left Casey's office, but he had no intention of letting her drive home alone. He would follow her, and if Eric wasn't there when they arrived, he would go next door and brief him on the situation. Clarise would understand if he was late, bless her. What she wouldn't understand was if he let her cousin go off unprotected.

He heard the last customer moving around in the back room, and then the bell over the front door jangled. He stopped for a moment, wondering if it was a late customer.

Casey tidied up the office, thinking what a strange day it had been. In five minutes, at 7 P.M. sharp, she would turn off the lights to the sign, get her purse and be ready to go. If Simon Drake hadn't reappeared by then, she would lock the door and unlock it for him when he left. Despite what she had told Paul, business wasn't so good that she could afford to ask a customer to leave.

She picked up her keys absentmindedly and jangled them in her hand. The bell over the doorway answered the sound like an echo. She moved from the desk to behind the counter to see who had come in.

Simon Drake had glanced at the title of almost every book in the store while he waited for closing time. His acute hearing had caught the sounds of the altercation in the office, and he had been relieved when Paul had come to the rescue. He would not have let that fool interfere with his intended pleasure, and it would have been easy for Simon to send him away, but he felt curiously reluctant to use his power tonight. Maybe it was the presence of the policeman. He had no wish to come to the attention of the authorities. Anonymity was his protection.

37

He heard the front door open again and the light slap, slap of tennis shoes on tile. Something was wrong. He could feel it. He headed for the office with a mixed handful of books for Casey to check out. It was close enough to closing time to make conversation with her until they left together. He had no doubt that Casey's date would be disappointed tonight.

The man in the coffin didn't have to look very far for a suitable mind. Anger, hate, bitterness and fear led like a thread to a mind that was just on the edge of madness. He struck at it viciously, crushing it with his power. He forced it to turn around and go back the way it had come, to her, closer to its own destruction. It made one feeble effort to stay free, but centuries of mastery made it easy to break the weak mind and impose his own will. He could see through its eyes now. It knew where to go, but there was someone else with it, a whining presence that irritated him. He caused an arm to strike out suddenly, felt it connect, and shared the fierce joy that his victim felt. This was something that the man had wanted to do for a long time, but had never found the nerve. He struck out again, letting it feel his own pleasure. He promised it more fun soon, and pointed it like a poisoned arrow at his brother's prey. Then he went along for the fun.

His bastard brother might feed tonight, but not on the one he had chosen. She would be dead, and after, he could direct the captive mind to borrow or steal a boat and pick him up. Otherwise, it might be a day, or even longer before the tides brought him back to shore. Then he would deal with his brother in person.

For now, he settled back to enjoy the look on his half brother's face when he was robbed of his pleasure.

Laura Harrington needled Billy Bazzel, of "those po' white trash Bazzels," as he drove north out of the city. She

38

didn't look up when the dark scrub pines changed to towering oaks hung with Spanish moss like thick, torn spiderwebs, and the stubby cyprus knees rose out of the still, black swamp waters. She laughed as he raved about that "pint-sized, half-ass runt of a cop tryin' to back me inta a corner. If he didn't have a badge on I woulda stomped him good. You coulda scraped him up with a shovel. I will yet."

Laura-Sue laughed derisively. "You ain't gonna do nothin' to him. You ain't got the balls to face him down, an' if you tried, you'd be the one scraped up. Assholes don't have no balls." Her insulting laughter broke out again at her last words, and she whooped with glee as he turned the car in a skid.

"Where you goin' now, Billy-boy?" she managed to ask.

"Shut up, bitch." His voice sounded strange.

She tried to get a good look at him in the fading light. His eyes gleamed menacingly and she tried to still her laughter as the car turned back the way it had come.

"You don't fool me none. You ain't goin' back there. He'll nail your hide to the wall, if the bitch don't get you first. Besides, they was locking up. They'll be gone by now."

"No!"

The word burst from him in a roar, and she was thrown back as he stepped hard on the accelerator. His right hand left the wheel as he reached across her to the glove compartment. It was as if his fingertips had eyes. He opened the glove compartment and she watched, fascinated, as his hand ignored the tangle of trash, papers, candy wrappers, crumpled cigarette packs, old combs with broken teeth, a screwdriver and a wrench, and other assorted odds and ends. It went straight to the .22 caliber revolver that lay on the bottom of the heap.

"Are you crazy?" she screamed at him. "You cain't use that. He's a cop. He'll kill you." She was still yelling at him when he backhanded her casually across the face, the gun still in his hand.

Her mouth dropped open and her eyes widened in shock. "Billy?" Her voice was almost a whisper. Her hand crept to her cheek and she winced at the stinging pain there.

"You bastard!" She sobbed the words as her breath caught in her throat. Shock gave way to fury as she realized that he was not reacting to her. She hit him lightly on the shoulder with her fist.

"You hit me," she said incredulously, but there was still no reaction. Emboldened, she beat at his shoulder with her fists, working herself into a frenzy. Her fists pounded wildly as he swung the car into a familiar parking lot. The brightly lit sign read: Casey's Book Stop. We Buy and Sell Used Books.

Billy stopped the car and turned to her, smiling. Her fist slowed, hesitated, then her fingers uncurled like the petals of a flower as she stared deeply into his eyes. A fierce flame danced there. She opened her mouth to scream, but his hand lashed out first. This time he hit her with the gun barrel, opening a bloody gash in her forehead. She cowered back against the far door, scrabbling to get out of his way. She stared down the dark barrel of the gun, waiting for the shot, but he just grinned at her and said, "Wait here for me. I'll be right back." Her heart fluttered as hope shot through her. Did he mean that the Billy she had known so long would be right back? Then she realized that whatever came back, it wouldn't be her Billy.

She watched just long enough to see him pull the glass door open, then she bolted for the road.

Paul Bellecourt was checking the windows in the Romance Room, taking his time, waiting for the last customer to leave, when he heard the jangle of the doorbell and moved quietly down the hall to the front room. He paused at the doorway, looking right to the outside door, but he was too late to see the person who had just entered. Over the racks that filled the room, he could just see the top of someone's head as the person moved toward Casey's office. Paul took one step into the room and stopped abruptly, his attention caught by a sudden movement to his left. A man came into view and stopped.

The tall blond man stepped into the room and stood, immobile, as if flowing water had been suddenly frozen. Paul felt his body draw into itself, ready for battle, but only the tall man's eyes moved, tracking from the one who had just entered to Paul. Even at this distance, Paul could see the brilliance of those blue eyes. He felt drawn into them. Slowly, the tall man's head turned toward him, drawing attention to his high forehead and dark eyebrows. The light glinted off his blond hair, then all Paul could see were those incredible blue eyes, bottomless pits with just a hint of angry red in their depths. He felt himself weighed and measured, then dismissed so completely that his body swayed back in release. He stood staring dumbly as Simon turned away from him and stepped farther into the room, moving left toward the office. Paul came back to his senses, and moved between the rows. He recognized the back of Billy's head and hurried to intercept him. Simon had already reached the corner and was turning toward Billy. Paul caught a glimpse of Billy's gun, but he was too far away. He shouted, knowing with a cop's instinct that it was already too late. There was a blur to his left as he sprinted toward them.

He was too late.

Simon had heard the bell and moved lightly out of the back room, down the hall, and paused in the doorway of the main room. The light pad of footsteps on carpet drew his attention to the front. All he could see over the racks was a shock of greasy black hair proceeding slowly to his left. He glanced to the right at Paul, then turned to face him. That was not where this feeling of danger was coming from. He dismissed Paul as, if not an ally, at least not an antagonist. He moved left along the wall, slipping quietly around the corner until he could see the entrance to the office.

Billy Bazzel stood in the doorway, pointing a gun at the counter area. Simon couldn't see Casey from this angle, but he could hear her. There was a quick indrawn breath, a small sound of protest, and a single footfall as she turned away.

41

"No." Simon barely whispered the word, focusing all his power of command at Billy. It was like hitting a shield, but Billy's eyes slid sideways to glance at him. Fear and confusion warred with the thrill of forbidden pleasure.

"Mine!" Simon growled softly.

Bazzel's lips drew back to show long tarnished teeth as he giggled at Simon's helplessness. His eyes flicked back to Casey and he fired the gun.

The sharp crack thundered through the shop. There was a dull thud as something soft hit the office wall, and Simon launched himself into the air, roaring, "Stop!"

He covered the ten foot distance too fast for the eye to follow. The second shot exploded as his left hand knocked the gunhand down. His right grabbed the nape of Billy's neck and squeezed once, briefly. He heard the crunch of small bones and a corpse dangled from his fist. He shook it once, just to make sure, then tossed the carcass disgustedly into a corner.

He took one long stride into the office and vaulted over the counter, landing with his legs straddling Casey's inert body. His hand touched slick warm wetness on the wall, and he looked up to see a splatter of blood at head height. It smeared down to where Casey slumped with her back against the wall. The coppery odor was intoxicating. It filled his senses and his anger grew at the waste. Kneeling, he felt the life spilling out of her. He stretched out his hand to touch her face, then shifted her head and shoulders gently until she lay flat.

"Is she alive?" Paul yelled from the other room.

Simon heard a thud, then a skittering noise and he realized that the cop had stopped to kick the gun out of Billy's hand. The action was according to the best police procedure, he was sure, but in this case it was totally unnecessary. He grinned savagely, showing his fangs as he answered, "Barely."

"I'll call the paramedics. Don't move her." Paul came around the counter to stare at the wreck that had been his friend.

"Call them then!" Simon snapped the words out, already knowing the worst. His sensitive fingers had found the soft, bloody groove in the back of her head. From the angle, she must have been turning away when the bastard shot her. He could feel the gritty movement of bone fragments through his fingertips. Even in his overwhelming rage, he knew that it was no coincidence that the bullet had found his chosen prey. A part of his mind wondered who was responsible and why.

As Paul turned to use the desk phone, Simon bent further over Casey, hiding her from a possible backward glance. There was still one way to save her, though he didn't know if it was wise. He didn't stop to think about it.

He released her for a moment, moving to balance on the balls of his feet. Drawing the sharp thumbnail of his right hand across his left wrist, he watched the blood bubble from the deep slit. He pressed it to her cold slack lips, feeling her heartbeat through his wrist. It was a weak, thready beat that said that life was almost over. He stroked her throat as one would a sick kitten, to make her swallow. Her eyes flickered open briefly as she tasted his offering, and the pulse gradually grew stronger and more regular. He willed his lifeblood into her, feeling the beat pick up until it matched his own. It thundered through him, a primitive, compelling drumbeat. The familiar, hungry ache in his cheekbones was a warning, and he reluctantly pulled his wrist from her warm, sucking lips.

The irony of it didn't escape him; he was giving to her what he had planned to take. The red depths of his eyes subsided to a distant glimmer and his teeth stopped hurting. He smiled with satisfaction as he closed the cut with pressure from his fingers and wiped a smear of blood from her lips. Staring at their mingled blood on his hands, he slowly raised his bloody fingers to his mouth. He tasted it thoughtfully, feeling the heat course through his veins, and closing his eyes against the hunger it raised.

"Some other time," he promised her quietly.

Paul had finished his phone call and checked on Billy. He

hadn't expected to find him dead, the counterattack had been too sudden, too brief, but he was relieved that he didn't have to deal with him. He hurried back to Casey and found her stretched out in the space between the counter and the wall. He put his hand on Simon's shoulder, then snatched it back as if bitten.

Simon stood up slowly, wearily. He towered over Paul, who stepped back a pace and spoke.

"I called the ambulance for her. Billy won't need one. How is she?"

Simon moved back without answering, and Paul slipped in to take his place. He checked her pulse and breathing, then looked up to see Simon heading toward the door.

"Where you going?"

"You have no further need of me, and I have done what I could for her."

"I think you better stick 'round. You leave now, it jus' muddy de water. There ain't no question dat you acted rightly in defense of her, and there ain't gonna be no problem 'bout it since you got a cop for an eyeball witness, but dere be a hell of a lot of forms to fill out." Paul's Cajun accent sounded thick after Simon's elegant dismissal.

"I dislike publicity. Perhaps . . ." Simon's voice trailed off suggestively as he turned his hypnotic eyes on Paul. The gesture was lost since Paul had already turned back to Casey.

"I'll do what I can do t'keep your name out of it, but don't you count on much. De newshounds, they'll be all over you soon's they figger out what de hell happened. You could be a hero in dis town." Paul looked up to see Simon shake his head decisively. "Yeah, can't say's I blame you. But you'll still have to stick around."

Simon spread his hands in acquiescence, then leaned gracefully against a wall. There was no hurry. He had fed well last night. The hunger he had felt was a reaction to the blood, an inconvenience, not a demand. He wondered idly whether his kind could starve to death, and how long it would take. There was no danger of that here. They would not be able to keep him if he chose to leave.

The ambulance arrived quickly, but then the paramedics encountered an unexpected problem. They worked in the confined space to brace her head and neck, but the space between the wall and counter was too narrow to put the stretcher down beside Casey and put her on it. And she was too heavy for one of them to lift and walk out with her. Simon watched them in detached amusement until one of them tried to lift her shoulders and duck walk her out of the confined space. He slipped as he stepped in a pool of her blood and his foot slid out from under him. He sat down with an audible thump. Casey's head bounced stiffly in his lap.

As Paul cursed the clumsy fool, Simon growled softly. "Move, fool." He reached over the counter, grabbed the man by the front of his uniform, jerked him over the top, and tossed him to the floor. Simon carelessly brushed aside the other attendant as he slid across the top of the counter and stooped to her side. Putting one arm under her neck and shoulders and the other under her knees, he straightened up carefully, cradling her head. He walked easily around the barrier and placed her gently on the stretcher. Then he took her hands and placed them precisely alongside her body. He tenderly stroked her cheek with the back of his hand, then leaned down and touched his lips to hers.

"Do you know her?" Paul asked, puzzled.

"No." Simon straightened up and watched them carry her away. "But I will."

45

Chapter Two

Clarise Bellecourt arrived at the restaurant a few minutes after seven. Her first reaction when she saw that her husband wasn't there was satisfaction; for once he was the one who was late. She would be reminding him of this for a long time. She went straight to their usual table, waving to the waitress as she went by. Casey's cousin was a trifle above medium height, slim from the waist up and disproportionately heavy from the waist down. When she walked, her hips swayed gracefully from side to side, slightly later than her shoulders. It gave her a sensual grace that was deceptive. Her real condition was one of shy awkwardness. She had been one of those unfortunate children who were all elbows, knees, teeth, and glasses. She had never outgrown a tendency to knock into things and to become flustered whenever she was the center of attention.

Marriage had given her a superficial poise that could still turn into awkward shyness in an instant. Her husband gave her confidence; she gave him tenderness. They each had an underlying stubbornness that caused enough disagreements to keep their marriage interesting.

Now she waited impatiently. It was not like Paul to be late. She drummed her fingers on the table and crossed her legs first one way, then another, but her smile stayed firmly in place. Her eyes brightened each time she glanced hopefully at the door.

She ordered two drinks from the bar and sipped hers

slowly. It was 7:20 P.M. He shouldn't be late tonight. He had called her at 6:30 P.M., just before he left the station. She had hurried because he was closer to the restaurant and she didn't want him to have to wait. Ten minutes later she was on her way to call him when his call came through. She left for the hospital.

Clarise and Casey had been raised together, friends and cousins. Their homes were only half a mile apart until Casey's parents had moved to New Orleans when she was sixteen. Even then Casey had stayed to finish her senior year in Florida and had come back frequently to spend time with her grandparents during the summers.

Casey had gone on to college in New Orleans, while Clarise had gotten married and moved to Texas and then to California, and it was those years she thought of now. Not because of the move, but because of Mark, their first love.

When they grew up, there were no Help Houses for Children like the one she worked at now. Kids who had problems had nowhere to turn except to neighbors and friends. Both sets of parents had acted as hosts for troubled children. It was known around the neighborhood, the school, and the churches that any kid who needed a break from his parents could come and stay for a week or a month or as long as the parents agreed to. And the adult Carsons and Brightons seemed to have a way of talking parents into letting the kids stay. Maybe because the parents needed a break from the kids as much as the kids needed one from them.

Mark had turned up one day when Clarise was fourteen. It had been love at first sight for her, while he, at the ripe old age of sixteen, couldn't have seen her with a microscope. For the next three years, long after Mark had moved back in with his parents and even after he had graduated from high school, she and Casey had shared endless talks about their crush on the "older man."

At nineteen, Mark had finally noticed them. He dated

each of them for awhile, then his affections settled on Clarise. They married a year after Casey and Clarise graduated from high school, and Casey had been her only attendant. They left the next day for Houston. The marriage had lasted for two years, which was four months after the first time he hit her, and one hour after the second. He had followed her back to Ft. Walton Beach and had stayed, calling her every day and begging her to come back to him. He often stopped by her parents' house to see her. He spent hours there, telling her mother funny stories to keep her laughing. After awhile, the stories weren't so funny anymore: they centered on how well he had treated Clarise and how much he loved her, how hard he had tried and how Clarise had run out on him when he was down. Casey arrived to spend the summer with her grandparents, and Clarise was invited to stay with them for awhile. The only condition was that Mark was not welcome in their home.

The first time he came, he was the perfect gentleman. His soft Southern drawl was soaked with words such as, "darlin', sugar, and honey." The elderly Brightons asked him politely to leave, and he did, although it took him half an hour to get out of his chair and walk across the room.

The second time was a week later. The older Brightons had left for a movie fifteen minutes before. When Casey had seen his car top the sandy rise, she had called the police and locked the doors. Clarise had wanted to talk to him, but Casey had turned pale and screamed at her, "Get out! Get upstairs and hide. Run! For God's sake, Clarise, it's you he's after!"

Now when she thought about it, it was the melodrama that she remembered most. Casey's sick white face, the wood on wood pounding at the door, followed by the rhythmic, rapid ticking sound of the window glass vibrating. Casey whispered, "Run," and she did. Up the stairs in leaps like a young deer, Clarise bolted into her

48

bedroom and pushed the button to lock the door.

It unrolled in her head like an old movie. She was helpless to stop it or to speed it up, and she drove with mechanical precision as she picked her way to the hospital.

There had been a rending crash from downstairs, and in her mind she could picture the heavy door slamming inward. Mark strode in and his pale hair shone like a bright cap. In one hand he held a cone of supermarket flowers, in the other a baseball bat. She had since asked Casey a hundred times to tell her what was said. Casey never would, but in her mind Clarise could still hear his yell of rage and Casey's defiant scream. He had hit her twice with the bat before he came upstairs looking for Clarise.

She had lugged a bedroom chair to the door and wedged it under the knob. It had held almost long enough. As he pushed through the barricade, she had seen that his lip was torn where Casey had gone down fighting. He had just begun to beat her when the police arrived. Officer Paul T. Bellecourt, recently from New Orleans, had pulled her husband off her and had demonstrated enough police brutality to disgrace the combined Florida and Louisiana police forces.

She had cheerfully lied about that during the investigation that followed, and Casey had remembered hitting Mark "at least once." It still didn't account for all the bruises, but it convinced the investigators.

Clarise and Paul had been married three years later, and Casey had flown down to Florida to be maid of honor again.

That was the part that Clarise hung on to. The happy ending of a Grimm's fairy tale.

Casey was in the hospital again. This time it wasn't just a broken arm and a concussion. This time she had been shot.

She tried to picture Casey as she had last seen her. All that came to mind was a silent image of dark blue eyes in a paper white face and bloodless lips mouthing one word. "Run."

Driving east from New Orleans, Louisiana, Interstate Highway 10 angles first north over Lake Pontchartrain, skirts the lake, then moves slightly inland from the Gulf of Mexico to head almost due east. The lakefront area consists of small villages, gradually being overtaken by apartments and condominiums, built on what was swamp land a few years before. The older houses have gray, weathered wooden fronts and are built on land so low that every footstep sinks and the tracks fill quickly with water. The surrounding marsh grass has saw-toothed blades that can rip skin and leave pick marks in clothes. Ten miles further north, where I-10 turns east, the ground becomes rolling hills topped with tall, long needle pines and broad leaf oaks. The road is dotted with signs for cheap gas and hotels for those who can't or won't afford the inflated New Orleans rates.

Seven miles from the turn, the Pearl River marks the end of Saint Tammany Parish and the road crosses into Mississippi. Soon the land becomes marsh, with occasional clumps of stunted trees and small creeks meandering through flat fields of four foot high marsh grass. Further along, weeping willow trees mark the banks of creeks with tongue twisting names: Tchoutacabouffa, Pascagoula, and Escatawpa. Old women lean against the bridge rails with cane poles rigged with string. The coffee cans beside them contain worms dug fresh from the garden. The trees are draped with Spanish moss, and fields of wild flowers brighten the empty stretches.

The land slants gradually upward to the Alabama border. Twenty-five miles on, Mobile is a scatter of bright lights leading to an overpass which cuts diagonally through the city. Visible in the distance are tall buildings and shipping docks on the bay. The new twin tunnels are well spaced and brightly lit. They run under the Mobile River and emerge onto the Jubilee Parkway, forming a half circle to skirt the deeper water of the bay. The bridges of the Parkway look down on Battleship Park where the *USS Alabama* is permanently moored, on hotels and motels, waterfront restaurants, bait and beer joints, and the glittering water of the bay. On good days, the blue water glistens and sparkles with reflected sun. On bad days, the water turns to a dull gray and surges with dirty brown foam and debris, and the air is fouled with the stench from the paper mills a short distance up river.

From the rise at Spanish Fort the whole bay, causeway, and city are laid out in picture postcard fashion, framed by blue sky and accented by wheeling gulls. It's a spot for tourists who appreciate scenery; the local residents take such views for granted, as natives usually do. The fifty mile stretch from Mobile to Pensacola, Florida is a boring repetition of small Southern towns and long expanses of scrubby, dwarfed pine trees which are being slowly strangled by sweet smelling honeysuckle and healthy blankets of kudzu. The soil is so sandy that the trees look like a forest of bonzai pine, twisted and shortened from the lack of nutrients.

At the Pensacola exit, long after dark, Ned and Kate Brighton turned south onto I-110, passed through downtown, and drove across the Pensacola Bay Bridge. The entrance was marked with signs warning motorists to check their gas before venturing on the long bridge. Ned checked his gas gauge automatically, but he had filled the tank in Mobile and the car was in good shape.

He drove with single-minded purpose, as he had for the last four hours. Kate had offered to drive more than once, but it gave him something to think about besides Casey. The phone call had come shortly after eight. Clarise had broken it to them as gently as possible. Beyond the bare fact that their daughter had been shot in the head, she could only tell them that the doctors didn't know anything

51

yet. They would start with x-rays and proceed from there.

They had left New Orleans at 8:30 P.M., after calling the airport to check on flights. It would be quicker to drive, and they had made good time. Two and a half hours to Mobile, a little over an hour to Pensacola, and still forty minutes to get to the Seaside Hospital in Ft. Walton Beach. It would be 12:30 or 1:00 A.M. before they arrived. Ned increased his speed unconsciously, ignoring the wonderful blend of all the geographical features that surrounded them. Lakes, bays, bayous, bridges, swamps, rivers and creeks, trees both incredibly tall and ridiculously stunted, sandy hills and flat beaches—all combined in the Ft. Walton Beach area.

Their conversation had been exhausted hours ago. Now their occasional comments were prayers for their daughter's life, or desultory remarks about driving conditions.

For the next forty miles they parallelled the Gulf, and just off the coast, Santa Rosa Island. The island was a narrow strip of sandy beach separated from the mainland by a few hundred yards of blue-green water. A part of it was owned by the Air Force, the rest was being developed into tourist property, complete with condominiums, hotels, and bars. Most of the commercial property faced the Gulf, the more peaceful and less popular waters of Santa Rosa Sound were reserved for private beach houses. As Ned and Kate drove along the coast, they could catch occasional glimpses of lights through the tree lined shore of the mainland.

At the Mary Esther cutoff, they turned left off Highway 98. They made another left on Beal Parkway, and then a right on to Racetrack Road. Ned threaded his way through the streets with easy familiarity, but he was going so fast that he almost missed the left onto Mar Walt Drive. The tires squealed a protest as he wrenched the wheel around. Kate's indrawn breath made him grunt with irritation. Neither of them noticed the new housing developments and subdivisions as they turned left into the hospital parking lot.

Eric Tyler was waiting for them in the main lobby. They had met him only twice, once shortly after he moved in, and once when Casey invited him for Christmas dinner. Kate noticed the droop of his shoulders and the paleness under his tan. Unconsciously, she prepared herself for the worst.

"Eric?" Ned's voice was tentative. He recognized him now only because he had expected to see him here.

"She's alive and she's doing pretty well. Clarise and Paul are up in the ICU waiting room." He guided them to the elevator quickly. It wasn't until later that Ned appreciated the concise brevity. "She's still in the intensive care unit, but they've finished the x-rays and tests for now. The doctor said that you could see her, but only for five minutes. She's in a ward with a lot of people who don't need to be disturbed. The bullet cracked her skull in the back. They thought at first that they'd have to operate to get the bone fragments, but she was very, very lucky. The break was clean. When it heals, she'll probably be as good as new, but right now . . . well . . ."

"Spit it out, boy."

"Mr. Brighton, she looks a lot worse than she is." He was trying to prepare them, Ned realized. He put a hand on Kate's arm to keep her from rushing off the elevator.

"Her face is swollen, and her eyes are black and blue, and she lost a hell of a lot of blood. That's normal for a head wound, they tell me. But she still looks pale and not like, well, like Casey. She's still unconscious. They don't expect her to wake up until morning, but they have all the monitors hooked up to her, so if she does wake up, they'll know it."

"Unconscious. Asleep?" Kate asked tentatively.

"She probably won't wake up while you're here." Eric strenuously avoided the word "coma" that the doctors and nurses had been discussing ever since they had brought her in.

53

Clarise and Paul spotted them from the waiting room, and made a beeline for them. Ned hugged Clarise hard, but Kate clung to her desperately.

"Have you seen her?" Kate asked.

"Oh, yeah. She . . . she . . ." Clarise's eyes filled as she looked helplessly at Paul. Her hands fluttered weakly.

"She just doesn't look good, but the doctors say that she may be just fine." Eric spoke rapidly.

"May?" Kate's whisper reflected her pain at the word.

"We'll know more in a few hours, when the specialist gets here." Clarise led her down the hall while she tried to reassure her. "They were going to operate immediately, but they wanted to give her some blood, and there was some problem about that, and they wanted to get her stabilized first. So Eric sent for a specialist from New Orleans, and they decided to wait until he gets here. The first x-rays showed bone fragments, but the set they took a few minutes ago didn't show the same thing, and they're all confused, so they're waiting to see what the new doctor says." Paul tried unsuccessfully to shut her up, to slow her down, but four hours of tension and medical discussions came tumbling out in thirty seconds.

"Why don't you just go in to see her now, and we'll talk afterwards." Paul opened the door, but Ned hesitated.

"What kind of specialist?"

Eric's eyes looked sick, but he answered firmly. "A brain surgeon. We may not need him at all, but as long as she can get the best, we may as well have him on standby. It's just a precaution. They were going to wait for her condition to stabilize anyway, so the delay is no problem."

"Oh my God." Kate's hushed voice came from inside the room, and Ned followed her in reluctantly. "She's dying, Ned. Oh, God, she's dying."

All the attempts to prepare them could not have softened the reality. Her face was puffy and swollen so badly that her eyes were mere slits of purple-black discoloration. Her mouth, slackly open, was dripping saliva around a thick tube. Lines ran from the inside of her elbows to monitors and tubes while machines puffed, beeped, and gurgled. Bloody splotches on her sheets and pillow were just beginning to turn brown.

"She looks worse than she is." Ned repeated the words firmly to his wife as he stared in horror. Even her eyelashes stuck out grotesquely from her swollen lids. Kate moved to hold her, but the intimidating tangle of lines and tubes stopped her from doing more than touching her daughter's hand.

When they came out of the ward, Kate was sobbing openly, but the silent tears running down Ned's face seemed worse to Eric.

"How did it happen?" Ned's voice was flat and expressionless. His back straightened as his arm supported his wife.

Paul gave them a brief summary. The only interruption was when he told them that Simon had already killed Billy Bazzel. Ned looked almost disappointed that he couldn't take care of that himself, but all he said was, "I want to meet Mr. Drake."

"What the hell are you trying to pull, Tyler? You drag me down to this shit hole in the middle of the night. You faked the damn x-rays and acted like this kid was going to die any minute. You even get the doctors here to back up your lies and I want to know just what the bloody hell is going on. I don't care how much of my hospital you built, this is totally inexcusable."

Kate Brighton winced at the language, but grasped at the fact that this rude, bald-headed man who was supposed to be the leading brain surgeon in the country seemed to think that Casey was not as seriously hurt as they had led her to believe. Or had he said that? Maybe he was just annoyed because she was hopeless. She tuned back into the argument.

55

"Fake x-rays? Are you crazy, Bill? Casey is a friend of mine. If I wanted you here to hold her hand, I'd just call and ask you, not go through the hospital administration. Now what the hell are you bitching about?" Eric's fist clenched as he responded angrily. His eyes were bloodshot from the sleepless night and from holding back the tears.

"Is Casey alright?" Ned interrupted savagely. They could fight some other time.

"Who? The patient? She has a hairline fracture and she's still in a coma. Other than that she's fine. No fragments, no hemorrhaging. She could walk out of here tomorrow if she wakes up before these quacks get to her." He turned deliberately back to Eric, ignoring the doctor who had just walked up. "If you didn't switch the x-rays, then I'd get her out of here. The plates you sent to wake me up were not from the patient I just examined. Those had fragments driven into the brain, here and here." He tapped the back of his head firmly. "It would have taken some fancy cutting to get those out and still have a live patient. That's why I came. But the x-rays they showed me this morning were from a still different patient; they showed a bad fracture, in the same place, but it was a clean break. No fragments involved. So I supervised a set of my own on the girl you pointed out. If that's the right patient, she should be fine." He paused to look balefully at the nervous doctor beside him. "Those show a rather long hairline fracture that should heal clean. If these crazy quacks don't get their hands on her."

"Oh, thank God!" Kate collapsed back into her chair, and tears of relief filled her eyes and overflowed.

"Don't misunderstand me." The short man held her glance in a vise. "She's not fine now. She's in a coma and her head took one hell of a blow. Her brain got bounced around in there. It's bruised at the least, and there may be damage we don't know about yet. We won't know until she wakes up."

"When will she wake up?" Kate was still pinned by

those sharp eyes.

"That, my dear, is a very good question." His gaze was suddenly sympathetic, which scared her much worse than the anger. "The longer she stays in a coma, the less chance that she'll wake up at all, and the more chance that if she does wake up, she'll have severe brain damage."

"Brain damage . . ." Kate repeated weakly. Her square shoulders slumped under the impact.

"Is there anything we can do?" Eric broke in quickly.

"Talk to her. There's no proof that comatose patients can hear a word, but there's no proof they can't, either. Most doctors don't believe that it helps, but it can't hurt. You can have the life support equipment taken off any time. She's not having problems breathing and it might give her brain something to do."

"Those x-rays were not switched!" The indignant tone came from the tall doctor who had joined them. His hospital greens reflected on his face and turned his sallow complexion an unhealthy shade of chartreuse. He seemed to be in awe of his colleague. "I was in the emergency room and I personally supervised the x-rays. The girl was dying. If he," the doctor looked at Eric with loathing, "hadn't called you, we would have operated immediately."

"In that area of the brain? You would have killed her."

"Do you agree that she's doing well now?" Eric asked.

"Dr. Meistershoorn is one of the foremost brain specialists in the world. I wouldn't dare argue about his specialty. But those x-rays were not switched. I can't explain it. I saw the latest ones, and she is . . . fine now, but she wasn't then. She had extensive brain damage, fragments, bleeding. We had to give her blood just to stabilize her enough to operate. She needed that life support equipment."

"But what about now?" Ned insisted.

"She's stable." He agreed reluctantly. "No splinters, no bleeding, no apparent brain damage, and no need for life support equipment. She's breathing fine on her own. I can't explain it, but I can't deny what I saw, either."

"You think bone splinters can vanish into thin air? Get me out of this hospital, Eric. Can you even get a decent scotch in this town?" the specialist demanded.

"I tell you I know what I saw," the local doctor protested.

"Then fire your x-ray technician. Or get new equipment. Try a CAT-scan, I hear they're real popular in the big city." Dr. Meistershoorn turned to face him, "Or do something, Doctor. But you better get your malpractice insurance paid up. And don't call me the next time you have an emergency. Come, Eric. I need a drink. Do we have time for a round of golf before my plane leaves?"

"Your plane leaves whenever you tell it to, Bill. It's yours for the weekend."

"I? I didn't call you . . ." The local doctor's belated protest dwindled off as the small man bounced jauntily down the hall toward the door.

Eric smiled at Ned and Kate, waved off their attempt to thank him, and followed him to the door.

Kate's eyes were shining like a child's when she turned to Ned. "She's going to be alright. She really is."

He hugged her exuberantly. He felt like yelling, dancing, laughing with joy. He kissed his wife instead.

Thursday, June 20, 1992
Article from the *Ft. Walton Beach News*

An apparent robbery attempt was foiled last night by Mr. Simon Drake, a resident of Ft. Walton Beach. William Bazzel, 37, also a local resident and owner/operator of Bazzel's Blues, entered Ms. Brighton's bookstore on Highway 98, and fired one shot from a .22 caliber revolver at her. Officer Paul Bellecourt, who was also a customer at the time, told this reporter Mr. Drake struck Bazzel on the neck before he could prevent the shooting. Bazzel's neck was broken.

Ms. Brighton is in a coma in the intensive care unit of Seaside Hospital. Her condition is listed as critical.

William Bazzel was dead on arrival at Seaside. No charges are anticipated against Mr. Drake. He was not available for comment.

Two weeks later Kate remembered her words.

"Why doesn't she wake up?" She stared down at her daughter.

Ned shook his head helplessly.

"I want the life support equipment taken off."

"They said they'd do it tomorrow."

"They've been saying that for two weeks." She looked at him and he knew there was more. He waited for it patiently. He had some news of his own to tell her, but that could wait. She finally took a deep breath and tried out the idea on him.

"I want to take her home."

"No, Katie. You can't."

"I already feed her with that tube. I can learn to put in the IV needle. Half the time, I'm the one who takes care of her. If I can do it here, I can do it at home."

"Katie, be realistic. You go home at night. It gives you a rest, and the nurses are always here if she needs something. What if something happened? You wouldn't know what to do."

"But if she was home, she might wake up. Maybe just being at home would do it." Her nervous hands patted the covers, pulled up the sheet, folded it down under Casey's chin, then patted the covers again.

"No. You can't handle her alone. I didn't want to tell you this just yet, but I have to go back on Sunday. I've taken all my leave and I have to get back."

"I knew it was coming. Don't look so upset. I can still stay here, even if I can't take her home."

"You couldn't do that anyway, Kate." He captured her

59

hands, marveling at the strength in them, and pulled her to him.

"I know. I know." She leaned against his shoulder. Just being held by him gave her strength. She couldn't tell him how much she dreaded his leaving.

They were much alike, so much so that some had mistaken them for brother and sister rather than husband and wife. Both were medium height and slim, both had dark hair, both were self-assured and had that special, happy, self-confident look that comes with loving and being loved. His eyes were the same dark blue as his daughter's, while hers were a deep, rich brown. Both pairs stared now at the unconscious figure on the bed. Kate sighed softly, and he felt her warm breath on his neck. It reminded him of happier times.

"Maybe without the equipment, maybe if she has to work a little to live, she'll wake up." She closed her eyes and clung to him.

"Maybe."

"How long can she stay like this?"

Ned squeezed her harder, but he didn't reply. It was something they both tried not to think about.

"What if—"

"Don't." The word squeezed out between clenched lips. The doctors had been brutally honest about her chances of awakening without brain damage. The odds got longer every day.

Casey. Bright, beautiful, vivacious Casey. Willing to fight everyone else's battles, adopting stray cats and dogs, caring. His daughter was a vegetable. But they had to keep trying, believing that there was still a chance. Would they be able to tell if there wasn't?

"I'll come back every weekend." He was talking to his wife, but the promise was to his daughter. He moved to her bed and took her hand. "I talked to Clarise and Beverly. They want to come over and help take care of her. Clarise will be here every Tuesday and Bev will come on

Thursday. Eric and Paul couldn't set a schedule, but they'll be here, too. I don't want you to stay here all the time. Get out, go shopping, do something interesting. I'll take care of her on weekends. I'll leave the Oldsmobile here and take a taxi from the airport. I hope the battery isn't dead in the Chrysler."

She hushed him gently. "It's alright, darling. It's no problem. There's no point in both of us staying. I'll take good care of her, and I'll call you if anything changes."

He put his arm around his wife and held his daughter's limp hand. "Maybe we should think about moving her to New Orleans."

"No. This has always been her home. If she's going to wake up, it will be here."

"Honey . . ."

"No. I know it's harder this way, but I'm afraid. I'm afraid if we move her, we'll lose her."

He nodded slowly. If she had healing to do, she would do it here. She had never been comfortable in New Orleans. As long as they could stand it, she would stay here.

His screams reverberated in the small space until it seemed that the wood and earth surrounding him screamed back in sympathy. He couldn't seem to control his hands anymore. The fingers kept wandering to the lid above him, and the scratching noise they made was driving him insane. Even in the darkness, he could see the gashes he had made in the hard wood.

One strong push. That was all it would take, just one strong push and he would be out. The air would be fresh again, and even if he didn't really need to breathe, he *needed* fresh air. He had almost forgotten how fresh air tasted.

He forced his hand down to his side, and gripped the already shredded satin over the ancient dirt. The scratching noise turned into a disgusting rustling as his fingers dug in and sifted through the dry earth. While he was awake, which was less and less each night as his strength slowly withered away, his fingers never stopped moving.

He was so hungry. The thirst burned in him, a constant searing pain that wouldn't let him rest; a nagging reminder that was destroying his brain. His mouth seemed filled with dust, but it didn't stop the screams.

It was the steady, nerve-wracking motion of the waves that was really driving him insane. The constant up and down, side to side swaying that never stopped.

Fresh air. Just one little breath of fresh air. He would sell his soul for one clean breath, without dust and the stink of his own body decaying. He could open the coffin, despite the locks the sailors had put on it. But could he seal it again?

The temptation was driving him crazy.

He could change into a bat and fly to the nearest land. But how far was the nearest land? And in what direction? His senses were too weak now to locate it. Pick a direction, north would probably be his best bet, and fly. It was so tempting. To just fly away. But his power was almost drained, and his wings would grow weaker and weaker. He would drop closer and closer to the water, until finally a wingtip would touch a wave and send him tumbling into the depths. Vampires didn't float. He would sink like a stone. Consciousness would die. He would die.

After more than five hundred years, he would cease to be.

He saw it every day in his dreams, and a thousand times each night. It was the thought that kept him in this cage, airless and echoing with his screams. As long as he was in it, he could live again. If he ever found the courage to open his coffin, just to breathe again, just to feel alive again, could he seal it back, watertight? The seal was not automatic. Would water seep in, a little at a time? As weak as he was, it would drain his strength even more, and faster. To be in direct contact with water would be mental and physical torture, and how much more could he stand?

The screaming began again. Maybe it was really the screaming that was driving him insane.

"You want to what?" The amused credulity came through clearly in Simon's voice.

"I want to take you out to dinner on me. You saved the life of a very good friend of mine and for weeks you've refused every offer of thanks that her parents and I have made, so the least I can do is buy you dinner." Eric was trying to be as reasonable and persuasive as he could be, but Simon's attitude was a little hard to take.

"And drinks, I suppose," Simon mused. "I could use a drink."

"You name it." Eric was relieved.

"I would love to," Simon was still talking more to himself than Eric, but Eric took it as an affirmative.

"It's settled then. Shall I pick you up?"

"I would love to, but I think perhaps it would not be wise—"

"But—"

"I have been overindulging lately," Simon said smoothly. "I appreciate your offer, but I think not."

"Dinner then?" Eric persisted. "How about a home cooked meal? Mrs. Brighton requested that I ask you. She's an excellent cook. Or we'll go to a restaurant, if you prefer."

"Mr. Tyler, I must tell you that that is the most generous offer I've had in many years, but I'm afraid my stomach has not been well lately. The thought of solid food, well, I really don't think I could take it. Recently I have confined myself to liquids."

Eric could hear the undercurrent of amusement that ran through Simon's voice. A sudden thought occurred to him.

63

"Am I interrupting something?" he asked tentatively.

"As a matter of fact . . ." Simon's voice trailed off suggestively, and Eric could hear music in the background. "Perhaps we could continue this conversation some other time? But I did want to ask, how is the girl? I have been meaning to stop by the hospital, but I haven't had time. Is she still in a coma?"

"Yes. The doctors don't seem to know when she'll come out of it."

"That is a shame. But I'm sure she'll recover sooner or later. I will call you back, Mr. Tyler, when I get thirsty."

Chapter Three

Estelle Wiltz had finished washing the dinner dishes and had stacked them on a dish towel on the stained, chipped counter. She was drying her hands when she heard David, the youngest child, cry. She turned from the counter abruptly, and her dress caught on the rough edge where the molding had broken. It ripped. She grabbed for the dress, and her elbow caught a glass. It smashed to the floor.

She held her breath, listening. The baby's distant cries were louder now. She tiptoed to the door and peeked into the front room cautiously. Thank God, Jerry was still sleeping. She might have time to quiet the baby down and change him, and clean up the broken glass before her husband woke up. Then she would be safe. All the rest of the evening's work was upstairs. He might not even come upstairs tonight. If she was lucky.

She started across the living room, forcing her tired legs to step softly. She stopped halfway, reversed course, and went back to the kitchen. She got a beer from the refrigerator and set it down quietly on the table by his right hand. There. Now there was no reason for her husband to go into the kitchen and see the mess she had made. Jerry was a tidy man. It was her own fault if he got mad at her sometimes. She was so messy. She just couldn't seem to help it. He had found dust in the boys' room yesterday, and he hadn't even raised his voice to her. Just stood there and watched while she cleaned it up. He tried so hard to be patient with her. If he woke up and found the broken glass on the floor, it would be her own fault if he lost his temper.

Even the thought made her whimper, but as scared as she was of him, she worried more about the children. If only she could talk him out of being so strict with them. And she didn't understand why he insisted that she keep the house so obsessively clean when he kept all that junk in the front yard, just where it looked so trashy. She rubbed her ear absently as she pushed away the traitorous thought. The last time she had dared to question him about it, he had hit her so hard that the sudden increase in air pressure had burst her eardrum. He had told her later that he was sorry, but it wasn't until after the hospital bill had come that she had believed him. Of course, that had set him off again, but it was almost worth it to see him have to fork out the money.

The baby's cries had turned to short, hiccuping screams of anger. He was too young to understand that in this house it was better to keep your pain and outrage to yourself. She changed him quickly, briefly cuddled him to stop his cries, checked the other children, and hurried downstairs to clean up the mess. She hid the fragments carefully in the trash, pulling out an empty milk carton and the scrapings from dinner to put the pieces on the bottom.

Once again she walked softly up the stairs, as she did a hundred times each day. She checked the baby again and told her eleven-year-old, Sally, to turn down the radio in the girls' room. Matt and Janie looked up apprehensively as she opened the door to the boys' room. They were playing "war" with Jake's toy soldiers. Jake, at age thirteen, was too old for such childish things but still touchy about the "little kids" playing with his precious old toys. He was oblivious to this heresy. His nose was buried in one of the comic books that his mother had miraculously brought home several weeks ago. He looked up with a guilty start as his mother opened the door.

"It's alright, Jake. Your father had a hard day today. He should sleep for awhile if y'all behave and be quiet. Janie, it's time for your bath. Come on, now. No fussin'. Your Daddy's asleep downstairs and he needs his rest. Now you get in there and start the water." Her hand lingered lovingly on the child's fair hair as they passed in the doorway. She wished Janie would do some fussing. She had been so quiet for so long now. There were weeks when she never said a word.

Estelle walked over to Matt, bending down to kiss his forehead. He brushed her away with the back of his hand.

"I tol' you, Momma, no more kissin'. That's mushy."

"You clean up this room now, y'heah? You know the rules." She headed into the bathroom to help her youngest daughter, just turned nine two weeks ago, wash her hair.

Simon Drake strolled casually into the hospital lobby just before the end of visiting hours. The receptionist looked up with a bored expression that changed almost comically when she got a good look at him. His bright blue eyes twinkled at her intimately as he asked which room Casey was in.

"That's 412, sir, but her visitor list is restricted. May I have your name?" The tone made it more than a casual request. He gave it, wondering if the family had thought to include him on the list, then mildly surprised when she waved him on. Paul and Eric had both called him shortly after the incident, to try to thank him and to invite him for dinner, but he had refused. He had thought little more about it. He had wondered occasionally if she had recovered, but each time he had tried to contact her mentally, he had been unsuccessful. Tonight, on a whim, he had decided to see for himself.

When she died, tomorrow or a hundred years hence, he would know. He would be her Bloodmaster. It would be his responsibility to teach her, and he took his responsibilities very seriously. He would have to train her himself, to keep her from making more of their kind.

That's all I need, he thought wryly, to have a horde of vampires invade the area. To be responsible, as the Bloodmaster always is, for keeping them under control.

He had given this Casey girl his own precious blood to drink, which meant that she would be one of the rare ones who retained their mental faculties through the transformation to Nosferatu. That was not something that could be undone and sooner or later she would die and rise again to drink the blood of life. He wondered again what malignant force had tried to take her from him and why. No matter, he thought, there has been no sign of it for three weeks now. If a Nosferatu was in the area, he's gone now. Perhaps the stranger discovered whose territory he had invaded.

He made his way to her room, ignoring the interest of the receptionist. He would find sustenance elsewhere tonight. Perhaps on the beach. He always enjoyed the beach. He pushed open the door to Casey's room, expecting to find her alone, but the room was a double and there was someone in the next bed. He inclined his head courteously to the old black woman and made his way to Casey's bed.

She has changed, he thought. Her skin was dry and slack, and she had lost so much weight that it hung loosely from her bones. The lack of exercise had caused her muscles to lose tone and strength. How much

68

weight has she lost in only three weeks? he wondered. Twenty pounds? Thirty? He had no way to judge, but he could see the terrible toll it had taken on her body. Even her hair looked lifeless. It hung in dry, brittle strands; all the curl had gone, as if even that were too much effort for her body to make.

It took a moment for him to recognize the emotion that welled up in him, tightening the muscles around his heart and making it hard to breathe. Pity. He thought he had lost the capacity for that long, long ago.

His rage returned as if it had never left. He no longer wondered why he had tried to save her. She had been worth saving, but this was sacrilege.

His rage gave him power, and he cried out silently, trying to touch her mind. His hand stroked hers, then moved to smooth her cheek. There was no response. He closed his eyes, gathering all his power. When he felt it deep inside him, like a hard, bright balloon of light expanding until he could no longer contain or control it, he opened his eyes and *looked* at Casey.

There was a bright red flash, as if lightning were seen through rose-colored glasses.

Casey didn't move. He bowed his head in defeat. Standing beside her, touching her slack flesh, he felt as if she was too far away to hear him. He leaned forward and gently touched his lips to hers. His hand hovered at her throat. It would be easy to take her now, without any preparation. She would die, be buried, and come back to him. But he would never get to taste her sweet blood again. She would wake hungry, not understanding the need within her. She would be confused, resentful, as he had been. She might never recover, and become a blood hungry zombie who would haunt the night until she made a fatal mistake, and a human caught up with her. And he would never know her as a human, as an equal. She would come to him as his slave, forever

69

adoring, begging to please him, when begging could never please him.

It was a terrible fate for one who had been so full of life. But why should he care?

He leaned back slowly, and became aware of the bright, curious eyes watching him. He had forgotten the old woman in the next bed. No matter, there was time. He would wait until Casey's muscles shriveled and twisted her bones, until he was sure that even if she awoke, she would have no chance to enjoy her life. When that time came, he would relieve her of her burden and she would come to him, grateful for his favor. He found the idea curiously depressing.

He kissed her again, slowly, with some lingering thought that his kiss might bring her back to life like a princess in a fairy tale, but her lips were slack and uncaring beneath his. He straightened abruptly, nodded once again to the old woman, and left.

He flew to the beach, enjoying the warm salt air, dipping and rising with the currents until he spotted a group of young people having a beach party. The warm summer air was redolent with the rich odors of wood smoke, boiling seafood and spices, and suntan oil, contrasting sharply with the pungent aroma of sweat from clean, healthy, youthful, and overheated bodies. The scents were intoxicating.

He could imagine himself swooping down among them, his giant wings reflecting the red firelight like a black mirror. He could almost hear the terrified screams as he danced in the air, avoiding their frantic efforts to beat him off. His jaws gaped open savagely, tasting the air as he singled out the strongest, most vital of the herd and cut him away from the rest. His sharp claws would slice into the tender flesh and he would lift him, screaming, and carry him away to feast on him at his leisure.

He pushed the fantasy away, shaking his head to dispel the vision as he found a secluded spot on the beach to change. He had gained control over his appetite over decades of effort. He no longer had to kill every night. He no longer had to kill at all, but in exchange, he gave up the vitality that draining the life force of others would have given him.

He studied the water thoughtfully. The ceaseless waves were like the beat of his own heart, a pulse that mocked life. The sea water was like his blood, full of life from other sources. Without those others, it would be as static and dead as he would be without human blood. He picked up a fistful of sand and let it drain through his fingers. He was being presumptuous. The sea had been here long before he existed, and it would be the same after he died the final death. It made a mockery of his extended span of existence, as he made a mockery of the human's. Was that why he had chosen to live in this area?

Simon stretched suddenly, enjoying his hunger. He felt a pang of loneliness as he approached the crowd of teenagers gathered around a fire of driftwood. They were laughing and talking, drinking and touching as they boiled shrimp and crabs in a big black iron pot. The fire was illegal, but that didn't seem to bother them. He sniffed deeply. They must have been out shrimping in the Gulf and come back to the beach to cook the fresh seafood.

He was greeted warmly. Someone thrust a beer at him and he took it to hold as camouflage until he decided on his prey. As so often happened, she chose him. A lithe Oriental girl caught his eye, and he planted a thought in her mind. She tilted her head and glanced at him from the corner of her eye, then looked away shyly. He smiled, but she turned her back and picked up a few shrimp from a platter. She blew on them to cool

71

them as she wandered in his direction.

As she came closer, the crossed light of the fire and the moon revealed her beauty. Her almond eyes were dark, and her straight black hair swept past her shoulders. Her mouth was almost a pout, with her full lips drawn together. She approached him and smiled mysteriously, an exotic gift from the Orient.

"Hi. You want a shrimp?"

She held out a spicy hot shrimp to him. It had been so long since he had tasted food, real food. Her hand touched his lips. It had been so long, surely one little bite wouldn't hurt him.

He took a small bite and chewed cautiously. The delicate flavor of the shrimp came through the tang of salt, bay leaves, red pepper, lemon, and spices. He chewed slowly, his enjoyment heightened by the threat of pain and danger.

"You ain't from aroun' here, are you?"

He choked, coughing. She was about as Oriental as Southern fried chicken. The blend of the accents had resulted in a Southern takeover, and the effect was charming. His throat closed as he tried to swallow, and he spit out the tasty morsel. She looked concerned.

"Did you git a bad one?"

"Must have been. No, I'm not from around here. I'm just a tourist. Have you lived here long?"

"Ten years. Are you hungry? We got plenty. You wanna join the party?"

"I'd rather talk to you. How about a walk on the beach instead?" he countered.

"I'd like that." She smiled over her shoulder, flipping her thick black hair back to look up at him coyly. He slipped his arm around her, feeling the beat of her heart as she snuggled comfortably against him. It was a game he played. She was not strong enough to fight his mental suggestions, but if she had been, she could have es-

72

caped him. It was no fun unless his intended victim had a chance. Hunting on the beach gave them a chance not only to escape, but to destroy him, if they were fast and strong and knowledgeable. Moving water was anathema to him. He not only couldn't swim, he could drown in water a foot deep. All she had to do was to catch him off guard and push him in. That moving, dark, oily-looking water would do the rest.

"Are you here with a group, or by yourse'f? How long are you stayin'?"

"Just a few days. I'm alone here. It's a beautiful night, isn't it?" He stepped to the edge of the water and waited. This was her chance.

"Yeah, real purty. What's your name?" She came up beside him and glanced coyly up at him from under her lowered lashes.

They were out of sight of the party before he turned to kiss her. He felt her surprise, but his control over her was so complete that the thought of pushing him away never entered her mind. His hands roved her back as he pulled her closer. He twisted his lips against hers and felt them take fire. Her hands came up to his shoulders, and she hesitated, then pressed her body eagerly against him.

He kissed the corner of her eye, then her neck and shoulder as his hands explored her body. He could feel her nipples tighten through the thin fabric of her swimsuit and he slipped the straps off her shoulders. Her body was trim and hard.

Her breath quickened, and he could feel her heartbeat speed up as she grew more excited. Her fingers tangled in his hair, pulling and releasing as he murmured softly to her. He could almost see the heat rising from her body.

There was an ache on either side of his nose. A small, familiar, welcome pain that meant the bones were

73

lengthening, growing, pushing his canine teeth out and forward. The teeth themselves grew longer and sharper and he hesitated, prolonging the expectation before the moment of joy. His lips found her throat. When she felt the sting, it was too late.

Her blood was strong and sweet, and her excited heartbeat frantically pumped it into his waiting mouth. She murmured one small protest, but he quieted her with his mind and his gentle hands. Her arousal had poured hormones and enzymes into her bloodstream and that, combined with her youth, meant he only had to drink a quart or less to get all the nourishment he needed for the next day.

When he finished, his fingers pressed her torn flesh closed and his mind helped it heal. He rubbed off the few drops of blood on her neck, then helped her to dress. His mind instructed hers as he sent her back to the party. The only memories she would have would be of an interesting stranger on the beach who had kissed her. Her subconscious would remember more, but her dreams would not last long.

He watched until she turned and waved at him with a vaguely dissatisfied gesture, as if there were something she had forgotten.

When she turned a final time from the safety of the fire, he was gone, soaring overhead with the flapping wings of a bat.

There was a storm in the Gulf. Lightning danced across the tallest waves and thunder made the water quake. The wind pushed at the small crate riding high in the water, and waves pounded the wooden walls like a hammer. At any moment, the seasoned ebony could splinter, and water would pour into his refuge. And this time he was too weak to find his calm center and block the fury of the wind and waves. He braced his hands against the sides of the coffin while it was tossed like a chip of wood. Dirt, dry as dust, showered around him, uncontained by the shreds of the satin cover still remaining.

He felt the pull of a great wave, sucking sideways at the box, and he screamed as the coffin flipped. He was jerked, twisted, then flipped to lie facedown on the lid, and a few hundred pounds of earth landed on his back, crushing him into the ebony wood. He could hear the roar of the water and feel the power of the waves, inches from his face. He moaned in terror, fighting the madness and losing.

He threw his head back and howled, pushing against the weight of the dirt, struggling to place his native soil between his body and the strength-sapping water. He managed to turn halfway, and his withered fingers clawed at the loose earth. He was burrowing upward when the crate flipped again, end for end and rolling at the same time. He braced his arms against the sides and let the soil cascade around him, buffeting his body from every direction.

When the motion stopped this time, the lid was above him but he was facedown, surrounded by the dirt. His insane gabbling had finally stopped, because the earth filled his mouth. He pushed his way up, coughed out the bigger chunks, wiped his eyes, then propped himself up on his elbows. His head almost touched the roof, his eyes burned, but there was not enough moisture left in him for tears.

Another wave rocked the box, and he made his decision. His fingernail slashed at his wrist as he screamed in horror, but his flesh had turned to leather and his fingers were too weak to break through it. He howled again, in frustration and madness, then his head bent and he bit through his own skin, through tough flesh

75

and stringy tendons and into the hard wall of the vein. The blood had congealed, drying and thickening into a paste. Another week and it would be a powder, useless to him.

He sucked avidly at his wrist, squeezing at the shrunken flesh to force the jelly into his mouth.

It was delicious.

There was enough moisture left to turn the dust in his mouth to mud, and he swallowed hungrily. It hit his belly like fire and he could feel the energy burn through him.

It wouldn't last long, he knew. He retreated into his mind, where all his strength lay. The power was still there. He concentrated all his mental ability on extending the calm center of his being to surround his body, then his coffin, then the water around both.

The motion of the waves lessened until the rocking was bearable again. He wanted to make it quit completely, but he was afraid his power would run out before the storm was over. He had no way of knowing how large the storm was, how long it would last, or in which direction it was taking him. The last shreds of his sanity washed away as he wondered how long his false power would last.

It was torture. Every time Casey tried to fight her way back to consciousness, the pain would overwhelm her mind and body and send her reeling back into darkness. No matter how hard she tried, her body would not respond.

Her muscles ached and burned. Sometimes they would spasm, and she would scream silently as they jerked. The pain in her head pounded with the rhythm of her heart. When the nurses or her parents turned her, as they did every few hours, the pounding became a sharp axe driven deeply into her brain, over and over again. She knew they all misunderstood her desperate gestures. She often heard people comment on her smile, when the muscles of her face, neck, and back were twisted into knots and she wanted to scream in agony.

"Doctor? It's the monitor in room 412 again. It's showing increased brain wave activity."

"Let me see."

The nurse ripped off the last six inches of the tape and held it out to him. He took one look and sprinted down the hall with the nurse at his heels. They flung open the door and rushed to her bed. Dr. Driscoll went through the motions, lifting her eyelids to check for pupil contraction and checking her breathing while the nurse took her pulse and blood pressure, but one look had convinced him that there was no change.

He straightened up finally, and turned to the nurse. "It must be a short in the system. With a reading like that, she'd not only be conscious, she'd be climbing the walls. Attach a note to her file with the tape. And have the damn machine fixed."

"Yes, doctor, but it was worked on just a few weeks ago when we started getting those crazy readings."

"Well, make them fix it this time. Until then, disconnect it. You don't need it bleeping all night."

Clarise knelt on the edge of the grass and dug furiously in the earth. The sweat dribbled off her face and rolled down her back until it dripped into the dirt. She attacked the weeds viciously, stabbing at the roots, then yanking the stems up as if they were personal enemies. Paul looked up from his trudge across the yard behind the mower and shook his head. It would have been easier on her if Casey had died a month ago when she was shot.

77

He pushed the thought away as he paused to wipe his face. It had been a hot summer, and the grass was a foot high in places. This was the first sunny day they'd had off together in over two weeks and the yard work was more a pleasure than a duty. He finished the last swatch and shut off the mower, then wiped his face again. At 9:00 A.M., it had been ninety-four degrees and now it was almost noon. He walked over to Clarise, took the forked spade from her dirty hand and pulled her to her feet.

"It's getting too hot and I'm hungry. Let's call it a day."

She nodded tiredly. Her shoulders were slumped and her eyes red, and she smelled of cut grass and fresh earth and sharp sweat. He pulled her head down to his and kissed her, his hand moving on her damp back.

"Paul!" She protested in surprise, but there was a smile in her eyes. "Not now, I'm all—"

"You certainly are," he said admiringly. He kissed the corner of her eye and nibbled on her earlobe.

"What's gotten into you? Mrs. Harris is watching."

"So? Maybe she'll learn something. Joe ought to thank me." His arm slipped around her waist as they walked up the drive to the house. "You can have the shower first. I'll fix us something tall and cool."

"Mmm, sounds good. What do you want for lunch? It'll have to be something quick, I'm due at the hospital at one."

"I'll see what's in the fridge. Git!" He slapped at her bottom lightly and she danced away.

The shower felt good. Even the warm water felt cool on her overheated flesh. She switched the shower head to massage and let it beat into the sore muscles of her shoulders. The bathroom door opened and she extended her arm through the shower curtain for her drink. Her soft hand touched his rough one. She waited, expecting the cool, smooth feel of glass, but it was the warmth of his lips that tickled her palm. She giggled softly and felt her love for him burst inside her. It touched every part of her and brought it to sensitive life before flowing downward, along her spine.

Just the thought of him could do that to her. She had never felt really pretty until she had met him; now she felt beautiful all the time. It was the way he looked at her. She sighed as she pressed her palm against his cheek, then twisted her fingers in his wiry hair. He moved back and she wriggled her fingers expectantly, but there was still no drink.

There was a sudden cool breeze as he opened the shower curtain and stepped in. She smiled as he slowly pulled her close to kiss her. She enjoyed it while it lasted, then stepped back and shook her head regretfully.

"I have to be at the hospital in a few minutes."

"No." He whispered in her ear, then nibbled his way down her shoulder. "I just called Kate. She said you needed the day off. She's a very wise woman, and I wouldn't think of arguing with her. Then I called the captain. It seems I have too much overtime built up and it would be a favor to the department if I would take the day off. So it's just you and me, kid. We're stuck with each other for the whole day. Think you can stand it?"

"The whole day?" She repeated dreamily. "It may be hard, but I think I can do it." Her eyes twinkled as her hands slipped down his chest and past his waist.

His indrawn breath was a quick hiss before he laughed at her boldness and the challenge in her eyes. He said casually, "I knew you could handle it." His hand smoothed her silky wet hair and traveled on down her back to her hips as she moved gently against him.

"Who're you? Wha'chu doin' here?"

The querulous voice startled him.

"Go to sleep, old woman," Simon Drake instructed. His mind touched hers and he suggested that she sleep, but he knew it was no use. Some minds were strong, like Casey's. Some minds were naturally resistant, and some were so near the end that nothing could influence them. The woman in the bed next to Casey's was very near the end. He had no power over her.

"What're you doin' t' her?"

"Just . . . watching."

"Comin' here, night aftah night." She grumbled, shifting carefully around the tubes. "Sneakin' pas' the nurses. You think I didn't see you? I been watchin'. You try t' do more than hol' her han' an' I'll call the doctors, you hear me?"

"I hear." He assured her smiling.

"You her boyfrien'?"

"No." He answered honestly, and was rewarded with a twinkle in the dark eyes.

"Good thing you don't lie t' me, boy. Her boyfrien' comes in here durin' the day with her fam'bly. Not sneakin' in here at two o'clock in the mahrnin'. Why you come so late?"

"I work days," he said briefly. He squeezed Casey's hand, then set it back on the bed and stood up. He shouldn't risk coming here again. But he knew he would. He hesitated at the door, then finally looked back at the white-haired, shrivelled woman in the bed next to hers.

"Alright!" he snapped, irritated. "What do you want?"

"Cigarettes!" she replied promptly. "Doctors say they're no good fer me, an' that lily-livered daughter of mine won't smuggle 'em in. Not charity. I'll pay fer 'em."

"Cigarettes." Only his eyes smiled.

"Get me the good kind. No filter, raht?"

"Right," he said firmly. Why shouldn't she have them if that's what she wanted? Humans lived such short lives.

"You best go now, boy. I'm gonna call the nurses fer my medicine. You go on, now. She'll be awrigh' till tomarrow. I'll watch out fer her till then."

"I'll be here."

"They come every week, you know?" Beverly Watkins swung her legs restlessly from her perch on the counter.

"Who?" Eric Tyler glanced up from the desk, noted her serious expression, and swiveled around to face her.

"The people who were in the shop that day. They all come back."

"Morbid curiosity, I guess." His tone was bored as he turned back to Casey's account books.

"Yeah, most of them, I guess. It's not often in a town this size that the corner bookstore lady gets shot. Everyone knows her."

"I had no idea her financial condition was this bad," Eric muttered worriedly. "She's making barely enough to live on. Why didn't she tell me?"

"Maybe because it's none of your business." Bev frowned at him. "The thing is, all the people who were here just before it happened come every week. Didn't you notice today? All of them were here at once this afternoon. You, me, Estelle Wiltz, Paul, even that boy who traded the books stopped by for a few minutes. Everyone who came in that afternoon, except the guy who saved her life."

"And Laura-Sue. No one's seen her since the day of the shooting." Eric replied absently. "Casey should have leapt at the offer I made her for the land. She needs the capital."

81

"It's more than curiosity. They're shook. Every one of them. We all seem to be . . . on the same wavelength. Even Estelle Wiltz feels it, and you know how dim she is. She brought her daughter in today. She said she tried not to let the kid know what happened, but that kid's sharp, even if she won't talk. She's had nightmares since it happened. So has Mrs. Wiltz."

"Estelle Wiltz? She was in the shop while I was. Casey gave her a stack of comics to give to her kids. She's barely breaking even and she's giving away her inventory. Why the hell didn't she ask me to look at her books?" He slammed the book shut and sat, brooding.

"Would you quit worrying about your damn money and listen for five seconds!"

"It's not my money, it's Casey's! Or rather, it isn't, because she doesn't have any! How's she going to pay the hospital? I can't even find her insurance papers."

"It's not about money, damnit! I don't know what the hell she sees in you, white boy. It's about my best friend being shot in the head. It's about Casey being a vegetable for the next twenty years. It's all I think about! A thousand times a day I think, 'I have to tell Casey about this,' or 'Wouldn't Case laugh at that.' And then it hits me. She'll never laugh again. The whole world seems tilted at some crazy angle. And everyone feels the same way. Everyone but you!" She glared at him accusingly.

"Me?" The muscle along his jaw twitched.

"Oh, sure, you help out once in a while."

His head whipped around and his cool green eyes looked hot as he glared at her. She backed down, slightly.

"Okay, more than a little. Here, and at the house. And the specialist. And the money, of course. With you it's always the money. But you don't really care about Casey, do you? You always thought about her as the fat

82

girl who lived next door and that didn't change at all. You didn't change and it didn't change you at all. Except for that first night, you haven't even been to the nursing home to see her. Did you even know they had moved her to the permanent care wing of the hospital? You go out with a different girl every night. I don't know where you find them all. The truth is, you never really cared about her, did you!"

"Shut up! Just shut up, you bitch! You think I don't hurt?" His hands clenched and the words rasped through his throat. His hazel eyes became gray and colorless. "You just have to keep pushing, don't you! You think you can just keep needling me, on and on, and I won't stop you because you're Casey's friend. Well, I've had it, you pushy broad. You didn't see her that night. You weren't the one who had to tell her parents. You didn't see the tubes or the bloody drip or the way her eyes were swollen shut or the way her skull looked lopsided at first or the blood even around her mouth."

Beverly sat stunned. She tried to speak once, cleared her throat and tried again. "I . . . I'm sorry."

Eric shrugged angrily. He had already said more than he had intended. His feelings were none of her business.

"I didn't know. You just act like you don't give a damn. You never want to talk about her. You ask how she is, but when I try to answer, you find something else to do. I just thought . . . I didn't realize . . ."

He had never seen her at a loss for words before. It was almost worth the outburst. He resolved not to say anything else, then thought of one thing he had to ask. "Bev? How does she look?"

"Oh, God, Eric, you should see her. She's lost a lot of weight. You know how she always despised people who told her how pretty she'd be if she lost weight? She said that either she was pretty or not, and it had nothing to

83

do with . . ." She caught the look of surprise on his face. "You didn't know? You told her that? How long did it take your Mama to teach you to come in out of the rain?"

Eric shook his head numbly.

"Men!" she said disgustedly. "You really are all alike. Stupid. She was so beautiful before, and you were too blind to see it. Now she's thin, but she's not pretty. She has as much life in her face as a wax doll. Kate started out just exercising her arms and legs, but now she even massages her face, to keep the muscles from sagging. It's working, I guess. She's thin, and her face looks like a, like a store mannequin's. All bones and angles. But she doesn't look like Casey!" The words seemed to have no effect on him, but this time she wasn't fooled.

"Go see her, Eric. You'll hate yourself forever if you don't. It isn't so bad, after you get used to it. She isn't bruised or swollen or bloody anymore. She's not scary, just kinda sad. She's just, sorta, like a house that's empty. It's like she just stepped out for a minute, and she'll be right back." She thought that she had finished what she had to say. She stared into those cold gray-green eyes and reached inside herself for the truth. "I'm afraid, Eric. I'm afraid she won't come back."

By the end of August, ten weeks after the shooting, Casey's parents and friends had settled into a comfortable routine. Kate rose at 7:00 A.M. every morning, and was at the nursing home by 9 A.M. Unless she was expecting someone to relieve her, she brought a thermos of hot coffee and her lunch. Every Tuesday, Clarise would come by to give her a free afternoon. Paul and Beverly alternated weeks. One or the other would turn up on Thursday afternoon and insist she take the rest of the day off, but Eric was the one who surprised her. She hardly saw him at all the first month, and then only at the house, but after that he made a habit of

84

stopping by the hospital whenever he was in town. He seemed uncomfortable at first, and she had wondered how long it would last, but then he seemed to adjust, talking and joking with Casey as if she heard and answered him.

August dragged into September, and Casey slept on. The Florida heat slowed movement, the humidity slicked the skin with sweat, and the combination made even breathing difficult.

Two tropical storms and one hurricane drifted into the Gulf, picked up speed, and hurled themselves at the coast. One tropical storm caused minor damage on the Mississippi coastline, but neither of the others came close to the Florida Panhandle. Afternoon thunderstorms dwindled to showers as the season progressed; the summer was hot and dry. Temperatures in the high nineties kept everyone but the tourists inside, and their fair skin burned quickly. They complained loudly of the heat, but the locals knew that they would go back to New York, New Jersey, or New Hampshire and brag about the warmth.

The heat continued as the year grew older. Old-timers talked about summers they had known, and the weatherman announced record breaking highs as if he were proud of them. Sweat dripped from unprotected faces and even the air conditioners whined complainingly. The water temperature hit eighty-five degrees and stuck there. Swimming in the buoyant water was like taking a warm salty bath.

With the prevailing winds out of the south, the heat brought more storms up from the Gulf. Meteorologists warned that conditions were right for formation of another hurricane and a tropical depression was spotted over the Atlantic, four hundred miles off the west coast of Africa. It was moving east.

In the Gulf of Mexico, the winds pushed the black

85

crate north, toward the Panhandle. The occupant had only brief periods of consciousness, usually in the small hours of the night. His awareness had been reduced to a few hundred yards from the box. His screams were only in his mind now, but they were constant. His power had faded until he had no awareness that land was near.

Chapter Four

Just after sunset, Airman First Class Michael E. Boyd left the flashy, trashy bright lights of Ft. Walton Beach and drove west along the Sound. It was amazing how quickly the scenery changed from the bars, restaurants, tourist traps and strip joints of any typical small town where eighty per cent of the income depended on tourists and military patronage. In minutes he was speeding along a divided four lane highway and the streetlights were too widely spaced to do much good.

Passing by Casey's bookstore, he noticed that the new hours were posted out front: 4-6 P.M. Mon., Wed., and Fri., 10 A.M.-6 P.M. Sat. It was a shame, what had happened to the fat lady who owned it. He had been horrified when he read in the paper that she had been shot less than an hour after he had been there. Last week he had stopped by and asked the black girl behind the counter if she was any better, but the girl just shook her head. Casey was still in a coma. She hadn't sounded very hopeful. It was such a shame.

He caught a glimpse of the lights of Santa Rosa Island through the trees, and momentarily wished he was going to the beach instead of fishing. This was his first tour; his first time to travel away from home. He had never thought to see anything more beautiful than the sun glinting off the lakes in Minnesota, but this incredible, limitless expanse of sea, sky, and sand of the island had filled an empty spot in his soul that he hadn't even known existed. He had seen days so hot that the burning sand could sear clear, white blisters on the tender flesh of his instep and toes, but to him it was warmth enough to make him forget the killing cold and the blinding whirl of snow needles that burned more fiercely than any tropical sun.

At work, they called this area the best kept secret in the Air Force because everyone who was stationed here talked about retiring here eventually. A good percentage achieved it. "You've got sand between your toes. You'll never get it out." He guessed they were right. Now, at the end of a hot summer, the words conjured up images of sun on tanned lithe bodies; the sweet flat smell of suntan oil on warm bare skin; and the salty tang of seawater on his tongue. To him the phrase was a promise.

The last time he had gone to the beach, he had taken his shoes off and walked south over sand dunes that slipped and shifted under his feet. At the water's edge, he had stood entranced, watching the setting sun break through the far edge of the gray-black storm clouds. A flash of light on the bottom rim of a cloud had transformed the sand to gold, then was gone before he could focus on it. The water was striped in shades of green and blue, turquoise and azure as the sun gently lowered itself beyond the Gulf waters.

He had been to the beach every chance he had gotten since his first day in Florida. He had yet to see it look the same way twice.

He loved the beach, but tonight he was out to gig flounders. Fishing was one of the few sports he had been able to continue since moving south, and even that had changed. The daytime heat was too much for him, even in September, so he did his fishing at night now, after it cooled off a bit.

How did the locals stand it? The civilians around here complained a little, but they still moved and worked and acted like it was nothing to worry about. Of course they moved slower than he was used to. Moved slower, talked slower, and worked slower, but he wouldn't make the mistake of believing that they thought any slower. He was no bigot, and to hear some of the guys in the mess hall tell it, a Southern accent automatically meant brain damage. He wasn't going to fall for that. In fact, if he lived in this climate year round he would have to slow down too, or risk heat stroke.

He turned right off the highway and drove on slowly, trying to remember Buddy's rather confused directions to his "private fishin' hole." It was a shame that Buddy couldn't come with him tonight, but Buddy was meeting one of the local girls.

Buddy went to all the local Baptist churches to meet girls. Every week, he tried a different one till he knew which ones had the best selection. "Just like goin' to a meat market." Mike could almost hear his slow drawl now. "Women's lib don't mean shit to them Baptists, an' that's how I like 'em."

Mike made a right turn to circle the bayou and ran into a light patch of fog. There was an instant of hesitation, then he switched the lights to bright. He had never believed that crap about fog being so thick that it reflected the light right back at you like a mirror. The gray tenuous substance suddenly became opaque. There was a bright wall of diffused light directly in front of him. He cursed as he slowed the car and switched the lights to low.

Buddy had been raised in this area and was born a Southern Baptist, but Mike was Lutheran. Still, it wouldn't hurt to visit a Baptist church once in a while, would it? It had always been hard for him to meet girls, and he regarded going to church as more of a social engagement than a religious experience.

He drifted in and out of the fog silently, as if he were

driving through clouds, then it thinned to patches. His speed was increasing when he caught sight of a small unmarked dirt road to his right. Damn! That was bound to be the turn. He had forgotten to notice the mileage at the last light, but it seemed about right.

He yanked the wheel to the right, then held his breath as the tires lost their grip on the mist slicked macadam. The car slid sideways. He watched the trunk of a huge old oak tree floating through the fog toward him for endless heartbeats before the tires caught. There was a sickening lurch, then a series of bumps and thuds as the car dropped off the highway onto a rough, oystershell covered, pothole pitted drive. He fought the car to a stop and his face dropped slowly onto the steering wheel. The plastic felt cool on his forehead and he realized that he was sweating. What was wrong with him tonight? All his reactions seemed half a beat slow, and he couldn't seem to catch up.

Never mind. Fishing would relax him, and if the spot was half of what Buddy claimed, he might even be able to sell some of his catch locally. He started the car again, wincing as the starter whined for a minute before catching, then drove on slowly, up and down the ruts. His headlights reflected a tunnel through the scrub pine and thick underbrush. This must be the right road; it was just as Buddy had described it.

He drove slowly into a patch of fog. For a moment, the wagon was creeping through soft, damp, white nothingness. His eyes strained to see farther than the hood ornament. When the fog suddenly ended, it was like having a blanket lifted from the car. He stepped on the gas in relief, made a narrow little turn, and accelerated.

The road ended.

He slammed on the brakes and stopped the car just in time before the road ran out abruptly at a steep drop-off. He backed the wagon up and turned it around to head out. It was a tight squeeze in the brush. Good thing the road ran out, he thought as he walked to the back of the car. The old Pinto wouldn't take much more of those ruts. But this has to be the right place.

He stood on the bank and looked across the water. Left, inland, the bright sparks of house lights reflected their twins in the water. They formed an irregular arc around the bayou, like a gap-toothed smile. To his right, the waters of Santa Rosa Sound surged inward, and the fog formed a holey gray wall. One navigation buoy shone a clear, bright red, blinking a repetitive pattern: on-off, on-on-off. The other buoy was visible only as a green, glowing spot in a shifting fabric of gray. The water formed a moving, black, oily-looking floor under it all.

He opened the hatchback and retrieved his fishing gear, a flashlight, and a gig. He should wear wading boots, but he had never been able to convince himself that water at night was any more dangerous than water during the day. He stepped back to close the hatch, felt a sharp prick in his left thigh, then glanced down to see a rapier point between his legs, almost brushing his testicles. He had backed into a wild yucca plant. It was a small bush, about three feet across and three feet high, composed of miniature swords, an inch or two across at the base of the leaf, and narrowing to a razor sharp point. His sphincter closed at the thought of what could have happened. "At least my luck isn't all bad." He breathed a sigh of relief as he very carefully removed his tender jewels from the danger area.

The flashlight was useful in tracing the faint path down the embankment. When he reached the water, he was relieved to find a flat sandy beach and still, clear water. It was as protected as Buddy had said. Clear water was a must for gigging flounder. He looked anxiously to his right. The fog didn't seem to be moving, and the temperature seemed stable. With luck, he would have a

91

couple of hours before the fog closed in.

He sat down on the beach to untie his standard issue boots, then, with an almost furtive look around, he shucked off his shirt, jeans, and jockey shorts. He walked up the beach a hundred yards or so from where he planned to gig flounder and slipped quietly into the water. He sported like a fish, diving and twisting almost soundlessly until his energy was released and his mind was at peace. Then he turned on his back and floated, gazing up at a hazy sky. The darkness seemed to close in around him; sounds were muted and distant. The water was as warm as milk, and his bare skin felt cool where the still air touched it. The moon was dodging between haze and fog, between a glowing atmospheric halo and streaky brightness. He wished that he could see some stars, but the airborne moisture was too thick, even away from the fog. The water pulled him silently from the bank and his gear, and he drifted inland.

The warm water tickled his groin and he felt himself stir. If only he had a girl; life would be fantastic. There could be nothing finer than working on jets during the day, fishing at dusk, and going home to a sexy woman at night. When he finally found the right girl, she would be sexy, that was one thing he was sure of. She didn't have to be a virgin, but he didn't want someone who had been around a lot. She would be more special than that. He was throbbing now, and he turned uncomfortably in the water. Something brushed his foot, and he jerked away. His head went under and he came up sputtering.

Must have been a fish, he thought, trying to relax. Wasn't that what he was there for? But his muscles seemed independent of his reason, and it really was a spooky night.

He twisted to look for the shore. He must have drifted longer than he had realized. It seemed he had been floating for only a few minutes, but the beach was only a

92

light streak in the darkness when he turned onto his stomach and struck out against the incoming tide. When he thought he must have come halfway there he lifted his head, stared ahead of him and shivered. He was swimming toward a black wall streaked and glowing with malevolent colors. High above, something vaguely yellow climbed the darkness like a spider. At eye level, there were giant demon eyes, one red and one green, looking at him. He blinked, and they shifted to arching colored fire. He blinked again, and they were mismatched cat's eyes, with elongated, slitted pupils. Then the red one disappeared, and he realized that a heavier patch of fog had moved between his line of sight and the buoy light.

He gasped, aware for the first time of the tightness in his chest. Feather soft, slimy, another fish or perhaps some seaweed brushed his thigh and the sudden warmth of the water near his groin made him realize just how scared he was. He resumed swimming, changing to the breast stroke because he had to be able to see and hear. Struggling against the current, he tried to ignore the tightness of his muscles and added to his problems by swimming with his head craned up to keep an eye on those changing lights.

Spooky night. Weird, spooky night. Maybe I shouldn't have tried this alone. How do I know what's in this water? Maybe there's sharks, or stingrays. This wasn't a good idea, he thought. He carefully planned every step he would take to get back to the car. I'll swim to the closest beach, that little point there, then follow the shore back to where I left my gear. The flashlight is right by the gig and I'll grab them and the pack and get the hell back to the car. I can dress there.

He reluctantly tore his eyes from the shifting glow. Out of the corner of his eyes, the lights seemed to leap toward him. He jerked his gaze back. Were they closer? Brighter? He stared for a long moment, then cautiously glanced at the shore. What the hell! The lighter strip was less defined, harder to see. He was still being pulled outward by the current. He twisted his body around and headed straight toward the beach, determined not to turn his head in that direction again.

It was perfectly natural, of course. His logic overrode primitive terror as his mind pushed each thought firmly into place. When I turned my head in one direction, my body followed naturally. He had been watching the lights and swimming, and therefore he had swum toward the lights without meaning to. (Yes, but he was no novice. He liked to swim watching birds or sky or whatever, and he knew how to keep from drifting and there was something out there and it wanted him.) No, that was nonsense. There was nothing out here, but fish and fog. (He could feel something watching him, sneaking up on him when he wasn't looking.)

He jerked his head around to find the lights glaring at him, spying on him . . . waiting for him. He was pinpointed in their spotlight. His swimming slowed, then stopped as they maliciously winked at him; first one, then the other. Above, the moon crowned the eyes with golden horns.

Those are harbor lights, he thought grimly. He tried to say it out loud, but his throat closed around the words. His hands grabbed the water and his body lurched forward. Usually he was a tireless swimmer, but now his muscles ached. He could feel the strain burn inside his legs as he frog-kicked. The beach was closer now, just a hundred yards to go. The sand gleamed in invitation. Ten minutes more, maybe only five if he really pushed. He would be safe and he would never, never go out swimming at night again. He would get his gear and his light, and he would get out of here. Oh, God, please, please, he would get out of here. And the spear-like gig could do real damage if the need arose.

94

His eyes began to blur with exhaustion and fear. His legs were trailing in the water, reduced now to short, trembling jerks at each stroke. He was terrified that the very slightest splash would bring the *something* out of the water behind him. He fought the impulse to glance at the fog again. The beach was so close now. He began to feel slightly foolish. A few more strokes and he would be home free. A giggle rose unexpectedly in his throat. Here he was, swimming for dear life from a menacing heap of humid air, spooked by harbor lights. His muscles were stretched to cramping; he was naked as the day he was born, his skin and other things were shriveled from the water and the fear. The giggle rose in his throat again, and this time he wasn't quick enough to stop it.

Something rough and hard grabbed his foot.

Casey moved uneasily in her deep sleep. She took one deep breath, then another. The woman in the next bed looked up through her tears, too involved with dying to notice any change. She wished vaguely for a roommate she could talk to and confide in. She was afraid of dying, but more afraid of dying alone. That was worse than the pain, worse than the disfigurement and torture of having her breast removed. She had begged the doctors not to do that. She had cried and pleaded, but her daughter and the doctors had worn her down until she had finally signed the release papers. The doctor had opened her up and sectioned her like a chicken. They cut off her breast one day and lied to her the next. She had seen the truth in their eyes, but they had been too afraid to tell her. Everyone had maintained a polite fiction to avoid the truth. Every time she had tried to bring it up, they had told her not to worry, she would be just fine. What she had really wanted to know was why had they put her through this? She had asked Mary Louise, but the only answer was that they were "trying to help." Help who?

She didn't need any help dying, and that was the only thing left now. She remembered watching her grandfather die. The whole family had taken turns sitting up with him so he wouldn't be alone. When the time came, they had each kissed him goodbye, and Momma had held his hand. Dying hadn't seemed so scary there, in the downstairs parlor they had turned into a sickroom. They had all helped to paint it a bright blue. It was so cheerful, and they had worked so hard to make it nice for Grampa. They had each donated something precious to him. She could still remember him lying in the big white bed, with her favorite quilt on top of the sheet. She had thought that it was the last thing she could give him. Ever after that, she would lie in bed hugging that old quilt, comforted by thoughts of Grampa. Now she knew it hadn't been their last gift, or even their best.

When he had quietly finished his last breath, they all went to the kitchen and cried, for him and for themselves at their loss. Daddy had cried hardest and stopped first. He had started telling them tales from when he was a kid and Grampa was still young. By the time Mr. Jack's men had come to take the body away, they knew that he was really safe with God and Gramma.

Now she was dying alone, and she knew that the only reason Grampa had been so peaceful was that he had had family around. She had no one. Not really. Oh sure, Mary Louise, her youngest, visited for one hour every day, sure as clockwork, but it just seemed to make the time before and after go slower. It wasn't the pain, though that was bad enough. It was the aloneness. Her own daughter wouldn't even let the grandchildren visit anymore. She'd made lots of excuses at first, but now she didn't even bother. The reason hung between them like a shroud.

"I want you to remember your grandmother just the

way she was, not like she is now." The old woman could almost hear her say the words to Susan, the oldest at fourteen. No unpleasant memories for those three. Like dying was something she ought to be ashamed of, something she had to hide from the young'uns. So they brought her here and left her so they didn't have to be embarrassed anymore.

She changed position in the narrow hospital bed, careful of the needle in her thin arm. She was always afraid that it would shift position and something terrible would happen. That was one fear she wouldn't have to worry about anymore, and at least she could shift positions, not like that poor vegetable in the next bed. She had plenty of visitors, and she couldn't even enjoy them. They were such nice people, too, especially her parents. They sat there for hours, just reading and talking to her.

The old woman glanced at her silent companion, wishing again for someone, anyone who would listen and care. She began to sob, short energy draining cries that came from her heart. Through her tears, she didn't see Casey's eyes open, wide and staring.

"Mrs. Wilcox? The monitor in room 412 just went off again. That's the third time this week." The young nurse looked at her supervisor anxiously.

"Well, turn it off, Dani. We don't have time to check out every false alarm. Make a note to take the monitor off next time you go in there. I've complained so much lately that they're going to trade it for a different one tomorrow."

"Good. I hope they don't give it to someone who's critical. Why does she even need a monitor, anyway?"

"The parents insisted," Mrs. Wilcox shrugged. "I guess the doctors couldn't find the nerve to tell them their daughter's a vegetable. Check room 420, would you? I'm going the other way."

* * *

Mike Boyd screamed as he thrashed desperately, trying to kick without extending his legs. He screamed again as his foot hit hard, then sank into something that closed around it and sucked gently as he jerked it back. His legs went high, his head sank, and his scream was choked off by the water. His hands struck out under the water as he tried to push away the terrible *something* that he couldn't see. His knees came down hard, scraping against the abrasive sand. His hands came out of the water with fistfuls of sand that washed away between his fingers.

The beach was two yards away. He was safe.

He scrambled up from his knees and staggered out of the water, gasping for breath. He wanted to collapse right there, but his terror was still too immediate. His whole body trembled as he tried to get his bearings.

Where's my car? His mind screamed the question. Is it away from the fog or toward it? He glanced back into the mist, and was captured by the sight. He watched the red and green spread and grow until they seemed to cover the whole bayou. The colors twisted, merging and mingling, twining around each other in a hideous embrace. He tore his eyes from that evil, winking glow. He had to get back to the car. It must be in the direction of the fog, but that didn't mean that he had to look at that slowly approaching mist. He concentrated on the light strand of sand at his feet, but his eyes kept slipping toward the water. He bent his head and dragged his feet as he walked along the beach.

His muscles still twitched, but his mind had begun to relax by the time he found his gear. He shivered once in the warm night air, and he grabbed his shirt to dry off the droplets from his skin. Scared shitless of nothing, he thought disgustedly. I panicked like a kid afraid of the bogeyman under the bed. Stupid, stupid, stupid. What would the guys think if they knew? Nevertheless, he carefully avoided looking up as he grabbed his underwear and pulled it on. Maybe I'll go ahead and do some fishing. The thought sent his adrenaline soaring and his hands began to tremble uncontrollably.

Not tonight. Some other time, maybe, preferably during the day, but not tonight. Not when even the sand tried to swallow him whole.

He picked up the rest of his clothes and the gaff. The hilt felt good in his hand. He stooped to get the flashlight, but didn't turn it on. Something might see it. He scrambled to the edge of the small bluff, and hesitated, ashamed. He couldn't leave like this. He had to take at least one last look. He turned resolutely back.

The light made a small hole in the darkness, like a tunnel leading directly to him. During the moment it took for his eyes to adjust, he felt vulnerable, exposed. He clutched his clothes to his body, as if to hide behind them. He aimed the light far out, trying to catch a glimpse of one of the buoys. They were too distant, but the flashlight dimmed their evil glow. The light just dwindled into a gray curtain. He breathed a sigh of relief as he swung the light toward shore.

Shock raced through him as the glint of metal stopped his swing. There was something coming out of the fog. Drifting on the tide, rocking silently, moving in and out of focus it came toward him. His eyes traced the sharp regular sides and the metal trim of a large crate before he dropped the light and bolted toward the bank. The soft dirt crumbled as he scrambled up the steep sides. His hands dug into the sandy soil. He went over the top with his last surge of strength, and stumbled to his knees.

"A crate. It's nothing but a big box. Off a ship." His breathy voice surprised him. He sounded almost rational as he knelt in the sand. "I'm safe here. Nothing can get me, it's just a box. Just a box. It can't hurt me."

He looked behind him, and the light was pointing directly at the crate. It brought him back to his senses. Nothing from the water could sneak up on him unseen. But what about from the land? At the thought, he whirled to look behind him, just to be sure. But all his senses told him the threat was from the sea. He took a step toward the Pinto, but glanced back nervously. The light caught the box full in its glare. An ordinary crate in good condition, it gleamed with moisture and the brass fittings were shiny and bright.

Nothing to fear. The words echoed in his mind as if they had been spoken by someone else. He hesitated, torn between the urge to run, and curiosity mixed with shame.

Almost eight feet long and four feet deep, the container rode broadside to him, bobbing easily, harmlessly in the current. As he watched, one corner caught on a sand bar, and the box swung to face him. It was outlined by a red glare. His eyes drifted. Why had he ever been spooked by a lighted buoy? It was a harmless light, a helpful light. A guide for sailors and a protection against storm and fog.

He focused on the box again. A harmless crate. There was nothing to fear. It might even be something interesting. Something to make up for a night of terror and lost fish. A feeling of peaceful relief stole over him. Everything was going to be fine as long as he didn't try to run away. Only cowards ran away.

He noted an emblem on the side and stood up to see better. Who would lose a fancy box like that? Why was it floating out there? What was in it? If he could get a little closer he might be able to read whatever was on the side. It looked sort of foreign. He edged closer.

An article he had recently read flashed through his mind. Something about a "green tide." Green as in

100

money, green as in grass. Some kids had found plastic garbage bags filled with marijuana. Sweet South American grass. The writer had theorized that smugglers had been pulled over by the Coast Guard and had dumped their illegal wares over the side. It was not even that unusual in this area.

How much grass could that container hold? How much grass could he smoke in a lifetime? How much money was he short this month? This year?

He looked at the clothes in his hands and hesitated. He was still shaky from the scare he had had in the water. Maybe it would be better to just go back to the base. He pulled his jeans on slowly. What else could that crate hold? Cocaine? Heroin? He wasn't very familiar with the hard drugs, but he knew they brought high prices. Did he really want to get involved with something like that? He glanced toward the car and the road beyond it. The fog hadn't reached that far yet, but it wouldn't be long. And if the patches he had run into on the way over were any indication, he was in for a hard drive back. The thought of going back empty handed and having to tell the guys that he had quit before he started was galling, but he took a step toward the car.

Coward!

A wave of embarrassment flooded him, leaving his face blushed with shame. He couldn't do it. He hesitated, then turned back, still clutching some of his clothes. The crate stood out like a monument, wedged solidly into the sandbar, just about where he had hit bottom and panicked. He couldn't head home with that memory as the only catch of the trip. He took a firm grip on the gig, picked up the flashlight, and headed back down the embankment toward his treasure.

There was an insistent keening sound, low in volume

101

but piercing in tone. It kept getting in one ear and rico-
cheting back and forth behind her eyes. Casey could
block it out for a little time and sink back into quiet
darkness, but it always reappeared. Soft and shrill, it
dragged her back with the ache it put in her head. Eventually, she tried to open her eyes to locate the source, but
she found that they were already open, they just weren't
seeing. When she concentrated, light gray areas became
walls and ceiling; a striped area to her left made her turn
her head to see moonlight streaming through Venetian
blinds; the single spot of brightness to her right was only
a reading light which illuminated the face of a dying
woman.

That was the source of the noise.

Casey saw the lips move, and heard the sound, and
still could not match the two. She tried to reach out and
touch the woman, she looked so close, but her hand only
flapped weakly. That infuriated her and she tried again.
Better. Her hand lifted off the cover and waved in front
of her face. At least it still worked, sort of. She didn't
feel as if much else would, but she gave it a try. Not
bad; she could see her toes wiggle under a sheet. Next,
she tried to sit up, but finally decided rolling over was a
better idea. She pushed hard, her wrists bent as if the
bones had somehow been removed, but she managed to
sit up. The noise was still there, more in her head than
her ears. She fumbled between the bars at the side of her
bed. One part of her mind acknowledged that she was in
a hospital, and another part thought that that was a very
good place to be. She hit the catch almost by accident,
and the bar caught the back of her hand as it went
down. She barely noticed the tug of the IV needle as it
abruptly left the inside of her elbow. Her arms helped
her legs over the side and she hung on to the bed for
dear life. She didn't know quite why her body was acting
like this, but it was making her more and more angry.

102

She looked down to see if her legs would move and her mind snapped into focus.

She tried to say, "Where's my body?" Her mouth was so dry that no words came out. It didn't stop her from wondering. "What happened to me? What the hell is going on?" The last question came out as a low moan, and she was startled to see the old woman turn and look at her. It distracted her from her own problems. She grabbed the bedside cart and used it to push her reluctant body to the other bed. Whatever had happened to her, she was alive and she planned to stay that way. This woman was dying; she wouldn't wait.

She reached the bed, lowered the side, and gratefully collapsed.

"C . . . ca . . . caaall . . . nurse?" Her voice had a funny croak to it, but it seemed to be working again.

"No. No, please don't. I've called 'em so much I don't lahke to bother 'em no more."

Casey listened carefully. The woman was not crying anymore, but she still seemed to hear it.

"You was asleep a long time, wahn't you?"

Casey started to ask her for how long and what had happened to the body she came in with, and why? Questions raced through her mind, but it seemed like too much trouble to ask, so she just nodded her head. There was a chain reaction of pain. The ache that she had ignored since she woke up suddenly crashed down on her and her eyes watered with tears. The muscles in her neck bent with the strain of holding up her head. Her shoulders and back felt encased in concrete. She tried to push the pain away, then settled for ignoring it again. If she couldn't talk, she could listen. She wondered if she would be able to make it all the way back to her bed when the time came. Would these stick thin legs hold her weight?

The room spun and she clutched at the mattress. Maybe she just needed a short rest. She propped her hand on the bed and leaned back for support as she forced her mind back to the dying woman. She looked down to see her crying and, on impulse, touched the wrinkled rivulet of a tear. The cheek felt as soft and thin as tissue paper and was still warm from the tear.

"Oh." The quiet sound was a surprise. "That's . . . That's nice." She couldn't bring herself to tell this poor young woman that it was the first time anyone but the nurses had voluntarily touched her since the operation. It was such a relief, just to feel the touch of a friendly hand. She reached for Casey's retreating fingers, but she was too weak. Casey saw the fluttering fingers and reached down to pick up her hand. She held it gently, noting the liver spots and age wrinkles. It was mostly mottled skin over knotty blue veins and sharp brittle bones. She was suddenly fascinated by the texture and color of the soft loose skin over round bulging knuckles and blade sharp angles.

There was a glow coming from that hand.

It was as if an invisible fire burned just under the skin. She could see neither smoke nor flame, but only a glow of colored light against the white sheet. She laid the hand on her knee and patted it gently, trying to feel the colors, but afraid to relinquish the support of her braced arm.

Yellow-brown felt sticky and clammy. Gray felt cold and slimy. She had never seen such ugly colors before, and certainly not radiating from someone's skin. She withdrew quickly, blinking and tossing her head to dispel the illusion, then had to fight the pain again to get it under control. She focused dizzily on the old woman's face.

"My mouth is so dry." The woman looked at the bedside table, unwilling to ask for help. Casey gladly put the still glowing hand back on the bed and reached for the Styrofoam pitcher and the plastic glass with the bent

104

straw. Water splashed onto the table and the floor, but she managed to get some in the glass. She helped the woman to wet her lips before she poured herself a glass. As she drank, she looked at the thin silvery hair over the rim of her glass. There were the flames again. Inert, unmoving, they hovered like a dark cloud close to that frail head. She jerked her eyes back almost guiltily to the dark brown eyes that met hers.

"Tha's raht, chile. I'm dyin'. I knows it."

Dark pain-filled eyes met confused blue ones.

"Iiii . . ." She forced out one word, but she couldn't continue.

"I'm tired o' lies, girl. They all lied t' me. Mary Louise an' them damn doctors. They tol' me I'd be fine, jest fine. They tol' me they'd take care o' me, then they shut me up in here all alone an' they jus' waitin' fo' me t' die. They jus' awaitin' fo' me t' die." She sighed heavily and a tear rolled down her cheek. "Guess they won't be awaitin' much longah."

Casey's eyes burned with unshed tears. She had to try twice, but her words finally came out. "No, I don't think it'll be much longer." Her head bowed, but her voice was almost steady. She was unprepared for the sobbing outburst that followed.

"Mah babies. All mah swee' babies. Why ain't they here? I'm so scared and they ain't even here to say goodbye. I don' wanna die."

Casey slipped to the head of the bed and gently cradled the crying woman. She shivered as her head entered that dark glow. Her first breath left her sick to her stomach; the smell was prolonged death, a fetid miasma of decaying flesh. She pulled her head back, then lifted the bird weight against her shoulder, careful of the needles and tubes. She wanted so much to help.

"You're not alone now." Her body rocked, futilely trying to console her.

105

The dark lady didn't have much time. She spoke in frantic spurts, wandering somewhere between the pain and the medicine, the past and the present. Her life, her loves, her children. She even laughed once when she talked about how scared she was on her wedding day. Before she died, she said quietly, "Mama, it don't hurt so much now." The room turned cold as the aura around her head and hands changed to a peaceful glow, then to a puff of gray smoke that faded before her eyes, and Casey realized that the old woman had gone elsewhere.

She sat for a long time, tears of weakness and grief pouring down her cheeks. Her arms were trembling when she gently laid the body out straight. She closed the dark gray lids over the dull brown eyes, fluffed out the tight white curls, and straightened the plain cotton gown before she made her way wearily back to her own bed. She slipped on the solution that had drained from the bag hanging above her bed, then fell half on the bed and crawled in the rest of the way. The room spun around her, and her mind spun with it. The feeling of death was almost tangible. She had expected the old woman to take it with her, but it was an overwhelming presence, making the air heavy and cold on her sweat soaked skin. Her hands and the crown of her head tingled almost painfully. The skin of her face felt stretched and tight, and her eyes burned as they searched each dark corner of the room. Her muscles ached and her head felt as if someone had driven a spike into the back of it. She tried to think back to what had gotten her into this mess. She remembered being in the bookstore, and the customers who had come in. When she reached the part where Billy Bazzel had entered the second time, she felt the tears on her cheeks.

Her thoughts were broken by a shrill, gloating laugh. It sounded maniacal, like wind chimes in a hurricane, an insanely frantic sound. She realized dimly that the sound was not in her ears, like the crying that had kept on after the woman had stopped.

Her mind grabbed for reality, but the bed seemed far beneath her and she had a sensation of movement. She opened her eyes and it was as if she were floating above water. Colors gleamed and sparkled around the figure below her and she tried to remember where she had seen him before. He was standing on the narrow beach that rounded the cove, and staring out into the water. She tried to turn, and was surprised when it worked. She revolved in midair and what she saw made her gasp. The crate was almost directly below her, and to her sensitive eyes it seemed to glow and pulse malignantly. The young man moved suddenly and her attention jerked back to him. She focused her mind and strained mental eyes and suddenly she could hear him talking to himself. It took a while before she realized that the dialogue was internal. She was eavesdropping on his mind.

"There's got to be something good in that crate," Mike Boyd whispered. "People don't toss something like that overboard for no reason. Every few weeks you read about a bale or a bag of grass washing up onto somebody's backyard or on a public beach. And those are just the assholes that turn it in. How many play 'finders keepers' with it? How many wash in at night and get collected by some lucky bastard like me? I'd be a fool not to even look, wouldn't I? How much could fit in there? How much would it be worth? Thousands? A million?" Beneath his outward bravado, Mike was scared. He desperately did not want to walk back out there.

Casey completely agreed with this undercurrent of fear. The clear voice tended to fragment and fade into a jumble of emotion. She tried to speak, to warn him to get out of there, but she knew she wasn't making any sound that he could hear. Something terrible was going to happen. She could feel it so clearly, why couldn't he? He

107

took a step into the water and she fought to bring herself back to the reality of the hospital bed. She caught a glimpse of white ceiling and broken moonbeams. The room was just stabilizing when she heard that insane laugh again.

She was more than scared. She was terrified. There was something evil nearby, she could feel it. It was pulling at her, trying to suck her soul out of her body. She struggled frantically, but the gloating laughter came again. This time words followed it. She knew it wasn't talking to her, but she was still helpless to resist it.

"Come. Now."

She found herself hurtling through space. There was no sensation of slowing, but suddenly she was there, hanging high above the water.

Mike pushed aside the undercurrent of fear and approached the water cautiously, like a man on the edge of a great pit. His feet scuffed through the sand and the gig in his hand probed the ground ahead of him. His eyes darted from side to side.

The tide had stopped, maintaining a delicate balance as it prepared to reverse itself. A mosquito whirred by and he noted how quiet the woods were: no night birds, no owls, no frogs, not even the splash of a mullet. The only sound was the blood hungry whine of that mosquito. He batted at it ineffectually, and found that he had taken another step toward the box. He stared at it fixedly, trying to make out the emblem on the side.

The more he stared, the brighter it seemed, as if it had been dipped in the phosphorescent algae that sometimes streaked the waves.

There is something special in there, he thought clearly. Something nice, just for me. Maybe more than grass, more than drugs. Something special. All for me.

He laughed at his fancy, but the smile didn't touch the fear in his eyes. Yeah, and maybe it's a pirate's treasure, with rubies and diamonds and strings of pearls and gold doubloons.

He reached the edge of the water and stopped. His head rocked from side to side as he tried to tear his eyes from the box. Dread dwelled up inside until he opened his mouth to scream, but he couldn't make a sound. He watched in horror as his right foot moved into the water and he couldn't stop it. He couldn't control his own body.

He panicked. He jerked away, throwing himself off balance, but instead of stepping back, he reeled forward. His left foot splashed into the water, his arms windmilled backwards and his head jerked up. His mind grew very still.

The container was blazing with light. He didn't need the flashlight, he could see perfectly despite the darkness. What was he so afraid of? Why was he fighting? It was beautiful. There was something wonderful inside, just for him. The box was there, waiting, but he had to hurry or it might get impatient. No, that wasn't right, it couldn't get impatient. He must have meant that the tide might turn and take it away. That was right. The tide might float it off the sandbar.

His mind was working very slowly now. He had been moving through the water but now he stopped. There was an immediate urge, like a pressure in his mind to get to the box. He swayed forward. The splash brought a flashback to the sudden terror when his foot scraped the sandy bottom and he thought that something had him. He felt a renewed flush of shame as he remembered how his arms and legs had thrashed against the water. For God's sweet sake, he was in the Air Force now. He wasn't supposed to panic like a snot-nosed kid. His white-knuckled grip on the gig loosened, and he took a deep breath. For the first time he was conscious of the muscle aches in his legs and shoulders. He took a step and the brackish

109

water burned the scraped places on his feet. He could see the emblem now. It was a wolf's snarling head against a background of stars and a full moon. The detail was incredible. When the box rocked slightly, the wolf seemed to snarl and the stars twinkled brightly. It was so beautiful.

He sloshed through the water until it was waist high. It slowed his movements, making his actions dreamlike as he rounded the crate to push from the other side. It rode high in the water. He touched the side gingerly, not expecting to feel the slimy sea growth that fouled his fingers. He snatched them away quickly, waving them through the cool water to clean them, then rubbing them together briskly. They still felt slimy and cold. Even through that brief contact, he had felt the stinging cold, like dry ice under a thick coating of rancid oil. It must have been in the water longer than he thought. What would be packed in dry ice? He didn't stop to think that the two conditions were mutually exclusive: Nothing that had been in the water that long should have retained such cold.

Again, he reached slowly toward the box. He could feel the cold from a foot away, and he shuddered. Out of the corner of his vision, he could see the glow from the buoy lights. The eyes were fainter now, more diffuse, as if the light had run and spread, absorbed by the fog. He felt a feather light push at the backs of his knees and there was a ripple leading away from him. The tide had turned. He saw the container shift slightly and he made his decision.

He used the point of the gig to lever it off the sandbar. It moved surprisingly easily, bobbing slightly in the deeper water. When it again stuck on sand, he pushed until it stopped moving and was out of danger of the receding tide.

He stared at the gleaming box, noting the glistening

brass fittings and a rusted padlock. He reached for the latter and gave it a strong twist. It held securely, despite the rust, so he prodded it with the gig, then inserted the point between the wood and the clasp and pushed. It seemed to loosen slightly, but he was afraid of breaking the haft, so he backed off. The fear was gone, and he felt pleasantly high.

"Can't get it open. Have to open it," he voiced aloud. His fingers fumbled numbly, picking at the lock with the point of the gig. It wouldn't open. "Open sesame." He giggled, then stopped. It seemed disrespectful. He could get it open. There was a hammer in the car. He patted the box consolingly, and grinned. "Be right back, sweetie."

He turned to go to his car, took two steps in the knee-deep water, and stopped dead.

He turned for one last look. It was wedged too solidly for the tide to take it back, but . . . maybe he shouldn't leave it. His thoughts dwindled and died as he stared at his treasure chest. It looked vulnerable. Small and beckoning. As if he could pick it up, tuck it under his arm, and walk off with it. And if he could, anyone could. Maybe a big wave could come in and wash it away; after all, what did he know about the Gulf and the bayous? Anything could happen to it if he abandoned it, even for a little while. It was his. He couldn't leave it like that.

This time he noticed neither the slime nor the cold. His hands grasped the bottom corner eagerly and he duckwalked backward through the shallows. He repeated the maneuver on the other side. In two more repetitions he had it on dry land.

He picked up the flashlight and traced the emblem with the light. The figures were raised and the detail was incredibly fine. He could see individual hairs in the wolf's ruff. The flashlight jiggled slightly and the figures seemed to move. A star twinkled, and the wolf's upper

111

lip snarled above an ivory canine. He moved the light up to the edge of the crate and traced the lid with both fingertips and light. When he reached the center, he jostled the lock slightly. It fell open.

He lifted the lock off gently. Cradling it in his palm, he touched the rusted mechanism, scraping idly with a fingernail. He must have weakened it before and the final tap slipped the lock. He flipped it into the water, braced his hands on the lid, and threw it open.

His first glance was incredulous. He swept the light back and forth, trying to comprehend what he was seeing and seeking something else. Marijuana, drugs, farm machinery for Christ's sweet sake! But not this . . . this putrid smelling, petrified figure.

He moved the light to the face. It looked like the *Return of the Mummy,* without the dirty bandages. There were faint white wisps of dirty hair still clinging to the scabrous scalp. The skin was stretched leather, rips and tears exposing the polished bone. A hole in one cheek revealed a long, gleaming tooth. A faint brown rim showed where the gums had receded from the root of the tooth. The eyes were open and staring. They might have been horrible, except that they were so dry and sunken that they looked fake, as if he should brush the dust off them. The whole corpse was too old and dry to even be scary, but the smell was gut wrenching.

He swept the light farther down. The clothes were in remarkable condition considering the apparent age of the corpse. It wore a black suit, pinstriped with a thread of pearl gray. The shirt matched the stripe and the tie was maroon. All were covered in dirt and dust. The skin at the throat clearly outlined ribs of cartilage. The hands were loosely crossed on the chest.

Damn! He'd been cheated. All that work and fear and it was just a stinking corpse in a lousy coffin that had probably fallen off a freighter. The rage swelled in his

112

mind until his face was distorted with it. His hands grabbed the lid, ready to slam it down when he caught a flash of red in the light. On the forefinger of the left hand was a ruby ring such as he had never seen. The ruby itself was carved into the gape-mouthed outline of a wolf's head. The ears extended back toward a hand that was nothing but leather over bones. The fangs were inlaid ivory. On one of them, a single ruby drop glowed.

He leaned a little closer to get a better look. In the back of his mind there was a niggling little thought: no one would know if I took it. I was cheated. I deserve it.

He squelched the thought harshly. The worst thing he had ever done was to "borrow" a car for joyriding. He hadn't been caught, but the agony he went through thinking that he would be convinced him that he was not meant for a life of crime. If he stole from a dead man, he would despise himself forever. But he had to get a closer look at that ring.

He dropped to his knees in front of the casket, then leaned over slowly. The light was focused on those long, bony claws; he didn't notice the slight movement as those dusty eyes followed him. His head was inside the coffin now. He held his breath against the smell of death, but that didn't keep his eyes from watering or his stomach from churning.

He reached to touch that glittering jewel, and a hand brushed his on its way up. He was slow, too slow. It caught his throat before he could move, before he could draw breath to scream. It locked the stale air in his lungs in a grip so cold that it sent chills throughout his body. The flashlight swung crazily as he raised both hands to try to break that grip. For one brief instant the face was in its glare. He saw the skin around the lips shred as wire-thin muscles tried to smile. The grip tightened and he was pulled inexorably down toward that gaping grin. He wrenched at those twig-like fingers and found that

113

they were stone hard. He beat at the arm, but the grip only tightened. His lungs were burning. His whole body felt as if it were on fire. He could feel his eyes bulging from their sockets.

It was more instinct and training than any higher brain function that brought the light crashing down between those dead shrunken eyes, but even so he noticed that they had become a bright, burning red in a black core.

His blow should have crushed that fragile skull, but it didn't.

I wanta go home, he thought dimly, as he saw his arm bounce upward after the strike. He didn't feel those sharp teeth as they plunged into his jugular vein and ripped out his throat in their haste to give him his desire.

The vampire drained every last drop, sucking at the opening long after the heart quit pumping. He tossed the empty husk back onto the shore like a torn rag, then licked his bloody fingers thoughtfully. They were still skin wrapped bones, but he could feel the strength that new blood gave him. He had to find more soon. He knew how quickly he would fade without it.

He had not stopped smiling since he made his move. Now his laughter rent the quiet bayou. He would have more blood. He would bathe in it; no, he would swim in it. He would bottle it like fine wine and hide it in his coffin. He would have warehouses of it. He would never go thirsty again.

He laughed until echoes came back from the far shore, muffled and distorted from the mist. He would have all the blood he needed to grow strong and young again. Then he would find Simon.

Casey felt the scream of madness bubbling up in her mind. When that dark eye had slowly turned, searching for its prey, for a terrifying instant she had had a vision of herself, pinned in its gaze. It would slowly peel her soul back in layers like an onion until the depth of her was revealed, black with the contamination of that gaze. Then the eyes fixed on the boy's throat and she felt giddy with relief.

The pressure on her mind eased as his attention focused on the boy, and she wrenched her thoughts back to the hospital bed. There was an abrupt, snapping sensation, like a rubber band stretched too far, then she was back in her own body. She screamed once before her voice choked off as she lost consciousness.

Chapter Five

Simon Drake stepped onto his balcony and stretched. He had already been out once tonight, but he was restless. All his senses were alert, his nerves were stretched to breaking. There was something out there. It had an interest in him.

One foot touched the top of the railing as he went over. He changed into a bat as he fell, his wings spread while he was still five feet from the ground, and he dodged sideways into the trees. Pine, oak, magnolia, dogwood, pecan, and wild cherry trees tangled into forest in all directions. Several streams wandered through the property, and willow and cyprus lined their banks. Moss hung in long strands, like torn spider's webs, and bushes and vines climbed upward toward the sun.

Simon headed into the thickest, darkest tangle of branches. His giant wings beat like a hummingbird's as he twisted, turned, leapt, and dove. He found a trail, followed it for a few moments, then darted in the opposite direction. From fifty feet, he dropped to twenty in a heartbeat. The moss rustled above and around him as he tried to slip through, and the backrush of air stirred both leaf and moss to life.

He reached a clearing and pointed his snout to the sky. The twitch of an arm muscle flipped him into a turn. He circled, then darted up again. The air was cool and full of scents: the sharp smell of pine, the dank aroma of moss, and the faraway tang of salt air. He could even smell the small lives below him, but the sky was his alone. His sensitive ears caught every returning echo of his squeaky little voice until his human mind formed a detailed picture of the terrain below him. Every leaf, every strand of hanging moss, every oak tree that hung its graceful, drooping branches to the ground was his. It was familiar, safe.

But something had invaded it. Something that pushed at his mind from all sides. Directionless, formless, it slipped away each time he tried to pin it down. He circled again, always climbing higher, focusing his mind now on the hunger that had invaded his territory.

As soon as he concentrated on it, he encountered the mist. It was as if hunger had taken form, but not substance. It clouded his mind and made all directions the same. The hunger ran through his veins like ice water. He needed hot blood to warm him. He fought the feeling, he had fed only an hour ago, but the hunger wasn't his. It surrounded him, overpowered him in the mist. He breathed it in. It had the smell of madness in it.

He would search the beaches first, he decided.

An hour later the thirst was worse than ever, coming in powerful waves as Simon worked his way along the coast from Pensacola Beach east along Santa Rosa Island. This was unfamiliar territory for him. There were too many places to hunt for him to risk crossing the deep Santa Rosa Sound. He flew faster, feeling the call from the north, but there were only two bridges. One was far behind him now, and the other only a few miles ahead. Over and over in his mind he asked, demanded to know, who the invader was, but the hunger was his only answer. He fought it, with all the control he had spent decades learning.

He was losing.

He could smell the humans below. Every passing car was a temptation, every apartment house a delicatessen. The hunger had reached the saturation point, like the fog rolling in from the sea. Except, the only fog here was in his mind. When he looked inland, he could see a dark bank, like a solid cloud that had come to rest on the ground.

117

Here the sky was clear and the moon shone, but across the Sound, there was only darkness. He had to find out what was in the fog. He opened his mind, listening for any hint. When he reached the next bridge, he planned to cross back to the mainland and search the inlets and bayous in the mist.

He flew low over a block of apartments and cottages. The sound of a car door slamming caught his attention. His mouth watered and his tongue tested the sharpness of a fang as the hunger boiled up inside him.

Not mine! The hunger isn't mine! His mind insisted. I fed once today. And twice yesterday. It is not my hunger!

He turned east again, but his hearing followed every step as the woman walked languidly away from the parking lot. The dark man in the truck waved once as he pulled away. The woman waved back, standing on the patio in the moonlight.

He controlled the urge to feed as he flew above her and on toward the bridge. He was fifty feet away when thoughts of Casey caught his attention. Casey? What did she know of Casey?

He turned as if jerked on a string. His strong wings flapped as he hovered over the building. She looked familiar.

She bent to lift the dangling, bell shaped blossom of a red hibiscus to the moonlight. She touched one long, delicate finger to the fine grains of yellow pollen.

He fought to ignore the hunger and his teeth clicked together sharply as he wheeled to avoid a branch. The slow beat of her heart was like a drumbeat in his brain. He could even smell the sweet blood pumping through her veins.

This is madness, he thought angrily. I can find the source now, if I can just control the thirst. His wings beat even faster as he tried to gain altitude, but his head swiveled to keep the girl in view.

118

She stretched languidly, pushing her arms up to the sky. She lifted her head and he could see the pulse of life in her throat.

He dropped like a stone and his fangs lunged into her neck, ripping the vein with the force of his blow. The hot blood pumped through the tear as he opened his mouth and let it pour down his throat. She grabbed his wings, trying to thrust him away, but her head jerked with pain as her grip jostled the fangs in her neck.

He drank for a long time, as her struggles grew weaker. When the first ravenous hunger was satiated and he regained control of himself, he realized that the source of the hunger was gone. He felt nothing. He turned his attention to the girl. She was lying half under the hibiscus bush, sprinkled with drops of blood and matching petals. Her heart was still pumping strongly; there was still a chance. He metamorphosed to human in an instant. He looked around to see if he had been spotted, then he picked her up in arms that barely felt her weight. He stopped abruptly at the door. It was a dwelling. There was no way for him to get inside without an invitation. He murmured to her sweetly, then again when she didn't respond. She finally moaned something unintelligible and he tried the door gingerly. It opened and he cautiously stuck his hand through the opening, like someone testing hot water. His hand passed easily through the barrier and he carried her inside. Her bedroom was the second door he opened.

He deposited her carefully on the bed, then smoothed the torn flesh of her throat back into place. The bleeding stopped when he touched it. He checked her breathing and pulse. She would wake in the morning or afternoon, sick and dizzy at first and very thirsty. He went to the kitchen and returned with a large glass of cold orange juice, sweetened with two spoons of sugar. More in penance for his loss of control than of remorse at her condition, he put it on the table beside her bed, murmured to her softly for a few minutes, and kissed her once before he left. She would

119

remember nothing, but her dreams and her throat would take a long time to heal.

The emaciated vampire finished his long awaited feast, and tossed the mutilated corpse aside. He levered himself out of the coffin with difficulty. His skin had an unfortunate tendency to shred when it brushed the hard surface. The boy had been young and strong, but one good meal was not enough to make up for months at sea. He needed more than one man's blood to regain his former powers.

His skeletal fingers closed over the edge of the box and he tugged until it slid through the soft sand. The effort of getting it up the crumbling bank exhausted him. He sat down on the top for a moment, willing strength into muscles that were little more than desiccated strings. Did he have enough strength to change to bat or wolf and find a food source? If he didn't find more blood soon, he would not have the strength to change back. It would be a hideous fate: to drop to Earth in animal form, unable to go farther, in vain hope that some small creature would wander into striking distance. If the animal was stronger than he, he would retain human consciousness while the body was torn apart and devoured. Human form was much safer, he decided. Besides, he would just have to come back and get his coffin. He needed to hide it before daylight. If he could get it into the car, he could drive to a house. That would mean at least one meal, and, with luck, a place to hide from the sun. He still had enough power left to take over any human with whom he came in close contact, but not enough to draw someone to him at a distance of more than a few hundred feet.

He glanced back at the water.

Free. He was free! What else could matter?

He could do anything now. Nothing could stop him. These pitiful mortals would make him strong as he bled them white. Even after their deaths, they would not escape him. When he finished with them, they would be feeding

120

on each other they'd be so hungry. He would move on when this place was a ghost town.

He realized that he was mumbling aloud, and he looked around warily. He was still too weak. They could gang up on him like they had on the ship. Dogs! All of them! But a thousand dogs could bring down one lone wolf. He had to be careful. There must be no witnesses. He would take care of them all. All the dogs would die.

He cowered for a moment, huddled in the protection of his casket as he felt Simon searching for him with his mind. He was tempted to change to bat form and escape, but that was tempting fate. The change required energy, which might be noticed. His mind was still strong enough to keep secrets from the brother who had been his slave, but Simon had changed. His mind was stronger. He was an unknown quantity now.

He was too weak to fight Simon. He needed food, then he would deal with his traitorous brother.

First, he would lie low and build up his strength. Then he would mark his territory, and in doing so, trap his brother in a circle of death. He had spent the last three months planning the perfect revenge. Now he had all the time in the world.

It must have been the feeding frenzy that had alerted Simon, because it was not possible for the slave to read his master's mind, unless the master willed it. But why hadn't Simon heard him when he mentally spoke to him? Was he really looking for Franz, his brother and master, or could he only feel the hunger Franz was broadcasting? From now on he would have to control his thirst, and hide until he knew more. He tried to suppress the hunger that still gnawed at him, but the meal he had drunk was not even enough to flesh out his fingers. It was like giving a starving man a single grape; just enough to get the juices flowing, but not enough to keep him from starving.

He tugged at the coffin until it was next to the hatchback, then levered it into the car with a heave. The end stuck out and he had to leave the hatch open. He went back to pick up Mike's body, then threw it into the water. There was no point in leaving it where someone might find it. When he opened the door, he wondered for the first time if he had enough power left to start it without a key, but Mike Boyd had seen no reason to take the keys with him in such an isolated spot. He sat for a long time in front of the steering wheel, waiting for the energy to drive without weaving.

The car started easily and he drove the rutted road with no problems. He hesitated at the turn onto the main road. He had to find a meal and a place to hide before daybreak. A place where no curious person might stumble onto his coffin and open it. In his condition, even a single stray beam of sunlight would incinerate him.

A car came whizzing by to his left, and he turned to follow it. One direction was as good as another until he could find fresh blood. He had driven ten miles when he felt Simon approaching. Panic seized his mind and his foot hit the accelerator. He had to get away. Simon was too strong. The tires screamed around a curve and his eyes searched the sky.

The feeling of Simon's presence grew. He was headed directly toward him. He wheeled the car in a U-turn, bumping over the shoulder and barely avoiding the drainage ditch. He concentrated on shielding his mind as he raced back the way he had come.

It was too late. Simon was coming for him. He whimpered in fear as he searched for an escape.

A narrow road opened to his right and he wrenched the wheel around. The car slid sideways through the entrance to a small subdivision. He almost had it under control when the back tire hit the curb. He cut the wheel, hard, and the Pinto straightened out. There was an old oak tree, thick with low-hanging branches, and he drove under its cover and cut the engine.

He could feel Simon, almost overhead. He cowered in

the seat, trying to make himself invisible. The sound of bat wings came clearly through the early morning air. High overhead, his brother circled, and the desperate vampire trembled. He bit his hand to keep from screaming in rage and fear while he fought for control.

Simon circled once, then continued north.

Fifteen minutes later, the smell of rubber and dust brought him back to reality. He was shivering on the floor of the car, but he couldn't remember why he was there. He climbed into the driver's seat, wondering where he was supposed to go, then drove straight ahead, waiting for a reason to turn.

He passed six houses in two miles before one caught his attention. To his sensitive mind, the place reeked of fear and secrecy. The house was separated from the others by a small stream and a stretch of woods. The yard was littered with parts of old cars, lawn mowers, and junk. The smell of fear had soaked into the very walls of the house and it pulled at him.

He turned off the engine and coasted the car into the yard. There were some lights showing on the second floor, but none on the first. It felt like the perfect place to relieve his hunger, without disturbing nosy neighbors. Judging from the well-kept houses surrounding it, even the most curious observers would stay far away from their less meticulous neighbor. He crept up to the house through weeds and tall grass. When he touched the wall, flecks of paint came off in his hands. He moved swiftly to a small window and peered inside. The downstairs was dark and silent. Putting his hand on the side of the house, he crawled up the wall, moving as silently and quickly as a spider. He reached a second floor window and paused. Two boys were sleeping soundly in bunk beds shoved against the far wall. There was a single olive drab dresser with nothing on the top of it. There were no pictures or posters on the walls, no clothes carelessly thrown on the bed or floor, no toys, books, records or tapes in evidence. The room looked un-

123

inhabited. Except for the small figures curled up on the beds, he would never have thought it was a room for children.

It was too risky. One of them could wake up and scream while he was busy with the other. He was too weak to take the chance that even two children represented.

He circled the house, moving easily along the vertical wall to peer into the next bedroom. A woman was reading in bed. She looked small and frail, with mouse brown hair and reading glasses. Her granny gown had seen better days.

There was a crib in one corner of the room, and he could barely see a small head at one end. As he watched, a young girl came in, rubbing her eyes. She stood staring at her mother until the woman noticed her.

"Janie, you gave me a start. You should be in bed."

The child shook her head emphatically, and her arms hugged her body protectively. He could almost see the tears in her eyes.

"Another nightmare?"

She shivered and nodded.

"It was just a dream and it's over now. Go back to bed."

The child stood and stared, not moving from the doorway. Her mother put down the book and held out her arms. "All right, you can come to bed with me. Daddy won't be back tonight." Janie scooted across the room and hugged her mother.

"There's just one condition, darling. You have to tell me, in words, what the nightmare was." The child shook her head negatively and her mother pushed her gently away. "Go back to your own room, then."

The girl twisted her old Snoopy nightshirt between her fingers and fidgeted.

"You have to start talking again or you might forget how. Tell Mommy what you dreamed."

She considered this gravely for a moment, then said softly, "Chased me."

124

"Something chased you?" The child shrugged. "Someone chased you?" She shrugged again. The woman tried to make the best of it, since it was evidently all Janie was going to say. She patted the bed beside her, and the girl crawled in.

"Where's Sally?"

Instead of speaking, she pantomimed. Her eyes closed, she laid her head on her folded hands as if sleeping, then looked down the hall.

"All right, then. Get under the covers and go to sleep. I just want to finish this chapter and check the baby, then I'll turn off the light."

The girl made a small lovely lump under the sheet, but his mouth was too dry to salivate. He moved again, around a bathroom window and to the last window on this side. This room was even smaller than the rest, little more than an extended closet. There was a double bed which filled half of the room, and a small dresser to one side. The opened door was directly against the foot of the bed. Again, there were no decorations, no untidiness. It was as personal as a cell.

The bedcover was thrown back on one side, and the pillow was dented from a small head. He could almost smell the warm, lovely, little girl scent.

On the other side of the bed, her head almost touching the window, was a sleeping child. She looked about twelve years old. If he couldn't control this one without alerting the others, he wasn't worthy of the title Nosferatu, he decided. He scratched on the window screen and she moved restlessly. He waited a moment, and scratched again.

"Sally?" The sibilant whisper could have come from inside her head.

"Sally. Let me in." The bright hair tossed restlessly on the pillow.

"Open the window, pretty girl. I want to come in and play." His mind was pushing at hers now. If she woke up enough to raise her head and look at him, just once, he would have the whole house.

"Mmmm . . ." The sound was a sleepy moan of protest now, he thought, but in an instant it would be a cry for Mommy.

"Sally, look at me. I have something nice for you."

She turned her head on the pillow, but her eyes were searching the small room like a trapped animal's. "Daddy?" Her voice was low and scared, and he enjoyed the fear.

"Over here, Sally. Behind you." Big brown eyes met black ones as her head twisted to see behind her. She stopped, mesmerized. His eyes enveloped her, smothered her with his power.

"Let me in," he ordered softly as his fingers moved restlessly over the flimsy screen. "I want to come in." She sat up and moved obediently to release the catch.

"Just ask me to come in!" He fought for patience against his hunger as she hesitated, confused. "Say it, you silly bitch! Say it!" He watched her flinch from his hunger and rage. Her hands extended to ward him off, but her tear-filled eyes never left his. "Damn you, tell me to come in."

Her head turned to the door, but her eyes rolled to keep him in view. He realized suddenly that he was too weak to hold her. He clamped down on his anger and returned to a strong, commanding tone. "Look at me. Come here."

She moved closer to the window, sliding on her knees in the bed.

"Just say, 'Come in,' pretty girl." Her ragged yellow night-gown slid up over her knees. "Invite me in, Sally."

Her eyes filled with tears. In a breathy, little girl voice that was rusty with fear, she whispered, "Come in, Daddy."

Simon gave up his search shortly after 3:00 A.M. After he left Beverly he circled the Bay area several times. Once he thought that he had pinpointed the source, but when he flew over it, the area was a blank in his mind. The waves

126

of hunger had lessened enough for him to ignore them safely.

He felt stronger, more alive and alert then he had in years. That's the advantage of frequent feedings, he thought with a lift of his snout. The gesture would have been a grin if he had been human at the time. Fresh blood always makes me feel younger and keeps the senses alert. But there are plenty of disadvantages, too. If anyone had been watching tonight, I would still have taken her. I was lucky. This time. But there IS another vampire around, I can feel him. Why can't I find him? His thoughts turned inward as he thought about all the old souls who had died in so many unpleasant ways. I thought I was the last Old One left.

It wasn't true that death was never pleasant or welcome for a human, but it was true for his kind. He had seen people glad to be released from their suffering, and people who were simply too tired to go on. They could welcome death with dignity, like an old friend who had come to stay. But his kind never died that way. Physical pain was a brief thing to them. Injuries either repaired themselves almost instantly, or they were fatal, such as a stake through the heart. Death by burning or drowning was slower and more painful, but even that usually lasted only a few minutes. He often admired the humans for being able to put up with months and years of pain. That took a special kind of courage. As long as there was young, healthy blood around, there was no need for him ever to be tired, or hurt, or to grow old.

Mental pain was a different problem. He had long since come to terms with his way of life. His longing for daylight, for endless sunny days and bright blue skies was like a dull ache in the back of his mind. It was never worth killing himself over, but it was always there. It was much the same with his food. He could never relegate humans to the status of cattle as did some of his compatriots. Blood was blood. He had tried living off cattle and sheep at various

127

times, but he always returned to people. The lower animals could never satisfy his hunger, they could only stave off starvation.

They were his own kind. In a curious way, they were his reason for living. He admired them all. They lived so frantically, aware deep down of their own mortality, but never admitting it to themselves. Each one was like a flicker of light in the dark. Each a different shape, size, color and intensity, but each aware that sooner or later the light would flicker and go out. That was the difference, perhaps. Animals had emotions: love, hate, joy, and fear; but one could never quite feed on them. He fed as much on human mortality as he did on human blood.

At least I haven't become a fear junkie, he thought as he landed in his courtyard, changing to human as he touched down. He stood for a moment, enjoying the soft coolness of the night air. The flight had been a good one. He had not been caught when he took the girl and the waves of hunger had almost stopped.

Maybe he was overreacting. The one who had been there tonight must have heard his threat. The stranger would leave without feeding again. Only one of the Old Bloodmasters could be so strong, and he would be too smart to start a feud. Simon's reputation was widely known among his kind. Over the years, others had learned a healthy respect for his power.

He lifted his head and faced into the wind. There was a strong breeze and the smell of rain.

Was there a storm coming?

Simon's brother tossed the small body back onto the bed. Franz's eyes were bright now, black pools streaked with livid flame. As he wiped the blood from his mouth, he felt the leathery skin of his chin start to crack and peel. The feeling in his fingers was coming back, and he scraped a swatch of skin from his neck where it itched. It felt papery and crackled with dryness in his hand. The new skin

128

underneath was still stretched tight over protruding bones.

He moved cautiously down the hall, his fingers still scratching at his skin. The boys' room first. He would take care of them quickly and quietly, not stopping to play. There was no reason to test whether or not he was strong enough to handle more than one at a time. A young towheaded boy slept in the upper bunk, near the door. He picked him up easily and carried him into the hall. With a strong mental command for silence, he woke the child.

He had not anticipated the effect that the sight of his ravaged face would have. The boy took one look, opened his mouth, and tried to scream.

Franz ripped out his throat regretfully. Air and blood bubbled out through the open windpipe. He hadn't wanted it to be this quick, but the experience taught him that he was still too weak to play around with them. Perhaps, after these two, he could take his time with their mother, and arrange it so that it didn't matter if she screamed.

Matt woke up when Jake's body hit the floor in the hall. He rubbed the sleep from his eyes, and on hands and knees in the lower bunk, he peered cautiously around the door. Jake's body was on the floor, almost at eye level. It looked funny, kind of yellow and shriveled. So that's what a dead person looks like, he thought wonderingly. He and Jake had discussed it just last week, and Jake had claimed that his baby brother would scream if he ever saw one.

"I'm not going to scream," he said aloud.

"Good." The voice was as velvety soft and smooth as a night wind.

Matt's eyes traveled up an impossibly long distance from dirty black shoes to thin legs and funny coat to a face that looked as old as God. Or the devil. He opened his mouth to scream, but a peeling claw hooked around his throat and dragged him out of bed. He writhed and kicked in that grip, but his feet were dangling off the floor. He was drawn closer and closer to those gaping fangs. His fist struck out, landed just under an eye, and he watched with horror as the thick skin shredded under his blow.

This wasn't the way it was supposed to be. Monsters were just in comic books, and on TV, not in real life. They weren't supposed to drag you out of your bed. They weren't supposed to kill your brother or hurt anyone. Monsters were for fun! They were like the roller coaster, where you got scared, but you knew that no one could really get hurt. This wasn't right. It wasn't fair. His chest hurt as he tried to suck in air. The little that got through made a whistling sound in his closed throat.

He watched the thick skin shred, but it didn't seem to hurt this monster at all, and the fangs slowly came closer. The grip on his throat relaxed a little as the fangs sunk into his neck. He shuddered with the pain, drew one deep breath, and died.

Franz finished draining the life out of Matthew Alan Wiltz and ran a sharp red tongue over his full red lips. He was beginning to fill out now. The skin he shed was dry and brittle, but the new skin under it was healthy and pink. His muscles were cords now, giving his bones substance and definition. Even his scalp was peeling, showing dirty brown strands under the lank white shreds. He needed more.

He would have it.

He moved confidently down the hall, striding soundlessly to the master bedroom. He paused at the door. The three of them were sleeping peacefully; the mother with her arm thrown protectively over her daughter's waist, and the baby, dewy pink in the crib. It was a scene to melt the hardest heart.

It made him hungry.

He moved the baby first. He put him on the bed in the first bedroom. Then he gathered the sleeping daughter into his arms, without waking her mother. He put her on the bed with her baby brother and her dead sister. The lock was a bolt type, unusual for an inside door, and he won-

130

dered for the first time what sort of house he had found, where one child called a vampire "Daddy" and there were bolts on bedroom doors. He put the thought away, and twisted the lock. His dessert would be safe until he had finished with the main course.

He moved quietly to the master bedroom. Estelle Wiltz slept as if drugged. He leaned over and kissed her gently. His lips lingered on hers, moved to her cheeks, then her eyelids as he slipped lightly onto the bed beside her. She sighed deeply and turned slightly toward him. He ran his fingers through her fine brown hair, touching, feeling, pulling her gently to him. She murmured softly and her lips curved into a smile as she opened her eyes. He saw the scream coming in her widened eyes and quick gasp. He kissed her hard, and thrust his tongue into her mouth.

She gasped in the putrid odor of the grave. She choked on fetid foulness, a sickly sweet odor of death and decay. Her hands came up to push him away and he let her fight. Her tongue squirmed against his, trying to push that foul gag out of her mouth, but he just thrust it in deeper. It twisted like a fat worm. Her brown eyes met his as she struggled, and she saw the satisfaction in his face. Without warning, she bit down hard, choking back her own revulsion at the taste of rotted flesh. A vision of gamy, green meat riddled with maggots flashed through her mind.

She couldn't believe that anyone could stand the pain of having his tongue bitten, but he didn't flinch from those strong white teeth. He felt her lips writhe against his as he pushed his pointed tongue deeper into her throat. She bit harder and his tongue was like hard rubber, thick and resilient.

She gave up trying to bite, and concentrated on trying not to throw up. She was terrified by the thought that if she did, he still would not remove that foul gag and she would strangle on her own vomit. She was probably right.

He waited until she had given up, then moved back

131

slightly, smiling as his right hand roamed her body. His left was still tangled in her hair, forcing her head back.

Without warning, she struck at his face. He closed his eyes, feeling her nails scrape the lids. There was no pain, no blood, only sheets of old skin that crumbled under her attack. He opened his eyes, then closed one slowly in a lewd wink.

His smile widened as he used one hand to rip her nightgown down the front and bent his head to run his tongue over her knobby brown nipples. His lips slid up over his long white teeth and the needle points raked her skin, drawing blood. She grabbed his hair in both hands and yanked upward frantically. For the first time, she screamed. His hair and most of his scalp peeled away in her fists. She shuddered with revulsion as she cast it from her. He looked up and smiled, licking her blood from his lips, then that horrid tongue felt the tip of one fang as if testing it for sharpness. He kissed her mouth again, then bit down hard on her lower lip. Her blood spurted into his mouth and he sucked at it avidly.

She screamed again. This time he heard the baby's cry echo hers. There was a loud banging on a door and he jerked up, tearing her lip in the process. He listened intently, then decided that the noise was from upstairs and could safely be ignored.

He worked his way languidly down her soft body. He kissed her breasts, then her stomach, enjoying the smell and taste of her. He bit suddenly, sinking his fangs deep into the hollow of her hip. He sucked for a long time, until her screams subsided into resigned sobs. His hands moved between her legs, pushing them apart. He slung his right leg over her right knee, unprepared for her sudden lunge. He could easily have prevented it, but he allowed her to bring her knee up sharply between his legs. He didn't even blink.

When he lifted his head and smiled at her this time, she gave up. Her eyes filled with tears and her head arched

132

back into the pillow. He noticed that the noises in the other room had stopped. He bit her on the thigh, working slowly inward with alternate bites and kisses. When he finally mounted her, she was slippery with blood. He kissed her deeply, letting her taste her own blood. His lips moved along the line of her jaw, under her ear, and finally he felt the big vein throbbing in her neck. His incisors went deeper than before, angling downward. Her blood was rich with adrenaline and the hormones of her fear. He savored every drop as his hips drove between her legs. As she died, he exploded inside her.

Janie woke up to her mother's screams. She could feel her sister in bed with her, and she knew she was back in her own room.

Daddy must be home, she thought, as her mother's voice grew hoarse. He must be very sick this time. He must be hitting Momma with the empty bottle again. He did that when he ran out of whiskey. Then he got sick, Momma said. He couldn't control himself. And sometimes, when he was very, very sick and Momma was lying in bed asleep or crying, then he would come and get her or Sally. Then he would hurt them in that special way he had.

She reached for Sally's hand, surprised that her sister wasn't already awake and holding her. Her eyes filled up with tears. A year ago, she had cried and begged him not to hurt her, but he got real mad. He hit her so hard across the throat that for weeks it had hurt to speak, so she had stopped talking. She had never found a reason to start again.

She reached up to turn on the light, and her hand brushed the baby's blanket. He rolled to the floor with a solid thud. There was an outraged gasp as he gathered breath to scream. She flicked on the lamp before she got out of bed to pick him up. She cuddled him ineffectually, then looked to her big sister for help.

Sally's throat was a gaping wound. Her head was turned to the side and her wide eyes stared straight at Janie. She screamed soundlessly, over and over, gasping for breath as she grasped her brother in one arm and bolted to the door. Her hand slipped on the knob, jerking at it frantically, but it wouldn't open. She pounded with one small fist, making the sturdy door rattle, but no one came to her rescue. David renewed his cries indignantly as her whole body shook with her effort and her tears.

Her hand was sore and swollen when she stopped, but her mother was still screaming. Janie turned to face the thing that had been her sister. The funny yellow colored skin was too big for the body and the teeth were too big for the mouth. Whatever had done that to Sally would do the same to them. If it was Daddy, she didn't care how sick he was, she had to do something to stop him. She knew better than to think she could stop him. She had tried before. She looked wildly around the room, searching for anything that might give her an idea. She put Davey carefully down on the bed, then tugged at the bedpost, trying to push the bed in front of the door, but her nine-year-old arms couldn't budge it. She picked up the lamp, and imagined herself throwing it at her father. She smiled at the thought, but her imagination worked too well. He batted it aside, his face leering at her. She moved slowly to the door and listened. Her mother was sobbing now. Daddy would come for her soon. She ran to the closet and opened it, searching wildly for some place to hide. Her closet was pitifully bare. On impulse, she grabbed her jeans and a shirt and pulled them on hurriedly.

She moved to the bed and flipped the covers back. They accidently landed over her sister's face, but she hardly even noticed. She patted David comfortingly as she knelt and looked under the bed, then she glanced back at the door. It was the first place he would look. She had hidden there once before, and he had made a game of it. He pretended to look in the closet and the dresser drawers and even out the window before he pounced on her. He had twisted her ankle as he pulled her out. She had limped for weeks.

134

The window.

She raced to it and looked out. The screen made a dark shadow in the backyard. It was a long drop. She looked left, then right. Left there was nothing but blank wall. To her right, about three feet away, there was a rain gutter. She ran back to the door and listened. Mommy was still crying, but softer now. Hopelessly. There was nothing she could do for her. The sound made her shiver.

She snatched Davey off the bed and went back to the window. She held him with one arm while she stretched with the other. When she leaned as far out as she could, she could just touch the rusted pipe. She looked down at the helpless baby in her arms. If I leave him here, maybe Daddy won't hurt him, she thought, but Daddy never did like him very much. He hit Mommy when she brought home a baby boy instead of a girl, and he always liked hitting Davey when he was even smaller than he is now. If he killed Sally like that, what will he do to Davey? If there was just someplace to hide him.

She looked around the room in despair. She had to do something. She went to the door and listened again. Far off, she could hear a night bird call: whip-poor-will, whip-poor-will. It almost obscured the pitiful whimpering sound that reminded her of a kitten she had found in the woods. She had brought the little tom cat home and fed him from an eyedropper, then from a baby's bottle. He had been her constant companion for years. Buck was probably out in those woods right now. The thought was curiously comforting.

She moved to the bed and sat down next to Sally.

What do I do now? she thought dismally. I've got to get out of here, but I can't carry Davey and climb too, and I can't leave him here. Her face hardened suddenly, matching the strength in her eyes. She grabbed a blue nylon windbreaker, and spread it on the bed. She laid him in it carefully, patting and rubbing him until he gurgled and smiled. He was always such a good baby, except when he got mad. Funny how such a little guy could make so much racket when he was angry. She pulled the cord that ran through the bottom hem of the jacket until it was tight, then double knotted it. She zipped up the front, and picked it up by the sleeves, and hefted it a few times to make sure he was secure. After the sleeves were tied together, she put her head and one arm through them. She had carried books this way, and even Buck, until he had scratched his way out and Mommy put a stop to it. This time she had to be extra careful.

She walked to the window, and put a hand behind her to shift the load. Davey was heavier than Buck, but he didn't squirm as much, and he didn't have claws. The jacket arms cut into her neck and shoulder, but there didn't seem to be much she could do about that. She climbed carefully over the sill until she could sit with her legs dangling. Staring down twenty feet into the dark yard, she hesitated.

Her mother gave one final agonized cry.

"Mommy." She whispered tearfully as she scooted far to the right and leaned over. She tottered for a moment, her hands grasping for the drain. She wavered and glanced down to see the ground ripple beneath her. The improvised pack gave a sudden lurch and she grabbed wildly for the pipe as she fell.

Her small hands caught it, slipped, and caught again. She hung by one hand. The rust cut into her fingers and flaked away her grip. Davey shifted and her left hand swung to the pipe. She grabbed it and squeezed for dear life. Twin tears of fear and pain leaked from under her closed lids. She took a deep breath and started down the pipe. It swayed alarmingly, and she held tighter, watching the rust rip her hands and listening to the pipe creak.

The trip down was endless. The pack cut into her shoulder and neck, and her muscles ached with the strain. Her hands were torn and bleeding after only a few moments. Her shoes scrabbled against the shingles and she tried to brace her knees against the pipe. She shifted each grip carefully, time after time, aware of the precious burden on her back. It wouldn't do to run away from Daddy just to smash Davey on the ground.

She inched her way down. When her feet finally touched solid earth, she dropped to her knees and cradled her hands in her lap.

She was about to take off the pack and carry him in front of her when she felt a chill run up her back. Her neck prickled, like the time she had almost stepped on a cotton-mouth water moccasin. Without a second thought, she struggled to her feet, overwhelmed by the fear she had blocked out for so long. She bolted for the woods, her feet pounding and her heart matching them. Her long blond hair streamed out over the pack, and Davey gave it a hard yank and gurgled in laughter. The long grasses caught at her as she threaded her way through the clutter and junk in the yard.

The first line of trees didn't even slow her down. She moved left, picking her way through the underbrush until she found the trail and was hidden by the forest. She turned to look at the house. There was a man standing at her window. Daddy? She held her breath as she watched.

Franz pushed the body off the bed and it hit the floor with a thump. He stretched languidly, enjoying the feel of strength and health that poured through him. I look a little more human now, he thought as he picked a flake of dried skin from his chest. His arms and legs had a touch of roundness now, hiding the bones of his skeleton. His chest was filling out. Although he still looked like the seventy year old victim of a death camp, he felt comparatively good. For the first time in three months, he was full.

He scratched a smear of blood from his thigh, and his thoughts turned to dessert. There was no hurry now. He would clean up first. At times he had dreamed of a hot bath or shower, but that was impossible without special

137

protection. He would have to be satisfied with wiping off. He got to his feet, moving lazily now, and walked into the adjoining bathroom. He wet a towel and began to wipe his skin. He rinsed the cloth frequently, watching the water become brown and scummy.

When he was clean, he picked up his own clothes, wrinkling his nose at the smell. He couldn't put those back on. He searched the closets and found some jeans and a shirt. They hung on him loosely, but they would do for now. He was humming as he thought about dessert, but halfway to the girl's bedroom, he knew something was wrong. There were no sounds from the room. Not a baby's cry, not even the sibilant hush of breathing. He sprinted down the hall and smashed through the door, bursting lock, wood, and hinges with one blow. His eyes searched the room. He ripped the sheet from the bed, mercilessly exposing Sally's gaping wound and staring eyes. The closet door splintered as he hit it more in rage than in hope of finding the children. He strode to the window and his keen eyes searched the area. It was a long drop, but there were no signs of bodies below. He looked toward the woods, his eyes easily piercing the darkness, but not the foliage. There was no telltale movement, no slightest hint of a small child running for her life. How long ago had she left?

He noticed the drain pipe to his right and climbed out easily, making a cruel mockery of all her tearful, painful effort. He crawled out head first and bent slightly to smell the fresh blood. He scurried down the wall like a roach, his hands and feet clinging to the rough surface. About six feet from the ground he pushed off, twisted in midair like a cat, and landed lightly on his feet.

The girl couldn't have gone far. He should be able to overtake her in wolf form in a few minutes, since he had enough energy now to change without problems. He glanced up to check the sky and stopped in his tracks. It was less than an hour until dawn. He had planned to spend the day here, but if she escaped, he would have to find a safe place before the sun rose. She might already be too close to the nearest house for him to get to her, even in bat or wolf form. If he wasted time now, there might be none later. He was strong again, but not to the point where he could risk even brief exposure to sunlight.

The girl hadn't seen him. She had been asleep when he moved her. She wouldn't know who or what had killed her family.

The rage in him was building. She had no right to escape him. He had waited too long for this, and she had stolen his final pleasure. Like a spoiled child robbed of a sweet, he could think of nothing else.

He changed quickly. His wings, fluttering like flags in a strong wind, carried him easily across the trashy yard, and he flew higher to clear the treetops. The growth of the forest kept him from scanning the ground beneath him, but worse than that was the light that appeared through the trees. He flew higher. The light was from a house just beyond the woods to the north. An old couple appeared on the porch with a flashlight. Even at this distance he could hear their words.

"I heard someone screaming, so I called the police. If he's beatin' those kids again, we've got to stop him, Bill."

Bill's voice was old and tired. "They was just out here last month. Ain't nothin' they can do but send those child welfare people out. An' Estelle and the kids keep lyin' to protect him."

The woman answered sharply. "I don't care. I'm goin' over there. Maybe if we interrupt him enough, he'll get tired of—"

"Maybe if we interrupt him enough, he'll come after us one night! You ever think of that, Mattie?"

The voices trailed off into an indistinct murmur as he flew back down the path to the other house. He had to get his coffin and get out of there. The cops were evidently accustomed to being called out to the house at all hours and they might be here at any moment. He had not anticipated that. Surely it was a man's right to beat his woman and kids if he felt like it? In South America, it was no one's business what a man did to his own property. Perverted laws like these might make his plans more difficult, but . . .

He caught a mental whiff of the girl and the baby. They hadn't run for the neighbor's house after all.

He paused, listening. He still had time. It would take the old couple several minutes to get this far down the path.

Below him, close enough to see the glint of his fangs in a stray beam of moonlight, Janie crouched. Her hand hovered over the sleeping baby's lips. Her breath came through her mouth as she tried to stifle her panicked breathing.

She had watched from a twist of the path as the man came down the wall head first. She had seen him lift his head from the drain and look straight in her direction. She stood, transfixed, as he leapt to the ground and changed into a bat. In her straightforward mind the conclusion was inescapable.

Daddy is a vampire, she thought. All this time he's been one and nobody knew it. That must be why he likes to hurt people, to see them bleed.

Her main emotion was one of wonder. Why hadn't she ever realized it before? It was so obvious. The only reason that no one had ever suspected was that vampires weren't supposed to be real. Now that she knew, she couldn't understand why everyone couldn't see it. What would they say when she told them?

She took one step down the path and froze as he passed overhead to the north. She would stop and think about it later. Now she had to hide where he couldn't find her. She headed straight into the underbrush, carefully pushing aside brambles that might have scratched Davey's face. She had lived next to this small stretch of woods for the whole of her nine years and it had been her refuge more than

140

once. She had hidden here from her father too many times to panic just because he had found a new way to torment and trick her. She wouldn't have been too surprised if he had sprouted horns, hooves, and a tail, and turned into the Devil Incarnate. She had seen him that way often enough, in her mind's eye. But it just didn't seem fair that now he could fly after her, too.

She dodged under a tree branch and stepped over a blackberry vine. Even in the darkness, she found her favorite hidey-hole. A fully grown pine tree, perhaps three feet in circumference, had broken about three feet from the ground and fallen to the side, still attached to the trunk. Over the years, brush and debris had collected on both sides and had been woven into a thick matting by vines. One small entrance had been left, near the trunk.

Of all her hiding places, this was the one in which she felt most secure. A hundred times she had hidden there, while her daddy had walked the nearby path, calling her name. She had peeked out from between the branches and watched him, knowing that if she could just hide until he passed out, he might not remember his anger in the morning.

Laying David down under a windfall of branches, she climbed carefully in beside him. She would have been happier if she could have poked around first with a stick, but right now, dying from snakebite didn't seem so bad. She cradled Davey closer as she watched that giant black form come flapping toward her from the direction of the Larson's house. The baby had had a hard night. Crying had worn him out and now he slept peacefully, but she kept her hand near his mouth in case he awakened suddenly. Davey would be alright. She would take care of him.

Bat wings filled the night. She could see the red glare of his eyes as he searched the path to left and right. He hovered as he came across from her, and she prayed desperately for something, a rabbit, a 'coon, a 'possum, anything, to break cover and streak past those deadly eyes. But the

141

animals were still, and the woods silent, as if the whole world held its breath in terror.

His eyes met hers and pinned her like a butterfly in a display case. She tried to look away, but she was trapped.

He ordered her forward. She fought it with all the determination and will of a born survivor.

She lost.

Her mind gibbered in fear as her legs moved against her will. Janie crawled out with leaves, twigs and dirt stuck almost comically in her hair and clothes. Inside, deep, deep inside, a small part of her shrieked in protest. It warned her back, fighting to the last, making her hesitate and stumble. Davey made a small, sleepy sound.

That other, silent voice thundered at her, hurting her mind, and forcing her to obey. She took a stronger grip on the baby and started forward obediently.

"Hurry. Hurry." It was sweet now, and gentle as long as she did what he said. She wanted to go to Daddy now. To please him. To make him love her and stop hurting her. She had always tried so hard, but she was never quite good enough. Now she would be.

A small part of her mind thought a naughty word and kept fighting.

"Come here." The words blasted at her, and she cringed back in fear. "I'm not angry with you, sweetling." The words were softer and reassuring in her mind. "Come here. You will see how kind I can be. Come to me."

The words went round and round in her head. She stepped forward to hear better. She tried to walk through the brambles to get to him faster and one long vine whipped across Davey's cheek, leaving a bloody trail of droplets. She ignored his outraged screech and kept blindly trying to push her way through.

"Careful, you stupid bitch." The bat wings beat in frantic rhythm with her heart, as she cringed again at the lash in his voice. Davey cried and screamed against this latest outrage.

142

"Shut him up." The voice beat at her cruelly and she squeezed Davey's mouth and nose closed as she stared into those bat-red eyes and crouched down to get around the briars. She moved slowly and cautiously, still blocking off the baby's air. She was almost within touching range of him now and she released the baby's mouth to stretch out her hand to him. Scarcely able to contain his impatience and anger, he flew closer. His wings fairly danced on the still air. His mouth opened wide and the long sharp fangs were exposed. Davey screamed in terror.

The pointed little head whipped around to look down the path.

She blinked dazedly as his mental hold was broken. She opened her eyes and he was gone, as if he had never been. Relief poured through her as she straightened up slowly and took the final step on to the path.

"Over here, Mattie. I can hear the baby cry."

She hugged Davey gratefully as she listened to her neighbors come down the path.

"I told you I heard something. You go on to the house and wait for the police. I'll take care of the little ones."

Aunt Mattie Larson's dear voice broke the spell. Janie ran to the light and threw her arms around the short woman, clutching her desperately.

"Good Lord Almighty! I mighta known it'd be you, chile. You're the only one with a smidgen of gumption in the whole bunch." She stepped back and played the light over the pale face, the ripped and dirty clothes. "Looks like it's been a rough night for you. Come on back with me. Your Daddy won't dare come for you there."

Janie hesitated, then turned back to face the house. Her whisper was too quiet for old ears to catch.

"Daddy?"

He circled once above their heads, watching as the children were guided to the Larsons' house. He marked it in his mind. He would return and repay them for taking what was rightfully his. Even if he wasn't hungry at the moment, this temerity would have to be punished.

The sky lightened, and he looked around uneasily. There were clouds on the horizon, but he had less than an hour until dawn and he had to find shelter. He flew straight to the house and landed on top of the car. His claws scrabbled on the slippery roof. He slipped off and changed to human as he hit the ground.

He thought briefly about going back to the cove, since it was the only area with which he was familiar, but he knew that there wasn't sufficient cover there to protect him from prying eyes. It would be better to drive away from the water and take his chances. Dawn light would be weakened by the clouds. He would have a few extra minutes between gray dawn and the full light of the sun. He hoped he wouldn't need them.

Chapter Six

Hearing returned first. Small sounds were magnified until they echoed in her head. Voices blurred and shifted until she didn't know whether they were real or dreams. Words trembled on the edge of understanding, then faded away. Footsteps clacked sharply on a tile floor, then multiplied until they merged into one continuous racket that made her head ache and throb. After a long time, one voice came clear. It was a dear familiar voice, calm and understanding, that soothed the pain until she relaxed into a light sleep.

"Mrs. Brighton, I don't want to upset you." The doctor spoke in those unctuous tones which never failed to do just that. "We had a problem here last night, but I want to assure you that your daughter is just fine."

"Fine? How would you know? The monitor was disconnected last night. She could have died in her sleep and no one would have even noticed. And how did she get that bruise on her arm?" Her eyes flashed as she flung the questions at him. She had waited all morning for someone to explain the dark black and purple bruise on Casey's poor, thin forearm. She had asked a nurse about it early this morning but the only response had been that it hadn't happened while *she* was on duty. It wouldn't have happened if Kate had taken Cassandra home two months ago. She could have taken better care of her there. Whether the staff liked it or not, even if Ned disagreed, she wanted Casey at home.

145

"Well . . . the monitor keeps malfunctioning, but we'll get a new one in this morning. As for the bruise, we aren't exactly sure how she got it. The nurses here are all very conscientious. They know that the bedrails must be locked in place at night . . ."

"You mean Casey's arm was under that thing when it fell?" Kate was indignantly horrified.

"Well . . . we don't really know, but the rail was down and . . . uh . . . when the nurse came in she found Casey, that is, she found the bruise on her arm."

"What else?" Kate glared at the doctor.

"The IV was out of her arm," he confessed. "The nurses are told repeatedly not to thread the lines through the rails, but it does happen, especially on inactive patients. I'm sorry about this, Mrs. Brighton. You know how careful we are here." He stood there, apologetic and helpless, until she finally nodded. Dr. Meistershoorn had told her privately that he had taken a look around the hospital and the care here was very good. He still hadn't been able to explain the discrepancy of the x-rays, but he had recommended that she leave Casey here. Eric had brought him to inspect the place after the last time she had mentioned taking Casey home. It had relieved her mind then, but now she couldn't help but doubt again.

"I'd like to talk to the nurse who was responsible."

"We don't know who was responsible." He was clearly miserable now. "No one admits it, and one of the nurses swears that the rails were clear and locked when she checked Mrs. Collins at 8:00 P.M."

"Where is Mrs. Collins? Did she see anything?"

He took a deep breath and stared fixedly out of the window. "I'm very sorry. I thought you knew. She died during the night. In fact, we even considered the possibility that Mrs. Collins woke up very disoriented. Instead of trying to call a nurse, she might have gotten out of bed and tried to wake Casey up. She may have accidentally hit the release and pulled out her IV before she got back into bed and died there."

"That poor old woman." Kate blinked back the tears, but

her doubts remained. "But she was so weak. She could barely raise her head. How could she . . . ?"

"I know. It just doesn't seem very likely. The night nurse heard a scream about 2:00 A.M., but she was in her own bed, and she was already dead. When she checked on Casey, she found the rail down and the IV solution was all over the floor. It must have happened about an hour or so earlier."

"That poor old woman. Screaming as she died, with no one there to hold on to."

"Yes . . . well. . . ." The doctor seemed at a loss for words. "She had been sick for a very long time. And in cases of that sort, it's almost impossible to control all the pain. The point is that Casey is no worse. I checked her over personally this morning. We'll have a new monitor in here tomorrow, but her vital signs are strong and her heart rate is even up slightly. There's just no medical reason why she won't wake up. Still, I'd like to run some more tests." He seemed honestly concerned, as he had from the beginning. She relaxed slightly. She could forgive a lot from someone who really cared about Casey. Still, the thought of that poor woman, screaming in pain as she died, made her blood run cold. Couldn't they have done something? Wasn't that why they were here? And what about Casey? What if she woke up some night, alone and afraid? Wouldn't that be enough to send her back under? Kate made a firm resolve to stop by the hospital at odd hours of the night to check on her.

The voices had changed from soothing and regular to disturbing and concerned. Casey's deep sleep lightened and turned to dreams.

She was dancing.

Her feet barely skimmed the grassy knoll. Her arms lifted and swayed, graceful as the tree branches above her. The soft night air smelled of honeysuckle and sweet olive, the freshness of salty Gulf air after a rain and something else. Something strong and alien: copper and electricity, ozone and salt.

She twirled lightly, quickly, her arms flung open as if to embrace the world, and her face lifted to the sky. It didn't

147

surprise her that her body was slim and supple, that it effortlessly obeyed every mental wish to leap and soar to express her joy.

Her eyes were closed when the first drop splattered against her cheek. It was warm, like a southern summer rain, and she opened her mouth to catch the next sweet drop on her tongue.

It burned and stung like acid, and her eyes opened in shock.

A giant looked down at her from the clouds. He had the face of a god. His eyes were as large as the whole universe. For a moment she felt the world tilt and she slid toward that void, but then her bare feet felt the grass beneath her and her toes clung to the wet earth. She couldn't take her gaze from those incredible, endlessly empty eyes.

Far back, in each eye, a spark was born. They grew as she watched, coming closer and closer until they were rivers of red, like winding streams of blood. They reached the corners of the god's eyes and spilled over, and she felt the warm rain on her bare shoulders.

Her flesh burned and smoked as the acid ate through to the bones. She tore her gaze from his face and bolted toward the woods, seeking shelter under the trees, but his eyes flashed and lightning struck in front of her.

She dodged left, up the hill, and glanced back in time to dodge the next stroke of lightning. This one ricocheted like a bullet and she heard it zing past her ear. She flinched violently away, turning left again across the meadow. The rain was harder and hotter. The acid tears were burning holes in her skin, leaving bloody red furrows in her shoulders, breasts, stomach, and legs. She could no longer tell the difference between the red of his tears and her own blood. Her cheek burned and she reached up to touch her face. Soft, yielding skin had been stripped away to hard, smooth bone. She tried to scream her agony aloud, but her jaws were locked and she couldn't make a sound.

The ground was clear and level ahead of her and she risked an upward glance. He was grinning, enjoying her pain and fear, feeding on it. She sprinted for the trees and a giant hand slammed down in front of her. The fingers stretched toward her and she zigzagged frantically, as fast and agile as a cat, but it was no use.

The hand grabbed her, lifted her off the ground kicking and screaming. One arm was pinned, but her right hand beat frantically on his index finger. She bent her head and bit him, and his laughter boomed deafeningly in her ears.

His mouth opened, as black, empty, and hungry as the void of his eyes. She knew he could swallow her in one small bite, and his hunger would be unchanged. His lips stretched up as his mouth opened wider and his teeth were revealed.

Two giant fangs, viciously curving incisors long enough to impale her, were surrounded by short, sharp teeth. His head drew back as if to strike, then darted forward and she could feel his fang puncture her heart. It felt as if her body was collapsing inward. She screamed . . . and screamed . . . and screamed again.

Kate and the doctor were at her side before the first scream ended. Her mother held Casey's arms tenderly as she thrashed and struck out at something only she could see.

"Casey! Casey!! Wake up, it's okay now. You're alive! You're alive and awake! I'm here. Momma's here. You're going to be alright now. It was just a bad dream." Tears streaming down her face unnoticed, terrified that Casey would slip back into that deepest sleep, Kate took her by the shoulders and shook her, while the doctor fought to get to his patient. Kate yelled at her. "Look at me, Cassandra! Look at me. You're safe now. You're alive!"

Casey's eyes were wide and staring. She gasped for breath as if there wasn't enough air in the world to fill her lungs. The doctor had already hit the nurses' call button, and he ordered an emergency tracheotomy tray as the nurse hurried in. She was back in less than a minute, but Casey's breathing was already easier.

An hour later they had run tests and more tests, and she was hooked up to more monitors than she could count. Apparently, being in a coma was not nearly so medically inter-

149

esting as waking up from one. Her father had been called and he would be on the next flight. Eric had arrived while the doctor was checking her condition and he had taken Kate downstairs for a cup of coffee after the doctor had almost forcibly evicted her from the room. They had been gone less than ten minutes when Kate had insisted on returning. Now she sat by the bed, gripping Casey's hand as if holding her to consciousness by her strength alone.

"Mom, how long was I gone?"

The doctor stepped in quickly. "You mustn't worry yourself, Casey, uh, Miss Brighton." He corrected himself hastily.

"Casey."

"Don't try to talk, Casey. Lie there quietly and let us do the worrying for a little while longer."

"But I want to know." Her voice was querulous and demanding, like a tired, spoiled child. She heard the tone and winced.

"Not now." The doctor's soothing voice succeeded only in irritating her more. "You aren't strong enough yet. You need time to recover, to heal."

Her mind struggled and fought for answers. She was still afraid, but she wasn't sure of what. She had to know what had happened. And the doctor sounded too smug to bear.

"You mean I'm not strong enough for bad news." She mused quietly, self-absorbed, as if the problem was simply an academic exercise. "For very bad news? I know I was . . . asleep? Unconscious? Dead? Gone? I don't know what to call it—"

"Coma." Her mother stated quietly, simply.

"Coma," she agreed, her brow furrowed. "It was a long time. I didn't get a body like this overnight." A small smile touched her lips. "How much have I lost? Fifty pounds? Sixty? So it must be at least three or four months. I don't think it's been over a year, 'cause you and Eric look just the same, except you look so worn and thin, Mom. Have you lost weight, too?"

Eric watched her dark hair tumble over the short cropped area at the back. Even her hair seemed to have come back to

150

life. He kept waiting, watching for some lapse of memory or reason, but this was the same old Casey, even to the nervous, concentrated nibbling on a fingernail. She jerked her hand out of her mouth as if she had read his mind. He grinned with satisfaction as she stared at her nail intently.

"My fingernails haven't been this long since I was six." Then her face fell and she stared at her hand mournfully. "If only I knew how fast they grew, I'd be able to tell how long I've been here."

"Unless we trimmed them," Eric teased.

"You wouldn't dare! Not after all the time I wanted long fingernails and could never grow them."

Eric couldn't deny her any longer. "Over two months."

She looked confused, then sad.

"Really, sir! If you can't keep your mouth shut for the patient's own good, I'll have to ask you not to see her again."

Casey smiled her thanks at Eric then turned to the doctor. "Excuse me?" she said politely. "But I don't think it's up to you to say who can visit me and who can't."

"The last thing she needs right now is to worry over what she's lost," the doctor continued, ignoring her.

"Dammit, Doc, look at her," Eric interrupted loudly. "Does she look like she can't handle it? Not knowing was worrying her more than knowing will."

"More than two months. June to August?" Casey asked tentatively, ignoring them both.

"June twenty-seventh to September first, darling," Kate agreed with Eric without hesitation. Casey was as bullheaded as Ned; if she didn't know something she would worry at it until she figured it out. If the answers upset her, at least it would keep her awake. Kate was deathly afraid of her going back to sleep right now.

"Well, I guess the damage is done." The doctor's tight smile was an effort to make the best of things and Casey felt a sudden rush of sympathy for him. "What is the last thing you remember, Miss Brighton?"

"I . . ." She turned pale as the memories rushed in. "Oh, God! Billy Bazzel! He shot me! I saw the gun and. . . ." Her voice broke and her body shook with sobs. Kate sat on the bed next to her and rocked her as if she were a small child again.

"It's okay, Cassandra. You're here again, that's all that matters. You're going to be fine. Just fine." Kate looked at the doctor hopefully.

"Uh, yes, I think she is," he said amazed. "If you remember that much . . . memory usually comes back in bits and pieces, if it comes back at all. It's a very hopeful sign. Very hopeful. And she's talking. And making sense. It's really quite remarkable. You'll have to take it easy for awhile. No excitement, lots of rest. Your eyes may be very sensitive to the light, and you may have trouble keeping food down. And there are a lot of tests we'll want to run."

"I'll be good, Doctor . . . ?" She strained to read his nameplate, and ignored the part about tests.

"Driscoll." His red complexion faded back to its normal sallow color.

"I'll be good, Dr. Driscoll. I just want to know what I missed. And I don't feel much like resting right now. I think I've done enough of that for a long, long time. You took good care of me while I was gone, and I really appreciate it."

"I think your family and friends deserve most of the credit. There wasn't much that I could do for you, but they never gave up. They sat here day after day and read to you and talked to you. They massaged you and exercised you so you wouldn't be too weak if, uh, when you woke up."

"They must have done a good job. I feel okay." Casey had examined him curiously while he was speaking. He was a tall, stoop-shouldered man. Distinguished rather than handsome, his nose was too large and his mouth too small, and he looked gorgeous to her. She noticed that she was seeing those funny colors again. They were all around him, mostly blue and purple. She tried to ignore them. "But I'm sure you were some small help," she said teasingly. He wasn't used to such behavior from his patients, she noted. He blushed when she smiled warmly at him.

"Don't bother to thank me." Eric nudged her legs aside as

152

he relaxed on the side of her bed. One hand rested negligently on her knee. "Of course, I had to force myself to massage you every time, but what I'm really going to miss is being able to talk to you without you interrupting all the time." His mocking grin said welcome back more clearly than any tender words would have.

"Well, if you did the talking, I guess I didn't miss much. Maybe I'll take another nap." Casey's flippant answer hit all of them harder than she would have guessed. She shuddered at the thought of going back to sleep, while Kate fought back her tears.

"I don't think we could stand the strain." She squeezed Casey's hand. "Are you really feeling okay?"

"I feel like . . ." Casey hesitated, then told the truth, "like I've been beaten with a brick. I think every joint in my body is rusted through, my muscles feel like overstretched rubber, and would someone please take the hatchet out of my head?" To her utter embarrassment, her eyes filled with tears of self-pity and she could feel her lips tremble. Her mother reached to hug her, but the tubes and wires got in the way.

"No, really, I'm fine. I'm just glad to be back, and I want to go home." Casey tried to stop whining.

"Some weakness is perfectly normal, Miss Brighton. You can expect weakness, headaches, muscle aches, memory loss, nausea, sensitivity to light, disorientation, some pain, and perhaps quite a bit of depression. We'd rather not give you anything for it right now. It's better if your body can adjust by itself. You may also have some trouble sleeping, either too much or too little. You may even be afraid to sleep." He looked and sounded thrilled at what she was going through. "You can't go the rest of your life without sleep, so just try to relax and enjoy the fact that you're alive. I don't pretend to understand it, but a few weeks of exercise and you should be as good as new. Well, even better, considering the weight you've lost."

"Every fat person's dream, right?" Casey looked up ruefully. "Go to sleep one day fat and wake up the next skinny. Except for me it wasn't the next day."

"The Sleeping Woman's Diet," Eric chimed in. "You look fantastic."

"It *is* what you've always wanted," Kate said, fighting back tears. But, oh Lord, not like this, she thought. We pushed her to lose weight, nagged at her, yelled and screamed at her, but we never wanted it like this.

Casey looked at her, easily reading her emotions. "What do they say?" she asked wryly. " 'Be careful what you ask of the gods, they may hear you.' " Her tone was of bitter understanding, but she swallowed bravely and tried to smile. "You'll just have to find something else to nag me about."

"I could make out a list," Eric grinned. Even though she knew he was joking, Casey had to close her eyes against the tears.

But the doctor seemed to understand. "Please don't let it bother you, Casey. Your body has been through a great deal, even if you don't remember it. Tomorrow we'll run some more tests."

"When can I go home?"

"Tests for what?" Eric interrupted.

"I don't anticipate any problems, Mr. Tyler. The preliminary results are quite good."

"But?" Casey prompted.

Dr. Driscoll seemed at a loss. But he looked at Kate and she nodded firmly, so he continued. "There's a possibility of memory loss, or even muscle or nerve dysfunction. But please don't anticipate problems. I certainly don't. It's just that your case is so unusual. I'd like to ask some other doctors to have a look at you, too."

Casey cocked her head as if listening to something the others couldn't hear. "It's unusual and you want other doctors to study me? I . . . I don't think so. You've been very kind, Dr. Driscoll. I know I owe you a lot, but I just want to get home and start living my life again. So, if you please, no more tests and no more doctors. Is there really anything that would keep me from leaving today? Or tomorrow?"

"That would be very foolish! I don't want to scare you, but if you do have brain damage your headaches could get worse, you could pass out, or even hemorrhage."

"But I've been lying here for months. If that was going to happen, wouldn't it have happened by now? Besides, I must be healed or I wouldn't have awakened." She wanted out of there, but she also had the feeling that he was more concerned about her "unusual case" than he was in getting her back home and to work. "What is the soonest I can get out of here with the minimum of tests?"

"That's another thing. You've been lying here for months. We don't want to take the chance that a blood clot has developed and could travel to your lungs or your brain."

Her expression hardened. "When?"

He looked at her calculatingly, and she could tell that he would stretch it out as long as possible. "Saturday," he said firmly.

She had the grace to look embarrassed. "What day is this? know it's the first of September, but what day is it?"

"Tuesday." Her mother filled in.

"Then I go home on Thursday, whether you've finished your tests or not."

"If you leave against medical advice, your insurance won't pay for it." The doctor's complexion had gone from sallow to flaming red again.

"If you okay it, I'll make myself available if you want to bring in some specialists to show them what you've done." She hit him hard on that one, she could tell, but he came back well.

"These precautions are for your own good, Miss Brighton," he started, but he stopped when Kate shook her head at him.

Eric was grinning like a fool as he leaned over to kiss her and say, "Forget your tests, Doc. Casey is back, and there's nothing you can say to change her mind. Welcome home, Case."

She returned his kiss with interest, trying to ignore her mother's approving gaze.

"Not home yet and I don't know if I can even wait till Thursday. In a way, it feels like I just left home this morning, but in another way, it feels like years. I can't wait to get home to my own things in my own house."

Eric's lips twitched convulsively and Kate turned her head away. Casey looked at them suspiciously.

"Uh, Casey?" He said hesitantly.

"Yeah?"

"Well, uh. . . ." He looked to Kate for help.

"Dear, I really didn't have anything to do when I got home at night. And it's been so long since the house was painted, and papered, and rearranged."

"Oh, no. Mom, you didn't really! Did you?"

"Eric and Ned and Paul and Clarise and I uh, we, uh . . ." she took a deep breath and blurted it out. "We just fixed up a few things. New paint, papered the walls, rearranged the living room and the kitchen. Nothing important."

"Oh, no! Not my house! Mother!" The last word was an agonized wail.

"Mr. Tyler? This is Simon Drake." The words were spoken with an unconscious arrogance.

"Mr. Drake, I'm glad you called." Eric recognized the name immediately.

"You did say that I should call when I was ready to take you up on that drink."

"What a coincidence. I was going to call you tomorrow. Casey woke up this morning. The doctors say she'll be fine. We'll have more to celebrate than we planned."

"That's marvelous! I thought they had given up hope."

"I think they had, but they just wouldn't tell us. I talked to her today and she's weak, but she really does seem okay."

"Incredible! I'd really like to see her again. When will she be out of the hospital?" Simon asked.

"That's a good question. I think if it was up to the doctor, he'd keep her for a few weeks, but Casey says she's leaving Thursday."

"Why do the doctors want to keep her? Is there some problem?"

"Oh, nothing serious. Or, at least, I don't think so. He said

156

something about her blood tests, but I don't know what that has to do with her head. Anyway, Casey thinks he just wants to keep her and show off his 'miracle patient.'"

"Who do you think will win?" Simon asked cautiously.

"Casey!" Eric replied promptly. "The doctor doesn't stand a snowball's chance. She keeps telling him that the problem isn't in her blood, it's in her head. She'll be home by Friday at the latest."

"Is there still a problem?" Simon asked delicately.

"You mean brain damage?" Eric said curtly. He had to remind himself that except for this stranger, Casey would be dead. Surely he had the right to ask questions, even indelicate ones. "As far as we can tell, she's still the same old Casey. She's lost a lot of weight, and you may not recognize her since you only saw her that once, but inside, she's the same. She woke up asking questions and she hasn't stopped since."

"You mean that she just woke up? No one awakened her, no medicine or treatments or unpleasantness?"

"Well, not quite. She wasn't really having any treatments or medicine, because they had kind of given up, but she woke up screaming. It seems she had bad dreams, which they say is rare in a coma, but once she accepted that they were just bad dreams, she calmed down. She's really doing well now."

"I see," he said cautiously. "Nightmares can be quite upsetting. I've had a few myself recently. Do you think that she would be well enough to come over here for a drink on, say, Saturday? You could bring her."

"I wouldn't count on it," Eric said curtly. "She's been through a lot. When I said she was doing well, I didn't mean that she could get out and run around. But why don't you plan to come over and visit? You could come for dinner on Saturday and we'll surprise Casey. Just don't be too surprised if she doesn't recognize you at first. So far, her memory has been pretty good, but she only saw you that once, and then she was shot in the head. It may have wiped out those memories."

"I think you may be surprised at what she remembers," Simon remarked carelessly. "But I won't be offended if she

157

doesn't. However, I won't be able to make it for dinner. Shall we say drinks instead, about eight o'clock?"

"That's fine. We live on the island. I'll give you the directions."

After he hung up, Eric thought about the coincidence of Simon's call. After three months of calling to invite him to dinner, drinks, anything to show their appreciation, Simon just happened to call on the very day that Casey woke up. It didn't seem very likely. Did Simon have some source of information at the hospital that he just didn't mention? If so, why was he so anxious to meet Casey now? The clerk at the desk had told him that he had stopped by to see Casey more than once, yet Simon had very carefully avoided mentioning it. Even when he made the remark about Casey's weight, Simon had not reacted.

Eric put it out of his mind. It really didn't matter. All that mattered was that Casey would be fine.

He was anxious to meet that mysterious voice on the phone. Paul had told him a dozen times about Simon's incredible actions that day, and he wanted to meet the man who had killed Casey's attacker. Still, why was he hiding the fact that he had seen her? Eric's hand scrubbed unconsciously at the twitching muscle in his jaw.

Simon's strong wings caught an updraft, and he circled thoughtfully. There was a feeling in the air: a vibration that left him throbbing, an electricity that tingled almost painfully through him, an excitement that tightened his body and mind and yet left him in watchful suspense, feeling hollow and empty.

There was so much water in this area. The land was low, and threaded with streams and creeks, lakes and ponds. During the rainy season when the ground was saturated, even the smallest rain filled the drainage ditches and run-off areas and overflowed into fields and roads.

It was the rainy season, which always depressed him. A season of afternoon thunderstorms with lightning powerful enough to explode tree roots like small land mines, leaving torn bits of sap-filled cellulose at the bottom of two-foot deep holes. Season of ninety-eight degree days, day after day until the Gulf water temperature rose to the high eighties. Season of fat pine cones and fatter squirrels, deep blue skies and darker blue waters and tall, limber pine trees.

Season of hurricanes.

Chapter Seven

Jeremy Wiltz peered blearily through the dirty windshield of the car and took another swig of beer from the can perched firmly between his thighs. It had been cold ten minutes ago, when he dropped Al off at his house. He finished the dregs and tossed it into the back with the rest, then fished on the floor of the passenger's side for another.

"Damn!"

They had left the fishing camp with a fresh case only four hours ago and the three of them must have killed it because he only found one full can.

He looked up just in time to jerk the wheel to the left to avoid hitting the kid on a bike.

"Fuckin' asshole!" he yelled out the window as he went wide around the turn. His house was in sight, but he slammed on the brakes. It looked like the whole police force and half the town were standing in front of his house.

He rolled the window down and tossed the can out, spilling beer down his shirt and the side of the car as it went. What the hell were they doing here? Had someone reported him for drunk driving? He fished in the glove compartment and found an opened package of breath mints. One left. He brushed the dirt and tobacco off and popped it into his mouth, just as a cop looked up and saw the stopped car.

Too late to run now. Jerry saw him yell to another officer and they all stared at him, waiting.

What had he done? Why send all those cops after him? For drunk driving? His heart pounded as he released the brake and the car slowly rolled forward.

It couldn't just be drunk driving. Had they found out about the still in the woods? They couldn't know it was his, and anyway, he hadn't cooked up any moonshine in months. His heart froze and the chill spread through his chest until it was hard to breathe. What had he done? Why did they look so serious?

The car lurched over the curb as he back kicked a beer can out of sight under the seat. He opened the door and hurried to meet them, hoping they wouldn't look in the car. There were five cops waiting now, and he tried to keep his head steady as his stomach rolled.

"Wha'sa madder? Wha'chu wan' with me?"

"Mr. Wiltz? Jeremy Wiltz?"

"Wha' chu wan'? I didn' do nothin'." He tilted his head back precariously to see the captain's faces.

"It's him, Captain," Paul Bellecourt said tightly.

That scared him. There was a tone of pity that pierced the alcoholic fog.

"Wha's happen'? Wha's wrong?" he closed one eye. The captain only had one face now, but it kept weaving unsteadily.

"Why don't you come with me, Jerry? We can talk down at the station. And have some coffee." Paul tried to guide him to the patrol car, but he balked.

"Don' wan' no damn coffee. Wanna know wha's goin' on. You here ta'rest me?"

"What've you done?" the captain snapped.

"Nothin'. Ain't done nothin'. Jes had a liddle drink on the way home."

"Read him his rights," the captain ordered, and a uniformed cop stepped forward as Paul continued.

"Home? Home from where?" Paul asked kindly.

"You have the right to remain silent."

"Fishin'. Camp. Me an' m' buddies."

"You have the right to have an attorney . . ."

"Who? Where? Where were you, Jerry?" The captain's eyes looked like bullets.

Jerry could feel the cold sweat on his face. His hand came away oily and he wondered if they could smell his fear like he did.

"Al. Al Sm . . . sm . . . mith." It sounded like a lie. He knew it sounded like a lie. What had he done? Had he hit someone on the way home? He wanted to look back at his car, but he was afraid he'd fall if he tried to turn. "Woul'ju shut up!" he yelled at the patrolman. "Cain't hear mysel' think! Don't need no damn lawyer 'cause I didn' do nothin'. Jes' tell me wha' the fuck's goin' on!"

"In a minute," the captain snarled. "How much you had to drink, Jerry? You got drunk and you did something you're sorry for. Why don't you tell me about it?" he leaned over threateningly. "What happened, Jerry?"

"Where'd you go? Did you catch any?" Paul asked easily.

"Nowhere. Didn't go nowhere," he said defensively. They couldn't prove he'd been driving. He thought about the beer cans in the back.

"You were here all the time?" the captain prodded.

"My wife'll tell you. I neve' lef' the house."

"You just drove up," Paul reminded him.

"Jus' drove . . . oh —" He fumbled for something to say, but the captain interrupted.

"Estelle won't tell us anything." He paused. "She's dead, Jerry. But you already know that, don't you." It wasn't a question.

He burst out laughing. They didn't want him. Estelle, it was something about Estelle. "Wha'd she do? Wha'd the bitch do?"

"She's dead, Jerry," Paul snapped. "And the kids. Three of them. And you were here all the time."

"No! No, I wasn't! I was fishin'. I was fishin' wit' Al. Ask him. You kin ask Al." He laughed again.

"They're dead, you son'bitch!" Paul yelled at him suddenly. After all his sympathy, it was like a friend turning on him. "Dead. Your wife and kids, you drunken asshole!!!"

"But I didn't kill them!" Jerry Wiltz explained triumphantly.

It was late that afternoon when the lieutenant drove him home.

"I can't believe we're letting him go," said the young patrolman, Alex Mann, who was driving. It was almost a question.

Paul appreciated the tact.

"What were we supposed to do? Arrest him for DWI on the day his wife and kids were murdered?"

"Yeah, but —"

"He was fishin'," Paul said bitterly. He stared at the house, watching Jerry walk inside.

"Lieutenant? You think he'll sleep tonight? In there?" He pulled away from the curb.

"He'll sleep," he said shortly. Something had been gnawing at him. He finally let it out. "Y'know what bothers me most? He never asked which kids were dead, and which were alive."

That question didn't occur to Jerry Wiltz until much later. The first thing he had done was to get the bottle of bourbon from the cabinet under the sink. He took a swig before he poured a glassful and added some ice.

He drank as he walked around downstairs. They were dead. All of them . . . or almost all. Some crazy murderer had gotten in while he was gone and killed them. The relief of his own release soon deteriorated.

Everything looked strange, as if slightly out of place. Familiar, but out of proportion. It took a long time to realize that the chair in the corner looked too big because Estelle should have been curled up in it. He tore his eyes away, and the stairs were in front of him.

Bellecourt had told him what the murderer had done, or at least part of it, just before the bastard took him to the morgue to identify Estelle's body. He had taken one look and thrown up, spewing half-digested whiskey all over the corpse. They didn't ask him to look at the kids.

Estelle was dead. How many times had he wanted to kill her himself? That constant nagging whine drove him crazy and she knew it. She pushed him into hitting her, then she crept around for a week, acting like he was some kind of monster just because she knew it irritated him.

He finished the drink and poured another glass. He kept gulping at it as he prowled around downstairs, taking short, jerky strides. His thoughts wandered upstairs before he could force his feet to take him there. He finally found the courage, but each step was a hard climb. At the top of the stairs, he tore off the police barrier tape and faced the hall. He was panting, sweat dampened his hair and clothes.

He walked down the hall as quietly as he could, aware of every click and tap his feet made on the old hardwood floors. He opened the door to the boys' room and gagged at the smell. He barely glanced in before he bolted to the bathroom at the end of the hall. Vomiting left him cold sober, but as soon as he went back to the hall, he choked again on the stench.

He turned away from the open door, passed the splintered one to the room that his daughters had shared, and stood in front of the door to the room that he had shared with Estelle for over fifteen years. He pictured her body, bruised and drained, on the other side of that door. He trembled as he reached for the doorknob and his hand slipped on the shiny metal. He wiped his palm nervously on his pants, and twisted the knob savagely. The room was quiet and empty. The sheets had been stripped from the bed and the mattress was slightly off. There was a light dusting of powder on the headboard and dresser.

He was almost disappointed at how ordinary things looked. There were a few dime sized bloodstains on the mattress, but his imagination had painted bloody splashes on the walls and his wife's body sprawled on the bed. He took a deep breath and this time he didn't make it to the bathroom.

"I'm sorry. So sorry." He told the empty room. He wasn't quite sure what he was apologizing for.

That night, he stayed downstairs on the couch with his bottle.

They were dead. After all that time wishing they had never been born, he was finally rid of them. Someone had killed them the way he would have liked to. He took another swig from the bottle.

Why did he feel so empty? It didn't seem right. He should feel something. Weren't you supposed to feel something when your family was wiped out, even if you didn't like them?

Estelle would never whine at him again. No one to tell him not to drink straight from the bottle, no one to bitch about him drinking too much, no one to nag at him about cleaning the yard or being late to work or going out with his buddies. He could do what he wanted, when he wanted, anything he wanted.

And right now he wanted another drink. So he took one, straight from the bottle. It wasn't that good. How many times did he have to tell that bitch not to buy the cheap stuff?

No one to buy his whiskey, no one to fix his meals or warm his bed, either. No one to yell at, no one crying in the night, no one to beat or blame.

No one. He started crying. He was all alone. It wasn't fair. So what now?

The bottle was almost empty. He would have to remind Estelle to pick up. . . .

No one.

He passed out with the thought.

Simon Drake strode rapidly through the upstairs hall of his home. He barely glanced at the rare and lovely paintings on the walls or the Grecian statues in the alcove. The doors slammed open ahead of him, and he winced at the long crack that appeared in the stained glass inlay of the upper panel.

It didn't matter. This house was too small for him anyway. He wondered why he had ever built a house with only seven bedrooms. Over the past four hundred years he had indulged his love of beautiful things, and on his last trip to Europe he had added some really exquisite paintings. There had never been enough room for his collections, and now some would either have to go into storage, or to one of his other houses.

Still, this house gave him privacy, and he valued that as much or more than his collections.

He stepped onto the balcony, and took a deep breath, tasting the air. Below him, the wooded hill fell away toward the sea. A horned moon was just rising, and he wondered if that were causing part of his agitation. That, and perhaps the fog he could see just coming in from the Gulf.

One long step and he was on the top of the railing, balancing delicately on the wrought iron. He dove off head first, a graceful swan dive straight toward the intricate pattern of the brick patio. Less than a foot from the ground, he transformed himself.

Black leather wings, soft as suede, sprang from his shoulders. Five feet from wingtip to wingtip, they cupped the air, forcing it ahead of him as he braked. One of his tiny claw-tipped feet ticked against the tiles and he winced internally at the miscalculation. His wings began to beat and he started to rise, reaching for the sky with all the power and grace of an aerialist. He stretched upward, feeling the wind rushing through the short thick fur that now covered his body. He aimed his snout at the stars and flew.

His giant wings moved with the speed of a hummingbird's. He twitched a muscle that, until a few minutes ago, had controlled his right arm and dodged under the limb of a pine tree. His spine arched, and he felt the pine needles, soft as a whisper, brush his back. His mouth opened wide in a grin of pure joy as he reached the open sky and continued to climb.

Higher and higher he flew, until the air tasted cold and sharp. He gloried in the power of his wings, and the freedom of the sky. He rose until gravity was a poor weak thing that tugged like a faint memory. Finally, when his wings were beating frantically in air that was too thin to support them, he flattened out his climb and looked down.

The world spread out below him. The glow from the lights of Pensacola and Ft. Walton Beach were far to his right and left. Ahead of him there was only the perfect blackness of the Gulf of Mexico. Directly below him, the lights of his house were like distant stars. Cars, streetlights, houses, even neon signs were petty flaws in a deep dark pattern.

He folded his wings and dropped.

Ten feet. Twenty. Fifty. Two hundred feet and more.

The weightless feeling started in the pit of his stomach and spread. A childhood memory came back with a flash. Bright sunlight on a hot, sweaty day. Towering rock cliffs binding the rush of water to a thin sliver of gorge. That single instant of incredible joy as he released the rope at the top of the swing, and plummeted into the ice cold mountain stream.

Five hundred feet and still falling. The joy reached the tip of his wings and he thought if he could step back and see himself now, he would be glowing with it. It was the joy of absolute freedom and power such as no poor earth-bound creature could ever know.

Eight hundred feet. A thousand.

The wind rushed at him like a live thing, pushing in one direction, then another. He tasted a salty breeze as a warm draft slowed him for a moment, then dropped out from under him, leaving a hint of cool pine. He let out a series of high-pitched squeaks, and his ears read the echoes like a topographical map.

He thought about turning his dive into a spiral, one wing spread and flattened slightly, and it was done. He rolled farther, then did a flip. He pointed one wingtip at the ground and spiralled around it, held it for another three hundred feet, then flipped again. On his back, he let his wings trail flappingly above him. He tilted his head back and watched the trees and ground rush toward him.

For over an hour, he soared and spun, whirled, dipped, and glided in an ecstasy of freedom. He danced upon the air until, his emotions spent, his wings pushed back the wind and he turned his aerial ballet into a gentle glide. The bright white lights of the hospital were directly beneath him. It was 3:00 A.M. A time when the hospital staff would be tired and most of the patients asleep. Hospital rounds weren't for another hour. The old woman in the bed next to Casey's was too far gone to worry about. Even if she woke up and saw him, no one would believe her.

This time he had no intention of going in through the front door.

He found the right window easily. His claws clicked and slid against the smooth glass, then stopped as they hit the inch wide sill. He changed to human, keeping his balance effortlessly as he looked through the glass at her sleeping form.

She was frowning.

His heart soared and he felt he could fly even without his bat wings. It was the first expression he had seen on her face in over two months. Without tearing his eyes from her face, a single finger pointed at the lock gestured upwards.

The rusted safety lock creaked open. Simon spread his hand on the glass and pushed gently. It swung silently ajar. He crossed to her side in a single stride, kneeling, searching her face with his eyes.

Her frown had turned to a grimace. She twisted restlessly as a single tear leaked from under her closed eyelid.

"Cassandra."

The word was the lightest breath in her mind. His voice invaded her dream in a whisper, bringing peace and strength. She sighed gently, and her face relaxed. Her eyes opened sleepily. They were the exact shade of midnight blue that he remembered and his breath caught in his throat.

"Cassandra. Beloved. You have returned to me."

The slightest smile touched her lips and she murmured, "I know you."

He gathered her into his arms and stood, straight and proud. Her head tucked naturally under his chin and one hand curled lightly just under his ear. He could feel her heartbeat, slow and steady. Her breath was a spot of heat on his chest, and he wanted to rip his shirt off just to feel her warmth against his bare skin.

"Forever." He whispered the promise to her as he strode across the room to the window. After all these months, he would taste her sweet blood again. The thirst raged inside him, but this time, not for just any blood. This thirst could only be quenched by her unique taste and scent, by her strength. After watching her night after night, now they would have eternity. After waiting for her to come to life again, he would share her life forever. One exquisite pain for her, one sweetly intoxicating drink for him, and their love would be immortal.

She rubbed her head sensually under his chin, then tilted her head back to look into his eyes. The half smile touched her lips again as she sighed, "Hold me . . . safe."

Her words cut him like a knife, and he froze in the very motion of stepping through the window.

Safe. She thought she was safe. She felt safe with him, not because he had ordered her to. Not because he had twisted her mind or hypnotized her into believing in him. But simply because, of her own free will, she felt that way.

He swayed; his own feelings at war inside of him. He could take her now. She would never complain that the decision had been his alone. She would never have the slightest regret for what might have been. In fact, she would never again have any feeling that he did not condone. She would be his, totally and completely. She would not be an individual, unique in her strengths and weaknesses. She would be his *slave*.

Her eyes were closed again, but that trusting smile was on her lips.

His head bent and his steps dragged as he gently placed her back on the hospital bed. His hand brushed her cheek and smoothed back her hair. His kiss was as light as a butterfly's wing.

Nurse Patricia Shell pushed the door open and walked into a whirlwind. For a brief moment, the whole room seemed alive as papers, flowers, cards, and even the sheet suddenly took flight and swirled madly around the room. Pat stopped in shock, then rushed to the window and slammed it closed.

"Who the hell opened the window?" she said loudly.

"Hmmm?" Cascy struggled to lift her head from the pillow, opened one eye, then shrugged and sank back into a deep sleep.

Chapter Eight

"You want that orange juice?"

"Hmmm? No, help yourself, Beverly. I'm about juiced out." Casey shoved the glass in her direction.

"Are they giving you solid food yet?" Beverly perched on the side of the old brass bed and downed the juice without taking her lips from the glass.

"If you consider scrambled eggs, soft boiled eggs, chicken soup and oatmeal to be solid food, then I'm getting it. What do you say we bust outta this joint and go for pizza? Didn't you promise me a pizza the last time I saw you?"

Bev nearly choked on the last of the juice. "Casey! You just got out of the hospital yesterday! And from what I hear the doctors weren't real happy about letting you out early, either. Give it a rest, kid. You don't want to gain back all that weight you lost, do you? You look terrific skinny. A little pale, but then it's always hard to tell with white folks." Bev poured another glass of orange juice from the antique white pitcher on the bird's eye maple bedside table. The table matched the triple dresser, the man's chest of drawers, and the inlaid wood on the cedar chest. The furniture had been handcrafted for Casey's great-grandfather, and it was one of the reasons she had chosen this room as hers after her grandparents had died and she inherited the house. The other reason was the room itself. It was beautifully proportioned. Twelve foot ceilings rose to a circular skylight of beveled glass. It was foolish extravagance in an area torn by violent storms and hurricanes, but it added light and grace to the room. The whole room was a study in elegant simplicity. The lines of the furniture were clean and simple, saved from plainness only by the intricate pattern of the wood itself.

"Besides," Bev continued, "that pizza offer is three months old."

"For you maybe. For me, it was only a few days ago. My how time flies . . ."

". . . when you're having fun. I know. It's kind of spooky to think about. Did you . . . ? I mean, when you were unconscious, did you . . . ?"

"You mean, what was it like to be dead for three months?"

Her friend nodded hesitantly; her short, brisk Afro haloed blackly by the evening light from the glass over head. She poured another glass of juice and sipped at it slowly.

"I don't know, Bev." Casey closed her eyes and leaned back against the pillow with a tired sigh.

"Hey, if you don't want to talk about it—"

"It's not that, or maybe it is. I lost three months of my life. It's gone and I didn't get to live it. It's like a hole in my mind. I keep asking, why? Why did he come back? Why did he shoot? Why me? But the biggest question of all is, why did I wake up? There must be some purpose, some reason, some lesson to learn from it, but what is it?"

"Maybe one day you'll find out. Don't you remember anything from those months?"

"Not much. There were dreams. Strange dreams. Some of them were so real, but of course they were just dreams. Terrible, bloody dreams." Casey noticed Bev flinch.

"You still having them?"

"Mmmm."

"Are they about the shooting?" Bev persisted.

"No. I guess that's strange, too. But I only have one about the shooting, and it doesn't bother me much. I can see Billy Bazzel's face and the gun, Paul is there and some other guy. Actually, those aren't bad at all. The other dreams are really horrible, full of blood and people I know getting murdered and chased and I just stand there and can't do a thing. They don't make any sense." She could hear her voice whine com-

171

plainingly, and she controlled it with an effort.

There was a long silence. Bev was reluctant to bring up bad memories in her friend, and just as reluctant to burden her with her own problems. She poured the last of the juice into the glass, then looked up almost guiltily.

"I finished the juice," she stated. It seemed like a nice, safe subject.

"You've been having dreams, too, haven't you?" It was more than a question.

"Bad ones," Bev confessed. "The kind that make you want to stay up all night."

Casey cocked one eyebrow. "I thought you looked a little white around the gills."

"If you weren't sick in the head, I'd make you pay for that remark."

Casey touched her scalp gingerly. The headaches really are getting better, she told herself. "You get headaches, too?" she asked Bev.

"Yeah," Bev replied briefly, still reluctant to talk about her own problems.

"Dreams about death? Blood?" Casey prompted.

"Yeah."

"Maybe you're having sympathy pains." She tried to smile, but Bev just looked up fearfully and didn't answer. "When did they start?"

"Monday night. The night before you woke up, I guess."

"Tell me about them." It was more an order than a suggestion.

"Case, uh, I really don't think I should. Your Momma said not to worry you."

She didn't ask again, she just stared, but there was something in her eyes that made Bev uneasy. She got up to pace the room, her long legs scissoring back and forth. She nibbled nervously at one long fingernail.

"The first one was bad enough. There was something after me. A bird or something, but it had long, sharp teeth. It was at night and I was on the patio. It bit my neck and I couldn't pull it off. I was so damned scared." She shivered theatrically

172

as her arms hugged her body. Casey nodded understand-ingly. "Then it changed. I was in bed and there was this guy and, uh, well . . ."

"I get the picture," Casey said dryly.

"Yeah, well, even that was strange."

"I don't think I want to hear this." Casey shook her head and looked away.

"No, you don't understand. The guy was white and you know white guys just don't turn me on. No offense." She looked at her friend and grinned. "But him! Oh Lord, Case, he could park his shoes under my bed anytime, and the best part was that what I remember most after we were in bed was that he just held me, and whispered in my ear, and I felt so loved. No, more than that. I felt treasured, as if I was someone precious." Her voice trailed off as a smile gently touched her lips.

"Wow," Casey said reverently. "Has it been like that every night?"

"Just about. Sometimes everything is really confused, and I feel like I'm the one who's chasing him. I slept through the whole first day and barely woke up enough to even talk to your mother when she called to tell me you woke up. I even took a few days off work because I felt so weak and strange that I thought I was coming down with a virus or some-thing."

"Is that what the orange juice is for?"

"Huh? Oh, come to think of it, I have been very thirsty lately, too." She looked at the empty glass in her hand and thought for a moment. "That reminds me of something. When I finally woke up, there was a glass of juice by my bed. I wondered at the time why I didn't remember leaving it there. It doesn't seem like something I'd forget. I don't even remember going to bed that night, and I woke up in my clothes." She shrugged expressively.

"That is weird. Mine haven't been nearly that interesting, except that I think I had one about that bird with the long teeth. Mine have been all about blood and killing and mon-sters." She stopped, reluctant to think about them again.

173

"Come on, Case. It'll do you good to tell someone."

It took a minute, because she wanted to tell them in order, but she finally started. "I dreamed there was an old black woman in the hospital bed next to me, and she died. Then a mummy came to life and killed the guy who opened his coffin. Then the mummy went to the Wiltz's house and killed Mrs. Wiltz and most of the kids. That was the really horrible part because every time he killed, he got younger. The only ones who got away were Janie and the little baby. It was awful and sickening, but it was kind of absurd, too. I could hear him sucking on the wounds and his skin kept peeling off, and then he changed into a bird or a bat or something to chase Janie." She broke off abruptly as her friend whirled away from the window to face her.

"Casey, stop it! Your Mom told me they hadn't told you the news yet. She made a big point of me not telling you or upsetting you."

"Bev, what are you talking about? Are you okay? You look sick. I'm sorry, I thought you were having the same kind of dreams."

"Never mind the dreams! What you're talking about really happened. You must have heard about it on the news."

"Happened?" she repeated stupidly. "It couldn't have. What are you talking about?"

"Just what you said. Monday night someone broke into the house and killed the whole Wiltz family except for the little girl and the baby."

"Janie and David. And Mr. Wiltz? He wasn't there."

"He's the chief suspect. Someone must have told you about it."

"I dreamed it Monday night, before I woke up from the coma. You think one of the nurses could have talked about it in front of me and I sort of overheard it in my sleep?"

"It didn't make the news till the next morning. You couldn't have dreamed it that same night. You must be confused about the time. It must have been Tuesday night, after it hit the papers."

"They wouldn't let me look at a newspaper. Doctor's orders. I couldn't even talk Eric into smuggling one in." She was quiet for a moment, her thoughts whirling senselessly. "Besides, that's the reason I woke up screaming. Twice. It was Monday. Not Tuesday." Her head tossed restlessly. "It was just a weird dream. It had to be." Her voice was rising unevenly.

"Settle down, kid. Take it easy. You must have been half-asleep and the nurses discussed it and later it got confused in your mind." Bev began pacing the room again. She strode back and forth, dodging chairs and furniture.

"No! It was Monday night! Damnit! I know it was! Bev, how could I dream something like that while it was happening?"

"You couldn't!" She came back and perched on the bed like a bird ready to take wing. "Get real, Case! Things like that just don't happen." Casey didn't answer. "That's as absurd as believing that the man I dreamed about really existed. Or that a bird really bit my neck. Except there's one other thing . . ." Her voice trailed off as her hand rubbed her neck thoughtfully. "There were scratches on my neck. And blood. Casey? Cassandra?"

Casey still didn't move or reply.

"Look, maybe we just better forget it for now, huh?" She got up slowly from the bed and headed for the door. "Casey? I'm sorry I upset you. Look, I'm going to send your mother up here, okay?" She waited again, but not even Cassandra's eyelids flickered. "I'll come back soon and we'll just talk about happy things." She twisted the crystal knob slowly and drew the door inward. "I have to go to Atlanta tomorrow, but when I get back I'll smuggle in a pizza." She backed into the hall, tears of fear leaking down her cheeks and her voice tinged with false joviality as she turned and bolted down the stairs.

Casey ignored her retreating footsteps and the cry for Kate that echoed through the house.

How had she known? Known was the wrong word. She had *seen, felt, been there*. She had stood between the bat and the children, willing them back, urging them to fight, trying to

175

control or change her dream. She had even thought for awhile that it had worked. Now she wondered. Vampires were dreams, of course, but leave out the bloodsucking, the bat changing, the skin shedding, and the eyes that floated blackly in and out of all her dreams now. Leave out all the supernatural absurdities and you still had a family that had been brutally murdered, and a murderer whose face she may have seen in a dream.

"Cassandra? Are you alright?" Kate Brighton ran into the room and bent over Casey on the bed. Beverly came in right on her heels.

Casey closed her eyes, trying to concentrate.

"Cassandra, what's wrong?"

She ignored the demanding tone and tried to remember the face under the peeling skin.

"Casey, talk to me. Please!"

What if I did see a murder? Okay, it's probably absurd, but what if? There was a hand on her shoulder. She shrugged it off impatiently. What about the thing in the coffin? Did it really exist? And the old woman who died, was she real or a dream? Why is this happening to me? Because I got shot in the head? The word psychic flashed into her mind. She tried to dismiss it, but it hung there, taunting her.

Is this what it's like to be psychic? Somehow, I'd always thought it would be fun. Maybe knowing which horse would come in first, or what numbers to play in the lottery, but if I have to have nightmares like these, I'll give it back.

Maybe I'm making too much of this. There is such a thing as coincidence. Of course, it would have to cover my dreams and Bev and everything. Could I be wrong about the date of that terrible dream? I was pretty groggy, even sick. I still . . .

Her attention snapped back to the room as her automatic alert system picked up a key word.

". . . hospital. The doctor's number is by the phone in my room. I'll stay here with her." Kate bent over to check her forehead for a fever.

"Stop right there, Bev! I'm not going back to the hospital,"

176

Casey snapped, trying to keep her temper. The feeling lingered that she had almost understood the key to what was happening to her, just before she was interrupted.

"Casey, are you alright?" her mother demanded.

"Of course I'm alright."

"Did you black out?" Bev asked.

"Is that a smart remark? No, I didn't 'black out.' I'm still too pale from the hospital."

"I'm going to call the doctor," Kate stated positively.

"No, Mom, really. I was just thinking."

"No wonder the strain put you out." Bev was still standing by the door, poised to run to the phone, but her tone was acerbic.

"Sorry I worried you," Casey said as Kate glared at Bev resentfully.

"You don't have a fever, sweetheart. Are you sure you don't want the doctor? He told me to call him if you had any problems."

"The last thing I want is the doctor. If he gets his stethoscope on me again, I'll never get free. He thinks I'm some kind of interesting freak. No, it's really not that kind of problem. I was just thinking about coincidence."

"Don't start that again. You've got that funny look in your eyes again. Case, I think I better be going." Bev looked as guilty as she felt. "I'm sorry I upset you."

"No, you didn't. Don't go." Casey started to protest, but Bev cut her off.

"I've got to get home and pack for the weekend."

She didn't know where the words came from. They just popped out. "Bev, be careful. Don't trust anyone."

"What? Yeah, right," she replied casually, but her eyes were grave. She went out of the room, then stuck her head back around the doorjamb to say, "I'll stop by Monday or Tuesday evening . . . with a pizza."

"Don't you dare, Beverly Watkins!" Kate shouted at the empty door, then she gave Casey a rueful smile. "No pizza. Your stomach can't handle it yet. But you can have chicken pot-pie tomorrow. And eggs for dinner

177

tonight. How do you want them?"

"On pizza with pepperoni and mushrooms. If you fix it right, I won't even be able to taste the eggs."

"Why can't your one-track mind be fixed on getting married instead of food?" Kate said, relieved that her daughter was back to normal. "I'll go fix your dinner. Milk or orange juice?"

"Milk. Bev drank all the juice."

"All of it? That sounds just like her! I don't understand why you put up with her."

"Mom, I'm really not hungry. Sit down and visit for a minute."

Kate moved to the edge of the bed and sat down, still talking. "There was a whole quart of juice. She knew it was for you because you need the vitamins and the fluid. Is she dehydrated or something? Now I'll have to go out tonight and get you some more."

"No! I don't want you going out tonight!"

"What?"

"I just mean I'm feeling kind of down and I wish you and Dad would stay inside, where I can call you. Forget the juice. I was getting tired of it anyway. The point is that she told me something that made me curious." She had realized long ago that most people didn't enjoy Bev's attitude the way she did.

"I knew she said something to upset you! I should never have let her in."

"I'm not upset. She wouldn't do that. Mom, was there an old black woman in the room with me?"

"She told you about Mrs. Collins? I warned her not to! She knew better than that," Kate said angrily.

"I'm not upset!" Casey snapped back. "I just want to know if I dreamed her or if she was real."

"If you're not upset, why are you yelling?"

"I'm not . . . !" she yelled, then abruptly lowered her voice. "I'm not yelling. I had some weird dreams and I'm trying to sort them out. Mrs. Collins? Was that her name? I think I remember her. She was in the bed next to mine, but

178

when I woke up it was empty. What happened to her? Is she alright?"

"She's just fine," Kate said firmly. "They moved her out before you woke up. Why don't you take a nap before dinner?"

She was lying. Why would she lie?

"She's dead, isn't she?"

Kate stopped at the door and came back to sit down wearily. "She died the night before you woke up. That's why I never mentioned her to you. She was pretty far gone most of the time. The cancer . . . she hurt for a long time." Kate stopped suddenly. There was certainly no reason to go into details. The thought had haunted her even through her joy at Casey's recovery.

"It's okay, Momma," Casey said gently. "The pain stopped just before she died. You don't have to worry about that any more. I think she was . . . well, not happy about dying, but she accepted it at the end. She wasn't the one who screamed."

"Casey! Were you awake?"

"I thought later it was just a dream, but the dream came just after that. I must have been awake, then drifted back off."

"But, Casey," Kate said reluctantly, "the nurses heard her scream."

"That was me." The sting of tears in her eyes surprised her. "I had a nightmare. Anyway, I'm glad I met her. We talked for quite awhile. She was very special."

"You think that about everyone." Kate kissed the top of her head. "Even Bev. But you're right about her. She used to listen when I read to you. I think maybe she talked to you when no one else was around. She was special, and so are you." She squeezed Casey's hand proudly, then turned practical. It didn't do to let your kids know how proud of them you were. They might stop trying. "I'll get your dinner."

"I'm just not hungry."

"I never thought I'd hear that from you. Or that I'd miss your appetite, but the doctor said you've got to eat."

Casey smiled as her mother left the room. By the time she returned, Casey was moaning in her sleep.

* * *

Franz looked around his new home and grinned. It was stark and bare, with a concrete floor and thick solid walls. It had taken two nights to find it, but there was more than enough room for a dozen of his kind, and he would worry about the luxuries later. It was safe, and that was what mattered.

The abandoned icehouse had once serviced both the nearby highway and fishermen from the bayou in back. The Interstate had taken away most of the traffic and the icehouse had been deserted. A small stream cut to one side, feeding into the bayou, and a concrete conduit ran along the highway. It was dry at this time of the year, but he could see that during a flood it would make this place into an island. He didn't relish the idea of being surrounded by water, but by the time the rains came, he would be safe in Simon's house.

He had been out flying every night, checking out the area. It had too much water, and the strong sunlight lasted much too long, but the people were young and healthy. Simon had been careful, and they didn't even suspect that a vampire was in the area. It was rich country. He would drain it dry.

Tonight would be the first small step. He would need a dozen coffins and dirt from the local cemeteries, and he must arrange funds from his broker in Switzerland, but tonight he would make the first sacrifice. The full moon was next week, so he would have to hurry to complete the ritual twelve sacrifices, one for each direction. He looked forward to finding twelve strong humans, to draining their blood and bringing them back as his slaves. They would be his warriors in this fight against his brother.

He would mark his territorial boundaries in blood and in the process, he would capture his brother. On the night of the next full moon, he himself would be the thirteenth vampire and close the Circle of Death. Simon would be at the center of the circle.

Simon's house had drawn him like a beacon. Twice he had

180

flown high above the trees while his brother was home. He could smell his native soil, built into the very walls. There were long expanses of glass windows and balconies exposed to the sunlight. One tall narrow wall surrounded the property which wouldn't stop a determined child, much less an army. It was all sheer arrogance, an announcement of his power.

He didn't understand why Simon couldn't hear him. It had only been a short time, fifty years, yet Simon had grown so much. Did he even know that Franz had called to him? Perhaps he had grown too strong and independent, or perhaps fifty years of freedom had broken the bonds Franz had imposed as Bloodmaster, as the one who had first tasted Simon's blood and sanctioned him as Nosferatu. Whatever the reason, Simon had betrayed him.

While Franz had starved, Simon had feasted on the blood of the young and the strong. While he had begged and screamed for help, Simon sat in his air-conditioned den reveling in the music of Mozart and the art of Matisse. When he had slit his wrist to control the storm, Simon had been sleeping in his ebony bed.

Simon thought he was invulnerable. Simon was a traitorous bastard, but he wasn't a fool. Franz knew his strengths and weaknesses as only a brother could. Simon was strong, too strong to challenge now. But soon, after he had destroyed everything that Simon loved, after he had killed everyone that Simon cared about, after he had surrounded him with thirteen of his own kind, then he would slowly and painfully kill his brother.

The girl was still alive. He had read about it in the local paper under the headline, Miraculous Recovery. It gave details of the shooting and her name, so he had looked up her address in the telephone book. He stared at the clipping now, wondering if Simon was still involved with her. Why had he saved her? What was she to him? Had he fed on her so often that she would become a vampire? Was he in love with her?

The questions in his head grew louder and louder until he beat his fists against his temples to stop the noise. The pain helped him to concentrate, and he knew he had to be very careful. Simon was strong and tricky.

He felt he was on the brink of understanding something very important, something he should already know about his own brother, but then the whispers started.

"Kill him." The words crept into his brain until he spoke them aloud without hearing his voice. "Kill him. Destroy everything he cares about first, burn his forests, kill everyone he knows, drive him out of his house, and then kill him, very slowly. Kill him!"

He paced restlessly up and down the concrete floor, clutching the newspaper in his long, bony fingers, waiting for the last remnants of the day to die.

Beverly Watkins walked out of Casey's house and closed the door quietly. The first star twinkled brightly at her.

I didn't mean to upset her, she protested silently. *I didn't think she'd react like that. I wonder if she really did dream those murders while they were happening. Mrs. Brighton will probably shit when she hears that. She'll never let me darken the doorstep again. I wonder how long she'll be in town.*

She caught a movement out of the corner of her eye and glanced up uneasily. Was that a piece of paper or cloth flapping from the branch of that old pine tree? It was hard to tell in the dusk. Maybe some kid had been flying a kite and gotten it caught. But what kid would be hanging around Casey's house? She shivered uneasily as she folded her long legs to fit into her new Fiat.

She made the engine roar as she pulled into the long driveway, and she could imagine the expressions upstairs. Casey would grin like a fool, because someone was enjoying life, but Kate's lips would tighten and she would glance nervously at the window.

Or would Casey grin? All her friends went around assuring each other that she was just the same, but was she?

Beverly turned onto the main road and moved left into the

fast lane. A dark streak swooped in front of the headlights, and she leaned over to peer out the window. A bird? Did birds fly at night? She drove a little faster, still thinking of her friend.

Her eyes had changed. The Casey she knew had looked out boldly at the world, but now she seemed unsure, as if she didn't quite remember the rules of the game. Or as if someone had changed them while she was away.

Bev looked uneasily over her shoulder as she changed lanes to make a right turn.

This is a hell of a time to go away, she thought. I wish I could put it off, but if I don't go to Cicely's wedding, the whole family will disown me. How could I know Casey would wake up now? She made the turn into her apartments, looking behind her again, this time in the mirror. There was nothing there. I've just got time to take a quick swim before I pack.

As she changed into her gold swimsuit, she wondered why she was dressing up. This time of evening, there would be only a few people in the pool. That's why she chose it. But tonight seemed special somehow, as if she was waiting for something or someone.

She used the lighted sidewalk instead of the path. It was longer, but she told herself that she enjoyed the night air.

Billy Bazzel has a lot to answer for, she thought as she gazed out over the still Gulf waters and headed for the pool. I hope he's in hell where he belongs. I just can't forget what he said about sharks. Then he went crazy and got killed. It was the last thing he ever said to me. I was never scared of sharks before. Tonight, I'll swim in the pool and be comfortable, but I'm going to have to start swimming in the Gulf again. I can't let that son of a bitch scare me even after he's dead. Maybe I'll ask Case to go with me the first time. She was there, she heard him. She'll understand. I'm not really afraid. It's just like going to see *Jaws* at the movies, then going swimming. You can't get the picture out of your mind.

There were only three people in the pool. She recognized a neighbor and his kids and they swam companionably for awhile. When the kids were ready to go, Bev watched them all leave, and fought the urge to go with them. She still hadn't finished her laps, and she was determined to get in all the exercise she could.

She swam, back and forth, stroke after stroke. It was her therapy for insomnia and it usually worked well enough. A half-hour swim and a hot shower would normally put her in a sound sleep until morning. Tonight she would make it an hour. Maybe that would stop the dreams. Her muscles were smooth and flowing. She breathed rhythmically and easily, turning her head to the side with each stroke.

"Beverly."

Her head came up and she wiped the water from her eyes. "Yes? Who is it?"

There was no answer. Her heart was racing and her muscles tightened as she swam to the side of the pool and listened. Nothing.

She turned back into the pool, but decided to swim breaststroke now. The idea of not being able to clearly see or hear bothered her. After a few minutes, she put the voice out of her mind and concentrated on her laps. She was beginning to tire now, and she decided to end with ten laps of backstroke.

"Beverly."

Her head whipped around as she sought the voice.

"Who's there? This isn't funny, damnit! What do you want?"

A hundred things crowded into her mind. This was still the South, and she had grown up in the sixties when racial tensions were high. Was someone out there waiting for her? Maybe in white sheets to hide the identity of a coward?

She wound up laughing at the thought. Things like that didn't happen today. Certainly not in quiet Florida communities where the people treated her as a friend. She was tired, and still upset about Casey and sharks. Her imagination was working overtime.

She continued her swim until her muscles were tired and loose once more. Ten minutes later, she had almost forgotten

184

the voice as she swam to the steps and climbed out reluctantly. After the warmth of the water, the cool air made her shiver. She reached for her towel and wiped the glittering drops off her dark skin. She rubbed her hair briskly, then draped the towel over her shoulders and started for the gate.

On the path beyond, she paused for a moment. It was such a small stretch of woods, just a border really. It screened some of the cottages, but it darkened the quadrangle and separated the pool, tennis courts, private bar and game room from the row of cottages on one side and the two-story apartments facing the Gulf on the other. She could turn left and circle the woods along the lighted path, or she could go straight ahead to her cottage.

She rubbed the towel slowly over her shoulders, crossing her arms protectively over her chest. The dreams had started four days ago, and the shooting was three months past, but she was still spooked. It must be because of that.

I can't let fear run my life. Now I swim in the pool instead of the Gulf, and hear voices, she thought firmly. Next I'll be hiding in my room, scared to go out. I've seen it happen to people. They just retreat more and more from life until they panic if they have to go anywhere. I've never been scared of life before. Am I really going to take a five minute detour rather than go through a few trees just because I thought I heard my name called?

How long do I put up with this? she thought, suddenly furious. Next I'll be putting bars on the windows and be scared to go out after dark.

She pulled the towel firmly around her shoulders and marched straight ahead. She could see the path light, just on the other side of the trees. She was halfway through, when he stepped out in front of her.

He smiled at her and she choked off her scream before it escaped. He was facing the pool lights as he came forward but all she could see were his eyes. They looked familiar.

"Beverly." It was the velvety soft voice she had been waiting for, but she took a step back.

He walked forward and she smiled hesitantly. Was this the

185

man of her dreams? He looked older, and his hair was darker, and he was taller . . . but his eyes were the same. Darker than black, deep as a universe without stars, and she wondered what trick of the light gave them red glints. He was beautiful, and he loved her. She wanted him so much. Her thoughts slowed and stopped as his hand touched her cheek. He bent to kiss her, and she lifted her head to meet him. Her fingers stroked his hair. It was thin and brittle, which was odd, because in the light it had looked so thick and soft.

He kissed her gently, and his strong hands roved the curve of her back until he crushed her body to his. Nothing in the world mattered except his touch. He picked her up tenderly and strode with her to the bungalow. When he kissed her again, all she wanted was more.

Chapter Nine

Saturday morning, Casey woke up crying, but for once she couldn't remember the nightmare that had terrified her.

The house had that special early morning stillness that whispered that she was the only one awake in the whole world. She decided it was the right time to prove to her parents that she was perfectly capable of taking care of herself again. She found a bathing suit in a dresser drawer and pulled it on, noting absently that it was a trifle large.

By the time Ned and Kate came downstairs, their coffee and breakfast were on the stove, and Casey had left them a note that she'd be on the beach.

The water felt good, warm and smooth against her skin. It combed back her hair in waves as she swam in the calm Gulf. Her hands cut the water ahead of her, then pulled in powerful strokes down to her sides. In minutes, she was out of breath and gasping for air. She turned onto her back and floated, staring up into the morning sky, swirling her hands gently through the water.

The weather had turned cool last night, and today the brilliant blue sky had an autumn depth. She wasn't deluded. Tomorrow or the next day, the heat would come again. Summer would come and go for another two months before the cool days outnumbered the warm.

Her arms were already getting tired, so she swam to shore, staggered up the small slope to her beach blanket, and collapsed happily.

Oh, what a beautiful morning! A deep breath of sweet salt air cleansed the last remnant of hospital antiseptic from her lungs. The warming rays of the rising sun touched her sickly white skin with color. A gull scolded her with the voice of a baby crying and the wash of the waves filled the background with serenity. Every shade of blue from the dark mystery of deep water far offshore to the medium brilliance directly above, to the lightest tinge at the horizon, to the turquoise stripe of a nearby sandbar was revealed like the colors of an artist's palette. She squirmed slightly and the blindingly white sand beneath her molded itself to her body.

It was a feast for the senses, and she found herself laughing aloud for the sheer joy of living.

"I have missed that!"

"Eric!" She had been taken completely by surprise. "Missed what?"

"Seeing you on the beach. Hearing you laugh. It's so good to have you home." He dropped to his knees beside her and kissed her gently on the lips. "And looking like that!"

She drew back, surprised again. Eric had never kissed her like that before. Or flirted with her like that. She clutched the oversized towel protectively around her on the pretense of drying her hair and shoulders.

"What's wrong? Are you feeling okay?"

"I'm fine. Why don't you go ahead and swim? I'm going to take it easy for awhile."

He grinned as he tossed his towel down beside her. His eyes wandered down her body appreciatively, then looked deep into her eyes as he said huskily, "I really like your new bathing suit."

"Mother picked it out." Casey's lips tightened as Eric's grin widened.

"I'll thank her later."

Suddenly, it seemed terribly brief. Her arms and legs stuck out too far and they weren't quite under her com-

188

plete control. The bright red color had always been her favorite, but now it seemed to intrude on her pale skin. Her insecurity got the best of her. She waited until Eric had swum out to the sandbar, then picked up her towel, waved goodbye to him, and struggled up the nearest sand dune toward her house.

She stayed downstairs until after lunch, then made it all the way up the stairs by herself and only had to stop twice to rest. Then she collapsed on her bed and slept the rest of the afternoon.

The crack of thunder overhead startled her awake. The thoughts in her head seemed dreamlike as she wondered if the old pine tree just outside had been struck by lightning again. Her mind pictured the stark, widespread branches and rough gray-brown flakes of bark. For an instant, she saw it as if standing by her window. A puff of smoke was being drilled full of holes by heavy, fat raindrops. A branch that she remembered was gone now, leaving a jagged stump pointing up like an admonishing finger.

It was just a flash. Then it was gone, leaving her curious enough to get out of bed and go to the window. The whole branch was there, not as she had just imagined it, but as she remembered it. She breathed a sigh of relief as she turned from the window. Being able to see through walls might have been fun, but it would also have required a bit of getting used to and she had been through about all the changes she could stand.

She moved to the closet and opened the door, glancing into the full-length mirror on the inside door. She decided that she just wasn't ready yet to face her new self, and turned away. Most of her old clothes had been removed and she made a mental note to ask her mother what she had done with them. There were some very fine memories in those large size outfits.

While she was still in the hospital Kate had taken her measurements and had gone shopping with Clarise so that Casey would have something to wear when she got home, but all these clothes looked ridiculously small. She would never be able to fit into them. They had been absurdly optimistic when they chose them. Or rather, her mother must have been. Clarise should have known better. Casey had always been able to be more honest about her weight with Clarise, because it didn't seem to matter to her friend. With her mother, on the other hand, she had underestimated her weight, her dress size, and their importance to her. Now, apparently, it had come back to haunt her. Kate had guessed Casey to be a petite size three. These clothes looked like they'd fit a Barbie doll.

She sighed with resignation, picked out a red cotton blouse with blue trim that looked a trifle larger than the rest, and a matching pair of navy slacks. She trudged back to the bed, prepared to struggle into them and wondering if the store would take them back.

To her surprise, the slacks pulled on easily with more than enough room in the waist. The blouse was actually too loose. She sat on the bed for a moment, then stripped back down to her underwear. She had to see.

She walked back to the closet, opened the door, and faced the mirror.

She didn't know whether to laugh or cry. The image was not hers. The mirror showed a pale, skinny, childlike figure with stick-thin arms and legs. Her cheeks were hollow and her eyes looked enormous. Her collarbones stuck out and she could see the outline of her ribs through her skin. Her legs looked impossibly long and slender. She poked a finger experimentally into her thigh, then pinched a fold of skin at her waist. It was as if her body had been stripped of all fat, then slipped back into skin that was a size too large for her. She was thin, but flabby.

She had always considered herself a strong person, but now she looked sick, weak, pathetic, and helpless. And vulnerable. It was as if all her protection had been stripped away and now her real self, her very private self, was exposed to the world.

Was this what she had wanted? Was this what she had tortured herself with diets for? To look like an undernourished child, weak and defenseless? And it wasn't just the way she looked; it was the way she felt, too.

She slammed the closet door and crossed the room so fast that she almost stumbled, then jerked her clothes on. She had what she had always wanted, and now she didn't want it. She wasn't attractive; she was exposed. She was pale and puny, her bones stuck out in odd places, and her body had no shape.

She stared at the closet door, wondering. If this was the real Casey, if this was what had been hidden under all that fat for so very, very long, then it was time she faced it. She opened the closet door again and looked into the mirror.

The clothes hid a multitude of sins. Dark blue eyes under thick black lashes and eyebrows looked back at her gravely, then started to twinkle. She had cheekbones. She had always wanted cheekbones. And only one chin above a neck that was slim and elegant. She had been wrong about the curves; they were in the right places, but they had a subtlety now that was offset by those long, slender legs.

She had what she had always wanted. She looked like a normal person. A little on the thin side and definitely not in the best of health, but a normal sized person who could buy her clothes in a nice store instead of slinking back to the fat rack in the back. A person who could enjoy food without wondering how many calories were in it, at least until she built up a little muscle. *Someone who would attract men.*

She took a deep breath. Oh, yes, there was that to consider. Eric had proven that to her this morning. No need to fool herself. In this weight-conscious age, very few men were drawn to heavy women. All things equal, what man wouldn't rather have a thin, conventionally pretty woman dangling from his arm? Of course, she readily admitted that part of her problem had been her own attitude toward herself and her weight. When she was fat, she had never felt pretty.

But this morning she still hadn't felt pretty. She had felt thin and awkward and terribly, horribly vulnerable. Was it just her weight loss that had attracted Eric, or was that only part of it?

She paced restlessly. She had always admired those self-confident people who were happy with what they were, no matter how heavy or thin, but that just wasn't her. She was one of those who continually strived, and always failed, to be something else. She had tried a hundred self-help books, a thousand diets. She always started off enthusiastically, but each time she looked in a mirror, the feeling died a little. Then the hunger would gradually control her life. She would faithfully keep track of every bite. She became obsessed with food. She even avoided parties and friends because get-togethers always involved eating. And even when the diet was successful, the weight always came back, plus more.

But now I have a chance. I've been given a real chance. I have what I always wanted. I'll enjoy it if it kills me.

Maybe it wasn't as bad as she thought. Had she over-reacted?

She was silent as her thoughts continued. She had wanted to be slim for as long as she could remember. Now she was. What had she been so upset about? To hell with weak muscles and flabby skin. She could fix that.

Hell, she could fix anything! She felt as if a burden had been lifted.

Suddenly she was frantically, deliriously happy. She felt as if she could float across the room. She twirled in front of the mirror, ignoring the tremor in her legs. She was grinning like a lunatic and the blood fizzed in her veins. Her palms tingled and her feet danced around the room and down the hall.

How long had it been since she went dancing? Maybe Eric would take her out next week. She tried to compose her face as she walked down the stairs, touching the ban-nister lightly for balance.

She paused on the fifth step from the bottom, just above the one that always creaked and next to the vent that ad-joined the living room. Her parents were in the living room, and it was always interesting to hear them discuss her when they didn't know she was around.

Kate's voice resounded clearly. "It's a miracle. All those people praying for Casey and God answered their prayers."

"I knew she'd come out of it," Ned answered smugly. "You think He'll answer the one about Casey coming home with us?"

"Maybe we shouldn't push our luck. I'm just grateful that Audrey's baby didn't come early or I would have had to leave before now. I just couldn't let our daughter have her first child without me there, but we just can't leave Casey here alone yet. She seems so delicate now, as if the first stiff breeze would blow her away."

Her father snorted derisively. "That's just on the outside. On the inside she's still Casey. It'd take a hurricane to do her any damage, and even then my bet would be on Casey."

From her hiding place, Casey grinned, and squirmed slightly. Eavesdropping was really a weakness, but an irre-sistible one.

"I just don't know . . ." Her mother's worried frown was almost visible to Casey. Or was it just the tone of voice? "One minute she's happy as a lark, just like she used to be; the next, she runs upstairs and hides in her room so I won't see her cry."

"You talked to Dr. Winslow?"

"Mood swings. He said it's perfectly normal. It comes with the weakness. She's just very lucky she doesn't have all the rest of the symptoms like nausea and sensitivity to light and all the others he warned us about. It will just take time to heal and she should take it easy for awhile. No excitement, no strenuous exercise."

Casey felt better already.

"Well, this is the perfect place to recuperate without any excitement. Or it was, before those horrible murders. Is she sleeping any better?"

"No. Last night she was crying in her sleep. I went in almost every hour to check on her. I wanted to wake her up, but I thought it might be better if I didn't."

The thought of her mother, so tired and yet sacrificing her sleep just to check on her, was heartbreaking. Casey felt ridiculously guilty and responsible.

"We've got her back. That's all that really matters. The rest will heal with time. Maybe I can take another week off to stay with her while you visit Audrey."

"You know you can't miss any more work. I just don't know what to do."

"You should have been twins." Casey grinned as she walked into the room.

"I thought you gave up eavesdropping," Kate said disapprovingly.

"I wasn't eavesdropping," she protested automatically. "I was just coming down the stairs and I caught a few words. Are you really going to stay another week, Dad? I love the way Mom did the kitchen, but the guest room needs painting and we can clean out the storage. And I wanted to plant some dogwood trees in the back and the grass needs mowing and the front garden needs weeding and you know I'm too weak and frail to do work like that. But I could supervise. And if things really get rough, I'll go take a nap so I won't have to watch." She smiled innocently as she perched on the arm of her father's chair.

"Are you trying to get rid of us?" Kate's brown eyes snapped.

Casey took a deep breath and blurted, "Yes! I don't need looking after. I need peace and quiet. Being looked after makes me nervous. I want to get back to normal."

"You're still too weak," Ned stated.

"But I won't get stronger if I keep leaning on people. It's

194

not that bad. I can cook my own meals and I'll exercise every day until I'm in shape again. I love what you've done to the house and everything's cleaner than it's been since the last time you were here. I've been so involved with myself that I forgot Audrey's baby was due. I guess what I'm trying to say is, thanks. I love you both very much and I think I would have died if you hadn't been there to bring me back. But I need to feel like me again. I'm not used to people waiting on me. If I get babied anymore, someone's going to wind up changing my diapers."

"You're kicking us out then?" Ned sounded hurt.

"Daddy!" she said exasperatedly. "I didn't say that." Then she caught the telltale twinkle in his eyes. "But if you leave tomorrow morning, you'll have one day together before Mom has to leave for Washington. Tell Audrey that I love the name Ryan, and I'll be up to visit as soon as I can." She looked lovingly at them both. "You were both here when I needed you. I love you so much. Now, please, go home. You've got to get back to your lives, too. I'm going to the shop tomorrow, I'll take a quick inventory on Monday, and Tuesday, I'll have a Grand Reopening. I won't try to do too much at first. Maybe I'll keep it at three days a week, like you and Bev and Eric did. Eric said I can use his pool, so I'll swim every day and you don't have to worry about the undertow or sharks, or anything," she added quickly to forestall her mother's protests. "The doctor said I should exercise."

Kate started to object, but Ned caught her eye warningly, so she said only, "Be careful and don't push yourself too hard. Why don't you invite Bev to stay over for a few nights?"

"No, Mom, I don't need looking after," Casey replied absently. At the mention of Bev, her joy had evaporated, leaving a vague chill behind. "Besides, Bev's out of town for the weekend. I think I'll try to call her before she leaves."

"Don't bother. I just tried five minutes ago when I heard

195

you moving around upstairs."

Casey wondered suddenly if she had been set up for the whole conversation. She often suspected that her parents knew her better than they let on. "What time are you leaving tomorrow?"

"You don't mind if we have breakfast before we leave, do you?" her father asked sarcastically.

"Not if you cook it." Casey kissed the top of his head.

"Speaking of food, are you hungry?" Kate asked. "The doctor said you could start with solid food today, so I made a chicken potpie. I hope you feel like eating it. How's your stomach?"

"Much better. I'd love some chicken potpie, Mom."

Kate started to get up, but Casey beat her to the door, calling back, "I'll get it, and I'll call Clarise while I'm in the kitchen. She said they might come over tonight. Anyone else want some pie?"

There was one place setting laid on the kitchen table, but Casey didn't feel like eating in there alone. She put the plate away, then searched the cabinets for a bowl. It took her three tries to find it. She was on her way to the stove, admiring the cheerful green of the new wallpaper, when she thought again about calling Clarise. Her blood turned to dry ice and sent a chill through her whole body.

Clarise was in trouble. The dish slipped from her hand and smashed on the tile, but she barely noticed. She concentrated on Clarise, trying to imagine her friend. She seemed to separate. She could still see her kitchen, but it faded into the background. Suddenly she was there, at Clarise's house, but it was like looking through a window into a dark fog. She hovered at the top of the nearest tree and watched Clarise through the kitchen window. A black shadow slipped through the rain just inside the trees and she knew it was watching her. It circled to the back door and the knock came clearly. Casey tried to move, to warn her, to scream at Clarise to lock the door and hide, but she couldn't move.

196

Clarise's quick footsteps were almost obscured by the lightning-thunder duo of the storm. In the quick flash of light, Casey tried to get a glimpse of the shadow, but it still seemed a large, shapeless mass. With one part of her mind, she was aware of her mother's footsteps in the hall. She bent to pick up the broken glass, turning her back to the door, and tried to learn more. She had one last glimpse. The scene had shifted. It was Clarise, lying in a hospital bed, pale and lifeless.

"Are you okay?" Kate called from the door.

"Yeah, okay," she said vaguely, then forced her voice back to normal. "I'm fine. Just trying out my new kitchen. It's initiation night. Go ahead, Mom. I'm going to call Clarise before I eat."

"Okay." Kate was doubtful, but Casey had already put the big pieces in the trash and was heading for the place she used to keep the broom. Kate watched carefully, but her daughter didn't move as if she were hurting. Kate fetched the broom from the hall closet and handed it to her.

Casey brushed up the slivers and put them in the trash. She made her way to the phone on automatic pilot, still concentrating on Clarise and straining to see more. It seemed that the harder she tried, the less she saw. She dialed the number without thinking. It wasn't until Clarise answered that she wondered what she was going to say.

"Hi, cuz. What time are you and Paul coming over tonight?"

"Casey? You sound funny. Are you feeling okay?"

"Fine. What time?" she insisted.

"Paul's picking me up about nine o'clock. What's up?"

Nine o'clock. Full dark for over an hour. No good.

"Could you come early? About seven?"

"I really can't. My car is in the shop. What's wrong, Casey?"

"Nothing. Look, I could drive over and pick you up."

"Are you crazy? You just got out of the hospital!

197

You can't drive yet, especially in this weather. Can't you hear that storm? What's going on? Aren't your parents there?"

"Yeah. Maybe Eric could pick you up."

"He was going to Pensacola today, remember? I'm kind of busy right now, but if it's really that important, I guess I could walk over about eight."

"No!" The word burst from her without control. No help for it now. She'd have to tell her something. Clarise could be stubborn as a mule if the whim took her, and it usually did. It would be better to concoct the wildest story than not to answer her. For the first time, Casey remembered the vision of the broken tree limb. If that was false, why was this one true? She couldn't take the chance of dismissing it.

"Reese, look, I . . ." It was harder than she thought to open herself up to ridicule, especially to her best friend. She forced herself to go on. "I want you to lock all the doors and windows and stay inside tonight. Don't open the door to anyone until Paul gets there."

"What in the world are you talking about?" Clarise tried to laugh. "Did that bump on the head flip you out completely?" Her voice changed slightly. "Does Kate know you're talking this way?"

"No, and she won't either. Reese, please, just do it. Right now. You don't have to go out for anything, do you?"

"No, but . . ."

"Clarise Amelia, I want you to put down the phone right now, and go and lock every door and check every window in the house." They had agreed, so very long ago, that if ever there was a serious problem, they would call each other by their middle names and no questions would be asked. Would she remember? "I'll hold on till you get back and explain when I see you." There was a thud on the line and for a moment Casey was afraid they had been disconnected, but the faint sound of footsteps reassured

198

her. She waited patiently while the phone gave off vague echoes. She stretched the phone cord to get another dish, then took the pie out of the oven, spooned out a small portion and let it cool. It was three very long minutes before Clarise returned, but the wait had given Casey precious time to think.

"Case!" The phone suddenly came alive with Clarise's voice. "If this is some kind of a joke, you just remember paybacks are hell."

She had decided to treat it like a joke. Casey started to relax, then tightened up again. "You won't let anyone in, will you? I'm serious, Reese."

"Unless you tell me what's going on, I'll open the front door and put a red light over it or something," she threatened.

"I had a feeling. A bad one. About someone trying to get into your house tonight," she said. Then she thought silently, How do I even know it's tonight? What am I doing?

"A feeling? C'mon, Case." Her voice drawled sarcasm and disbelief.

"Reese, I swear. I just have a strong feeling that someone is going to try to get in your house tonight. It was like a premonition."

"You called me and had me in a panic and even used my middle name because of a 'premonition?' "

"Reese, please . . ."

"I can't believe you did that! Do you know how scared I was running around the house, locking doors and—"

"Reese, listen to me. Please."

"You abused our code, Casey, and now I'll never—"

"Damnit! I did not. I saw him. I saw him trying to get into your house and trying the back door and I saw you," she choked back the words "in the hospital." There was no need to tell her that and scare her even more.

"You saw who?" She was listening now, very seriously.

"I don't know. It was just a shadow. You were going to the door to let it in."

199

"Then what happened?" she asked, caught up in spite of herself.

"Mother came in. I can't explain now. I'll tell all when I see you. If nothing happens, you can have a big laugh on me. But please, please don't open that door to anyone but Paul, not even if you know them. Promise?"

"Well, uh, yeah, I won't. I mean, I will. If you meant to spook me, it worked."

The storm announced its arrival and the line crackled a warning. They hung up quickly, and Casey began to shake. What was happening to her? She leaned over the sink, letting the reaction run its course. Her knees were weak, her hands shaking, and she was drenched in cold sweat. Thoughts kept crowding in, and she kept pushing them away.

Not now, she begged herself silently. Not with Mom and Dad in the next room, watching for any sign of weakness. I'll think later. I promise.

She turned on the tap and splashed water on her face, pretending she didn't hear her mother's questioning call. She dried her face, grabbed the bowl and took it into the living room. Ned was in her favorite chair so she curled up on the couch. The news had just started so she had two and a half hours until Paul and Clarise arrived.

She took a bite of the potpie and choked it down. She had never felt less like eating, but she complimented her mother on it. Kate smiled, satisfied, and turned her attention to the TV. Casey forced herself to finish half the serving, then escaped upstairs to her room as the announcer stated that Tropical Storm Di had hit Cuba. The first thing she did was to try to call Paul. The sergeant at the desk said he'd give him the message.

The thought occurred to her that she could ask her parents to drive over and pick up Clarise, but she dismissed it immediately. The thought brought back the cold sweats and there was no way to put it off any longer. She lay on her bed and cried. What was happening to her?

Was she flipping out completely? Had the bullet wound resulted in permanent brain damage? Would she have fits like this for the rest of her life?

"What the hell!"

Beverly's eyes popped open and she stared upward into total darkness. Not a glimmer of light, but then she didn't really need her eyes to tell her that she was lying in a coffin on a bed of dirt. She was a vampire.

Damn! Yesterday I didn't even believe in vampires and tonight I am one. The space was too small to really stretch, but there was a tingling in her that urged her to move. So she tightened all her muscles, like a cat. That was when she first noticed it.

She felt wonderful. Alive or dead, she had never felt better. Not an ache, not a pain, not a sore muscle or a tender joint or even a hangnail. She flexed the knee she had dislocated in a white water rafting accident. It didn't pop or catch and she could tell just by the feel that it wasn't swollen. Her whole body felt vibrant and alive.

No, it was more than that.

She felt young! Was this what it was like to be a vampire? Were the legends true? Would she feel this way forever? Was she actually immortal? Would she live forever?

Well, as long as she stayed away from crosses and stakes.

And sunlight. She could feel the strength coursing through her body and she realized that the sun was setting. She smoothed her hands down her body and felt the luscious curves. If she felt this fantastic, she could just imagine how she looked. She could hardly wait to open the coffin and see the changes in her own body.

Oops. Slight problem with mirrors, if she remembered correctly. She was surprised at how disappointed she was, but it would still be fun to see the look in the eyes of certain friends, especially the ones who were younger, or had been better endowed.

This could be fun. Young forever. Beautiful forever. I've had worse days.

As the sun set, the hunger hit her. Not the ordinary, empty stomach hunger pangs, not some nagging little reminder that it was time to eat, but a raging, burning craving that seared through her veins and demanded satisfaction now!

She threw open the casket lid, and saw him.

At the front of the room on a raised dais, a huge, ornate, ebony casket with the most magnificent, gorgeous, powerful, and perfect man she had ever seen standing beside it. Her breath caught in her throat and her heart stopped. She floated toward him, unaware that she was even moving. All she wanted was a touch, a look, a glance from him, but he regally ignored her until she was standing in front of him, gazing adoringly up at him.

Finally, he deigned to notice her. He lifted one hand lazily to the side and brushed her cheek with the back of two fingers, trailed them down to her chin, then traced her lips sensuously. Finally, his eyes turned to her and he whispered her name intimately.

"Beverly. You are mine now."

She glowed with pride, and tried to ignore the hunger growing in her. She didn't want to think about it. Didn't vampires have to kill to stay young and alive? She didn't want to kill anyone, but this roaring craving was already more than she could stand. To appease this burning hunger she could kill. *She would kill.* Maybe, if she were selective, she could even benefit mankind. Cull the rejects, so to speak.

"You will feed soon," he said, as if reading her mind. "You are young and strong and smart. I made a good first choice. Tonight, I will teach you many things." His hand tightened on her chin and his eyes glared madly into hers. "And you will teach me, everything you know about Cassandra Brighton."

Casey? Did he want her to kill her best friend?

He smiled.

Well, if he wanted her to kill Casey then he must have a good reason. He was so wise and kind and good. Casey must have done something terrible. If he wished it, then she couldn't even conceive of disagreeing in any way. She couldn't even think of arguing. Of course she would kill Casey for him.

And she was getting very, very hungry.

Casey watched the shadows creep into her room and imagined that other shadow creeping around Clarise's house. Imagination. Was that it? After all, she had seen the broken branch and it hadn't really happened. The storm added to her nervousness, and she began to pace back and forth across the room. She finally decided that using the time to plan and exercise would be more productive. She lay on her back and concentrated on the stretching exercises the therapist had shown her. Her thoughts gradually became more coherent as her muscles stretched and relaxed. The storm continued and dusk was early. When the phone rang, she leaped for it with considerably more flexibility.

"Paul?" she didn't have time for polite conversation.

"Casey? Dispatch said it was urgent. You okay?"

"Fine. What time are you picking Clarise up?"

"Eight-thirty. Why?"

"Cabin fever. I've got to get out of here, even if it's just a drive around the corner. Could you pick me up? If you pick me up as soon as you get off, we could both go to get Reese. We could go with you to do your errands." She had rehearsed the words and they sounded it.

There was a long silence.

"What's goin' on, Casey?" His voice was flat and she remembered the way he had looked in the bookstore.

"I really need to get out." She controlled her voice carefully.

"In this weather?"

As if to punctuate his words, there was a bright flash and the simultaneous crack of thunder rattled the window glass. The phone line sputtered ominously. Casey turned slowly to the window, afraid and confused. A puff of smoke was being drilled by raindrops. A tree limb, almost opposite her window, toppled and fell in slow motion. The noise as it crashed was muffled.

"Casey? What's wrong? Are you there?"

Tears stung her eyes as she stared at the tree. One broken finger pointed a warning at her.

"Casey?"

She took a deep breath. "Please." Her whisper broke, then dwindled away.

"I'll be there in fifteen minutes."

Casey moved down the stairs lightly, retrieved her raincoat from the hall closet and slung it over her shoulders. Then she waited upstairs until she saw the headlights top the rise in the driveway. The stairs were easier each time. She stuck her head through the doorway to the living room and spoke to her parents. "I'm going with Paul to pick up Clarise. We'll be right back."

"In this weather? Are you crazy? You just got out of the hospital!" Kate was outraged.

"And the doctor said I was fine. A little rain won't hurt me. I really need to get out for awhile." A honk sounded and she moved to the door. "There he is. I've got to go. Be back in a little."

"Casey, this is stupid. You can't leave." Kate was on her way to the door when Casey pulled it quietly shut from the outside, wincing as she pictured her mother's face. She slipped in a puddle and slid into the car door. She yanked it open and got in.

"Get me out of here. Mother's on the warpath and I can't say I blame her." As Paul hit the gas, she looked back to see the door open. Kate and Ned would be fuming by the time she got back, but she couldn't worry about that now. Besides, Kate would understand. She wasn't too fond of being coddled either.

There was still a glow in the sky, but the rain was washing it out. Five minutes, ten at the most, and Clarise would be safe with them. They would be laughing about this. She tried hard to picture it in her mind, but her usually reliable imagination let her down. She pushed back the hood of her raincoat and a trickle of water ran down her neck. She shivered involuntarily.

"What de hell is goin' on?" He was so upset he didn't even try to control his accent, and his Cajun blood was ready to boil.

"Nothing. Mother didn't want me to go out in the rain."

"Don't play me for no fool, you," he snapped back.

"Can't we just wait till we pick up Clarise? Then I'll tell you both." Even her voice was reluctant. Paul was a level-headed, seen-it-all-before cop. If she told him now, he'd probably take her straight back home.

"No, we cain't. I t'ink you tell me de truth right here an' now, or I just drive yourself back home." He brought the car to a stop instead of turning onto the main road. The last glow of daylight was fading.

"It's almost dark. We've got to hurry."

He sat and looked at her.

"I'll tell you. Just drive!"

He turned right and speeded up until the needle held steady at fifty-five.

"I don't know quite where to start." The car slowed noticeably and she hurried on. "I had a premonition." There was that word again. She glanced sideways at him, but he was concentrating on driving. She explained as calmly as she could, but her voice started to rise before she finished.

Paul's foot hit the accelerator and the needle leapt up to seventy and kept going. There were advantages to being a cop, Casey thought with satisfaction as the tires screamed around a curve. She grabbed the dash and held on.

"But you done said nothing happened to the tree," Paul

205

commented neutrally.

"Not then. I called Reese and warned her. I think she took it as a joke, but she did promise not to open the door." Casey watched as the needle crept back down to sixty-five. "Don't slow down. Please. It's so dark tonight. When you called back, I was standing by the window. You heard it. The lightning hit just where I had seen it."

"What exactly did you see?" His fingers whitened on the steering wheel.

"A shadow. Of a man I think, but shapeless. Even in the bright light from a window, I couldn't see his face."

"You're sure it was a man? You said 'it' a while ago."

"Did I? It must have been a man. Don't miss the turn."

"I'm not likely to, though you've got me het up enough."

"You believe me?" she asked incredulously. Was he humoring her? He didn't act like it. Would he really take her word on such a thing?

"It's easy enough to prove, one way or de other. I t'ink you're telling de truth, but dat's a slight bit of difference. Here we are." He turned right off Beal Parkway, went to the end of the block, and turned left. He pulled into the last driveway on the right, and parked just short of the carport.

"She's got every light blazing." There was a touch of relief in his voice.

It was a quiet subdivision in a well-to-do section of town. Fences and hedges blocked off each backyard, and the fronts were decorated with azalea and camellia bushes. Streetlights alternated on each side of the way, throwing little illumination through the pouring rain. Heavy woods to her left made her glance that way apprehensively as Paul turned off the engine.

"You comin' in?" Paul asked as he opened the door.

"No. I think I'll stay out here."

"It's raining pretty hard again. Maybe you shouldn't get out in it. I'll get Clarise and be right back." He reached for the keys and she stopped him with a gesture.

"No!" The word came out too harshly, so she tried again. "No. I might want to listen to the radio. Do you mind?"

He shook his head, obviously not believing her, but too polite to call her a liar. He left the keys where they were. When he got out, his hand went to the back of his belt where he kept his gun when he was off-duty. She felt a little relieved. He was taking this seriously. She watched him walk around the carport to the back of the house and she barely stopped herself from shrieking at him. But he stopped wide of the corner, stood for a moment, and started back. He tapped the car hood as he passed and gave her a thumbs-up gesture. She forced herself to smile back and watched him hurry to the front door. As soon as Paul's back was turned, she scooted into the driver's seat. It was so dark, and she felt chilled in the damp. A cold trickle went down her back, and she checked the door to make sure it was locked. She waited until he was at the front door, protected from the rain by the overhang, then she started the engine. He jerked around nervously at the sound, his curly hair sparkling with rain. She waved at him to go on, then made a circling motion with her hand. He shrugged, nodded, and knocked on the door, fitting his key in at the same time. She could hear his voice as he called out to Clarise, but she couldn't make out the words.

She pushed the automatic lever into reverse and cramped the wheel to the left. The car rolled slowly back and she split her attention between Paul and the rearview mirror. Clarise was justifiably proud of the azaleas that lined her driveway on each side, and Paul loved his bright blue Ciera. If she hurt either one, they would skin her.

Casey glanced ahead and saw the door open and catch. Reese had the safety chain on. "Hurry, hurry, hurry," Casey muttered as she caught a flash of white in the opening door. She inched the car forward when she wanted to make the engine race. The windshield wiper squealed and she jerked nervously again. If only the rain would let up so she could see more than three feet in front of the car. She saw the tops of the azaleas wave and bend as the front wheels of the car dropped into the flowerbed.

The drive was too narrow. She would have to reverse again, and probably a third and fourth time before the car would be headed out. She crimped the wheel again and started back, but she still switched her gaze back and forth between the mirror and the front door. The car was pointed straight across the drive when she stopped to watch the door open wide. Clarise practically jerked Paul inside and slammed the door.

Casey breathed a sigh of relief and shifted her full concentration to turning the car around. The apprehension that had grown as she sat in the dark car alone suddenly mushroomed into panic. The car had to be ready to go when they came out of the house. What if someone was watching them, waiting for them to come out of the house?

She glanced in the mirror again, half expecting, half dreading that someone would pop up out of the bushes behind her. She put the car in reverse and eased her foot onto the gas. The car inched backward, then stopped. She stepped harder on the accelerator, trying to get the front tires out of the flowerbed. The back wheels spun, then caught, and the car lurched backward suddenly. Casey glanced in the mirror, then twisted around to see.

There was a man standing behind the car.

Reflex slammed on the brakes. She stared, her hand gripped the back of the seat until the tendons writhed like tiny snakes. She gasped in air, wanting to scream, but it seemed so useless.

He was tall and slender, dressed in black. A cloak, lined in red, flapped behind him in the wind. His face was hidden in the shadows, but he took a step forward, bent over to put his hands on the trunk, and leaned forward to grin at her through the back windshield. The red brakelights reflected on his skin and eyes, and even glinted bloodily off

208

his gleaming, sharp teeth. His bones were sharp under his skin, and his dark hair was long and swept back above his forehead. His eyes were polished onyx with red flames reflecting the red glare of the lights.

She watched, paralyzed, as his hand came up and beckoned to her, slowly, imperiously, deliberately. There was an answering pressure in her mind.

Come to me. I am everything you ever wanted, everything you ever dreamed of. I am power and excitement and danger with no fear. I know everything there is to know about you, and I want you. I can love you the way you have always wanted to be loved. I am life everlasting.

It would be so easy. He wanted her, cared about her, loved her.

A slow, sensuous smile lit her face. He was strong and wise and powerful and he loved her.

Come to me. His hand beckoned silently.

She wanted to. His eyes promised ecstasy, if she would just give herself to him. She longed to feel those red, red lips on her, and the strength of his arms as he enfolded her. He would take care of her. No one would ever hurt her again if she would just give herself to him. She would belong to him . . . forever.

Her mind was working very slowly now.

Herself. Her self. Forever. His.

The words formed in her brain and ice formed around her heart.

"No." Her lips were frozen, numb. The word was only in her mind, but he read it there.

He frowned, and she was overwhelmed with guilt and fear. She had hurt him. He had offered her the world and more, and she had rejected him.

Come. He forgave her. He was offering her another chance and her heart leapt with joy.

Come.

She smiled and stretched out her hand, but her mind screamed a warning. Her hand curled into a fist and her head jerked as she fought him. Her whole arm began to shake as she fought for control of her own mind and body. His smile turned to a grimace as the force on her mind increased. His lips curled into a snarl revealing two long incisor teeth that grew as she watched in horror.

A door slammed. His head jerked up, and her whole body swayed back with the release as his mind was distracted. She wrenched her eyes away from him to check the house. Paul and Clarise were moving toward the car, their heads bent against the lashing rain. She screamed a warning as her eyes were drawn irresistibly to the rearview mirror. Rain, azaleas, and darkness. Her head whipped back again.

He was there. He had moved back slightly and she could see him from the legs up. She caught a flash of white as he smiled at her. Then he lifted one hand, as if in farewell.

His flesh dwindled and shrank.

She watched in horror as he changed. His cheekbones shone white, then disappeared. His canine teeth shifted forward and his skull compacted. His arms flattened and spread as his legs dwindled upward until he hovered without support. Only the eyes were the same black pits with volcanic centers. Shadow dark wings flapped as he passed over the car.

"No," she whispered blindly. "No."

She wrenched her body forward, and saw the giant bat dive at Clarise. Paul must have caught a glimpse of the movement out of the corner of his eyes, because he jerked Clarise toward him with one arm and shielded her head with the other. Razor sharp fangs sliced across the back of his left hand and the blood looked black in the headlight beams.

"NO!!!" Casey screamed as she hit the accelerator. "No vampires!"

Clarise stumbled and went to her knees, clutching at Paul. He struggled to pull his gun, but her hand was in the way and the bat was hurtling down on them.

Casey hit the horn and drove one-handed, bumping over the flowers and sliding over the rain softened grass. There was an instant of absurd regret for ruining the lawn, then she wrenched the wheel to the left and splattered Paul and Clarise with mud and grass as she stopped.

The passenger door was less than a yard from the couple but they didn't move toward it. She scooted across the seat and opened the door as Clarise began to scream.

Blood splattered on Clarise's rainsoaked hair as Paul waved his hand wildly over his head, trying to fend off the creature. His right hand jerked at his gun as Clarise staggered toward the car. He gave her a helpful shove and fired two rounds, but it was moving too fast. It dove at Clarise, missing only because of the push he had given her. It sheared off before it hit the car and he shot again as it climbed. The second shot hit it. He saw the impact as it tore through a wing and it wobbled slightly, then came back to dive again.

Casey shoved the door open, grabbed Clarise by the first thing that came to hand. Her fingers tangled in her friend's hair and she pulled, hard. It was enough to tumble her into the car, but then Clarise leaned back out and grabbed at Paul, screaming, "Get in! Get in!"

Casey moved back to the wheel, dragging Clarise with her. Paul took one last shot at the gape jawed creature hurtling toward him. Clarise screamed again as the bat ripped a furrow along his jaw. He hunched his shoulder up and ripped at the wings beating at his face. His fingers finally got a grip on a wing and he flung the bat away. He dove into the car and slammed the door behind him.

"Go!" he yelled, but he was too slow for Casey. She had hit the gas before the door was closed and now the tires were cutting furrows into the soft grass. She didn't slow as she bounced over the curb and swerved left. She didn't even pause at the stop sign, but kept accelerating until Paul yelled at her to slow down. She looked at him with

211

blank, staring eyes. He yelled again, "Casey!" and she gasped for air, sobbed, and eased off on the gas pedal. Clarise was sobbing uncontrollably as Paul pulled her to his chest. He made comforting noises and looked at Casey helplessly.

"What the hell happened?" he asked helplessly.

"No vampires. There are no real vampires," she deliberately muttered too low for them to hear, but she had to say it. She wanted to keep saying it, to scream it out, but she couldn't. She shook her head and concentrated on taking deep breaths.

"Clarise, are you hurt? Did it hit you?" Paul tried to tilt her head up to look at him, but she just clutched him tighter. "Darling, take a deep breath. Another." He kept his arms locked around her securely as he spoke to Casey. "I think we're both okay, but you better head for the hospital. I don't—"

"Hospital?" Clarise interrupted, alarmed.

"Well, I don't think I'll need stitches, and it doesn't really hurt, but it's still bleeding."

Casey's mind raced with questions. Was there something in the bite to make it bleed more? Was that how he drained them so fast? Weren't there certain insects and other creatures that had an anticoagulant in their saliva? Didn't mosquitoes have a pain killer that deadened the area around the bite so that sometimes when you noticed them they were already bloated with blood? She shuddered at the image.

"Let me see your hand," Clarise said as she reached overhead to switch on the light. She looked at his face and gasped. The scratch along his jaw was still dripping blood on his raincoat and had smeared up almost to his eyebrows. She grabbed a box of tissues from the backseat and began blotting his face. "Hurry, Casey. Please hurry."

Casey glanced at his face and tried to figure out the best route. The fastest might be to go back the way she came, but she couldn't bring herself to turn around. She could make a wide circle and bypass their house. Maybe fifteen minutes if she circled. If she turned back, it would only . . .

"Go around." Paul's order startled her out of her reverie and she nodded. Clarise looked from one to the other, then behind her. She shuddered violently and agreed, "Go around."

Paul reached around his wife for the police radio, called in and told them to warn the hospital that they were coming.

Casey drove a little faster, and blessed the empty roads that had made her so uneasy earlier. The road only claimed part of her attention, the rest of it was concerned with what she had seen. She kept telling herself, over and over again, that there were no such things as vampires, but it was harder than she would have imagined to deny her own eyes.

"There's got to be a rational explanation." She was unaware that she had spoken aloud until Paul looked at her sharply.

"It was the biggest bat I've ever seen," Paul stated. There was a warning look in his eyes that she didn't understand.

"I've never heard of one attacking like that, either," Clarise said reluctantly. "Do you think, I mean, could it have been . . .? I think we better tell the doctor that it might have been . . ."

"Rabid," Paul finished the difficult sentence for her.

"No!" Casey hadn't even thought of that, but as soon as he mentioned it, she knew it was wrong.

"Casey, we have to . . ." Clarise sputtered.

"Bats don't usually attack people, unless they're rabid," Paul declared.

"It wasn't rabid. You can tell the doctor anything you want, but it wasn't rabid. It may have been diseased, but not that way. It was . . ." she couldn't say it. She turned left, the tires sliding as she pulled into the emergency entrance, still shaking her head. A nurse was waiting at the

213

door, and Casey recognized her instantly. She greeted Paul and Casey like old friends and introduced herself to Clarise as Patricia Shell. She hustled Paul into a wheelchair and rolled him into the emergency room while she told Clarise to stop by the office to fill out the forms. Casey followed Paul and the nurse, wondering how she was going to stop them from giving him the rabies vaccine.

It was the first time she had been to the emergency room when she was conscious, and she looked around curiously. Large and brightly lit, it was divided by curtains into separate cubicles for the patients, and a large desk area for the staff. Even though she knew she couldn't possibly remember it, it still seemed vaguely familiar.

There was a scream from a curtained room, and she flinched violently.

"What's going on?" Paul asked curiously as a security guard rushed toward the room.

"You name it. If I didn't know better, I'd sware it was a full moon. I think every crazy in the city has gotten violent this week. We've had to cancel vacations and work double shifts. They even pulled me from my ward to help down here. We're so shorthanded even the doctors are doing double duty. But don't worry, Dr. Marshall is on his way down to take care of you. A bat bite, huh? Did you kill it?"

"No. I shot at it and I could have sworn I hit it at least twice, but it didn't seem to faze it. It was huge! It must have had a five foot wingspread," he explained disgustedly.

Pat tilted her head and smiled indulgently.

"I'm serious! Ask Casey!"

Casey wished he had kept his mouth shut.

"You really shouldn't be in here." Pat noticed her for the first time.

"I was curious. I was in here after I was shot and I wondered if I had dreamed it or imagined it."

"And?"

"It's just like I remember. I was in that cubicle." She pointed to the middle curtain. "You were there, but you weren't in uniform. You helped put a tube down my throat. I didn't like it much, even if I couldn't feel it."

"You really remember that? That's incredible. You were unconscious the whole time." Pat stared at her curiously, and Casey remembered why she had decided not to talk about it.

"How are you feeling?" Pat was a woman of average size, brown hair going gray and gray eyes that smiled brightly on the world.

"Fine."

She looked at Casey closely. It was more than a nurse's professional scrutiny. There was an element of understanding and compassion that brought tears to Casey's eyes. "Not many people have come back from a coma the way you did. It must be very hard and disorienting to be gone so long. Have they recommended a counselor for you?"

"Yes, but I haven't been yet. I really don't think I need one," Casey answered honestly.

"Well, if you ever do feel like talking, give me a call." She pulled a card out of her pocket and handed it to Casey, who held it as if it were a treasure. This was someone she could talk with, if she needed to. She grinned like a fool and got out of the way as the doctor came in.

"Did you bring in the bat? We'll need a necropsy to check for rabies," Dr. Marshall commented as he tilted Paul's head up to check the wound along his jaw, then took his hand and examined it closely.

"Sorry, no can do." Paul winced as the doctor probed carefully. "I shot it but it just made it mad."

"That's bad. We need the brain for examination. If you really wounded it, it may die in a couple of days. We can wait for a few days, I guess, just in case someone else brings it in. I think you should notify the news media and publicize it. Tell them that people should bring in any dead bats they find to the Health Center. I'm afraid it's not

215

likely they'll get the right one, but we can try. If you really shot it, there shouldn't be any problem identifying it."

"There won't be any problem with identification anyway. It was the biggest damn bat in the world." Paul made a face as the doctor injected him with a local anesthetic. Casey decided to find Clarise and wait with her.

Pat wheeled Paul out a few minutes later with neat bandages on his face and hand. "The doctor said he could go back to work." She shrugged noncommittally. "If he wants to."

"Not a chance!" Clarise protested. "You're going home and to bed . . ." Her voice trailed off as she realized that home was the last place she wanted to go.

"Exactly," Casey added. "My home and the guest room for both of you. And don't give the bat a second thought. It wasn't rabid."

They were silent as Pat frowned at her. "May I speak with you?"

"Sure." Casey smiled, but she felt as if she had been called into the principal's office. Clarise helped Paul into the car while Casey stayed behind.

"You shouldn't say that to them. I know you don't want them to worry, but what if the bat was rabid? The treatment is very painful, but it's a lot better to have it than to reject it and die from rabies."

"Yeah," Casey didn't try to explain as they slowly followed Clarise and Paul to the car.

Pat put her hand on Casey's shoulder. "I know it's hard, especially after everything you've been through, but you really can't afford to give him false hope. A bat that would attack a human without any provocation is probably sick."

Casey barely heard her words. The hand on her shoulder was as cold as death and she was finding it hard to breathe. "Pat, you . . . don't go home tonight."

"What?" Pat stepped back, watching her as if she were an alien.

"Don't go home. Stay here. Stay with a friend, but don't

216

drive and don't go home. You'll die if you go home."

"What are you talking about?"

"You don't believe me," Casey said sadly. "I can't force you, and maybe I can't change what's going to happen, but what harm would it do to listen to me? Go home with a friend. Call a taxi and go to a motel. Just please, please don't drive home alone." She turned away from the disbelieving look and climbed into the driver's seat. She started the car, then rolled down the window for one last try. "Please don't go out alone, Pat. I can feel death all around you. A lot of people will miss you."

Pat's mouth hung open as Casey drove off, shivering. She knew it was no good. Even if she stayed and offered to drive Pat home, she wouldn't accept. She was dead. She just didn't know it yet.

"Paul? Where are we going?" Clarise questioned.

"I think Casey's right. There's no reason we shouldn't stay at her house tonight."

"In fact, why don't you both move in until this is all over? If you move back home, then Clarise might be left alone if you're called back in to work unexpectedly. You don't want to be home alone, do you, Reese?"

"Paul?"

"Sure. Sounds great," he said with relief. "And if I have to go into the hospital for those shots, she'll have some company."

"The bat wasn't rabid," she insisted. A vampire, maybe, she thought silently, but not rabid. How can I tell them what I saw? They won't believe me anyway, but shouldn't I warn someone? All those legends are true. I'll have to go to the library tomorrow and read up on vampires. Or look through my occult inventory at the store.

"We can't take the chance," Paul interrupted her thoughts. "If they don't find the bat, I'll have to go through the shots. They inject the serum directly into the stomach." He rubbed his stomach thoughtfully.

"No! It wasn't rabid. I know it wasn't."

"You mean, you hope it wasn't," Clarise corrected.

"I know it. I just don't know how to convince you."

"Right," Reese said dispiritedly.

"I know it the same way I knew that you were in danger. You didn't really believe that there was any danger, did you?"

"A bat attack is a little different from a homicidal maniac," Paul said derisively. "If you hadn't dragged me over there, we wouldn't have been outside and the bat—"

"But he was there!" Clarise interrupted wildly. "He was there! He came to the door and knocked but I wouldn't open it. Then he scratched at the back screen and called to me. I wanted to open it. He said he needed my help. If Casey hadn't warned me, I would have let him in, but I screamed at him to go away." Clarise was sobbing with fear. Paul reached awkwardly over the back of the seat to pat her shoulder, but Casey poked her in the side with her finger.

"Ouch! What was that for?"

"No more crying, damnit! We're ten minutes from my place and Mom and Dad are there. They're planning to go home tomorrow and I don't want them to have even a hint that anything is wrong."

"You're right. I don't want to worry Kate. She's been through enough lately. The last thing she needs is to find out the bat was rabid." Clarise dried her eyes.

"It wasn't rabid! Would you quit that?" Casey snapped at her, then grinned. "Trust me," she drawled sarcastically.

"Right now we have to worry about how not to tell your parents about a strange man scratching on windows," Paul pointed out, "and a bat attack. My cuts are easy enough. I was cut in a knife fight at work and the delay was because I wanted to get cleaned up. Casey, you can even use that as your excuse for running out this evening. Tell them Clarise needed you to help. It's lucky you two cleaned my shirt at the hospital. We won't look too bad."

"Clarise, you must have had one of your terrible allergy

218

attacks today," Casey chimed in.

"In the rain?" Clarise looked confused.

"Well, if you'd clean your house more often you wouldn't have such a problem, and your eyes wouldn't look as if you'd been crying," Casey said virtuously.

"Oh, your mother will love that."

"Yeah, I know," Casey smiled tightly. "Maybe she'll come over and redo your house next time."

"Casey, I'm sorry I tried to blame you. If you hadn't called . . ." Paul's voice choked off as he reached over to gently stroke his wife's hair.

"It's okay. I just wish you'd believe me about the bat. Before this is over, we'll have a lot more to worry about than rabies."

Chapter Ten

At home, Casey stopped in front of the hall mirror to check her hair, and to avoid the furor when her parents saw Paul. The rain had turned waves into curls and framed her face with a sparkling, unruly mass which she tried to tame as she heard Eric ask Paul for the name of the woman who had scratched him. She walked into the room as Paul repeated the story they had agreed on, but her smile died as she noticed that one guest was not listening.

The voices receded and the rest of the room blurred. Her eyes burned with unshed tears and through them, dark colors flared and danced above his head.

She had thought he was another dream. His blue eyes were just as she remembered, bright and clear, with just a hint of darker gray. His eyebrows were darker than his blond hair, and his lips curved as he stared back at her. His name was . . .

She was having trouble breathing. The conversation wound down as Eric looked at her like a naughty kid at a surprise party. "Casey, I wanted to introduce you to someone."

Paul noticed the stranger for the first time. "Drake? Simon Drake?"

Simon turned languidly to greet him as Paul bounced over to shake his hand. Eric's intended surprise had popped like a balloon, but he presented Simon to Casey as if introducing royalty. "Cassandra Lane Brighton, allow me to introduce the man who saved your life, Si . . ."

"Simon Tepes Drake." Her eyes never left his as she offered him her hand. He took it gently and inclined his head, just the slightest bit. "I thought you were a dream. I . . . I . . ." she paused, trying to find the words. "Thank you. That just seems so inadequate for what I want to say."

"Then don't say anything. You have changed, Ms. Brighton. But I would have recognized you anywhere." He lifted his eyes to hers, then lifted her hand to his lips and kissed her fingertips slowly. The sensuous thrill caught her breath and held it.

"I think that saving my life entitles you to call me Casey. But I haven't changed that much. I'm still me," she protested. I am! I'm not crazy. It was defensive and she knew it, but this man threw her off balance. He was too powerful. It radiated from him like the colors and threatened to overwhelm her. Still, she was disappointed when he released her hand and stepped back.

"Even more so, if that is possible. More intense. More aware. And even more beautiful, I think." He smiled softly, intimately.

Her eyes widened in shock and she tossed her head back abruptly. His hand had brushed her cheek. A light caressing gesture that made her want to dip her head and rub against his fingers like a cat.

There was only one problem. He was three feet away from her and his hand hadn't moved. A fingertip sensuously outlined her lips and she stared at him in disbelief. The sly smile told her that he knew exactly what he was doing to her, and was enjoying it. Her memory flashed back to the last time she had seen him smile like that, and the reason for it.

"Casey?" Eric put a drink in her hand and she turned to him in relief. "Are you alright?"

"Sure. I'm fine. It's just such a . . . pleasure to meet Mr. Drake again. Could I have a cigarette, Eric?" Her hand trembled as she brought it to her lips, and her annoyance grew as she noticed Simon noticing the tremor.

Kate walked by just as Eric lit it for her. "I thought you were going to quit smoking, Cassandra."

"Now?" Her mind screamed at the thought, When there are bats and vampires and murderers running around? When I felt someone touch me who couldn't have and I think I'm losing my mind?

"Listen to you! Your voice is croaking like a bullfrog! I told you not to go out in this weather. I don't know what gets into you."

"You're absolutely right, Mom. Eric, could you get me another drink? And this time put something in it?"

"And drinking! Didn't the doctor tell you not to?"

"I don't think he mentioned it."

"Well, he should have. Mr. Drake, I'm so glad you finally accepted my invitation, but I have to admit it was a shock. Casey, did Eric tell you that he called the very day you woke up?"

She could see the expectant smile in Simon's eyes. The last time she had seen that sly, superior smile was in the bookstore, when he seemed to take it for granted that women would admire him. "What a coincidence," she said innocently.

"Fate!" he snapped. Was the girl blind? Did she have no sensitivity? Or was she that stupid? He had waited for her for over two months and she thought it was coincidence!

"Whatever it was," Eric said soothingly, "you can see why we'd hate to lose her." He casually put his arm around her waist.

So that's how it is, Simon thought, then revised his estimate as she shrugged off Eric's arm and moved to join her mother.

"Mom, did you hear about the storm moving in? What time were you and Dad planning to leave in the morning?" Casey asked.

"Yes, it was on the news," Ned commented as he walked up with Paul. "They named it 'Tropical Storm Diana' and

222

it entered the Gulf this morning. People are already calling it the Princess. We shouldn't be getting any feeder storms from it for several days, but you never can tell. I thought we'd make sure your supplies are okay, and try to leave before lunch."

"A 'D' already? You mean I slept through three hurricanes?"

"I always said you could do it," Ned grinned.

She made a childish face at him as she realized that the other three probably hadn't come near the Florida Panhandle and may not have even become hurricanes.

"You know we'll take care of her," Eric commented.

"If the storm comes near here, we'll all stick together," Clarise said, and Paul nodded firmly.

Ned smiled quietly, then put his arm around his wife's shoulders. "Ready for bed, darling? I'm about worn out." They said good night to everyone and kissed Casey and Clarise before they went upstairs.

Casey breathed a sigh of relief, and then wondered, Why is it so important to get them away from here? A voice in her mind added, Before the trouble starts.

"Mr. Drake, I've just been dying to meet you," Clarise beamed at him, her smile irresistible. "I can't wait to hear how you saved Casey's life and killed Billy Bazzel. To hear my husband tell it, you came out of nowhere, crossed the whole room in a single bound like Superman, then crushed his neck just by grabbing it."

"How could I possibly argue with that account?" Simon's laugh boomed through the room and Casey looked at him in surprise. She had never even imagined him laughing, but this exuberant noise suited him perfectly.

"Maybe we shouldn't talk about this right now." Eric moved closer to Casey and put his arm around her. "We don't want you getting upset."

Her surprise was almost comical. "I think I can handle it. After all, I managed to live through the shooting," she said dryly. "I'd really like to hear it from

223

someone else's point of view."

"I can't believe it was the first time you were ever in the shop and you managed to save my cousin's life. Wasn't it closing time?" Clarise asked.

"The truth is," Simon hesitated, looking curiously at Casey. If only he could hear and understand her thoughts like he could with others, but she was closed to him. Only her emotions were evident, and he couldn't tell if he was reading her heart or her face. "I was waiting for everyone to leave so I could ask Cassandra out."

"Really?" Clarise asked.

Casey's eyes sparkled, but there was still a trace of doubt. She remembered how interested he had seemed at first, then that amused glance, and she had decided she was imagining it.

"Really," he said honestly, staring into Casey's eyes. "I thought that you had the most beautiful, the wisest eyes I had ever seen."

"Casey and I had a dinner date planned that night," Eric said.

"That wasn't a date, that was a business appointment." Casey shook her head, confused, then smiled as she looked up at Simon. Her smile died slowly.

There were those colors again. Eric radiated a spikelike, jagged orange-red, shot with an ugly green. He said something to Simon and his words were surrounded in a red haze that cut into her brain. But it was a different red that surrounded Simon. A wine-red, blood-red field of energy that was edged in black, as if encapsulated and contained.

They were looking at her, and she had no idea what had been said. "Pardon?" she asked politely. She didn't mean to sway.

Eric was closer but it was Simon who swept her off her feet before she fell. He laid her gently on the couch. The world spun as Paul put a pillow under her feet and Clarise dipped a cloth in ice water. Simon put his hand on her forehead and his mouth was moving, but she couldn't hear

224

the words. She could only see his eyes. They were dark as night and big as the universe and she was falling straight up into them.

Her disorientation lasted only a minute, then the world snapped back into focus just as Clarise said, "It was just too much for her. She shouldn't have tried to get out in this weather, then that bat attacked and we had to go to the hospital. Maybe we should call Kate."

"Don't you dare," Casey shook her head. She tried to sit up, but Simon pushed her gently back down.

"A bat attacked you?" Simon asked sharply.

"Just relax, Casey. I won't tell Kate, but you just lie there quietly," Clarise ordered, then she turned to Simon. "It was the weirdest thing . . ."

"No," she choked out the word and the room started to spin again. "No." But it was too late. Nothing short of a hurricane could have stopped Clarise from telling such a fascinating story. Casey closed her eyes, lay back, and thought her own thoughts.

I saw a man change into a bat, tonight. I dreamed I saw a tree struck by lightning, and later it happened. I had a "premonition," her mouth puckered at the sound in her mind, that Clarise would be in trouble, and she was. And I saw a vampire.

Her thoughts stopped, unable to go on. It was like a stuck record, playing the same notes again and again. I dreamed I saw a man come out of a coffin and kill people. And those people are dead. I saw a man who had no reflection in a mirror. He changed into a bat and flew away. He was a vampire. There are no vampires. But I saw a man with no reflection turn into a bat.

Stop. Logical, rational thought. That's what you need. Listen, Brighton, you can either believe your own eyes and legends that have been around for thousands of years, or you can believe modern science and thought.

I don't want to believe in vampires. Stop it! It doesn't matter what you want. We're talking reality. So what do I

225

do about it? RUN!!!

She pushed the attractive idea aside. There was a part of her that knew that something had to be done. And if she was the only one who knew that vampires were real, then she had been elected.

But I can't be the only one. There must be people out there who know. How do I get in touch with them? And avoid getting locked up with them.

The logical place to look was the local insane asylum, because everyone would think they were crazy. That idea wasn't appealing. She could put an ad in the newspaper, but that would be even worse. Not only would everyone in town laugh at her, every kook in the area would probably answer it.

She opened her eyes and looked around the room. Paul was telling them about the bat. Clarise caught her eye and grinned. A dim haze of yellow surrounded her, but a darker thread ran toward her head.

What is that? Casey wondered, and the answer was in her mind. Clarise was horribly, frantically terrified that Paul would develop rabies. All she could think about was that huge bat and how crazy it had acted.

Great! So I'm going to relieve her mind by convincing her that the bat wasn't rabid, it was a vampire?

But that was the answer, and she knew it. These were the people she knew and trusted, they knew and trusted her. If they wouldn't believe her, no one would. Maybe no one should. Maybe she was crazy.

Simon. She concentrated intently on him and he gazed calmly back at her. The colors around him became intense. The red seemed to shift and flow like fresh blood, and black rimmed it like an early frost. It was incredibly beautiful, sparkling with power. The patterns captured her eyes until it was all she could see and her dizziness returned.

She closed her eyes. He was the unknown quantity. There was no reason for him to be in on this. Even if he

226

had saved her life, she didn't really know him. He had crushed Billy's neck with one blow, but that might have been a fluke. That touch on her face, it must have been her imagination. There was a lull in the conversation and she realized that Clarise and Paul had told Eric and Simon the whole story. At least as they knew it. She decided firmly that she would wait for Simon to leave and then she would tell the others.

"I met a vampire tonight," Casey heard the words come out of her mouth but she had no understanding of what, why, or when she had changed her mind. Laughter burst from Eric, and slowly died as he realized she was serious. Simon's eyes narrowed. He had an utter stillness that was so intense it was almost frightening. Paul turned a cop's stern eye on her, and Clarise gave Casey her familiar, "Oh, shit! What are you pulling this time?" expression. Still, there was such a feeling of relief at having said it that Casey almost grinned.

"Now that I have your attention," she continued as she sat up. "I'd like to tell you about a woman who woke up from a coma and began seeing and hearing things that other people didn't." She saved the worst until last, but she hadn't realized how bad it was until she had to force the words out, stuttering and stumbling over them. She ignored her trembling lips and concentrated on keeping her voice level. She tried to make her description absolutely factual as she told about the red glow of his eyes in the lights. He withered again, his body shrunk upwards while his arms flattened and spread, and she relived that terrible metamorphosis. Tears ran from her eyes unnoticed, and the only way she could deal with the fear was to cut it off, to pretend it didn't exist.

She came back to the room with a start. Her gaze lifted from her clenched fists to meet Simon's guarded eyes. Clarise's face was set firmly on neutral, but Eric's expression was puzzled and sympathetic. Paul looked as if he had bitten into a sour, green apple.

She hit rock bottom and dug in. "He came out of a coffin. He drank their blood. He changed into a bat. He's a vampire!"

"Casey, cuz, you know it didn't happen that way." Clarise's smile was uncertain, but her voice was positive. "There was a man and a bat, but they weren't the same. The bat was crazy or sick, but it wasn't a vampire."

"Not even a vampire bat," Paul tried to smile. "But I did hear the thunder while I was on the phone with her, and I told you what she told me in the car."

"You mean you believe her?" Clarise demanded incredulously.

"I didn't say . . ."

"It's all a joke, right, Case?" Eric smiled with relief. "You're just making it all up."

"I didn't make up the man outside their door. I didn't imagine the bat."

"Stop it, Casey!" Clarise ordered. "I think we've had enough."

"Eric?" she appealed to him.

"Aw, c'mon, Case. Maybe you think you mean it, but be real. You were shot in the head. You were in a coma for almost three months." Eric's exaggeratedly patient voice rose slightly as her calm look didn't change. "You still have headaches and you just collapsed a few minutes ago. You're weak and sick, you need help. You need to go to bed. You can't take this seriously."

"I have to take it seriously. It's happening to me." She still fought for calm. "I'm not having hallucinations. Paul can vouch for that. I'm not sick, and I don't think I'm crazy. What do you want me to say? That it sounds insane? I know how it sounds! But I can't say it didn't happen when it did. And someone has to do something."

"Casey, please." Clarise was distraught. "I think . . . Eric is right. You don't mean . . . it's a joke, you can't be serious. In a few days, all this will make you laugh."

"Paul?" Casey appealed to him. "I knew something was

228

out there. You even caught my slip when I said it, not him. You have to believe me."

"She did say 'it,' " he admitted reluctantly. "And she warned you about the prowler before it happened. The rest? I don't know . . . but the Casey I know wouldn't lie about something like this."

"She's crazy! And if you believe her, you're crazy too!" Eric exploded, outraged that anyone should be so gullible.

"Stop that!" the normally meek Clarise snapped at him. "She . . . she's not crazy! She's not! She's just . . . weak. She hasn't recovered yet. Casey, why don't you go up and lie down for awhile?" Casey ignored her and Clarise turned back to the men. "She's still sick and she needs help, not someone screaming at her, or encouraging her. Paul, I think encouraging her to believe in vampires is cruel. How could you!"

"Me? I just said she isn't a liar," he said defensively. "Just that she believes what she's saying, not that I believe it."

"You're encouraging her."

"I am not!" Paul heard the protesting tone in his voice and he backed off. His small delicate hands made a pushing motion.

"Hospital. She needs the hospital or a doctor. I'll wake Kate up and we can call someone," Clarise decided.

"No!" Casey stated flatly. "Absolutely not. If you say one word of this to Mom or Dad I'll . . ." She couldn't think of any threat drastic enough. "I'll mourn you as if you had died, because to me you'll *be* dead." She watched Eric shake his head and wondered. Indecision? Or disgust? Her face burned as she saw it was amusement.

"Let me get this straight," he said, barely able to control his laughter. "You want us to go vampire hunting? Shall we start digging up graves? Should we hang garlic from the doors and windows, or maybe get some Holy Water from the local priest? Maybe we should check all unidentified bats in the area. And what do we do if we find one? I'm sorry, my vampire lore is a little rusty. Is it a stake through the heart, or a silver bullet?"

"That's for werewolves," Clarise said scornfully. Paul stared at her in amazement. "Well, I read to the kids at the shelter and they like to hear scary stories, so I just remembered, that's all."

"And you said I was encouraging her?" Paul asked sarcastically. Then he turned on Eric. "As for checking all bats, if you had seen the one that attacked us, you wouldn't think that was quite so funny."

"What about it, Casey?" Eric asked. "Do you really believe you saw a vampire? Do you really want to convince Paul, knowing that that bat could have been rabid? What if he doesn't go in for treatment? Do you want to be responsible for that? You still want to insist it was a vampire, knowing it might cost him his life?"

Her face was expressionless as she stared at him, then she turned to her last hope.

Simon.

He desperately wanted to laugh, to ridicule her, to make fun of her in front of her friends. If he could just do that, it would be the last straw. They would never believe her. They would be too embarrassed to even consider the notion. He would be safe to deal with the intruder in his own way. Even if he had to give her up, never to see her again, at least there would be no vampire hunters searching for him and his kind.

Her eyes were so hopeful, so vulnerable. She trusted him. She wanted so desperately for him to believe her. He watched silently as the hope turned to doubt, then pain. He couldn't add to it. He said nothing.

The bat dropped from his perch and scuttled awkwardly along the ground. The limb was too far away from the room for him to hear properly. He waddled under an azalea bush and stopped directly under the window. It had not been hard to follow them from the hospital, but find-

230

ing Simon here had been an unexpected bonus.

The humans were plotting to kill him. He kept waiting, expecting Simon to say something to throw them off the track. Simon was well-fed and strong. He could have taken the whole room of them and drained them dry, but he said nothing.

"Casey?" Paul prodded her gently.

"Yes," she cleared her throat, looked up at Eric's face, and tried again. The first time hadn't come out so well. She hadn't realized how humiliating this would be. "Yes. I believe in vampires," she repeated firmly. She thought of all the ways she could have avoided an answer.

"And what do we do if we find one?" Paul asked calmly.

"We destroy it!" That answer was easier.

"A stake through the heart?" The muscles in Eric's face made sharp ridges from his cheekbones to his jaw.

"If that's what it takes."

"And what if we don't go along with this insanity?" He watched her closely and didn't like what he saw.

"Then I try it alone," she said miserably.

"I can't believe it! I just can't believe you want us to do this!" The muscle in Eric's cheek twitched violently.

"Nobody's twisting your arm, damnit! I said I'd do it alone!"

"No way. You need a keeper. If you won't agree to a psychiatrist, I'll have to go with you, but there's one provision. If we find a reasonable explanation for what you think you saw, you won't change your story to witches and werewolves. No more arguments, no more farfetched theories. Or you go into a hospital for evaluation. Agreed?"

"If you can find any other explanation for what I saw, we quit." That was a nice thought, but she didn't try to hold on to it. It was enough that she wouldn't be alone in this. She hadn't realized how much that thought had terrified her. She turned to Paul next.

231

"Yes," he said simply.

"Reese?"

"You're crazy! You're all crazy! I'm going to call the doctor."

"No. No doctors. No cops but Paul. We need you, Reese. I need you."

"Oh, great! Emotional blackmail. Alright, alright. I'll go just to keep an eye on you. I don't believe it and I know I'm going to regret it, but I'll go."

"I don't care how much you bitch at me, cousin, as long as you're there," Casey laughed with relief. Three down, one to go. "Simon?"

"You people are really going to do this?!" He could barely check his angry sarcasm. "The four of you are going to track the mighty vampire to his lair and pound a stake through his heart?"

"With, or without you," Eric spoke levelly, careful to keep any hint of challenge out of his voice. Simon slowly looked over the group, as if he were assessing their capabilities or their sanity.

"You could help us, couldn't you, Simon?" Casey spoke impulsively.

"What?"

"You can help us, if you want to. You know about things like this. When you first came into the bookstore, you wanted information on reincarnation. Have you studied metaphysics?" He didn't answer, and she rushed on. She was sure of what she was saying, but she didn't understand how she knew. "You have. You have experience with psychics and you know a lot about things that go bump in the night. You could find him."

"No, I'm afraid you—"

"Bullshit!" she snapped. "You've never been afraid in your life. You don't even know what the word means, do you? You were the only one who didn't laugh at me when I said I saw a vampire. Your silence speaks much louder than words. You could find him. You know how, don't

232

you? Don't you!"

"No! I can't find him." The words burst from him before he could stop them. He shook his head ruefully. "I can't help you. I'd like to, but it's impossible."

"Yes, you could," Casey said sadly to Simon. "But I can't blame you for refusing."

"So, it's just the four of us, then," Eric tried to keep from smiling. "Where do we start? I guess we better figure out how to kill it before we find it."

"That does seem reasonable," Simon murmured.

"I don't even know where we can get information on vampires."

"All I have at the shop is the popular fiction type. I think we need more legends and stuff. Maybe the library, but I have to admit I've never seen anything there. We need more than a small town library. Maybe Mobile or New Orleans would have more."

"Perhaps, I *can* help you," Simon said reluctantly.

"I knew you would." Casey's quiet smile was a thing of pure joy and beauty.

"I have quite a collection of folklore and legends in my library. I'm sure I have some books on the subject of vampires. And there is one other thing I might be able to do," he added slowly.

"What's that?"

"You've only been awake from the coma for a week, and already you've experienced clairvoyant dreams, visions, and premonitions. Psychics are very vulnerable when they first awaken. I might be able to teach you to protect yourself, and to use and develop your gift. You may have trouble controlling it at first."

"Oh, this is wonderful. Now we've all lost our minds," Clarise remarked.

"I have been having trouble. You really think you could teach me to control it?" Casey asked hopefully.

"I didn't say that," Simon corrected her hastily. "I don't know if it can be controlled. Most of what I've read indi-

233

cates that although some psychics can call on their power at will, it may also come and go at its own whim. But first you must learn to protect yourself. If he can invade your dreams, then he may be able to do other, more concrete things."

"Like what?" Eric demanded.

"If I remember correctly, vampires are known to have a certain 'calling power.' "

Simon was plotting to kill him!

Bastard! Traitorous bastard! I'll kill you for this. I'll make you beg for the final death. I'll stake you out in the sun until your eyes bubble and your flesh melts. If I had not chosen you to join me, you would have grown old and died. You owe me, brother! And I will collect.

Franz felt such a flare of hate and rage that he could not believe that Simon could not feel it. He controlled it quickly, and tried to think of other things. He had left Beverly at the hospital after he saw that Casey and the nurse were friends. He wanted as many of her friends as possible.

He had heard enough. He moved back to the limb, wondering. Who was this woman who enthralled Simon to such a degree that he could not or would not hear his own brother? What hold did she have on him? If he wanted her, why didn't he just take her? What kind of game was Simon playing with her? And with his own brother? Or was it the woman's game?

Too many questions. They were all against him, that was all that mattered. His own brother, this woman, who else was in on it? He looked around uneasily. Maybe they had known the sailors who had thrown him overboard. Maybe they were all in it together.

He could find out. He was close enough now. He could probe her mind, or one of the lesser ones in there, but it took concentration. He had to block out every outside fac-

234

tor. He had to go deep into his subconscious. When he did that, he was totally vulnerable. For that time, the outer world, including his own body, faded into a minimal background awareness. It was much like his sleep during the day.

Was that what Simon was waiting for? He would wait until Franz's defenses were down, then attack.

It was all a trap. Everyone was against him. Everyone except Beverly.

His back claws released the limb and he dropped, then flew frantically away. There was only one he could trust now.

Soon there would be many.

"I've seen that in movies!" Clarise said excitedly. "Where he stands outside the beautiful woman's window and she wakes up and goes to him. I always thought it was kind of corny."

"It may be, but what if it's true? What if he senses her interest and calls her to him before I can teach her to find him?"

"You don't know Casey very well," Clarise tilted her head, trying to find the words to explain. "She's feisty. Contrary. I don't believe he could—"

"Why do we keep saying he and him?" Eric asked sarcastically. "If Casey really saw one, don't they create more of their own kind? There may be fifty of them out there. If you believe in one; why not in more than one?"

"No, there can't be." Casey turned pale at the thought and her voice gradually became loud and shrill, "Don't say that. Not more like him. Don't even think it!"

"Casey, stop it! You're scaring me," Clarise seemed as much angry as scared.

"I think we should all be scared," Casey responded.

"I don't mean of vampires! For Christ's sake, Casey, I'm scared for you. You really believe this." Clarise was near tears. She looked at Paul helplessly and caught the warning shake of his head.

"You said you'd help," Cassandra replied flatly.

"That's not the kind of help you need. I'm scared for your sanity."

"Reese, please. I know what you think, but I don't need another doctor. I need some friends who will stand by me." If Clarise backed out, Paul would go with her. Simon would probably go next. Would Eric stay if the others left? She didn't want to think that he would desert her, but he might. Then she'd have to do it alone. The thought scared her even more than the memory of that glowing face.

"I know that none of you believe me." She tried to force a smile. "If I were you I probably wouldn't believe me either. Treat it as a game, if you want, but please, please, don't make me do this alone." She stopped abruptly.

What am I doing? If they treat this as a joke, they could all be killed. They have to be convinced to take this seriously. But not now, she thought helplessly. If I push too hard now, I'll lose them.

Clarise moved closer and put her arm around Casey's shoulder. "I won't leave you, kid. We'll all do everything we can until . . . well, until you agree to stop."

"Then let's plan what to do. Paul? You've been so quiet."

"I've just been thinking about the police investigation. It's been almost a week now, but they've refused to release the coroner's report and the lab findings. It shouldn't take this long. Something's up."

"Can you find out what?"

"I'll work on it. There's one other thing."

"What?" Casey prompted.

"You're forgetting that there were two survivors to the attack."

"Janie and David." Casey considered carefully before she continued, "Could I talk to Janie?"

"I thought you knew . . ."

". . . that she doesn't talk. Yeah. I still want to see her.

236

Can I?"

Paul looked at his wife. "You're the expert. What do you think?"

"I don't think it'll hurt. I'd like to go, too."

"You're a child advocate. I'll see if I can pull some strings to have you appointed to this case. I'll set up an appointment for tomorrow."

"I'll drive them over," Eric volunteered, unwilling to be left out.

"Not to their house! They didn't go back there, did they? What about Janie's father? Is he home yet?" Casey asked slowly.

Paul gave her a funny look. He couldn't have remembered the names of the children if he had tried, but perhaps Casey had known them from the bookstore. He wondered what else she knew. "Yeah, Jerry's home. How did you know their father wasn't there?"

"I told you, I was there, sort of." She smiled at him gently. "It's kind of foggy, almost like a dream, but I do remember. I wish I could forget. Ask me questions if you like."

"Maybe later. Jerry Wiltz is still a suspect, but it doesn't seem like he could have done it. He was out hunting near Montgomery, four hours away. Two men were with him the whole time. As for the kids, he didn't seem in a hurry to get them back so we left them with the Larsons."

"So now what do we do?" Clarise asked.

"I guess we have two priorities: find out how to kill it first, then find out where it is."

"Seems to me," Eric spoke hesitantly, "the mistake everyone makes in the movies is to get there too late. After dark, I mean. So whatever we do, we do it on the brightest, sunniest day we can find."

"That hardly seems sporting," Simon said softly. "I don't think that I could go out in the sun to hunt a vampire."

"Fair?" Clarise looked at him, puzzled. He believed Casey. She could tell.

"Surely even a vampire deserves a fair chance. Once, he was a man."

"Maybe, but what is he now?" Eric remarked.

"I think the question is a little academic for me," Paul broke in. "Besides, if we wait for a sunny day, we may all be vampires. We're in the middle of a rainy spell, remember? There's also a tropical storm in the Gulf, and even if it doesn't turn into a hurricane, we'll probably get rain from it in a few days."

"Paul's right. Forecast was for clouds and thunderstorms. If sunlight kills vampires, I wonder if they can go out on cloudy days?" Clarise shrugged as she asked the question.

Everyone looked at Casey.

"I don't know!" she snapped defensively. "I just saw one, I'm not an expert. Maybe one of Simon's books will tell us."

"Wouldn't there be other indications?" Clarise asked hesitantly.

"Like what?"

"Well, people disappearing or dying or something."

"I'll check the files," Paul volunteered.

"Simon, my parents are leaving tomorrow morning. I wonder if I could come over and look through your library."

"You really shouldn't be driving yet, Casey. I'll take you," Eric volunteered, but Simon shook his head.

"Sorry, but I will be in Pensacola all day. Why don't we meet back here tomorrow night? Then, if you want to check my library, I'll drive you."

They didn't come until after 1:00 A.M. Jerry Wiltz woke slowly at the scratching on the screen. He could hear his wife whisper, "Jerry? Let me in. I've missed you, and I'm cold."

His head was spinning and his stomach lurched, and Jerry knew he was suffering more than a hangover.

238

"You fergit your key again, stupid? I'm thirsty. Did you fergit the whiskey, too?"

Her voice came again, soft and sweet. "Le' me in, honey. I'm thirsty, too."

He got up reluctantly and staggered as he stepped toward the door. "Wha' time is it?" he muttered groggily.

A giggle at the window answered him.

"Y'all kids quit foolin' aroun'," he yelled. "Where y'all been this time o' night?"

"Hurry, darlin'. I got somethin' real special for you," Estelle's voice sounded strange. He wondered if she'd been drinking.

He reached for the doorknob and his eyes widened. Fingerprint powder still dimmed the brass and he jerked his hand back as the memories flooded in. They were dead. He had identified Estelle's body in the morgue before he got sick and Bellecourt said he was too drunk to see the kids.

"They're dead. They're all dead. I'm jus' dreamin'." He whirled from the door as his wife's voice drifted to him.

"Jerry? Let me in. I'm thirsty."

His eyes jerked to the window and he stared blindly. There was no one there. There couldn't be. Estelle was dead. The kids were dead. He had buried them all today. The shock and the whiskey had just ganged up on him, that was all there was to it.

But he didn't want to go to that window.

The giggle came again, and he recognized it. He had never been able to beat it out of her. Sally was out there. But Sally wasn't one of the ones who survived, was she? He flattened himself against the wall next to the window.

His wife's voice was sharp now, more the way he remembered it. "Jerry?"

He was shaking as his mind insisted, "She's dead. The only thing out there is grass and trees and bushes. An' if I see anythin' else, it'll probably be pink elephants and giant purple spiders."

That damn giggle again. He jerked away from the wall and slipped. Off-balance, he reeled unsteadily and his nose flattened against the glass.

There was nothing out there but the windblown bushes, waving at him.

His breath whooshed out in relief and he closed his eyes. Too much whiskey, that was all that was wrong with him. The glass felt good against his forehead, cool and smooth. He rubbed the back of his neck where it had "cricked" because the couch wasn't quite long enough for him to stretch out on.

"So tired," he mumbled vaguely. "Maybe I should go upstairs to bed." His eyes snapped open as he remembered what had happened on that bed.

Estelle stared back at him, smiling through the window.

He shrieked wildly and turned to run. He fell over the couch, got up unmindful of the pain in his shin, and sprinted to the door, then stopped.

What was out there? Estelle? Whatever it was, it wanted in. It wanted him to open the door. What would happen if he did? He backed away from it slowly, and looked around the living room.

What was she doing out there? She was dead. Dead is dead is dead and no one walks around after. He staggered to the couch and drained the rest of the bottle. Then he remembered the giggle.

How many were out there? Was Sally still alive? They had told him that the kids who survived were with that old couple who kept calling the cops on him. If they wouldn't let the kids go to the funeral, they sure wouldn't let them come home in the middle of the night. Maybe Sally had snuck out, and seeing Estelle was just his imagination.

He had to see, had to know if he was going crazy or if they were really there.

He crept back to the window and peeked out. Estelle was standing in the moonlight, in full view. She looks dead, he thought. He could see the children behind her.

240

Matt, Sally, and Jake. They all looked dead.

"Go away!" he yelled. "You're dead and I didn't kill you!"

She ignored his words and smiled at him. "Let me in, Jerry. I'm cold and thirsty." The kids stood around as if sleepwalking.

They looked dead. He had no doubt that they were dead. He knew that if he opened the window, they would smell dead. The same stench that was in the room upstairs. They were dead. And if they touched him, he would go insane.

He pulled the curtains and ran through the rooms, making sure each window was closed and locked. Then he forced himself to go upstairs to do the same. Back downstairs, he barricaded the doors, shoving furniture around and trying to figure a way to block the windows. The voice called and screamed at him, until he peeked outside to see if she was trying to break into the house. She stopped when she saw him. She seemed to have forgotten what she wanted him for.

When he closed the peephole she screamed at him again. He turned on the radio and the TV to drown out the sound. He wondered briefly if he should call the cops. What could he tell them? That his dead wife was outside and wanted in? They would think it was a guilty conscience. They might even lock him up.

The radio and TV blared at him, and he found that it was worse not being able to hear what was going on outside. He turned the noiseboxes off. He spent the night going from window to door to window, peering out at them. Sometimes he screamed back at them. Sometimes he crept around softly so they wouldn't hear him.

They left, just before dawn.

Chapter Eleven

It was after midnight when Pat Shell splashed through the hospital parking lot to her car. The rain had stopped, but a heavy fog lay on the ground like cotton wool. Individual droplets hung in the air like a fine spray and the combination of heat and humidity was stifling.

Pat held her head up straight, but her shoulders were beginning to slump. Her normal assignment was the terminal cancer ward, Death Row as some of the less sensitive called it. That was bad enough, but eight hours in emergency had taken everything she had to give and left her emotionally and physically worn out.

She looked around the sky vaguely, trying to spot a full moon. Despite all the experts and the scientific studies, she knew that a full moon brought out all the crazies, that critical patients got worse, and that the terminal ones would choose that time to die. Tonight the ER had been a madhouse. One patient after another and all of them scared, desperate, and hurt, and looking to her for help, comfort, and reassurance.

If there was a moon out there, she couldn't find it. Just a wet gray fog, seamless, formless, distortingly directionless. She made her way through the first three rows of cars, then turned left and tried to use the lights above her as markers, since they were useless for illumination. Haloes of light surrounded the top of each pole, expanding dimly but never reaching the ground. She walked down the middle of the lane, ignoring the yard-wide puddles that

242

stretched from one side to the other. Her shoes squelched wetly as she wondered if she had parked on the fourth row or the fifth, and was it closer to the side door, or the street?

She peered through the gloom, trying to spot her car by the shape and color, but all the corners were blunted and the colors were washed out. It was no use. She would have to inspect each car as she came to it instead of cutting across the lanes.

She shivered, and really couldn't say whether it was from the damp or the eerie atmosphere of the night. A door slammed and she looked up hopefully, but sounds ricocheted in the mist and she couldn't tell from what direction it came. She decided she couldn't have parked this far out, and was crossing to the next lane when she spotted a familiar shape. Her big Oldsmobile squatted comfortably in the darkness, as if waiting for her. A smile lit her face as she hurried forward.

The light above flickered and she glanced up, wondering if the bulb was about to die. The dimness above was steady, but there was a tremor in the dark fog behind her. She flinched, and her foot disappeared as she stepped into a puddle.

There was a splash, and an answering echo behind her. Her foot sank out of sight in a pothole. She screamed as her ankle twisted, then began to collapse, but twenty years of nursing, of walking, bending, stooping, and lifting patients, had strengthened her legs. She caught herself before she fell. The muscles in her left leg felt pulled and she was wet to the knee, but the ankle hadn't sprained and she felt lucky. She gingerly put her weight on the injury.

It held. She took the first step to her car before she heard it. A whirring, flapping noise, like a fan with a noisy blade. It set her teeth on edge. She put her foot down too hard, and the pain shot through her ankle and up her leg. She bit back a whimper as she tried to hurry.

Her car was beside her now and she leaned heavily on it

243

for support. The fog distorted sounds, but the pounding of heavy steps behind her was unmistakable. She reached the door and frantically thrust the key in the lock, twisting and turning it in the same motion. As she heard the lock click she remembered Casey's warning.

There was a movement behind her. She whirled, her keys held as a weapon in her hand. A huge shape, distorted by fog and fear, came rushing out of the dark. Pat screamed for help, hopelessly, knowing that they were alone in the parking lot.

"Whut is it, lady? Whut's wrong?"

She opened her eyes, ready to scream again, when she saw the uniform.

"Where is he?" The burly security guard had his gun drawn, peering through the fog, looking for an assailant. "Whut did he do to you? Which way did he go?"

"He? Who?" Pat asked, confused.

"I heard a scream. Was there someone after you?"

"No." She collapsed against the car, trying to keep from laughing with relief. "No, I just stepped in a pothole and twisted my ankle. Then I heard someone coming and got scared."

"Well, I heard the scream so I come arunnin'. With those murders last week, I jist thought . . . well, hope I didn't scare you none."

"That's the understatement of the year! I guess I'll never have to worry about a coronary. If my heart was weak, I would just have died of fright." Her hand was trembling so badly that she couldn't open the door. The guard reached around her and opened it easily.

"Well, don't you worry, little lady. I'll stand right here and watch till you're clean outa the parking lot." She started to say something, but he anticipated her. "If I cain't see, I kin hear the engine. You just git in and set a minute, till you git your breath back."

She nodded with relief, put the key in the ignition and listened gratefully as he rambled on about his job in the hospital and how careful the guards were to take care of the nurses. "Nex' time," he concluded sternly, "you jist wait by the door till I git back and I'll walk you to your car. Don't you come out here alone again late at night. Ain't nothin' gonna happen, but it don't make no sense to take chances. You okay now?"

"Yeah. Thanks," she said sincerely.

"Lock the doors and roll up those windows. I'll stand right here and listen, and you jist beep that horn once when you turn onto the road. Any trouble, and I'll come arunnin'."

She did as ordered, sighing with relief as she made the turn and beeped the horn.

It had been so absurd to get scared like that. Casey's warning must have made more of an impression than she wanted to admit. After all, the girl had been in a coma for months. She was entitled to a few fearful fantasies. Pat decided that she should be touched that the girl had cared enough about her to warn her. After all, Casey had slept through most of the care that Pat had given her. She couldn't know if Pat had been tender, or rough and uncaring.

Maybe that's why we always have to be so careful, Pat imagined herself explaining it to one of her student nurses. Because we never know what God has in store for our patients. And just when we're too tired to change another bed or turn a comatose patient one more time, she wakes up to thank us. That would make an impression. The young trainees were so idealistic. Some of the nurses liked to disillusion them as fast as possible, but Pat thought that the longer they could hold on to those illusions, the better nurses they would be.

She turned right onto Racetrack Road and the fog cleared. There was no thinning and shifting and gradual clearing; it just stopped. On one side, there was fog. On the other, it was clear.

Weird, she thought. But it felt so good to be driving

245

without being surrounded by that maddening fluffy gray blanket that her foot just naturally got heavier on the accelerator. She was humming despite her tiredness. It was Saturday night. She checked her watch absently and corrected that thought to Sunday morning. She wasn't due back at the hospital until Wednesday. Unless of course someone called in sick and they asked her to substitute.

She put that thought out of her mind. She had a long break and she would make the best of it. At the end of Racetrack Road, she turned north, away from the Gulf. It was only a short drive home, and she was so very glad. A mile more and she made the turn into a subdivision. The car weaved through the maze to the other side, and came to a dead-end street that very few people even realized was there. A single streetlight dimly illuminated the turn.

The car was going too fast. She didn't realize it until someone stepped out in front of her and she slammed on the brakes.

There was no way she could have stopped.

The car plowed into him, tossing him up and over like a bull goring a matador. He flew through the air ahead of her.

The brakes locked and the car slid, went under him, and she screamed as his body came down on the windshield, shattering it. Glass peppered her face and hands. She wanted to stop thinking, to stop hearing and seeing and reasoning, but her brain kept right on working, explaining every sound. He bounced again, onto the roof this time, and she could hear each individual thud as he rolled across the roof and down. A larger, harder sound, and reason told her that he had just hit the trunk. A rolling thud and then a splat as he hit the wet pavement. The car swung to a stop and she realized that she was still screaming. She shut her mouth, but she couldn't stop the anguish in her mind. Her hands were shaking so badly that she had trouble unlocking the seatbelt.

Her vision blurred and she wiped the blood from her

246

eyes, fighting to hurry. Her nurses training told her that no one could survive such an impact, but she had to make sure. There was always a chance.

Her hand groped for the door handle, finally found it, and jerked the door open. The body was a huddled mass twenty feet away, under the light. She tried to run, took two steps, and her legs collapsed beneath her.

I'm trained to save lives, she told herself sternly and a snide voice inside her retorted, Well, you sure as hell fucked this one up and I don't think you're going to be able to put him back together.

She got up and staggered toward the lifeless form. He was lying on his side, his face toward the ground. She felt his neck for a pulse, but there was no sign of life.

She knelt beside the body, sobbing uncontrollably. One finger twitched. She knew it was probably a postmortem reaction, but she checked the pulse again, then pushed lightly on his shoulder to turn him over. She brushed her tears away as his head rolled limply toward the light. Except for a smear of blood on his lips, his face was undamaged. She had expected a look of terror, or the peaceful countenance the dead sometimes wore, but this corpse was grinning as if he had played some strange joke on fate. His eyes were closed. She opened one to check for pupil reflex.

Her hand jerked back uncontrollably and her whole body shook. The sightless sockets were filled with black blood. It gleamed wetly in the stark light, pools of darkness permeated with red highlights. She told herself that there must have been massive trauma to the side or the back of his head, but her probing fingers found nothing.

He winked at her.

"Oh, my God!" she screamed, scrabbling backward, but his hand whipped out unbelievably fast and clamped around her throat. He rose easily to his feet, still holding her.

"Beverly," he said quietly, and the most incredibly beautiful black woman she had ever seen was suddenly beside him.

"Please," Pat tried to say. Her fingers dug into his hands, but he didn't seem to notice. If she tried very hard, she could force air past his hands into her lungs, but there was none extra for conversation. The beautiful woman looked vaguely familiar, and Pat looked at her, silently pleading for help.

Neither of them noticed.

"Now you know one way to get food. There are many others that I will teach you. You did well tonight. I know how hard the first hunger is to resist, but you watched and waited until I returned and sacrificed the guard. She will be your first kill and third in the Circle."

He tossed Pat to her effortlessly. She didn't even have time to scream before Bev tore her throat out, gulping the blood down in great mouthfuls, ignoring the arterial spurts shooting past her onto the pavement.

"You do have much to learn," Franz commented dryly. He waited impatiently until the flow of blood had slowed to a trickle and Pat's eyes were glazing with death. Now was the time. Only a few drops of his blood would insure that when she awoke, she would retain her faculties. She would learn and grow, and she eventually would become Nosferatu.

"Move away." He put his hand on Bev's shoulder.

She whirled on him and snarled, exposing her great teeth, protecting her prey. The back of his hand exploded against her face, sending her flying ten feet away.

"Don't you ever, ever defy me again." Without seeming to move, he towered over her, his fists clenched in fury.

His mind beat at her until she cowered back, whimpering. It pleased him and he finally, reluctantly stopped. He remembered Pat just in time and hurried to her body.

Her eyes were glazed but he could hear a last, desperate heartbeat. He used his fingernails to slit open his wrist, and let a drop of blood fall lazily into her open mouth.

He waited. Another drop fell.

A third.

She swallowed once, and her heartbeat stopped.

And he knew victory! So many things could have gone wrong: she could have worked until dawn; or gone to a populated place; or someone could have come along while he was dealing with the guard; or she could have died before he protected her from Simon with his own blood. But fate was on his side and he had won another convert. Two in one night! He was marvelous, incredible, brilliant! Simon could never stand against him.

Still, he wanted as many as possible who knew Simon or his whore. The more he knew about them and their habits, the easier it would be to trap them. Tonight he had three. Soon he would have eleven. Casey would be the twelfth sacrifice. He himself would close the Circle of Death to make thirteen.

"Bring the woman's body," he ordered. "I will carry the guard's."

Casey took her second cup of coffee into the living room and lit a cigarette. It had been a rough night. Twice, her own whimpers had awakened her. By 7:00 A.M. she was up and dressed. She had wanted to talk with Paul before he left, but he was already gone. She had fixed breakfast for her parents and Clarise, then shooed them out of the kitchen while she did the dishes. She was already exhausted, but she had to convince her parents that she could take care of herself. Now she slipped gratefully into a chair in front of the television.

"Have you finished your packing?" she asked her mother.

"Just about. Clarise, I'm so glad that you and Paul decided to stay here for a few days. I don't think I could leave if Cassandra had to stay here alone." She turned to frown at her daughter. "Just don't pull any more stunts like last night. I want you to stay home and rest, like the doctor said. You . . ."

"Shhh," Ned said impatiently. "The news is on."

Casey smiled gratefully. He had just saved her from a lecture that she'd rather not hear. As long as the news was on, her mother would try not to disturb him. Ned was a news hog. It was a harmless addiction, but as long as the morning, evening, nightly or in-between news shows were on, the rest of the family had a tendency to tiptoe. In most things, it was a pretty equal household, but each person admittedly had his or her quirks, and the family bowed easily to these prejudices.

Maybe by the time the show ended, her mother would forget about all the warnings she had stored up. It wasn't likely, she admitted to herself, but there was a chance. She picked up the newspaper from the coffee table next to her and began to read the current account of the Wiltz murders. She had almost finished when her father interrupted her.

"Casey, the chart's in front of you. Get the numbers, will you?"

She looked up in surprise. She hadn't been listening to the announcer, but now her attention snapped to the small screen. The weatherman had dropped his usual mindless grin and looked grim as he stood in front of the map. Casey grabbed a pen and the hurricane tracking chart and started scribbling. Lady Di was at latitude 25.3N, longitude 87.8W, right in the middle of the Gulf of Mexico. She filled in the tiny dot in the right place, but when the screen changed to a satellite photo, it showed a frighteningly large mass that filled most of the Gulf. She wrote the important information next to the dot. Four hundred miles in diameter, sustained winds of eighty-five with gusts up to one hundred miles per hour. Barometer reading 28.34. Moving north-northwest at four miles per hour. Expected landfall: Louisiana-Texas border.

Princess Diana was now a Class One hurricane.

She breathed a sigh of relief. It should miss both Florida and her parents' house in New Orleans, then she realized something. "That storm last night. It was a feeder storm from the hurricane, wasn't it?"

"You haven't been paying attention," her father said sternly. "They told us that on the news last night. Of course, you weren't here to hear it. Did you notice the wide arc when they projected the landfall?" She shook her head. "It covered half of the coastline of Texas and Louisiana. They don't know where or when she'll hit. They think she'll sit still awhile, building strength, and then she'll probably start to wobble." He got up to pace restlessly. "Devil storm, or evil spirit. Did you know that's what the word 'hurricane' means? It's more likely to hit near New Orleans than here, or I'd insist you come home with us." Casey shook her head firmly. "Then I'll get out the boards and have everything ready in case you need it. Kate, would you check the supplies?"

"No need," Casey said quickly. "Unless you moved them, they're in the hall closet."

"They're still there, but you may need new batteries. And if she even looks like she's heading this way, be sure to clean the bathtub and fill it with water. And you better start making more ice now, just in case."

"I know what to do. The important thing now is for you all to get home so you can tend to your own house. I hate it that you live in New Orleans. It should never have been carved out of the swamp. There's just no way to stop the flooding even when it's just a small storm. Between Lake Pontchartrain and the Gulf, and smack dab on the Mississippi River, the only thing between you and the water is the levees. Maybe you should stay here." Shut your mouth, stupid! Their chances are better with the storm. "I just wish the weatherman could give us more information," she concluded grumpily.

"The weather service tries hard, and they improve every year," her father lectured her. She knew better than to even hint at criticizing the weather bureau, so she took her punishment silently. "But there are just too many factors to consider, and the government keeps trying to cut their funding. Do you know that for the last three years in a row, they've taken away the funding for the Hurricane Hunter flights, out of Biloxi? They reinstated it each time because the Southern congressmen raised hell, but those flights are the best source of information for wind strength, barometric readings, and a dozen other factors. Can you imagine actually flying into a hurricane in a small plane?" His eyes looked dreamy and his mind was faraway.

By 11:00 A.M. they had completed first stage storm preparations. They had filled water containers, brought in loose objects from outside, and checked the fuel for the kerosene stove. By the time her father had come back from buying batteries, tape, and gas for the car, her mother had finished her packing and they loaded the car. Casey wistfully said goodbye to her parents and watched them drive away, then went inside and collapsed on the couch.

"I'm beat," she admitted to Clarise. "I think I'll take a nap right here."

"Stay awake long enough to eat some lunch. Then you can have an hour or two before Eric picks us up. We're supposed to be at the Larsons' house to talk to the kids at 4:30 P.M., remember?"

"Right." She wasn't looking forward to it.

Eric picked them up in his van at 4:00 P.M. and drove them to the Larsons' street. The police car was easy to spot in this quiet neighborhood, and Paul opened the door to their knock. The white bandage along his jaw stood out sharply.

"C'mon in. Mrs. Larson is in the kitchen. Janie is here, but I don't know what good that will do us. She isn't talking." Paul gestured to the doorway where the little girl

252

stood poised for flight. Casey smiled at her and approached her confidently.

"Hello, Janie. Do you remember me? I helped you pick out some books once. Did you finish those books yet?"

Janie moved back slightly and shook her head.

"Well, I guess you won't want these." Casey pulled two paperback books from her purse. Janie smiled shyly and lifted her hand to take them. Casey handed them over as Mrs. Larson entered the room with a plateful of cookies. The old woman frowned when she saw that Casey had been talking to the silent child. She put the tray down and walked briskly up to Casey, as Eric, Paul, and Clarise gathered around the table.

"I'll tell you the same thing I told Paul. I don't like this. If he'd done his job, this would never have happened. That child's been hurt enough, and she don't need you remindin' her of it. If I see any sign of y'all botherin' her, I'll stop you right there. No more questions, y'heah?"

"I'll try not to upset her," Casey replied easily. The woman wouldn't have been so fierce if she hadn't cared. "Janie and I are old friends. She likes books, and I think she's a very smart girl."

"You think a dummy could have got away from that crazy father of hers? And've taken her baby brother with her? She's sharp as a tack, she is." She remembered her earlier objections and her mouth clicked shut.

"Her father?" Casey asked.

"I already said you could talk to her. Just you don't upset her." She walked back across the room, turning once to give Casey a warning glance.

"Janie, you want a cookie?" Casey asked casually.

Big brown eyes looked at the crowd around the platter and she shook her head slightly. Casey strolled over to the table casually and came away with two cookies in her hand. She sat down on the floor near Janie and began to munch slowly, enjoying the flavor. Janie sat down next to her and put out her hand demandingly.

"You aren't a bit shy, are you?" Casey handed over a cookie and they ate in appreciative silence. Casey used the time to inspect her. Her long blond hair was clean and neatly combed. Her jeans were new, and so was the cotton blouse. She wore socks, but no shoes. She looked like a kid recovering from a long illness, who had been dressed in her best for company. Casey sympathized. She felt a bit of that herself. She had changed into a dark green dress for the occasion. It seemed larger than it had when she tried it on in her room, and her stockings felt too tight, as if her muscles were not used to being bound.

"You know why I'm here?" she finally asked.

Big brown eyes regarded her gravely.

"I know what happened that night." She paused to breathe. She knew what memories she was dredging up. To her it was a nightmare, but to this frail child, it was real. It wasn't fair to ask this sad child to help her. She turned away suddenly. Memories of what had been done to Janie's mother were suddenly overlaid with the image of Janie's sweet face, smiling through her new fangs. A small hand on her arm chased the image away and she was left to wonder — vision or hallucination?

"You know not to let anyone, anyone at all, in at night, don't you?" she said urgently. "If what I saw was real, and I'm still not sure it was, you have to be very careful, you understand? You can't trust anyone."

She stared into her eyes until the child nodded solemnly.

"I want you to promise that no matter who it is, if someone comes to the door or the window, you won't let them in. You call Mr. or Mrs. Larson, and you let them handle it. You promise?"

Janie's eyes narrowed as she thought, then she offered her hand as a pledge. Casey shook it solemnly, breathing a sigh of relief.

"I want you to be very careful because I know what happened that night. But maybe you saw, or heard, or felt something that I didn't. I know it won't be fun, but maybe

254

it will help you to know that someone else knows about it, too. I'll believe whatever you tell me, Janie, so I want you to be very careful about what you saw and heard. Okay?"

Janie nodded.

"Do you know who the man was?"

Another nod.

"Who was he, Janie? Whoops, I forgot. You don't like to talk, do you?" She scrounged in her purse for a pen and notebook, then handed them to the child. "Who?"

DADDY.

"Your Daddy was chasing you?"

Her eyes got bigger as the child realized that Casey really did know what had happened. She nodded silently.

"Okay, let's make sure we've got this straight. When you woke up you were already locked in your room. You didn't see the man till you were outside and he was in the window. It was your Daddy who chased you through the woods?"

A nod.

Casey felt her eyes fill with tears. She didn't know whether to be glad or sad. If she was wrong about this, if Jerry Wiltz had murdered his family, then all the rest were just nightmares and she could forget them and move on. She could forget the creature who killed a man even before he crawled out of his coffin, looking like something that should have been buried a thousand years ago. She could forget the way he grew younger as he killed, and the way he shed his skin, and the way his eyes turned black and the way his fangs glinted in the moonlight. She could forget watching a man turn into a bat and feeling the pull of his mind. What am I supposed to ask this kid? Have you ever watched your father shed his skin?

"Are you sure it was your father?"

An emphatic nod.

"Did you see his face?"

Slowly, Janie cocked her head to the side.

"He climbed down the wall, remember?" Casey

prompted her gently. "You were standing in the woods holding Davey. He climbed down the side of the house where the drainpipe is, and he was outlined by the light on the front porch. Something happened. What was it?" She pushed the notebook at the girl and waited again.

SNIFF DOG.

Casey leaned over to see. For a moment she was confused, but the memory of that nightmare was so clear she could almost see him climb headfirst down the pipe, sniffing like a dog at Janie's tracks.

"That's right, Janie. Then he climbed to the ground slowly, right?" She held her breath, waiting.

Janie disagreed sharply. She pulled at Casey's arm impatiently and the movement caught her guardian's eye.

"You're right, you're right," she smiled and tried to calm Janie down. She didn't miss the glare from Mrs. Larson, she just ignored it.

"Okay, he didn't come down slowly. He jumped." Now if Janie said that she had seen the vampire and it was her father, Casey couldn't shrug it off. "Could you see his face when he came down the pipe?"

A negative shake. Janie moved restlessly.

"Could you see it when he was on the ground?" Casey held her breath again.

Janie twisted around to look at Mattie Larson, then looked back at Casey. The negative shake was a long time coming. Casey let out her breath with a sigh. The men in the white coats would have to wait. She tried not to show how relieved she felt as she went on with the questions.

"Now he's on the ground. Does he walk toward you?"

Janie moved away slightly, and Casey caught her arm. Mattie slowly levered herself out of the chair. Her attention was on the child.

"What did he do, Janie?" Casey demanded urgently as Mattie walked toward them. "Janie, answer me. Did he walk . . . or did he fly?"

Janie took the pad Casey shoved at her and looked at it

256

vacantly, tears running down her cheeks. She scrawled something on the paper, then scratched it out violently, holding the pen in her fist. She looked at Casey and wailed, an animal sound of pain. She jumped to her feet and hurled the notebook across the room. Her feet almost left the ground as her arms flapped wildly. Mattie Larson swept her off her feet and held her protectively.

"Get out of here! No more damn questions! Hasn't this child been through enough?!"

Paul pulled Casey to the door while Clarise tried to apologize and calm Mattie down. Casey could hear Janie's soft whimper, but she couldn't see her.

"You're upsetting her," Casey yelled at Mattie. "Put her down. Janie, was it a bat? Did he change . . ."

"Get out of my house!" Mattie screamed from across the room.

Janie wailed even louder.

"Let me go!" Casey tried to push past Paul, but he dragged her out the door. She was trembling with reaction. The gasping sound of Janie's cries tore through her and she realized that she was crying, too, in rhythm with those pitiful wails. Her legs wobbled as Eric helped her down the walk. She felt as if a spike had been driven through her skull.

"What de bloody hell you doin', girl? You say you wan' to talk to de kid, not scare her t'death!" Paul was coldly, furiously angry, and the red aura seemed to pour from him and surround her. It made her headache worse.

"Why did you do that? What's wrong with you? You've changed, Cassandra Brighton. I wouldn't have believed that you had a cruel bone in your whole body and listen, just listen to what you did to that poor child!" Clarise didn't wait for an answer. She stalked to Eric's van and climbed in.

Casey brushed the tears from her eyes and turned to Eric, realizing for the first time how quiet he had become.

"Eric?"

He held out his arms and she went to him gratefully. For a precious moment, she felt safe, warm and secure in his arms, then he destroyed it with a quiet murmur.

"Why'd you do it, Case? That poor retarded kid couldn't help you if she wanted to. Why did you torture her that way?"

She pulled away from him, betrayed. He was a stranger. She hugged her arms to her body and looked at her friends. They were all strangers. She hadn't changed, but they had. Before she was hurt, they would have at least asked for an explanation and waited for the answer. She was their friend, and they might have been curious, even upset and hurt, but they would have trusted her enough to listen.

Had she tortured Janie? Of course not. Why didn't they understand, or at least stop yelling at her long enough to listen? Janie was· crying because she was scared. She had seen a vampire, and that was enough to scare anyone. But they would never believe it. They were strangers, and she was alone in this. She always had been. She was just too dumb and trusting to know it.

"I'm not the one who scared her," she said stubbornly. She stumbled to the van and crawled in the front. "Take me home, Eric."

Dinner that night was a silent meal. Clarise picked at her food while Eric nursed the bourbon in the living room. Casey didn't even pretend to eat. Afterwards she cleared the dishes herself, declining help. She heard Paul come in from work, but she postponed her entrance to the living room until she could wait no longer. When she finally entered, Simon was sitting in the same chair he had used last night. Paul was still standing. She stared at them dully.

"Paul called me." Simon was appalled at the change in her. Last night she had been vibrant and alive. Now she looked like a rag doll thrown away after years of cruel abuse.

Casey tried to think clearly, but she was so exhausted that her feet dragged on the carpet.

"Shouldn't you be at work?" She spoke to Paul, but she couldn't look up to meet his eyes.

"I checked out early. I have plenty of overtime to compensate," Paul spoke softly, as if in the presence of illness or death.

She put her hand to her forehead and fought the waves of light-headedness. Hadn't she felt like this just before her vision of Clarise? Oh, God, please, she prayed. Not now. I can't flip out now. That will be the last straw. They'll have me committed. She sat down quickly.

"Cassandra." Clarise dragged a footstool over in front of her, sat on it, and tried to take Casey's hand, but she winced away. "You need some rest. You're not strong enough yet."

"You're quitting," Casey's voice was flatly emotionless.

"We tried it your way. Really we did. Janie thinks her father did it. Paul will pass that along to the detectives. Maybe they can break his alibi."

Paul touched the bandage on his jaw uneasily, opened his mouth as if to object, then closed it abruptly.

"You're quitting, too."

"We're all quitting, Casey. You most of all," Eric ordered. "We tried to play your game until you got tired of it, but you went too far. You took a poor retarded kid and browbeat her until she broke. I'd never've believed you could be that cruel. We never should have started this."

"Janie's not retarded. I didn't mean to hurt her." Casey still wouldn't lift her eyes. *Alone.* She would have to do this alone.

The house drew him like an addiction. He knew it was dangerous, but he couldn't stay away. The wolf shape sniffed cautiously around the yard before he padded between the bushes to the window. They were all here. They

259

were plotting against him, and he had to hear.

He had planned to take Clarise tonight. Beverly had warned him that she would be here, protected, but he hadn't expected to find Simon here again. If he could just separate one of them from the group. . . . But humans were herd animals, seeking safety in numbers. The rest thought that Casey was the leader, but he knew that Simon was the real power. The bitch was only his tool, and he could deal with her later.

Now, there was a different problem. He hadn't realized that Janie could be a danger to him. He would have to take care of her first, then come back for Casey when Simon wasn't around.

"May I interrupt?" Simon inquired with barely concealed rage. "They told me what happened today. I'd like to hear the story from you."

"Why?" Casey asked dully, not really interested in the answer. She would have to start over tomorrow and make a plan. Not now. She was too tired, and her head hurt. All she wanted was rest and sleep. Deep, dreamless sleep.

"Eric, would you get her a drink, please?" Simon directed. "I don't understand why the child became so upset. What did you say to her?"

"I asked her if the man who chased her walked or flew." Her voice was detached. She took an absentminded sip, and then another. At least she didn't feel like she was going to flip out anymore. Maybe a few drinks would help her sleep.

"Is that all?" Simon didn't believe it.

"We talked about what happened. I described what I had seen, and she agreed. She even corrected me. She thought her father had done it, but I don't think she ever saw his face. She didn't get upset until I asked if he could fly." Her voice was a little stronger now.

"That's absurd," Simon said firmly. "Surely, any child,

260

even one who had been through such a terrible experience, would laugh if you asked her if her attacker could sprout wings and fly! Certainly she wouldn't scream and have a fit."

"She didn't scream and she didn't have a fit." Casey looked up for the first time. Simon's eyes were warm and comforting. "She got too upset to write it down, so she flapped her arms. Like wings. Like a bat. Not a fit."

"Keep drinking," Simon instructed firmly. "What about the scream?"

"There was no scream. Mattie rushed over and Janie got scared when we started to argue."

"Telling Mattie that she was the one who was upsetting the kid sure didn't help any," Eric put in.

"Was that what made her so mad?" Casey was beginning to understand now. "Anyway, when I asked if he changed into a bat, she started to cry. I saw a man change into a bat. I wanted to cry, too." Her voice drifted off again. What was the use? They saw things one way and she saw them another. Maybe she *was* crazy. She would think about it tomorrow.

"Casey, are you trying to tell us that you think Janie saw a vampire, too?" Eric asked incredulously.

"Of course she saw a vampire! I told you that last night. She thinks it was her father but it wasn't. I'll have to start looking for his hiding places tomorrow," Casey answered. Simon noted that she had a little more color in her cheeks, and her eyes looked more alert.

"You're not going ahead with this?" Clarise was aghast.

"I have to," Casey replied sadly. "But it's okay, Clarise. You and Paul," she looked at Eric with a level gaze, "and Eric have done enough. I'm well enough to stay alone now. I wonder if I can still use your library, Simon?" She turned to him and he smiled but said nothing.

"Where do you go from here?" Eric asked.

"I don't know. Maybe Eglin Air Force Base. I dreamed the vampire's first victim was a young airman. He looked

261

so familiar." She shuddered at the memory. "I'll check the AWOL list. Maybe that will tell me something. Then maybe, the police files for missing persons. If they're all in the same area, it will narrow down the search." Her voice brightened as her mind slipped back in gear.

"How long are you going to keep searching?" Eric demanded. "You promised me you'd quit if we proved that there are no such things as vampires." He punched out the last words.

"Do you think you've proved it?" Simon looked at him coolly.

Eric took a deep breath and let it out explosively. "No! No, I don't. So I guess I'm stuck with this until you give up."

Casey smiled at him gratefully. I don't want to do this without him, she thought. I don't want to do this at all.

"No more child abuse," Clarise said tartly, "and I'll stay, too."

Paul nodded but didn't speak. Simon was the only one left, and Casey looked up into those blue, blue eyes.

"My lovely lady," he smiled at her secretively. "When I go after something, I never quit."

Chapter Twelve

Franz circled the Wiltzs' house twice before he landed on the roof and listened for signs of life. Every light was blazing, and the windows were boarded up from the outside. He would have bet that the doors were boarded up from the inside, too. The person in there was terrified. He could tell that the upstairs was deserted, so he checked the outside of each window on the bottom floor. Someone was moving around, but the footsteps were too heavy for a child. He had been invited into the house once, and once was all it took. He could come and go freely, but it wasn't the man that he wanted. He hadn't been thinking clearly that first night, or the girl would never have gotten away. Now he had come back to correct his mistake. She was the only person who could possibly have seen his face.

He wondered idly when the man's playmates would show, and if any of them were worth his attention. He made a mental note to find out how many there were now. They were nominally under his control, but he had no reason to contact them, yet. If he could not convert twelve others and condition them against Simon by giving them his blood, he could always resort to calling these pitiful, mindless creatures to complete the Circle. If he called, they would come. As the Nosferatu who had created them, he was their Bloodmaster. But without his blood to strengthen them, only one in a thousand, usually the youngest and most adaptable, would retain their mental acuity.

The logical place to start searching was the long, low house toward which Janie had run. He found four people there, located the children's room, and changed to human form. There was a small night-light burning, he noted through the window.

The girl will let me in, he thought arrogantly. Older people have better defenses. They're wary of strangers, and feeble bodies often develop strong wills. But that little brat can't keep me out. She's already used up her share of luck. Now it's my turn.

He watched her sleep for a moment, her cheeks pale even against the white sheets. She was restless; she twitched and turned, her head tossed on the pillow. He imagined her in his arms, frozen with fear and the power of his mind. He could almost taste her blood, rich with youth and terror. His tongue eased out to stroke his lips. He moved closer to the window, and his long fingers reached out to lightly scratch the screen. The rasping noise made the girl jerk, and he wondered if she were awake. He reached out with his mind to touch hers, and then wondered if he should have tried that first. She was awake and alert now. Her fists were clenched rigidly by her sides, and her breathing was fast and shallow. He called to her, sweetly with his voice and imperiously with his mind.

"Janie? Come here, Janie."

A soft, animal whimper escaped those fragile lips. He stepped up the pressure.

"Come to the window, Janie. Invite me in."

She didn't respond.

He commanded her angrily. "Come here. Come now."

She turned on her side in the bed, and he could see her huge eyes, wells of darkness in the faint light, slide in his direction. He smiled enticingly and scratched the screen again. Such a flimsy barrier to keep him out. It was so unfair.

Unfair. Like Simon. He had to find a way to fight Si-

264

mon and his whore. If Simon could use Casey, then he could, too.

He called again, impatient at wasting so much time on a weakling child. "Janie, open the window. I have something for you, dear little girl. Get up and let me in." Her eyes bulged with terror and her lips twitched and jerked, but she refused to look at him. Just one glance was all it would take. He fumed impatiently, as her clenched fists slowly rose to her chest. He peered at her eagerly and ordered her out of bed.

As soon as he thought she was doing as ordered, his mind drifted back to Casey and Simon. *Is he trying to find me now? Are his friends sitting beside him? Does she know what he is?*

"Come on!" He said impatiently, barely glancing at the child. *Could Simon feel his hunger? He had to! He wanted to drive him mad with hunger.*

I'm starving, Simon! Feel my thirst! He drew on the memory of his months at sea and blasted his hunger at the world. Even if Simon had grown so much that he could no longer hear his brother's thoughts, he would not be able to block his former master's hunger. That hunger could spread madness through every unstable or vulnerable human within fifty miles. Maybe Simon would lose control and attack those pitiful humans he spent so much time with. Then Franz wouldn't have to worry about his half brother's friends.

Franz gloated over it, enjoying the fire that spread through his veins, burned from his eyes, and lengthened his fangs. He gloried in the power the blood hunger gave him. He wanted to howl his hunger at the waxing moon.

He turned savagely to the girl inside and realized his mistake.

She was sitting bolt upright in bed. She looked at him for the first time, her eyes wise and knowing as she recognized him for what he was. She nodded once, firmly, then opened her mouth and screamed as his mind reached for her.

"Go away, monster! I won't let you in!" She broke into sobs as lights went on in the room down the hall.

"Janie? What's the matter?" a wondering voice called. "Janie?" The light brightened suddenly as a door opened, and he backed away from the window.

"Fool!" he cursed himself angrily. No one here would invite him in tonight. He turned and changed, and his four legs dodged the shadowy bushes and trees. He raced headlong, venting his fury in motion and watching his shadow race ahead as the lights were turned on in Janie's room. In seconds he was in the woods and he changed into a bat. He headed automatically for his next destination, adding to the Circle of Death that he was drawing, but his mind was occupied with other things.

"Jerrrrry." Estelle Wiltz scratched on the window. It was the third time they had visited him, but this time he was prepared. He didn't need to run through the house, checking to make sure that all the doors and windows were still boarded up. He didn't need to, but he did.

"Just to make sure," he mumbled as he crept quietly upstairs, wondering how they always knew which window to come to. And how did they get to the second floor windows, anyway? He pushed the thought from his mind. It was better not to think while they were here. It was better to act.

In the closet in his bedroom was the shotgun. He took out the light load of birdshot and fumbled with the deadly 25/12 gauge game load. It took him three tries, but he finally reloaded the twelve gauge.

He was in a cold sweat as he cautiously crept down the stairs. His eyes darted from side to side as he searched every room, checked every closet to make sure they hadn't gotten in while he was upstairs. In the kitchen, he spotted a butcher knife and stuck it in his belt. Finally, he gath-

266

ered all the courage that he had left and peeked out the window.

"Jerrrrrry," Estelle called again. Her voice twisted eerily around in his head, like smoke spiralling up from a cigarette. "Jerome, my love. Let me in. I want to love you."

They were all calling to him now. All of his dear family. The family that he had worked so hard for so many years to support. He looked dreamily at the window and wondered why he had cut himself off from those who loved him. He moved to the window and reached to pull aside the curtain, but the shotgun got in the way.

"Jerrrry. Let me in. Please. We love you." They were all calling to him now.

He looked out the window at them, standing there so patiently, waiting for him. Estelle glided closer, and he noticed her figure for the first time in years. Her hips and breasts were full and tight, not like the slat-thin, sharp-boned body he was used to. Her skin was luminous and all the teeth he had knocked out through the years had grown back.

Why didn't he let her in? He couldn't remember now.

He had knocked out those white even teeth. She had talked back to him one night and he had belted her. She deserved it.

She was dead now, and she deserved that, too.

Estelle grinned back at him. Her inch long incisors glinted in the light, growing even as he watched. Her lips writhed away from the sharp points, grinning at him. Her eyes were glowing black holes. Her hands reached for him. "Come to me, darling. Let me in."

He shuddered at the thought and his thoughts snapped into focus. He did what he had always longed to do. He jerked the shotgun up and fired point-blank into her open mouth.

Her face jerked out of sight, and he thrust his head out the shattered window to see. He caught a glimpse of her on the ground before his head was yanked to one side by

267

Jake. Glass sliced his cheek as Sally's fingers reached for his eyes from the other side. He tried to jerk his head back through the hole, but his son's fingers were tangled in his hair. Sally's fingernails cut a furrow down his cheek. She screamed with joy and put her fingers in her mouth. Estelle was off the ground and in front of him. She grabbed the front of his hair, just as he braced his hands on either side of the window frame. His head was being jerked back and forth like a seesaw, when he shoved as hard as he could and lunged backward.

He succeeded in an unexpected way. Estelle's hand was drawn through the hole when she wouldn't release him. It turned red, as if immersed in boiling water, then the flesh blackened and became crisp. He pushed harder, trying to pull her arm in farther, but the flesh crumbled and she lost her grip. He grabbed the knife from where it had dropped to the floor and whirled, ready to slash the first thing that came through the door.

Nothing.

He approached the empty window frame cautiously. Angry voices rose from outside. He peeked around, carefully keeping his head out of reach. Estelle was up and moving, but her arm was burned to the shoulder. She saw him watching, and she hissed like a snake. Then she gathered the children together and they spoke too softly for him to hear.

They turned to smile at him with long, sharp teeth, then they drifted silently into the woods. He took advantage of their absence and barricaded the doors, shoving furniture around and trying to figure a way to block the window.

An hour later, Estelle came to the window and smiled at him. There was something dark smeared around her mouth. He avoided looking at it too closely as she licked her lips with her sharp, red tongue.

His eyes drifted down her body and he noticed the changes. Her arm was healed. Her legs were long and shapely and when she walked, her whole body undulated gracefully. She had a poise and assurance that made him want to beat it out of her.

She looked more beautiful than she ever had as a teenager, but there was the lure of an adult woman about her. She finished cleaning her lips with her tongue and smiled at him.

"Jerry? We're not hungry anymore." Her voice was soft and suggestive, but her eyes were vacant. "Can we come in now? It's so cold and lonely out here." Her voice was sweet and reasonable, and he listened and wanted to hear more. There had been years when he had wished she had had a voice like that, instead of the meek whine that grated on his nerves and drove him to violence.

"You're dead," he told her hoarsely. "Go back to your grave and lie down, bitch. And take your bastards with you."

"Look at your children, Jerry. They're strong and beautiful. Remember when we made them? We could have fun again, and this time I won't cry if you hit me."

He shuddered at the thought. She was the one who drove him to it. She had to be corrected. Punishment had to hurt, or she wouldn't learn from it. If it didn't hurt her, what was the point? He listened for awhile, refusing to answer.

He went to the corner, the one farthest from the window, then pulled out his whittling knife and picked up a piece of wood. Long, slow strokes, the way his Daddy had taught him. Long, slow strokes to make strong, sharp points.

"It's a miracle, Janie. It was just a bad dream, but it made you talk. You can talk again, child. You mustn't lose the knack this time." Mattie Larson was sitting on the side of Janie's bed. She had listened patiently as the child tried to describe the monster in the window, but her old bones were aching and she wanted to go back to bed. But after months of silence, the girl couldn't shut up.

269

"It wasn't a dream! And it wasn't Daddy! Miss Casey was right, Daddy didn't do it. Daddy is mean, but he can't turn into a vampire, can he?"

"No, of course he can't, child. There ain't no such things as vampires, Janie. You're just upsetting yourself more by gabbing about it. I want you to lie back and think good thoughts and go to sleep."

"But . . ."

"No more, sweetie. Go to sleep." The child's thin face looked so anxious that she couldn't leave her like that. "Would you like to come in with Uncle Bill and me, Janie?"

Anxiety turned to terror. "Do I have to?"

"Of course not! You just get those bad thoughts right out of your head! Nobody's ever gonna make you do nothin' like that again! And I want you to know that you and Davey can stay here for just as long as you want. Ain't nothin' bad gonna happen. You get some sleep now, y'heah?"

"I hear." She smiled sweetly as Mattie turned off all the lights but left the door open a crack as she walked out. She glanced back to see Janie's small smile.

Janie's practiced smile faded as soon as Mattie turned away. She was alone, and it was hard to smile when you were all alone in a dark world waiting for a monster to come back. She knew it would return, and she was determined to stay awake all night if she had to.

Davey turned restlessly in his sleep, and she could hear his quiet breathing. He was just a baby, and he didn't really count. He couldn't protect her and he couldn't make her feel less alone. He was really nice and everything, but he couldn't understand, so there was no point in talking to him.

She didn't see what the big deal was about talking anyway. Seems like everybody knew how to talk, but not many people knew how to be quiet. Ever since Momma died, people kept talking and talking at her; asking questions, telling her how sorry they were, and saying that things would be okay. Momma was dead, and sorry didn't help. The tears trickled slowly down her cheeks.

This feeling inside her said that things would never be okay again. Her family was gone, and even if Mattie said that she and Davey could stay with them, Janie knew that sooner or later Daddy would want her again, and nobody ever said no to Daddy.

Her hands curled into fists and she rolled over on her side. Mattie had left the light on in the hall and the door slightly ajar. She stared at the small pool of light on the floor through her tears. Everything felt wrong. It was too quiet. The only sound was Davey breathing, all the way across the huge room in that cute little rocker bed. This bed she was in was too large and too empty. Sally should be curled up next to her, stealing the covers and breathing in her ear.

There was a loud bumping noise. She jumped, clutching the covers as the air conditioner clicked on. Now it was too noisy. If something came to the window, she wouldn't be able to hear it. A cool draft hit her neck and she turned over in a panic to face the window. It was closed, and the drapes were drawn just the way Mattie had fixed them.

She squirmed restlessly, pulling the covers up to her chin. Facing the window, she couldn't see the light from the hall and that made her nervous. It was so dark. She had never seen dark like this before. It was dark like it would never be light again.

Dark and quiet and lonely and afraid and so very sad. She couldn't stop thinking of her family, and sobs racked her small body. Everyone she loved was dead.

Her eyes closed tiredly, but she didn't notice until the air conditioner clicked off. She jerked her eyes open in panic. They had adjusted to the night and she could see the room clearly now.

Except for Davey, her whole family was gone except her father, and he was the only one she really wanted to see

271

dead. There was no one in this world who could help her if the monster came back, so she began to pray.

"Please, dear God, don't let the monster get me. I know I've been a bad girl. It's my fault they were all killed. Daddy told me I was a bad girl an' I tried, really tried so hard to be a good girl. Jesus, I'm so sorry I'm bad an' stupid an' lazy an' careless. I'm sorry, God. I'm so sorry. I didn't mean to be bad. If You would only bring them back, I'd be such a good girl. I'd never be bad again.

"If You'll just give my family back, I won't cry no more when Daddy does those things to me. No matter how much it hurts, I won't think no more bad thoughts about him. I'll do like You told us to in the Bible and obey my father, even when he tells me to do those nasty things. Even if he wants to tie me up, and You know what he does. I won't cry or beg or anything, God, if You'll just bring my family back to me. Please, God, I want my Momma. I want my Momma. Please dear Jesus, I want my Mommy."

She sniffled back the tears and ended the prayer as she had been taught. "In Jesus' name we pray. Amen. Oh, I forgot. An' please God don't let the monster get me. Amen."

It made her feel better, because everyone knew that God was stronger than monsters, but she still couldn't go to sleep. The monster might sneak in while God was busy answering the prayers of some good little girl who deserved it more. She couldn't stop thinking, either. Even though she knew her Daddy wasn't the killer, when she thought about the monster, he had her Daddy's face.

It wasn't fair! God killed them all but her and it just wasn't fair. If she was so bad, why didn't He kill her, too? She wanted her Momma. She wanted to tell Sally that she could have all the covers. She wanted to hug Matt and tell Jake that she'd never borrow his things again. She wanted to tell them all how much she loved them and if only God would give her another chance, she'd never be bad again.

272

But most of all, she wanted her Mommy. Why didn't God kill her, too?

"Janie . . ."

Her head came up from the pillow and whipped around, searching the room.

"Janie . . . ?"

"Momma?" Her voice choked on the word. "Where are you?"

"Janie . . ."

She rushed to the window and threw open the drapes. They were all there. Momma, Jake, Sally, and Matt. She pulled at the window, realized it was locked, slipped the old-fashioned catch, and threw open the window.

"Oh, Mommy! I love you. I love you all! I'm sorry I was so bad. I'll never be bad again!" She was babbling through her sobs of joy.

"We love you, too, darling. That's why we came back for you." Her mother smiled, a glorious, glowing, loving smile that warmed her daughter's heart.

"You came back. . . ." They were dead. She had forgotten for a moment, but they were all dead.

"Let us in, Janie. Let us in and we'll be together forever."

Dead. Vampires. They wanted her to be a vampire, too.

"Janie? Don't you love us? Don't you love me anymore?" Her mother looked at her so longingly that it broke her heart.

"I love you."

"Don't you want to be with me forever?"

Life alone or death together? There was no real choice.

"Yes, Momma, I love you. I don't want to be alone anymore. I want to be with you forever." She took a deep breath and said very calmly, "Please come in."

The children scampered gaily to the crib and the other rooms as Estelle gave her favorite child her gift of eternal death.

* * *

Hurricane Diana did exactly what the meteorologists had feared. She found a nice warm spot in the Gulf and she sat there, gaining strength. Her winds increased gradually from ninety miles an hour to 110, with gusts up to 130. Her barometric pressure began to drop, pulling the water up in what would become a tidal surge. What had been a sprawling storm became a cohesive, spinning mass. As it spun, the heavy, water-filled clouds were driven outward by the winds and the center began to clear.

The hurricane's eye formed.

Calm and serene, in the middle of the storm, the skies overhead were blue. The waters were mild and the waves were small. The winds were gentle and caressing, with only a hint of the gusts that could rip apart buildings and trees. Here, the storm did not exist.

Yet only five to ten miles away in every direction, the winds built a wall of force around the calm center. Wind, rain, lightning, thunder, and the tidal surges created an organized chaos of destruction.

Spinning drunkenly, gaining speed and strength, she began to throw off feeder storms. They ran northeast, toward the coast, in thin lines of clouds. The rain and wind of each hit the coast in a matter of hours, but only lasted for minutes as they fled across the land at speeds of twenty or thirty miles an hour. Some areas received as many as six a day.

Chapter Thirteen

He was tired. So very tired.

He felt as if he hadn't slept in a week. His eyes were bloodshot and red-rimmed with fatigue, and when he rubbed them they felt gritty and sore. He stretched his arms over his head and his shoulders popped loudly. He poured the cold beer down his throat and reminded himself to get another case in the morning. It was times like this that Jerry Wiltz missed Estelle. Now he had no one to blame. It left a curiously empty spot, that he mislabelled as grief. He pulled another tab and belched loudly before he drank.

He finished that beer, then opened another and took it upstairs with him. He added his dirty, mudstained clothes to the growing pile in the bathroom, and stepped into the hot shower. The spray beat out the soreness in his muscles while he thought back on the week.

He had learned a lot about vampires lately. He had made a special trip to a bookstore and bought some books. Amazed at the selection, he chose some with covers showing white-faced vampires with blood dripping from their long fangs. At home, he called a buddy, a horror movie fan, who had revealed that they couldn't come into a house without being asked, and that wood was better than bullets against them.

Yesterday, he had checked the graveyard shortly after sunrise. The graves of his wife and children were sunken and the cheap wooden coffins were gone. He could still see the marks of bare hands and long, sharp fingernails in the packed graveyard mud. His usually limited imagination presented horrifyingly vivid pictures of his wife and children digging their way out of the graves.

Sitting on the cold gray marker, he tried to think of where they might hide. He had wasted a day searching that area, before he realized that they arrived too soon after sunset for them to travel far. They needed protection from sunlight and prying eyes. They needed a place large enough to hide four coffins, unless they were smarter than he gave them credit for and had split up. Since they arrived and left together, he discounted that idea. He had seen no evidence that they could change into bats or wolves, like the movies on TV, so they must be hidden in the area of his house.

This area had no caves, no basements or cellars, no crypts to shield caskets from prying eyes and deadly sunlight. Where the hell would the bitch go to ground? Would she keep the brats with her, or were they smart enough to split up?

He had left the house at dawn this morning. He searched the obvious places first: the shack down by the stream that had once been a fishing camp, his still and the storage shed in the deep woods where he kept the supplies for his corn liquor, and finally, the old abandoned house where the Campbells had lived and died. When he was still a hundred yards from the house, he noticed the silence.

The track he walked on had once been a dirt road, but now it was almost obscured by scrub pine, dewberry and honeysuckle vines, dollar weeds, and even a twining of poison ivy that poked its perfectly matched leaves into a stray patch of sunlight. The hot air should have been filled with the rhythmic throb of insects, the angry screech of a bluejay, the liquid song of a mockingbird, and the occasional chatter of a gray squirrel. Now the scrub oak trees were nine feet tall in what had been a serviceable road five years ago, but the surrounding woods were silent.

His steps made no sound on the dusty ground, and the tall, overhanging trees dropped the temperature by ten degrees to a comfortable eighty-five. The sweet scent of honeysuckle came and went with the fitful breeze. Jerry's eyes wandered to the trees, but he didn't notice the cobalt blue sky framed by tall, sparkling green pine trees. His steps dragged as he approached the clearing. His thoughts began to waver.

Maybe he should just leave. Leave this unnaturally quiet road, leave his house, leave this haunted city to the vampires. Let Estelle and the kids have it. It wasn't his job to exterminate the vampires. Let Estelle win. If he could only find a hole deep enough to hide in.

He spotted a young sassafras tree and picked a leaf, crushed it, and inhaled the sharp aroma. Estelle had loved sassafras tea. When he was courting her, he had dug up the sweet roots and they had drunk the root beer flavored drink until he was sick of the taste and smell. She had served it after dinner one night, a few months after they were married. He had thrown the cup at her, missing her face by inches and scalding her with the hot liquid. That had been their first fight.

He smiled at the memory.

Now that spineless bitch, that whining, nagging whore who could never do anything right, was trying to kill him. He would fix her. He would fix her good. He set his pack down on the pine-straw covered ground, and rubbed his shoulder where the strap had cut a crease in his flesh. He turned toward the woods as if to hide his actions from the house, then knelt beside the pack and opened the flap. He pulled out half a dozen wooden stakes, a fourteen pound short handled hammer, a string hung with a cross and garlic pods, and a flashlight. He hung the string around his neck, wincing at the smell. He put the flashlight in his back pocket and picked up four of the stakes and the hammer. He took a long look around, and breathed deeply of the pine-scented air.

It had once been a neat, one bedroom, white frame house. Now the paint was almost gone, the wood was cracked and rotten, and the roof sagged. The silence had

277

grown more intense, as if the world were waiting to see what he would do.

The porch steps were rotten. He stepped near the side support and went up cautiously. The door leaned to one side and he pushed it gingerly, wincing at the screeching sound. Would noise wake a vampire during the day? The thought made him check his watch. Almost noon. As he pushed the door aside and walked in, his stomach growled loudly. He hadn't had a decent meal since Estelle turned. If he wiped them all out today, he would go home, take a nap, and go out for supper tonight. Some place fancy to celebrate. Maybe that new steak house in town.

The smell struck him suddenly and he put his hand to his mouth to keep from retching. Maybe now wasn't the right time to plan the dinner menu. He was glad he hadn't eaten earlier, that smell would have made him bring it back up. It was like a skunk had been dead a week before it cut loose. It hung in the air like an invisible blanket, covering everything with a hot, oily film of putrefaction. He hesitated, then advanced stealthily into the living room.

Undisturbed dust and mildew covered every surface. Forcing his reluctant feet to take him in, he stood in the middle of the main room and turned slowly. His tracks were plainly visible in the dust and dirt. No one had been here for years. Five years, to be exact.

He thought back to the Campbells. Mean, stingy, son of a bitch. The old couple had lived here for years before Jerry had moved his family in down the road. The old woman had been alright at first, bringing cookies and pies, and helping Estelle can preserves and freeze vegetables. Then she got nosey. He knew she was telling Estelle things about him, but she had been useful for awhile. He still grinned when he remembered coming home early one day and overhearing her tell Estelle that she should take the kids and leave him. He had stormed into the kitchen and pulled the chair right out from under her fat ass.

The old man had raised quite a fuss. He had called the cops and complained. But since Jerry hadn't really laid a hand on her, and she hadn't been hurt, the police just gave him a warning. Even back then he had known better than to hit another man's property. He had forbidden his wife to visit her. He had always suspected that Estelle snuck behind his back to see her, but he had never been able to prove it. No matter. A man didn't have to prove things like that with his own wife. Knowing was enough to convict and punish her. Anyway, the old woman had died a few years later, and her husband had followed her within a month. It had been a week before anyone had found him. Even when Jerry had snuck in a few weeks later to scavenge, the smell had been enough to bring tears to his eyes.

The smell had been a lot like this.

He looked again at his tracks in the dust. No one had been here for five years. No human, that is. But they were here. He could feel them in the silence, and smell them in the fetid air.

Three doors led from the main room. The kitchen would be straight ahead, he guessed. His eyes were watering so badly from the smell that he bumped into the couch on his way to the door. The furniture was still solid, although the faded blue fabric had rotted and fallen away in places. The stuffing was brown and water stained, and he glanced up to see a matching stain on the sagging ceiling.

He pushed the door open and walked into the bathroom. A brief glance showed that there was no place to hide, but he opened the door to the linen closet anyway. Nothing but spiders and bugs, scurrying away from the light. He left the door open and walked across the living room to the door on the right. This was bound to be the kitchen. It was, but there was still no place to hide. The appliances had been torn out and the pantry door was off its hinges. He gave the room a cursory look and turned to the final door.

His hand went to the cross at his neck and he gripped it fiercely, wishing he had brought a bigger one. His mouth was as dry as the dust in the house as he tried to swallow. His stomach clenched violently and he tightened his sphincter muscles to keep from voiding his bowels.

The smell was worse on this side of the room.

The cold doorknob felt slimy to his touch and he snatched his hand back, scrubbing it on his jeans. He shoved the hammer into his belt. The weight dragged at his pants and the handle bumped his groin and thigh, but he ignored it. He grabbed the cross and held it at chest height, then turned the knob and flung the door open. It slammed against the wall with a force that cracked the old plaster. The stale air clenched his nostrils and closed his throat.

The room was empty except for a flimsy dresser in the center and an old bed against the far wall. The quilted bedspread had held up better than the mattress. It draped across the bed to the floor, and its bright colors were faded and covered with dust. The dresser had been dragged across the floor, leaving tracks in the dust and a clean spot of wallpaper near the closet door that matched the once cheerful curtains. Now they hung in faded, tattered green strips. Bright sunlight slanted through the dirty windows and highlighted the dust motes dancing in the air.

So it was the closet, or under the bed.

He went to the closet first. He put two fingers in the indented notch and tried to fling it to one side. The door grated loudly and slipped partly off the track. He shoved his hand into the opening, and wrenched it off the rails. It slid to the floor, scraping the wall and rapping his foot sharply on the way down. He jerked out of the way, almost grateful for the dust that choked off the stench for a few precious moments. A jangling cacophony made his heart jump and he pushed the cross out in front of him.

Coat hangers! His nervous laugh came out as a harsh croak. Except for the musical hangers, the closet was empty. He turned slowly, fearfully to the bed.

There isn't room, he thought, then choked back a giggle. How many vampires can fit under a bed?

He got down on his hands and knees, creeping cautiously around the dresser and trying not to breathe. The smell was worse down here. He angled sideways to see through a rip in the quilt, but it was too dark. He crept around the side of

280

the bed to the end, but the footboard came all the way to the floor.

He took the hammer from his belt and put down the stakes, then changed his mind, set the hammer down and picked up a stake. It was against his good sense, but he knew from Al that wood was the better weapon. He held the stake in his right hand and the cross in his left. The wood trembled with his fear as he used it to lift a corner of the quilt gently. It slipped off the stake and dropped to the floor.

He took a deep breath, filling his lungs with the stench, then jabbed the stake at the cover, and flipped it onto the bed. He thrust the cross in before he peered in cautiously.

It was empty.

He let out his breath and watched the dust bunnies dance away. His legs suddenly felt weak, and he dropped to a sitting position on the floor. The muscles in his thigh jerked and trembled as he tried to figure it out.

They had to be here. He could smell them. He could almost feel them listening to him, laughing at him, maybe even watching him. He wanted to get out, to run, to get away, but he fought the panic. His eyes darted around the room uneasily, and he noticed again the scratches where the dresser had been dragged from the wall. The lines were blurred now, where he had scuffed across them.

He scooted across the dusty floor.

The dresser rocked slightly as he put his palm against it and pushed, but it didn't fall. He hesitated, then put his nose almost to the floor and sniffed. His stomach lurched and he thought he was going to vomit. He jerked his head back and gasped air through his mouth.

He was right. The stench was stronger around the dresser, and worst of all near the floor. He stood up quickly, eager to get it over with now. Palms flat against the old wood, he shoved hard. It fell over with a tremendous crash, rattling the windows and shaking the whole house.

There was a two inch crack in one of the floor boards. The smell coming from it was almost visible. It left a dark brown taste in the back of his throat.

He held his breath and put his eye to the crack. He should have noticed it when he climbed the front steps. The house had a crawlspace under it. It was about three feet deep, and very dark, but the crack let in enough light for him to make out the outline of a coffin. Taking the flashlight out of his pocket, he shone the light through the hole. There was another coffin behind the first.

Outside again, he breathed air that was fresh and clean. He circled the house until he found the entry point, almost hidden by an upended wheelbarrow propped against the lattice-work sides. The weeds had been crushed and broken in a clear trail to the hole. The little one must have had to drag his coffin in.

He got a bottle out of his pack and took a long swig, then sat on the pack and smoked a cigarette while he drank. The feeling of laughter in his mind had faded to a dull whisper. She knew he was here. She knew he was coming for her and she couldn't do anything about it.

He laughed, sure that she could hear it.

He tossed the cigarette butt into the weeds and watched it smoulder. Maybe he should just burn the house down. It sure would save a lot of trouble. He imagined the flames licking at their coffins while they were helpless in the light of the sun, and was rewarded by a soundless whimper. He enjoyed that fearful cowering.

No, burning was too easy for them. They had put him through too much. He wanted to see the stakes pierce their flesh. He wanted to see their eyes open in terror and hear their screams, just like in the movies. He took a long swig from the bottle.

He lit another cigarette and checked his watch. 1:30 P.M. Damn! How could he have spent over an hour searching four rooms? No matter, he still had five hours until dusk. By that time, they would be history and he would be home. He noticed his cigarette had burned down to his fingers, but he still felt tired and listless. It was so hot, here in the sun. Maybe he would just have one more cigarette before he dug them up out of their hole.

The fresh air and the bourbon were making him drowsy and reluctant to move. He had stayed up most of the night, watching them watching him, too afraid to sleep, and it was taking its toll on him. He leaned back comfortably and closed his eyes against the glare.

He was sure he hadn't slept, but the next time he looked at his watch, it was almost three. He jumped to his feet, horrified by the time lapse. He could almost hear the soothing murmur of their voices, telling him that there was no reason to be alarmed, there was plenty of time.

He jerked the wheelbarrow away from the wall and the light showed four coffins, lined up side by side. The voices in his mind turned to fearful squeaks.

He crawled under the house, pushing his way through weeds and debris. Spider webs, paper wasp and dirt dobber nests dotted the sides of the crisscrossed wood slats, but there were no signs of the insects. He crawled farther. This deep, the shadows were black against gray. The light on the coffins made them shine like polished mahogany, but he had paid for them. He knew they were made of the cheapest wood. The sides were clean and bright. They looked as if they had never been touched by dirt or dust, but he had seen them buried in the dirt.

He touched the first one. It was cool and slick and he wanted to snatch his hand back; but instead, he struck it lightly with his fist, announcing his presence. It boomed like a drum. Amazed at the weight, he wrestled the first box into the light. He didn't open it, but went back in immediately for the next.

The heat was incredible. Sweat soaked through his shirt and stung his eyes. He could feel it running down his thighs as he crawled backwards, dragging the heavy boxes. He gasped for breath in the still, heavy air. The stench made him sick to his stomach and his harsh panting ricocheted in the narrow space. The coffins dug deep grooves in the hard packed earth and he estimated that each one must weigh a couple of hundred pounds. Each trip out was a passage through hell.

283

The last was the worst. When he touched it, he knew the coffin was his wife's. He struggled with it for what seemed like hours. It got caught going around corners formed by the support pillars. Once he jerked too hard, lost his grip; tried to catch his balance and hit his head on a beam. He sat stunned for a moment and imagined his wife's laughter, then his very rage enabled him to manhandle the box out by a series of jerking pulls.

He checked his watch as soon as he entered the light, terrified that the sun would go down before he finished. It was only 5 P.M. Time was traveling at a normal rate again. He breathed a sigh of relief and decided to have another cigarette. He made sure that all the coffins were out of the shadow of the house and in direct sunlight before he lit up. Then he walked around the caskets, laughing and talking to them as he drank. Finally, he sat on Estelle's coffin, rapping his knuckles on the lid and drumming his heels against the side as he talked to her softly.

"You never could do nothin' right, Estelle. I always tol' you that. You couldn't keep the house clean, you couldn't control yer brats, you couldn't even cook a decent meal. You were a lousy fuck, too. You even make a lousy vampire, you know that? You fucked up again, ya stupid bitch. I know you were tryin' t'delay me, but you're too stupid t'do it right. A real vampire could've stopped me, but you were always too weak and stupid t'do anything right. A real woman could've kep' me happy, but you were lousy at everything. You can't even hide good. You shoulda split up the boxes and hidden the kids somewhere else. You fucked that up, too, not that it woulda made any diff'rence. I would've found 'em and killed 'em one by one. It would've taken longer, but it woulda been lots more fun." He giggled at the thought, then jumped lightly off the casket and flipped his cigarette butt away.

"Are you awake, dear?" he asked solicitously. "Can you hear me? Will you hear our dear children when they scream? You always cared more for those brats than you did fer me. Do you still? I wonder. I think I'll start with Jake

284

first. It's only fittin'. Where is he now?" He pretended to make a great effort to figure out which child was in which coffin. He tapped on each box carefully, calling to the children and asking if they were awake in there. He finally settled on one, and to his surprise, the lid lifted easily. Sunlight struck the pale skin and it began to smoke. He coughed hoarsely. "You smell like burning dogshit."

His firstborn son's eyes were open. For a moment, Jerry hesitated. There had been good times, it was just hard to remember them. He tried to picture the first time he had taken Jake fishing, but all he could remember was making fun of the sissy because he didn't want to bait the hook. Jake had run away crying. Now his face was blank of expression. The green eyes stared up at him, watching without seeing. He put his hand on his son's forehead, trying to remember the sound of his laughter. The skin was cold and clammy to the touch. He pressed his hand gently over the eyelids, holding them closed for a moment. When he took his hand away, slowly, deliberately, they opened again.

Cursing to himself, he picked up a stake from the bundle next to the pack and put the point to his son's chest. The sweat made his hands slippery.

For the first time, the eyes moved. They looked downward at the approaching stake, and then up at his father. Jerry could read the silent pleading in his eyes.

It was just like old times. It gave him a feeling of power.

He brought the hammer down in one powerful stroke. The stake drove in, piercing the flesh and sinking deep. He winced away as the shell of his son screamed, and his hands came up and clutched the shaft. A high shriek beat at his ears, and he realized that his wife was screaming, too. He brought the hammer down again.

This time it pierced the heart. Dark blood welled up around the stake, stained the white burial shirt, and spilled onto the bare earth below. The body writhed and his hands pulled ineffectually at the wood. Jerry hit the stake one more time, just to be sure. The movement ceased abruptly. He slammed the lid down and leaned on the coffin, shaking.

His hands were trembling violently and he choked back the urge to vomit.

It was harder to open the next casket. His daughter gazed at him with knowing eyes. He remembered the times he had gone to her bed and the way she had pleaded and cried and begged, but he hadn't given in then, and he wouldn't now.

He was used to the screams now, and the sight of blood had never bothered him. He thought about all the times he had hated her for trying to deny him what any daughter should be pleased to give her father. It was easier than killing a stranger would have been.

At least he'd never have to listen to her giggle again.

He found that it was like wiping out his past, and the third casket was even easier. Matt had always been such a whiny, snot-nosed kid. He concentrated on that image of him while he drove the stake to rest.

"Did'ja hear that one, Estelle?" he asked her quietly, sitting on her coffin again. "You gonna scream that way fer me? I always liked to heah you scream. You allays had such a purty voice, singin' in the church choir an' all. Mebbe I'll jist open the lid and let the sun burn you t'death. That'ud be awful slow, wouldn't it? Bet it'd hurt, too. Those blisters look just like the time I poured that boiling water on you. It'd take a long time, but I bet you'd just keep bubblin' till nothin' was left but sludge. The movies all show it as bein' s'quick, but it ain't like that with y'all. Mebbe it's 'cause y'all ain't been dead long enough. Mebbe y'all were too close t' bein' alive to burn quick."

He stepped away from the box, unconsciously wiping his palms on his pants to get rid of that cold, slimy feeling. He threw the lid back with a crash. His wife lay there. Her eyes were closed.

In life she had been a spiritless creature, pale, almost sexless. He had seen her since, but always at night. Now she was more gorgeous than he had ever imagined. She looked like the woman of his dreams. Her cheeks, flushed with color, had not yet started to blister from the sun, and her mousy brown hair had a golden honey hue. She had found a white robe someplace and it was drawn tight across her breasts. Her legs had always been her best feature; now they stretched out impossibly long and slender. Her lips were red and full. She must have found some way to clean herself because he didn't notice the odor that had pervaded the kids' coffins.

His hand touched her ankle and moved slowly up to her knee. Her skin felt smooth and taut. He squeezed her thigh tentatively and heard a sweet, low murmur in his mind. She was so beautiful. He could feel his body responding.

She opened her eyes slowly. As soon as the sun touched them, they started to smoke. The steam rising from her body smelled of burned flesh, but he hardly noticed. He moved his hand under her robe. Her flesh was cold, but young and firm to his hands. Her lips moved as if she were trying to speak, but no words came. She smiled and he bent down closer to listen, drawn to those exquisite red lips. His hand moved from her leg to her waist, then he touched the swell of her breast above the robe.

"Cold as a witch's tit," he muttered, but it no longer mattered. He was hot enough to warm her up. He wanted her so badly; what harm could she do to him now? It was hours till dark and anyway, this was his wife, Estelle. Stupid, mousy, incompetent Estelle. Estelle, his body slave and his punching bag, could never find the guts to hurt him. And if she could, she didn't have the nerve or the power or the brains. As he'd told her so many times, without him, she'd be helpless. She'd be out on the street begging for food because she wasn't good enough at anything to ever get paid for it.

Her lips moved again, begging for his pleasure, and he bent to kiss her. She tasted sour but he no longer cared. His eyes caressed her breasts, more full and lovely than they had ever been in life. Her new body fascinated him. If she had looked this lovely in life, he wouldn't have had to turn to the kids for satisfaction. It was all her fault. Her lips moved again and he brushed them lightly with his own before he turned his head to see her body better, and to hear what she

287

was trying to say. Blisters were forming on her lovely face and arms as he leaned over his wife.

"Love me. . . ." It was the merest whisper of sound, but it inflamed him. She smiled and her teeth had suddenly grown into fangs. He looked up just in time to see the shadow touch her eyes. In seconds, her eyes changed from brown to black. The darkness spread and he watched, fascinated, until her eyes were all black; iris, pupil, and cornea.

Shadows? His mind snapped into focus and he looked around wildly just as her teeth clicked shut, just inches from his neck. The shadows were slanting to the east as the sun sank low in the west. All his hatred and resentment of her came back in full force.

"You no-good bitch!" He screamed at her. He hit her face twice with his fist, but his savage blows didn't even break a blister. Her flesh felt like the coolest, softest silk over hard rubber. There was no point in hitting her. At least, not with his fist. He picked up the stake and hammer eagerly.

"Now you'll get it, bitch. If you hadn't tried that, I might of let you off." They both knew it was a lie. "I'll give it to you good. Like I shoulda before. Better late than never." He chuckled at his witticism, put the stake to her breast and held the hammer high, waiting for some reaction. He wasn't disappointed.

The smile on those rich, tempting lips turned into a snarl. Her eyes sparkled with hate and defiance. He could see her struggle to lift her arm, then she glanced frantically toward the sinking sun.

"You can't move till it's all gone. Right, bitch?" He laughed harshly as he held the pose, watching her. Her expression changed from hate to fear, from defiance to pleading. It was what he had waited for.

He brought the hammer down hard.

The first stroke pierced her heart and her blood spurted over his hand. He struck twice more, just to be sure. Her blood seemed fresher, sweeter than the children's. The copper odor filled his nostrils, washing away the foul odors that had gone before.

288

He left the four coffins where they lay. If anyone found them, that would be their tough luck. He smeared the shiny tops with a rag, just to be sure the police wouldn't find his fingerprints. Even if they did, what could they arrest him for? Mutilating corpses? But the corpses had bled as if they were still alive. The police had already proved that he couldn't have killed them. He had nothing to worry about; still, it didn't hurt to be careful.

He wearily headed for home. He spent a long time in the shower, then lay down on the bed for a nap. It was the first time he had felt comfortable in the bedroom since Estelle and the kids had died. For awhile, he was too keyed up to sleep. The killings had excited and stimulated him. He wondered if he should pick up a woman before dinner tonight, or wait until after. That was definitely a problem. He had had some leftover chicken with his beer when he got home and his stomach was not his main concern, but if he picked up a woman from a bar at the wrong time, she would expect dinner before pleasure. He didn't feel like paying for some bitch's meal just because he needed a little nookie.

The tourist bars would be the best place. He hadn't had to go out cruising since Sally had turned eight. She had been good, but Janie was always better. He had had her at the age of five. She was the best there was. Maybe he would just go over to the Larsons' before he left for dinner. He could bring her back here for the night. A father had a right to have his own daughter, didn't he? No court order could keep him away from her. Maybe he would keep her for awhile. She was old enough to clean house, and she could learn to cook.

He tossed restlessly on the rumpled sheets and made a mental note to get her to change them in the morning, before he drifted off to sleep.

He awoke with a start. He'd been dreaming of Estelle, beautiful and sexy and with fangs so long that they curved under her chin. The banging noise that filled his dream changed from efforts to get out of her coffin, to someone trying to batter down the front door. "I'm comin'," he yelled, as he stumbled out of bed and headed down the hall. Christ, it sounded like the whole house was being shaken apart.

"I'm comin', damnit!" he screamed again. The last knock reverberated through the house as he took the stairs two at a time, trying to knuckle the sleep from his eyes at the same time.

He stopped abruptly on the last step, and glanced at the clock in the living room. Who the hell would be coming here at 9:00 P.M. at night? He went to the front door cautiously. His wife and kids were dead, really dead this time. He had nothing more to fear. Or did he? Who had changed them into vampires? Wasn't there supposed to be some kind of vampire king who gave them orders and sicced them on people? Maybe he was out there waiting. Maybe he was pissed off because he had lost four recruits this afternoon.

Jerry detoured around the door and approached a window that overlooked the porch. "Who's there?" he yelled.

Janie opened her eyes and stared at the underside of the bed, only inches from her face. The smell of dust tickled her nose. It was like being a very young child again. It brought back memories of the many times that she had squirmed far back into places where no hurtful grown-up hands could reach. She flinched away from the memory and rolled out from under the bed. Even at the tender age of nine, she had learned that if you didn't remember, if you pushed the thoughts away every time they came, then you could go on living as if life were a good thing.

She stretched languorously. She felt marvelous, alert and energetic, not sad at all. The smell of dust was replaced by an assortment of familiar odors. She identified furniture polish, perfume, people and blood. She could even smell the pork chops and turnip greens she had had for supper the night before and there was a faint trace of soap from the bathroom down the hall. She tugged the blanket down from the window where her mother had fixed it the night before, and opened the window. She breathed in the night, absorbing the scents of animals and birds, car exhaust and mown grass, and the magically alluring odors of the forest next

290

door. She could hear the small creek meandering through the woods, the chirp of crickets and the buzz of mosquitoes. She wondered idly if the mosquitoes would still prefer her as they had all her life, now that she was dead.

Dead. Something her mother had said once now came back to her. "Everybody wants to go to heaven but nobody wants to die to get there." Well, now she was dead, but she wasn't going to heaven. Why was everybody scared of dying? It wasn't so bad. She felt wonderful. She didn't feel sad or hurt or scared the way she used to.

"Mama . . ." Davey's voice came from the closet and she smiled as she let him out.

"Momma should be here soon," Janie said uneasily. She should have been here by now. She had told them she'd be back as soon as the sun set because they had a lot to do before it rose again. They needed boxes to sleep in, and dirt to sleep on to give them strength, and a safe dark place to stay.

"Mommy?"

"No, not Momma. Janie. You can say 'Janie.' "

"Mommeeee," he wailed piteously.

Why did Davey sound like that? Was he hurting? Where was Momma? Why wasn't she here?

As soon as she asked the question, the answer came as a picture in her mind. Janie saw the scene as if she herself had experienced it, as if Estelle had projected it as her dying gift to her children, impressing it on their minds even while they slept. Estelle was lying flat on her back and looking up at Jerry's face mercilessly grinning as he brought the hammer down.

Estelle had felt the dull stake rip into her body, as Janie felt it now. She gasped for breath as the massive pain crushed her chest. It wasn't a sharp, clean pain like a knife, but a mangling agony that spread sideways as well as down. Her ribs splintered and she could feel and hear each individual crack. She looked at Jerry's face through a spray of blood, then the stake tore into her heart muscle, and she was gone.

Janie screamed. An agonized cry of grief for losing her

mother twice in one week.

David hurtled his small body at her, sobbing. He clung to her legs as she crumpled to the floor, crying.

It was a long time before she gathered him into her strong young arms and left the house. They passed Mattie in the hall, but her eyes were dull and lifeless. She didn't seem to see them, and when Janie spoke, she didn't reply.

Outside, there was no place to go but home. The woods were delightful. Davey must have thought so too because he squirmed and laughed until she put him down and let him walk. He was getting better at walking. He didn't trip or fall or even wobble as he padded down the path. Even though the clouds hid the moon, they could see clearly. The forest was a wonderful place, full of sights and scents that she had never noticed before. A couple of times she started sniffling when she remembered her mother, but she pushed it back into the dark corner where she kept all the rest of the pain. By the time they reached the edge of the trees, she didn't want to leave them, but there was no choice. The most important thing now was shelter, and soon, she knew, they would be hungry.

The door was locked and she knocked, timidly at first, then she pounded frantically. At last, her father's voice came through the door, and she could hear the fear in it.

Jerry detoured around the door and approached a window that overlooked the porch. "Who's there?" he yelled.

"Daddy?" The answer was a frightened wail that made his blood run cold. "Daddy, let me in."

"Who is it?" he pushed the curtain aside as the answer came back.

"Daddy, it's me, Janie. And Davey. Let us in. I don't wanna stay with the Larsons no more. I wanna come home."

Janie! He peered cautiously around the yard. A fat, bright moon peeked out from the clouds long enough to show that there was no one lurking in the bushes, waiting to jump out. Even a master vampire couldn't come in unless he was invited. Could he? He went to the door and opened it a crack. "You alone?"

292

"Jus' me an' Davey. Please open the door. It's scary out here. Can we come in?"

"Yeah, but jus' Janie and Davey can come in," he said loudly. "No one else is invited."

She stepped forward and he jerked her in by the arm and slammed the door. Davey was settled on her hip, just like he used to ride his momma's.

"It's about time you got yer ass home, girl. Wha'chu doin' out in yer nightgown?"

"I snuck out. They didn't want me to go, but I missed you somethin' fierce. So I came home. Please can I stay, Daddy?" Her brown eyes looked up at him hopefully.

" 'Course you can, sweetie. I been wantin' you here. We're gonna have a good time, jus' you an' me. You git upstairs now an' I'll be up in a minute." He turned to check the door and windows to make sure they were secure.

"Yes, Daddy." She scampered up the stairs while he checked the doors to make sure they were locked. He grabbed a beer from the fridge as he walked by, and drank to wash the sour taste of sleep out of his mouth.

Upstairs again, he heard giggles coming from his bedroom. This was going to be fun. She hadn't even tried to hide in her bedroom. She had gone straight to her mother's bed and taken over. Maybe that had been the problem all along. Maybe she had just been jealous of her mother and she wanted to be the lady of the house.

He opened the door and grinned at the scene that met his eyes.

She was lying on her back, the sheet pulled up to her chin. Davey was on her stomach, bouncing up and down and chuckling gleefully.

"Tha's the happiest I've ever seen that brat," Jerry said as he picked up the baby and headed for the crib. "But we don't need him right now."

"No. Please let him stay," she pleaded with him prettily. She reached for Davey and her father held him just out of reach. "Please, Daddy. He won't be in the way." She smiled at him, but he frowned back.

"You sure got mighty talky since yer Momma died. You think you can do her job?"

"I kin do better than Momma ever did. Jus' you come here an' find out."

He hesitated at the change in her.

"Put Davey down here," she patted the far side of the bed. "An' you sit here." She indicated the space between them. His good mood vanished. He slapped her brutally across the face, but it seemed to take an instant before the force of the blow flung her across the bed. He put the baby down in the crib.

"Don't you never tell me what t'do, you little slut! I'll fix you good fer that." He shucked off his pants and turned to her. He was already full and hard with excitement. She lifted the sheet as he climbed into bed and reached for her.

She came to him eagerly, lifting her face to meet his kiss. He held her roughly, almost disappointed that he didn't have to force her.

A small, excited cry came from the crib.

He heard a thump from the side of the room and twisted his head to look. Davey had climbed out of the crib and was waddling quickly across the floor toward the bed.

Janie struck at her father's neck. Her long incisors slashed at his carotid artery, caught and held. He screamed and tried to jerk away, but every movement was agony. He yanked at her head and screamed again as her teeth jiggled in his neck.

He didn't notice the small weight as his son climbed onto the bed. His arms flailed uselessly as he tried to sit up, to move, to push her away, but her strength was too great. She held him easily. His neck burned, and the sucking sound next to his ear was more than he could stand. He felt as if little pieces of him were being pulled out through those small holes. He screamed again, weaker this time. He barely felt the added pain as his son grabbed a small fistful of hair to help pull himself up to the head of the bed. He crouched on his father's chest.

Baby teeth that were anything but babyish sunk into the

294

other side of his neck. The weight on his chest made his screams sound gasping and hoarse. They fed with eager sucking noises, using their tongues to lick up every last drop.

With his last conscious thought, he raged against the unfairness of it.

Chapter Fourteen

Lady Diana danced ponderously in the Gulf. Her skirts swirled counterclockwise, 125 miles per hour at her innermost ring. Feeder bands of storms, accompanied by funnel clouds, broke off in waves from the northeastern rim. They hurried for hundreds of miles, running before the storm. The northeast winds pushed the water ahead of her, building waves and tides to flood level a hundred miles away. She absorbed moisture from the Gulf like a sponge.

Her barometric pressure was down to 28.08 inches. Clouds squatted at thirty thousand feet instead of rising to thunderstorm height of sixty thousand to seventy thousand feet. The Princess was a warm core system, and she followed the heat in the air and water.

Overnight, she had crept north and west a hundred miles. Now her leading edge was located only fifty miles south of New Orleans, Louisiana. Early in the morning, she met a weak cold front coming off the coast and her forward speed dropped from fifteen miles an hour to less than five. She sat and thought a while, gaining strength and power, then slowly, gracefully, turned east, sweeping the coast with her wide skirts. Waves of storms from the feeder bands battered the Gulf Coast and scattered north and east all the way into Tennessee and North Carolina.

By midmorning, the inner ring was forming a double wall, the mark of some very big, very bad storms. The small, calm spot near her center didn't change. Mild, tranquil, with clear blue skies and soft gray water, it moved like the beat of her heart.

"Casey, I think we owe you an apology," Paul put the phone down and faced his friends. His eyes were grave as he said, "The residue in the bed and in the sink at the Wiltzs' place was human skin. Enough to conclude that most of the skin of at least one person was sloughed off, like an old sunburn. A patch of scalp was pulled completely off, but the ME has refused to give an estimate of the suspect's age. The victims were drained of blood."

"No," his wife whispered. "I won't believe it. There are no such things as vampires. They don't exist. They can't exist. I can't believe it." Her face was sick and pasty; her lips trembled uncontrollably. Wild and frightened, her eyes sought Paul's desperately.

"You're probably right, love." Paul's calm tone brought her back to earth. He put his arm around her shoulder and pulled her close. "But some nut out there thinks he's a vampire, and that's as dangerous as the real thing. And it also means that Casey's right. We can't give up."

"Reese?" Casey said slowly. "If it helps any, I felt the same way when I saw him. I still don't want to believe it. I hope Paul's right. I hope it was some nut who just made me think that he changed into a bat."

Clarise looked at her doubtfully. "You're only saying that to make me feel better. And after the terrible things I said last night to you about hurting Janie."

"Did it work?" Casey grinned.

"Yeah," she said softly.

"Well," Eric said diffidently. "I guess our work is just starting. What do we do now?"

Everyone looked at Casey, but she couldn't think. Last night, even through her exhaustion, things had seemed so simple. Tonight they would decide how to find and kill the vampire. Then Tuesday, in the sunlight, they would do it.

But after a day of resting and thinking, she still didn't know how, and no one else was volunteering any brilliant ideas. They had to find him and kill him, but where did they start?

"Perhaps my library might give us some clues," Simon suggested gently. "If you and I go over there tonight, I could also teach you some techniques for protecting yourself. Your psychic self," he added, forestalling her objections.

"What should we do?" Eric asked, frowning.

"Why don't you make yourself useful? Go find some garlic, or crosses, or something," Simon drawled insolently as he slipped his arm around Casey's waist.

"Maybe I'll sharpen some stakes," Eric glared back. "I can think of the perfect place to put one."

Paul stepped between them and spoke to Eric. "We can look at some of the maps I brought. With Clarise's help, we ought to be able to narrow the area to search."

Simon was walking out the door with Casey when he said curiously, "I haven't seen you wear that before. Is it a new necklace?"

She blushed with embarrassment, but answered boldly, "No, it's very old. It was my grandmother's. I guess it's silly, wearing a cross. I mean, how scared of them can vampires be if they come and go in cemeteries filled with them? But it just seemed . . . appropriate."

"Lovely," he commented, but his eyes never left hers.

Twenty minutes later, they crossed a bridge over a small stream, turned left to pass through enormous brick gates, and drove down a long lane bordered by ancient oak, magnolia, and sycamore trees.

"You didn't tell me it was an estate." She turned to look back at the massive gates, framed by thick stone columns.

"You didn't ask."

The driveway became a circle and he parked directly in front of the house. It was a huge brick structure with tall thin windows and black wrought iron balconies. He got

298

out of the Jaguar and walked around to open her door.

She slid her legs out first, aware of his appreciative glance, and smiled her thanks. There was a heady feeling of power in having such a man look at her in such a way. She walked down the cool terrazzo path and up the steps to an enclosed entrance with an iron gate. He opened the door and stepped aside for her to enter, watching her expression.

It wasn't what she expected. From the outside, the house resembled an ancient fortress, but on the inside it was bright and airy. The entrance was the base of a Y that broke on each side to lead naturally one step down into a living room on the left and one step up to a library on the right. In front of a wall of books she could see a single worn, comfortable-looking armchair.

Simon led the way into the living room and said, "Go ahead and look around. I'll make some coffee. Or would you rather have a drink?"

"Coffee would be great."

The room was long and spacious and full of contrasts. It was dimly lit by indirect lighting set in recessed panels just under the high ceiling. The carpet was a light cream color that almost matched the walls, but the furniture was a heavy, dark wood. The arrangement gave an effect of dark islands in a pale yellow sea. The curtains matched the dark brown of the furniture, but added touches of green and gold.

She started toward the library, then noticed the paintings. Entranced, she wandered from painting to sculpture, from priceless jade carving to ancient Greek statue, until her eyes were filled with wonder and beauty.

She walked into the kitchen with a dazed look on her face. "Now I know what you are."

His back was to her as he leaned over slightly to pick up a black lacquered Chinese tray, but she could sense the shock and utter stillness. Stillness so complete that he appeared to have stopped breathing, stopped even his heart from beating. "Oh?" The word was hardly a breath, more like a sigh.

"You're a gentleman thief. You must have robbed a museum, a hundred museums to collect such treasures."

He turned, smiling, and revealed an exquisite china coffee pot with a matching cup and saucer. "Sugar?"

"Just some milk, if you have any." She opened the refrigerator and stared in shock. It was empty. Not just bare, but totally, completely empty. A breath of stale, warm air hit her and she realized that it wasn't even cold.

Simon walked by and, balancing the tray easily in one hand, he gave the refrigerator door a casual shove. The handle jumped out of Casey's hand and the door slammed closed. "Sorry, all I've got is that wretched powdered cream. Will that do?"

She made a face. "I'll take it black. Simon, don't you ever eat at home?"

"Occasionally." A grin played about his mouth.

"But your refrigerator . . ." She realized how ridiculous she sounded. Surely it was his business if he didn't keep any food in the house.

"Sometimes, I even have it delivered." He smiled again, and she decided that she must be overly sensitive about it because she was used to stocking too much food. There had been times when she could not fit it all in her refrigerator. It was her security. She followed him meekly into the living room and sat down on the couch. He hesitated a moment, then sat down next to her and took her hand.

She watched his fingers, amazed that a man could move so gracefully and subtly, yet have no trace of the effeminate about him. His fingers curled around hers and she felt them absorbing her warmth. Her eyes traveled up the light blue shirt to his muscular shoulders. She liked the strong column of his neck, and the definite curl of his ear. His deep-set eyes were shaded; they looked almost black. Impressions came to her with his touch. Strength, knowl-

300

edge, aloneness, an incredible hunger for experience, and wisdom.

Stop it, she warned herself firmly as she pushed the thoughts away. At least find out what he's really like before you start fantasizing about him . . . but I already know so much. He saved my life by attacking an armed man. He's brave, kind, intelligent, and handsome. He has a sense of humor; he's sensitive and charming. He loves fine art, and has the money to collect it. He's everything I ever dreamed of in a man, and so very much more. She thought for a moment that he would kiss her, and she wondered, Am I ready for this? But he moved back slowly, poured her coffee, and set it down in front of her.

"Casey, sometimes, when you look at people, I have the feeling that you're seeing more than just their bodies."

She was reaching for the cup. Her hand stopped in midair as she stared at him in shock. She choked the word out, "Colors."

"Hmmm." He nodded understandingly. "Auras. They are different around each person?" he confirmed. "And sometimes strong, sometimes not?"

"Sometimes I don't even notice them." It was a relief to talk about them. "It's so hard to explain. Sometimes, if I'm curious about someone, or if I ask myself a question about a person, all I can see is his aura. It's as if the answer is there, if I just knew how to read it."

"Have you learned?"

"Some. I can usually control whether or not I see them. I finally realized that I see them more easily on a white background. And the more curious I am about the person, the more I forget myself and wonder about him, the more I see and understand. But there are so many contradictions. Red, like yours, is energy, except when it's anger. Fear is a kind of yellowish-green, that can also mean illness, and the aura gets real small and close to the head. Pure green means that the person is healthy, but sometimes it means that the person needs healing." She shook

301

her head at the contradictions, but he nodded calmly for her to go on. "Yellow is happiness. It makes me think of sunshine and flowers. Clarise is usually yellow."

"Seems like you've learned a lot."

"You wouldn't think so if you could see what I do. Or can you?"

"No, I wish I could. My talents lie in other directions."

"What directions are those?"

"We will talk about that some other time. Not tonight." He rose and began to pace the room. "Someday you will understand. What other changes have you noticed since you woke up?"

She tried to laugh, but it came out sounding like a crow's caw. "Too many to talk about."

"I think you need to talk about them." He was so understanding.

"I . . . I . . ." she finally shook her head. "Shouldn't we get to work?"

"We have time." He sat down next to her and she decided that his eyes were just the shade of a hot summer sky. "Have you been having bad dreams?"

"I told you I saw that vampire kill those people. I don't think dreams can get much worse." That single spot of light in his blue, blue eyes was just like the sun, so bright that it hurt to look at it.

"What else have you seen?"

"I don't understand." She felt so calm and relaxed. Her breath came out in a deep sigh and it seemed like too much trouble to talk.

"Have any of your dreams concerned me?"

She snapped back to reality, color flooding her cheeks. "No! Why should they?" She realized too late how rude that sounded and tried to soften it as she poured another cup of coffee. "I mean, I've had nightmares about the shooting, but you were just a blur." She'd be damned if she'd confess her dream about him coming to her hospital room one night. She got up, picked up her cup and sau-

302

cer, and started toward the library. "I think I better get to work."

He stared after her, his eyes thoughtful.

Three hours later, she closed the last book and put it on the library table, then got up to stretch her legs. "I think that's all for me tonight, Simon," Casey said. "I wouldn't have believed that a private library could be so complete."

"As I said, legends and myths are my hobby," he replied, watching her move.

She wandered slowly around the library, pausing to run one finger over a Chinese jade temple dog, then stepped closer to take a look at a dark Rembrandt on the wall behind it. The styles complemented each other.

On the far wall was an extraordinary painting. She realized it was a portrait of Simon, but it was unlike any portrait she had ever seen. It was magnificent. The artist had captured some essential mystery surrounding Simon. High in the right corner, a sliver of moon turned the edge of a cloud to silver and sent a shaft of light to brighten his hair to gold against a dark night sky. His features were clearcut in the light, and his blue eyes glowed with a knowing gaze.

"It's remarkable."

"Thank you."

She jumped slightly as the voice came from directly behind her. She hadn't even realized that he had moved from the chair. "Who is the artist?"

"Glenna. A rather remarkable American talent I stumbled across in Switzerland."

"I wouldn't have suspected you of such vanity," she teased him gently.

"It's called 'tradition' in my family," he retorted.

"It runs in your family, then." She couldn't take her eyes off the painting, but her hand reached automatically for the glass of wine he offered to her. "What else runs in your family, Simon?"

He wondered what she would do if he told her, then

303

thought without surprise that he would find out soon enough. He stood less than a foot behind her, and the scent of her hair filled each breath with a spicy, sweet fragrance. He could feel her warmth, only inches from him. He propped one hand on the wall next to the portrait, and leaned forward. His other hand found its own way from her waist, up her back, to the silken strands of her black hair. He lifted the heavy waves from her neck and lightly kissed her earlobe.

She slipped out of his grasp and moved to another portrait on the far wall, but she couldn't resist looking back at the painting.

"Long life," he said, raising his glass to her.

"What?"

"Long life runs in the family." He smiled at her as he drank, but she was absorbed by the painting over the mantel.

"He's gorgeous." Her remark was almost involuntary.

"Yes." His voice was completely neutral.

A man on horseback posed at the top of a hill. There were mountains, craggy and bleak, in the background and a black stone castle brooding on a hillside. The effect was of a man surveying his domain.

He was magnificent. The long, strong lines of his body melded into those of the horse. The curve of muscle in his leg showed the power of his control over the animal. His back was straight, but his strong shoulders were slightly turned as he stared arrogantly out of the painting. His dark hair was long over the collar of a loose white shirt, open almost to the waist. His short, black cape was thrown back over one shoulder to reveal a dark red contrast. His black boots blended into the ebony hide of the horse.

He was almost too handsome, like a model in a very expensive whiskey ad. His thick brows formed a strong arch, fit for the compelling dark blue eyes. His mouth seemed about to speak, and surely if it opened, it would be to

304

give an order. His jaw formed a firm line and his cheeks were flat planes.

"He looks so familiar." Casey shivered with a sudden chill.

"There is a family resemblance," Simon admitted reluctantly.

She looked at his blond hair and Nordic good looks. "Was he your grandfather?"

"My brother."

"But . . ."

"My half brother, to be accurate."

"But . . ."

"You mean the clothes and the apparent period? One of Franz's little jokes." Simon turned away from the portrait. "Why don't we complete our work in the living room?"

"Does he really look like that?" Casey studied the painting incredulously.

"The portrait did not do him justice," Simon said shortly. When he turned back to her, she was still staring at the picture. His irritation grew.

"Where is he now?" She didn't notice his pique.

"He died shortly after that painting was finished."

"No!" She rejected his statement instinctively. "How?"

"We were in Berlin. I was out late. The house we were living in was bombed."

"Oh, no! Terrorists?" Her eyes reflected her horror.

"Yes, terrorists." The agreement came without hesitation. "There was a . . . psychic link between us. We were attuned to each other. I had always believed that if he died, when he died, I would feel it, it would shake my very soul, but there was nothing. No warning, no pain, just a void where he used to be. I searched the city for weeks. I couldn't believe he was really gone, but he was."

"How horrible. I'm so sorry. You must have loved him very much." She felt for his pain, but she could sense layers of meaning underlying everything he said. The conventional words were all she could think of to say.

"He was my big brother. I adored him when we were much, much younger. When he grew up, he changed." He threw the remark away casually as he reached to place his glass on the mantel. She stepped back unexpectedly to have a last look at the brother he had once adored. Her head was almost against Simon's chest as she looked up. Once again he inhaled the fragrance of her hair. His hand rose to lightly touch her arm and a wave of hunger hit him. His hand clenched into a fist above her shoulder.

"He looks so familiar." Again, the chill ran through her and she turned, suddenly aware of him. "But there's really no family resemblance, is there?"

"I hope not." His fingers found the nape of her neck and he pulled her to him. His lips sought hers fiercely, even as he fought to be gentle, but she more than matched the fire in his kiss.

His arms wrapped around her until her body was crushed to his. He kissed his way to her ear and he could hear the blood pounding in her veins. In his arms, she seemed smaller, more vulnerable than when she stood alone.

His eyes burned blackly and he felt the familiar ache in his cheekbones as his fangs grew longer and sharper. His teeth were at her throat when he felt her shiver, and realized that her arms, which had been wrapped so tightly around him, were now pushing him away. "No, Simon. Please, don't."

His teeth clicked together, less than an inch from her fair skin. His hand pressed her head to his chest and his arm covered her face as he fought for control. In a moment, the hunger and the changes it wrought in him were only memories, but he was weak with reaction. He turned from her abruptly and said, "We still have a lot of work to do."

"But, Simon . . ."

He walked quickly through the entrance hall and to the living room, unwilling to face her while he was still fighting the urge to take her by force. He had not waited these months to be turned down and pushed aside, but neither had he waited this long to force himself on her like a common rapist.

She followed minutes later, slowly, looking hesitant and unsure. "Simon . . . I'd like to explain."

"There is no need. I assumed you felt as I did. I was mistaken," he said bitterly. He wanted more, he realized with a shock, than her blood and her life. He wanted her love. He wanted to feel her desire for him, and only him. He wanted her respect, even after he told her what he was. Was he asking the impossible?

"Maybe," she said enigmatically. She walked nervously back and forth across the room, glancing at him from the side of her eyes. Finally, she turned to face him with a sigh. "The truth is, I don't know. I don't know how I feel about you, or even about me. I woke up and I'm different. I feel different, I look different, I'm a different person. It's like one of those stupid movies. You know, where the guy gets hit over the head and has amnesia? And at the end of the movie he gets hit again and gets his memory back? I keep expecting someone to hit me again and I'll go back to being the old me again. I keep waiting for it." She tried to laugh, but tears made her eyes sparkle. "I don't know who I am anymore. I don't even know what I am."

He strode to her, moving across the room so quickly that she just looked up and he was there, holding her. His embrace this time was tender and comforting, and she cried on his shoulder until the sobs that shook her subsided. Then he gently put one finger under her chin and kissed her again, sure that he was completely in control of his emotions now. Her lips opened against his, and his tongue gently tasted her lower lip. Her body was warm where it pressed against his, and he could feel the beat of her heart. The skin of her throat felt velvety soft against his lips.

He gripped her shoulders and held her away from him. "Now, we work on your mind," he said firmly, taking a deep breath and steering her toward the couch.

She dried her tears unobtrusively, sipped the wine he brought her, and resisted the urge to apologize. She paid strict attention as he began to lecture.

"Thoughts are things," he began. "Very powerful things. They can affect changes not only in the thinker, but in the . . . receptor. Like a hypnotist who plants a suggestion in a vulnerable mind. Most people are very vulnerable, and they don't even know it." A small smile touched his lips, and was gone. "You have natural reserves and protection that you were unaware of until the accident brought them out."

"Protection? I'm the most vulnerable of all. The vampire even invades my dreams." She protested.

"No, I don't think so," he said slowly. "It's true you're receiving impressions from him, but I don't think he's deliberately sending them to you. So far, he seems totally unaware of your involvement. You see, receiving is such a passive psychic activity, that there may be nothing to alert him. A receiver is simply open, waiting. This vampire is broadcasting like a radio station, not focused on any one receiver, but anyone who has the capability can receive. Since the shooting, you have that capability."

"Great. So what do I do now?"

"You relax. Let me do the work for awhile. We'll see how good a hypnotic subject you are and whether we can learn more from your subconscious."

"Like?"

"Who he is, where he comes from, why he's here, where he's hiding, where he'll strike next."

She couldn't help smiling. "You really think my subconscious knows all of that?"

"We won't know until we ask. If you're receiving information psychically from him, you may know much more than you think." He leaned forward in his chair, his eyes

308

gazing intently into hers. "Cassandra, do you trust me?"

"I . . ." She closed her eyes against the power of his gaze, and looked inside herself for the answer. There was a thrill of excitement, of fear? Yes, but not of Simon. She knew on some level deeper than instinct that Simon would not hurt her. "Yes," she finally answered.

His eyes shone with pride as he took a deep breath and leaned back. "Then I want to try an experiment, okay?"

She nodded, slipped her shoes off and swung her feet up on the couch, then tucked her skirt modestly around her legs. She stretched out, and by the time she was laying her head down, Simon was slipping a pillow under it. He sat back down and stared at her, his eyes glowing.

"You're remarkable. You don't really need me to tell you what to do, but I want you to let me guide you now. Let me do the work. Your mind is going to become very open and vulnerable now. A total receptor. To do this, you have to relax your body completely. You feel totally safe and secure. Put your body aside. Put your ego aside." His voice was calm and soothing. She knew exactly what he was doing as he led her through the relaxation of each part of her body. Her mind became detached until she felt like she was floating on a cloud, high above all the tension, worry, and planning of daily life. There was only now, this moment. She relaxed even more, listening to Simon's questions and her own answers, and knowing securely that she would remember every word.

"Casey, I want you to think back to the impressions, the feelings and vibrations that you feel when you dream about the vampire. Remember one of those dreams. Do you remember?"

"Yes. Her face wrinkled in a frown as she saw the ancient, shriveled vampire lock his boney hand around the young airman's neck and lunge at him.

"It's alright, Casey. It's in the past, and it can't hurt you. You can stand back and watch it as if you were seeing it on a TV screen. Do you want to do that?"

309

"Yes," she said with relief. Before he even finished telling her how, she had transferred the images to a safe little box in front of her.

"Now, do you see the vampire?"

She didn't want to look. It was too horrible. "Yes," she finally whispered.

"Who is he, Casey? What does he look like?" Simon leaned forward eagerly.

"Can't . . . look."

"Yes, you can. He can't hurt you now. Tell me. What color is his hair? His eyes? Who is he?" He forced her on.

"Old. Like a mummy. Horrible." His skin was leathery and peeling and his fangs dripped blood. "White hair. Black eyes, and red flames. Teeth. Oh, God, his teeth." Her head twisted as she tried to resist Simon's mental control.

"Open your mind to the impressions he sends. What do you feel, Casey?"

"Evil! Sick anger, hatred, madness, insanity." The words tumbled from her until she found the one that described it best. "Power. He is the power of evil."

"You can identify this feeling of him whenever and wherever you sense it. You now know exactly what it feels like and you will instantly recognize it. When was the first time you ever felt his power, Cassandra?"

"The day I was shot," she replied instantly. Her eyes were closed, so she couldn't see his surprise. The words poured from her in a flood. "I was in the shop, sitting at my desk. I was wondering how I could pay all the bills. He tried to get inside my mind, but he couldn't." There was an expression of smug self-satisfaction on her face, that changed suddenly to pain. "Hurts!"

"What hurts?"

"He hurt me. But he still couldn't get in, so he went away."

"When . . ."

"Then he came back with Billy Bazzel. Inside him . . .

310

wearing him like a coat or a suit of clothes."

Simon was careful not to let his feelings show in his voice. He knew all too well what she was talking about. "And then? When was the next time you felt his presence?"

"A long time . . . he was gone . . . too far away, too weak. When he came back he woke me up. I didn't want to watch him, but I had to."

"Can you see him now, Casey?"

"No," she whispered. "Don't want to."

"Try, Casey. Where is he? What does he look like now? What is his name? Answer me!" Simon leaned forward, pushing her mentally until she cried out.

"No. Won't go there. Cold. Scared."

"It's okay." He backed off quickly, shocked that he had tried to force her, and afraid that he might have overwhelmed her and broken her fragile, human mind. "You don't have to. Next time, Casey. Next time you will be able to see without pain or fear." He brought her back to consciousness gently and slowly. She was amazed at how good she felt, rested and relaxed. She glanced at her watch casually and was shocked to see that she had been under his spell for over two hours.

"Wow," she said quietly.

"You alright?"

"I feel great. Even after resting most of the day, I didn't realize how nervous and upset I was. Now I feel so relaxed and calm. I'm sorry I couldn't see him tonight. Maybe I could have told you where he was and we could have ended this tomorrow, in the light."

"No, no. I should not have tried to push you —" he stopped abruptly. "You defied me. Even under hypnosis, you defied me. I have not seen such a thing since I told my brother to go to hell when he tried to force me to, to . . . Well, there is no need to go into that."

She looked at him curiously, but she was too tired, too relaxed to question him. "I guess that was useless."

311

"We accomplished a great deal. And I learned even more."

She looked at him, wondering whether he was just trying to comfort her. "Like what?"

"We learned that you are an excellent hypnotic subject, but only when you want to be. We learned that you were psychic before the accident, and had enough power to keep him from taking over your mind the way he stole Bazzel's. And I believe that you will be able to locate the vampire when the time is right. Tomorrow night we will try again. I will give you some exercises to practice until then."

"Great." She stood up. Her body felt stiff, but her mind was relaxed and alert, even though it was almost 2:00 A.M. "We better make it quick, though. I need some sleep."

"Before you go to sleep tonight," he explained to her on the drive home. "I want you to relax your body the way I taught you tonight. When you are completely relaxed, imagine a brilliantly pure white light filling up your whole body, from your feet to the top of your head. Then extend it outward from your body in every direction to form a shield around you. This will be your protection from the evil vampire. You said that he drifted in on the tide. He could have been starving since the incident in your shop. He's not quite . . . rational. He may even be insane."

"You mean as opposed to a sane vampire?" her voice rose with sarcasm. "Isn't that a contradiction in terms? Or maybe a sane vampire wouldn't have enjoyed it so much. Maybe a sane vampire wouldn't have terrified them before he killed them. Maybe he wouldn't have left Janie and the baby in that room to hear their mother scream her life away." She was shaking now, but she couldn't tell whether it was fear, rage, or reaction. His arm slipped around her and pulled her comfortingly close. She brought herself to a deliberate stop and took a deep ragged breath, then another. The tears were close to the surface again, and she fought for control. She realized that she was more than a

312

little annoyed at the lack of control she had over her own feelings. "Give me an example of what you mean by a sane vampire." She choked the words out.

She stared at him, unexpectedly bereft when he withdrew his arm from her shoulders. He stared blindly out the window and the night was suddenly chill.

"Perhaps you're right. Maybe there is no such thing as a sane vampire." She heard the pain in his voice and reached out to lightly touch his wrist on the steering wheel. His voice gained strength. "But I doubt it. If every vampire acted like this one, if they attracted the publicity that these murders are getting, the whole world would know about . . . them. And in a week they'd be exterminated. Their only protection is that the rest of the world doesn't believe they exist. A vampire would have to be mad to kill as this one has done."

Casey shuddered. Simon sounded as if he were quietly musing to himself, but all she could think of was that he was right. This could not be the only vampire in the world and that meant her world, the real world, was perched precariously on a dark underworld of vampires and . . . what? If there were real vampires, then what about demons and ghosts and witches and—

Simon interrupted her train of thought, and she was grateful. But only for a moment. "We have to deal with an insane, ravenous vampire who killed six people in one night. But does that mean that we have to assume that all vampires are the same?"

She didn't answer for a moment. Finally she lifted her head and gave him a long, steady look. "A difference which makes no difference is no difference. A vampire is a bloodsucking monster who kills people to live. How can any monster like that ever be considered good? I've met an evil vampire. I'd have to meet a good one before I'd believe in him."

"Touché, my dear." He smiled at her. "Who knows? Perhaps you will." He almost missed the turn into her driveway, but she hardly noticed as the Jaguar slid, then caught.

"All the lights are on," she remarked as they topped the hill. "Paul's car isn't here, either. He must have been called in to work. I hope Clarise asked Eric to come over and stay with her while Paul was gone." Casey peered through the windshield, trying to see through the gloom. The rain had stopped and the wind had picked up speed. Clouds scudded across the sky and left an impression of a moving roof, just above the trees. The house lights blazed in protest of the darkness.

Casey caught a movement in the shadows on the far side of the veranda. She made out a familiar form in the old porch swing.

"Beverly!" She wanted to scream the word joyfully, but all that came out was a whisper. She was out of the car almost before Simon brought it to a full stop. He followed at a more dignified pace, as she ran toward the house.

"Beverly?" Casey watched, puzzled, as her friend leisurely rose to her feet and undulated across the veranda.

"Hello, Casey. I came to see Clarise . . . and you. But she won't let me in."

"Casey! Get back!" Simon said urgently.

She ignored him as she paused on the top step and rested her hand on the wooden railing. "When did you get back in town? I've been worried. I tried to call, but no one answered. I was afraid something had happened to you."

"What could happen to me? I'm fine. Just a little thirsty. You got any more of that orange juice like last time? Could we go in and check?" Beverly smiled at her, and Casey repressed a shudder of revulsion. Her mind whispered a warning, but logic and familiarity overrode it. Casey smiled back tentatively as Simon reached the steps.

"Bev? I want you to meet—"

"Inside. We can talk inside, if you'll let me in now. It's damp out here and I've been waiting for so long."

314

Casey hesitated, moved by an impulse she couldn't explain. Suddenly resolute, she stripped off her necklace and held her clenched hand out to her friend. "Sure, just let me get my key. Hold this for me, will you?"

Bev reached eagerly for her wrist, but Casey's hand opened and the necklace dropped into Bev's waiting palm. She was unprepared for the shriek of pain and outrage that followed. Bev hurled the cross away as Simon took the steps in a bound. He shoved Casey out of range, just as Bev lunged for her. His right arm struck the vampire high in the chest and the shock jolted his arm. Bev bounced back against the railing and flipped over. She landed in a crouch, facing him.

"Go!" The mental command rang through Casey's head until she covered her ears to try to block the sound, only to succeed in capturing it between her ears. She twisted around to see Bev, and realized that that terrible order had been directed at her friend. Bev was already halfway to the woods. Her hands covered her ears, and her body jerked with every bound.

Casey gingerly removed her hands from her ears and watched, feeling ill, as her friend disappeared into the forest. Simon moved to her side and held her tightly. "Are you alright? Casey?"

He swept her into his arms and carried her to the door as Clarise opened it and helped them inside. Casey stared at Simon numbly. Her arms were securely around his neck as she murmured, "You're right, Simon. I had to meet a good vampire to believe in her."

"What? Did she hurt you? Are you okay?" Clarise asked worriedly.

"I think I'm fine. Are you? Where's Paul?"

"He was called back to work. I tried to call him, but Beverly broke the wire."

"How did you know not to let her in?" Simon asked curiously.

"I was looking out the window for y'all. I just happened

315

to look, and Bev came strolling out of the woods. I couldn't, just couldn't believe it. She was walking and you know how she hates . . . hated . . . I mean she just never walked anywhere. Casey, what's going on? She acted so weird. I watched her walk to the side of the house, so I ran to the side window and peeked out and she grabbed the wires and tore them. She just jerked them apart. It sounded like giant threads popping. I couldn't believe it.

"Then she went to the front door, and knocked, and I couldn't think what to do so I asked her what she wanted. She just kept changing her story, then she'd ask, 'Aren't you going to ask me in? Aren't you going to ask me in?' And I almost did except that she was so weird and not like Bev at all, so I just told her she'd have to wait until you got home. So I tried to call Paul, but the phone didn't work. Then I knew which wires she had pulled and I got really scared. Is she really dead, Case? Is Beverly really a vampire?"

The tears Casey had been fighting all day finally came to the surface, and Casey was afraid she'd never stop crying.

Chapter Fifteen

Tuesday morning dawned bright and clear, with the promise of heat to come. Eric was up early and in the pool before seven. He started out gently, giving his muscles time to warm up. Then he lengthened and quickened his stroke until he was slicing furiously through the water. When his arms and legs began to feel leaden, he slowed gradually and swam for another ten minutes before he showered and dressed. He threw on an old shirt and a pair of faded jeans, then ate breakfast while he waited for Paul. It would have been easy to call Paul at Casey's house, or to walk over and ask him to hurry, but Eric resisted the temptation. He didn't want to take the chance of seeing or talking to Casey this morning.

Casey had gotten home after 2:00 A.M. this morning. He hadn't meant to stay up and wait, but sleep had been a long time coming. When he had finally seen the car lights top the hill, he had turned the stereo up loud to drown out his thoughts. What had they been doing until two in the morning? Casey was just too vulnerable right now. She didn't need the pressure of someone like Simon to add to what she was already going through.

At Ned and Kate's request, he had attended the exit interview with Casey's doctor, who had explained carefully about all the problems she could expect: headaches, sensitivity to light, nausea, and weight loss. Sickness of her body, but what about her mind? It was her mind that was disturbed. She needed rest and quiet to stop the crying jags and the sick fantasies that weakness had created. The doctor hadn't realized what a bizarre way it could twist her mind. Eric had decided last night that if she didn't stop these delusions soon, or if she just dropped vampires in favor of little green men from Alpha Centauri, he would go to the doctor and get her some badly needed help. Until then, he would stay with her as much as possible and if Simon didn't like it, he could damn well lump it.

Someone had to be responsible for Casey.

"I'll tell her at lunch. I don't want her getting too involved with this psychic stuff," he concluded to Paul in the car. "I avoided her this morning because I didn't want to start a fight. She gets so defensive. I know she's going to cry when I tell her I don't want this Simon character hanging around her any more."

"She's more likely to laugh," Paul muttered. "What exactly are you going to tell her?"

"Well, of course, the best way would be for her to come out of it on her own. She might be a little embarrassed, but that should be the least of our problems. We've got to get her away from Simon. He just encourages this vampire nonsense."

"What if she isn't crazy?" Paul asked in a carefully neutral tone.

"I didn't say she was crazy," Eric snapped back. "She's not. She's just . . ."

"Mentally incompetent? Psychotic?" Paul supplied helpfully.

"Tired! I was going to say tired and weak!" Eric yelled.

"Bullshit! You think she needs a keeper, and you want the job. Well, I think you better ask her about that." Paul came to an abrupt halt, then brought up the subject that had been preying on his mind. "Beverly came over last night. I want to stop by her apartment on the way to the warehouse area."

"What's wrong?"

"She came over, but she didn't get in. She didn't drive and the phone lines were pulled apart."

"I don't get it. You mean Bev cut Casey's phone lines?

318

That's absurd." Eric grinned at Paul in disbelief.

"Well, not cut exactly. Broken. Clarise watched her pull them apart with her bare hands." Paul watched the remark sail over Eric's head. "When Simon and Casey got home, they said Bev was there waiting for them, and acting strange. Casey got suspicious, and handed her a cross to hold—"

"You see what I mean? Casey has flipped out," Eric interrupted. "She comes home after two and she thinks that all her friends are vampires. How much more are we supposed to take before we get her to a doctor?"

"You're not listening," Paul said loudly. "Bev came out of the woods. Clarise saw her *break* the phone lines. She pulled them apart. Casey gave her a cross to hold and they said she screamed like a scalded cat. Bev attacked Casey and tried to kill her. If Simon hadn't been there, they couldn't have stopped her."

"Are you trying to tell me that Bev is a vampire? You believe that shit?" His voice rose incredulously.

"It isn't just Casey now. If you won't believe her, maybe you'll believe Clarise and Simon. They both saw her. And I believe them. Maybe you'd like to have us all committed."

Eric remained silent until they turned into the apartment parking lot. Entry to the cottage was easy. Casey had given them her key, but the place was a disappointment. It looked as if Bev had just walked out for a minute. Dirty dishes were still in the sink and the residue on them had started to turn odd colors. There were a few small spots of dried blood on the sheets and pillow, but hardly more than a cut or scratch would leave. Eric looked around with a caution that Paul found admirable, if surprising.

They called Casey's house to see if the phone was repaired, but there was no answer. Back in the car, Eric resumed his thoughtful silence until they were almost at the warehouse district.

"Do you think we'll find anything?" he finally asked Paul.

"I thought you didn't believe there was anything to find." Paul's tone was carefully neutral.

"I was wrong."

Paul looked at him in shock. He had expected another argument, or at best a "wait and see" attitude. Eric caught his look and shrugged.

"I was wrong," he repeated. "The idea of real vampires turns my stomach. It's like diving into my own swimming pool and coming up with leeches. They have no right to even exist, much less to be *here*. But I've never known you to jump to conclusions or to believe fairy tales. I guess I'd rather believe that you're all crazy, but I can't. Do you think we can search this area in four hours?"

"We ought to be able to cover most of it. I think we can leave out the places that are used the most. The last thing a couple of vampires would want is people tramping in and out all day. After we finish here, I want to check the daily reports again. As of yesterday, there haven't been any more unexplained deaths reported. They have to be feeding on something."

"Or someone," Eric corrected quietly.

Two hours later, rain splattered the windshield as Casey turned onto the highway. Ordinarily, when she had something on her mind she went for a swim, but the Gulf was too rough and she didn't feel like risking Eric's appearance at his swimming pool.

She concentrated on road conditions and didn't worry about direction. Every station on the radio was announcing that Hurricane Diana was on her way. If she didn't stall or change direction again, she would hit Mobile, Alabama sometime tonight. Casey let out a sigh of relief. Mobile was sixty miles away. This area could expect high winds, heavy rains and flooding, but the worst of the storm would miss them.

Poor Mobile, she thought sympathetically. Hurricane Frederick, a class four storm with 140 miles an hour winds, had hit that lovely old Southern city in 1979. Now Princess Di's winds were up to 110 mph, and she was heading straight for it. Dauphin Island, which protected much of Mobile Bay, was being evacuated. Anyone who had survived Freddy would be more than happy to abandon every beloved possession, to flee and live to start over again. Mobile itself would not be evacuated, but the shelters were already starting to fill. The announcer started comparing Di to Hurricane Camille in her strength and erratic path.

Casey had been just a child when Camille hit Biloxi, Mississippi, but she had seen pictures that her parents took when they went in with a volunteer clean-up squad. The one she remembered most was of a little red Volkswagen, cradled in the arms of an old oak tree. It was parked fifty feet off the ground. Her parents told stories of an empty oil tanker that had been lifted over a line of pine trees, each over a hundred feet tall, and set down in a vacant lot. The trees were not even bent. A mile and more inland, the high water marks on what trees and houses were left, was more than six feet high.

The initial body count had been over five thousand. It was wrong. The water had scooped bodies out of cemeteries and spread them along the coast. The roads along the beach had been washed out in places to a depth of fifty feet. The roads inland weren't in much better shape. Broken trees and downed electrical lines kept people off the roads. The water was contaminated and there was no electricity in most areas for weeks. The only ones who were not affected were the human vultures who would sweep through neighborhoods stealing anything they found, even down to the lumber and metal the houses had been built of. They were shot on sight.

If Diana kept gaining strength, picking up water and spinning off tornadoes, changing directions and speeds, she could become another Camille.

Casey turned north onto a small highway, heading in the general direction of Simon's house.

Simon. What was she going to do about *Simon?*

A squall hit and suddenly the car was deluged with water. She flipped the wipers on high, but she still couldn't see more than ten feet past the hood ornament. She peered forward, trying to find the middle line, then looked up just in time to swerve out of the path of an oncoming car. The blare of a horn followed her as she jerked the car off the road onto an overgrown side track. She drove automatically, slowing the car as she passed through a narrow strip of woods and over a concrete bridge that spanned a deep drainage ditch. The water was only a few inches deep now, a fast running trickle that threatened greater things. The concrete broadened into an asphalt parking lot that was overgrown with weeds and pitted with potholes. Behind the overgrown lot was a squat, square building.

She brought the car to a halt, cut the engine, and leaned her face into the steering wheel. Her legs felt weak. That had been too close.

She started to turn the car, but her eyes were caught by the deserted building ahead. A broad loading dock with a faded sign faced the parking lot, but the corners had been broken off and there was a huge crack running through the front. The concrete face had no windows, and the broad sliding doors that covered half the width of the structure had been boarded over.

"Where the hell am I?" she wondered aloud. She twisted to look behind her, but the highway was hidden by the trees. It was so quiet. There were no traffic sounds, no bird or animal noises, not even the chirp of a cricket. It should have been peaceful. It wasn't. The chill started between her shoulders, traveled up her neck and made her scalp tighten.

She licked her lips, nervously looking back and to both sides as she started the car. She had to drive forward to make a circle. The closer she came to the building, the more she noticed the silence. The tires spurted gravel as she forced the car into a sharp turn, and drove back over the bridge. The back of her neck crawled and she couldn't control a shudder as she pulled back onto the highway. Within a mile, there was a sign, and she realized that she was only ten minutes from Simon's house.

It was a spur of the moment decision.

She banged on the door again. Perhaps he was in the

322

shower and hadn't heard the first three times she knocked. His car was parked out front and she knew, *just knew,* that he was there.

Perhaps he didn't want to see her. After all, she hadn't been invited and some people didn't like unannounced callers. The more she thought about her action, the worse her idea seemed. She gave one more timid knock, and turned to go.

The door swung open into darkness.

"Simon?" she called tentatively.

"I'm in the study. You may enter, Cassandra." It was odd. She could hear him quite plainly, even though his voice didn't sound as if he were calling to her from two rooms away. The timbre and tone, in fact, almost sounded as if he were speaking quite softly, just in front of her.

She stepped forward hesitantly, her eyes adjusting to the gloom. Glancing toward the windows, she realized that behind the heavy drapes, all the glass was highly polarized to block the sunlight.

She jumped nervously as the door slammed behind her, then made her way through the entrance hall and the library, and into his study beyond. It was an inner room without windows, made even darker by the black floor and dark walls. It was large enough for a round conference table and four chairs, a couch against one wall and an onyx fireplace against the other. Simon walked in through the opposite door, pulling his robe closed and tying the belt as he came.

"Simon," she said with relief.

He took one look at her, crossed the room with long strides, and folded her into his arms. "What is it? You're trembling."

"I'm okay. Just a little shaken." But when he tried to step back, she clung to him. "The strangest thing just happened. I was driving around and someone almost hit me, I think I'm still shaking from it. I swerved down this cow-track into a parking lot, and there was this weird building, an old abandoned icehouse, and I got the strangest . . . feeling." There was nothing under the robe, and the strange feeling she had had at the icehouse was nothing to what she was feeling now.

"Are you sure you're alright?"

"Yeah. I guess I overreacted. I shouldn't have come." She tried to step back, but he didn't let go.

"I wasn't expecting visitors, Casey. I was taking a shower. Please forgive my appearance." He hugged her and gave her a brief kiss and she noticed that his hair was wet. "But I'm glad you came."

"If it's a bad time . . ." she said awkwardly.

"Not at all. I'm afraid I became too involved with my study of vampires last night and after I left your house, I read until almost dawn. My eyes are still burning from the strain and the sunlight is extremely irritating. I hope you don't mind the dim light."

"Of course not." It really wasn't as dark as it had first seemed. Her eyes had adjusted quite well. "It was just unexpected."

"Shall we work in here?" He didn't wait for an answer, but seated her at the table in front of a dozen books. "My research took me into a different direction this morning. It's utterly incredible. I don't know why it never caught my attention before, but there are vampire legends all over the world. They're so common that there must be some truth behind them. In Eastern Europe, they're associated with incubus and succubus, sexual demons. In China, they're known as shape changers and their favorite form is the tiger. Europe, Asia, Africa, even South America, all have their vampire legends. All over the world, the dead rise to drink the blood of the living."

He leaned against the onyx mantel, gold and white against shiny black, and his eyes reminded her of a hawk's, fierce and proud. "They've existed for thousands of years, Casey. Did you realize that in the Bible, over and over again, there are warnings against drinking blood? It's okay to eat the meat, but the blood should be drained out first. Do not drink the blood. It's utterly fascinating. What causes it? A virus? Or some occult magic? Their power must come

324

from the blood, but how? Concentrated energy? There must be something more."

"You almost sound as if you admire them."

"To change your shape by the power of your will? To fly? To live for a thousand years and be forever young and strong? Have you ever really thought about what it would be like?"

"To kill your own kind to live? Did you think about that part?"

"But perhaps there is an alternative. Of course they must drink blood, but how much? Do they really have to kill or can they just take what is needed and leave the donor alive? After all, if the blood loss is not severe, the human body can quickly and easily replace it."

"That's not what he's doing. He's killing people, Simon. And he's enjoying it. We can't afford to admire them too much. We have to destroy him."

"Yes," he said with a sigh. "You can put this under the category of knowing your enemy. They have so much potential that it's hard not to regret the loss." His voice was soft and reminded her of something. "Think of it, how would it feel to change into a wolf? To run for miles without tiring, to know the world through the power of scent, to be wild and free and utterly without restraint?"

She realized with a start what his voice reminded her of. It was just the same tone that her father used when he talked about flying with the hurricane hunters.

"Have you ever dreamed you were flying?" he asked.

She nodded silently, remembering that soaring feeling.

"How would you like to have that feeling while you're awake? To fly high above the world by the power of your own wings? To glide and soar without restriction or restraint? Don't you have any curiosity, Casey?"

"Of course I do." She rose to pace the room. Even his presence was disturbing to her. His body was like a magnet, and she had trouble taking her eyes off it. "But you keep leaving out all the negatives. I don't want to have to kill people, or even to steal their blood, to live. I want to walk in

325

the sunlight and swim in the sea. I don't even want to have to believe in vampires, much less become one. I understand your fascination with them, but I saw the change you're talking about. I saw a man turn into a bat, and it wasn't this romantic fantasy of soaring and freedom. It was horrible. His body twisted and shrank. In seconds, his arms flattened out and his fingers became claws." She shivered as the memories overcame her.

His eyes were filled with sorrow as he stared after her. At last he sighed, took her by the arm again, and led her to the couch. "As long as you are here, we may as well do some work. It's up to you to find him. You must learn concentration first. To focus all your mental powers on one goal. It won't be easy. Why don't you relax while I put some clothes on?"

"This should be fun." She smiled optimistically. "I've always been able to concentrate."

He tried not to let his amusement show. "Just sit back and relax. I'll be back in a few minutes."

She was so relaxed that she didn't even hear him come back into the room, but the sound of his voice, soft and intimate, sent a tingle through her body.

"The most important thing I can teach you, as a psychic, is to look inside yourself for answers. There is a light inside you, some would call it the soul. If you cannot find this light, then imagine it; it is your connection with the universe."

With God, she thought.

"It can give you answers to your questions, and guidance when you need it. It is the fountain of strength and power, and true wisdom is never achieved without recognition of it."

Where is the kingdom of heaven? It is within. Her private thoughts continued without volition.

"Today I will teach you to channel that power. Picture yourself on the bank of a river." He led her downstream as the river narrowed, then into the water so that she was standing with her back to the force of it. She could almost feel the rushing power in the imaginary water.

"Now, open yourself to the force. It enters through your back, fills your body from head to toe, then overflows and spills from the crown of your head. Direct it along your arm. See it pool in your hand. Watch it glow as the power becomes stronger and stronger. Now, open your eyes, Cassandra."

She opened them. He was sitting in the chair across from her. On the table in front of her was a single piece of paper. A heavy, ivory, 5"x7" inch sheet of stationery.

"Feel the power in your hand, Casey. Look at the paper. You can feel the weight and texture of it. You can pick it up, if you want to. Do you want to?"

"Yes."

"Then do it."

She tried to lean forward, but her body was so relaxed that her muscles didn't respond.

"Not that way, Cassandra. With your mind. Touch it with your mind."

It seemed like a reasonable suggestion. So much easier than moving physically. She could still feel the power in her hand, so she just stretched it out and let the power flow.

The paper exploded into flames. They shot almost to the ceiling as Simon cursed and shielded his eyes with his arm. Casey jumped from the chair, immediately awake and alert. In less than a second, the paper was consumed and the flames died. Ashes, almost invisibly fine, drifted through the air and began to settle on the table. Curious, Casey held out her hand and watched it accumulate on her palm.

"It's cool," she said, surprised. "Almost cold."

"All the power was consumed instantaneously. I've never seen anything like it." Simon laughed as he pulled her to him and hugged her.

In admiration, confusion, or amusement? Casey wondered. "Then you weren't expecting this?"

"I would have been surprised and pleased if you had moved it the merest fraction of an inch."

An hour later, they had talked of nothing else.

"I should go," Casey said reluctantly. The last few min-

327

utes, she had noticed Simon's increasingly passive languor. She studied his face in the dim light. His eyes looked heavy and red with fatigue.

"We were going to try to locate the vampire," he objected slowly as his fingers played with her hair.

Casey felt the weight of his hand on her shoulder. She looked into his warm, knowing gaze and was trapped. She wanted him. He was everything she had ever desired in a man: strong, intelligent, wise, and caring. And last night he had shown that he felt the same way. Her cheek dipped to brush his hand. She leaned forward, trailing her fingers down the front of his open shirt. Her lips brushed his, as lightly as a butterfly's wing.

The muscles of his arm bulged and tightened as he pulled her to him and kissed her. His lips were cool at first, but in a moment they burned on hers, and the fire spread through her. His arm circled her waist and she felt as if she were losing herself in his eyes.

She was losing herself. And she found that she wanted to let go, to be so completely his that they were one.

He leaned back, releasing her. She saw that he was fighting to keep his eyes open as he took her hand and kissed it apologetically. "I'm sorry, my love, but perhaps you are right. I am feeling . . . very tired. It would be best if you left now. I will get some rest. I will pick you up tonight and we can continue this later. Will you forgive me?"

"Of course," she stammered the words as he rose and escorted her to the library door. "I hope you're not coming down with something."

"I can assure you I'm not." He smiled, shaking his head. "I will be fine tonight. Shall I pick you up at seven o'clock?"

"That'll be fine, if the weather holds." She remembered putting her purse down and she looked around for it. She spotted it under the tall window of the library and walked forward. He watched her for a moment, then turned away as she continued. "You'd better think about preparing your house for a hurricane. It looks like this may be a bad one. If it hits near here, or even Mobile." She reached for the drawing cord of the curtains. "These windows will have to be boarded up." She gave the cord a hard pull.

He whirled around and gaped in shock. One tremendous leap took him across the library as filtered sunlight streamed through the expanse of polarized glass. His hand slammed down on a switch near the door. She could hear the steel shutters as they crashed down to protect every window in the house. Rage battled with relief as he leaned back against the wall.

The innocent surprise on Casey's face brought him a small measure of control. "I told you it hurts my eyes," he snapped.

Casey looked from the window to the switch that he had bent with the force of his blow. "I guess you don't have to worry about the windows."

Chapter Sixteen

Eric and Paul arrived back at Casey's house; they were hot, dirty, and disgusted. There was a note on the door from Clarise. She had gone out to pick up a pizza and would be back soon. Casey was upstairs taking a nap. Paul claimed the bathroom first and went up to take a shower. Eric got a beer from the refrigerator, and put some glasses in the freezer to cool. Clarise drove up before he finished the first beer.

"Where's Paul?" she asked, handing him the boxes.

"Taking a shower. What kind did you get?"

"The top one has everything." Clarise smiled sensuously at him as she sidled to the door. "How long has he been up there?"

"Just a few minutes."

"He might need me to wash his back." She gave Eric a wicked grin and waved him to the pizza. She drifted down the hall, humming. "Save some for us."

He watched jealously as she swayed up the stairs, her heavy hips making a circle eight. "Not a chance. Hey," he yelled suddenly and she stopped and looked back. "Tell Casey to meet me at the pool at six o'clock." He grabbed one of the boxes and headed home.

"Casey? You awake? Case?" Clarise knocked discreetly on the door.

"Jus' a sec." Casey's voice sounded strangled, and Clarise didn't wait.

"You've been crying."

"No . . . well, just a little." Casey wiped at her eyes and sat up in bed. "C'mon in."

"What's the matter?"

"Nothing." Casey's response was automatic. She corrected herself quickly. "Everything. Sit down and cheer me up."

"Are you having headaches again?"

"It's not too bad. What's up?"

"The hurricane has changed course again. It's sitting out in the Gulf, gaining strength. Eric and Paul are boarding up the windows. I've checked everything, at least I think I have, but there are bound to be things I've forgotten."

Casey lifted her head and caught the distant sound of hammering. "What time is it?"

"Just after three. We let you sleep until after we finished at my house. Just relax, the weatherman said it probably won't hit land for another day or so."

"You think it'll hit here?" Casey may have been the psychic, but Clarise's weather sense had been proved over and over through the years.

Clarise's face was pale. Her head tilted as if she were listening to something only she could hear, then, slowly, she nodded. "Yeah, I do. I've already told Paul and Eric, and, of course, Eric didn't believe me. But Paul did. He called the station and took another day off, but if the storm heads this way, they'll need every man available. He'll have to go in."

"When?"

"When the storm hits, of course." Clarise looked puzzled, but Casey just grinned and rephrased her question.

"When will the storm hit?"

"I don't know. Tonight? Tomorrow? The sooner the quicker, as Daddy used to say. The longer it sits out there, the worse it gets."

"Yeah. Well, I guess I better get up and get busy." Casey tried to throw the sheet aside, but Clarise was sitting on it.

"Can I have a minute? I want to talk to you."

"Sure, about what?"

"Simon. And you."

"What about Simon and me?" Casey's tone was carefully

331

neutral, but her friend noticed the danger signs.

"Don't start that with me, Case. I know you don't like people intruding into your private life." Clarise's long, slender fingers plucked nervously at the sheet. "But this could be important. Just what is going on between you and Mr. Drake?"

"Nothing!" Casey blurted out before she thought.

"Case, I'm serious. You can tell me."

"I know I could, but there isn't anything."

"Casey!" Clarise stretched the word out to four syllables. "I've seen the way he looks at you. And you act like he was some kind of Greek god. You've just spent two days with him. It's important. How do you feel about him?" Clarise sat up straight with tension and Casey looked at her closely for the first time.

"You're really worried about this, aren't you?"

"You bet your ass I am. I remember Mark too clearly. Simon—"

"Simon's not like Mark," Casey flared. "Mark was a sadist. He liked hurting you and anyone else that he could bully."

"And you think you can't be bullied? You're wrong, Cassandra. It can happen to anyone. Simon's so strong. I don't want to see you hurt like my first husband hurt me."

"Simon's not like that. He would never hurt me—"

"But he's strong enough to, and you're not used to—" Clarise interrupted, but Casey interrupted her right back.

"Simon wouldn't! He doesn't want to control me. He just wants to teach me to use my mind in ways I've never—"

"You're blinded by gratitude because he saved your life, but I can see the problems. Don't you know that's why I have to warn you? Because you can't see what you're getting into?"

"Okay, Reese, you've got a point. I do think he's pretty terrific. Not just because he saved my life, but I admit that might be part of it. You don't meet many men who would risk their lives for a stranger. What problems are you talking about?"

"Well . . ." Now that the initial resistance was over, Clarise retreated to her usual flutter of indecision. Casey waited patiently, knowing that the longer the silence continued, the more important the issue. "It's not just that he reminds me of Mark. Not physically, but more his attitude . . . it's just a feeling, but if you weren't so blind about him, you'd see it, too."

"Since I don't see it, would you like to point it out for me?"

"No, but I think I have to. He acts like he's some kind of lord of creation. Like he will destroy anything, or anyone, who gets in his way. Mark had that same attitude. Simon acts like he just doesn't care about people."

"You mean he doesn't care about me," Casey said miserably. "That's what I've been trying to tell you. He doesn't care about me."

"No, no, that wasn't what I meant. He acts like you're the only person he does care about, but that's not the point."

"It is to me!" Casey protested.

"Mark liked me. Maybe he even loved me, in his own way. Simon has the same . . . undercurrent of violence," Clarise fought to express herself clearly. "It's like a riptide. You can't really see it, but it can take you and roll you under and you'll never come up again. And . . . and—"

Clarise stammered until Casey asked impatiently, "What is it?"

"He gives me the shivers," she blurted out.

"What?" Casey asked, astonished and laughing.

"I don't see how you can look into his eyes. He's too powerful. He's too strong. He's overwhelming. He'll eat you alive!"

"What are you talking about?" Casey yelled at her and Clarise sat back immediately with a stricken look on her face. Casey felt the guilt hit her and shoved it back. "Simon is the most considerate, caring person I've ever met. He risked his life for a stranger. He knows more about life and living than I could ever learn." She threw back the sheet and got out of bed, pacing the floor furiously. Suddenly, she threw up her hands and started to laugh. "I don't know what we're fighting for," she finally gasped to Clarise's curious questions. "I thought he was interested in me, too, but he's not."

"Casey . . ."

"No, really. I kissed him today, and he couldn't get me out of the house fast enough," she confessed, her face turning red.

"You what? *You* kissed *him?*" Her eyes were wide and she was trying not to laugh. "What happened?"

"Never mind. You don't need the details. He was just sitting next to me and I kept thinking about him, and I leaned over and kissed him."

"I can't believe it!" Clarise screamed with laughter. "What did he do?"

"At first, I thought he kissed me back. Then, well, he said he was awfully tired, and it was time for me to go."

"Tired? Did he yawn or something?"

"No, not exactly. He just acted kinda bored."

"God, that must have been humiliating!" Clarise said with satisfaction.

"Oh, well, thanks heaps for all the sympathy and understanding," Casey said sarcastically, but she couldn't help smiling. "There's just no one like your best friend to really enjoy your suffering. Even when I was fat I don't remember any man running away from me," she concluded wryly.

"Was that what you were crying about?" Clarise was still laughing, and her words were choked out between giggles.

"No, of course not."

"You lie!"

"Well, what if I do? It's a cinch I can't confide in you."

"I can just see it." She put her hand to her forehead dramatically. "Not tonight, dear, I have a headache."

"I'm so glad you're enjoying this," Casey continued her sarcasm. "Was there anything else you wanted? Before I throw you out?"

"Oh, yeah. Eric wants to see you."

"Does he have the maps that Paul brought? I took a wrong turn this morning and wound up at the back side of nowhere. I want to find out where I was."

"He wants you to go swimming this evening. Meet him at the pool at six o'clock."

"I can't. Simon is picking me up at seven. If I go swimming I'll have to wash my hair and I won't have time."

"Heaven forbid you should be late for Mr. Drake," Clarise prodded her.

"Yeah, well, maybe he'll have caught up on his sleep," Casey said defensively.

"Nothing like a little humiliation to get you interested, right?" Clarise remarked as she sauntered to the door. Casey picked up the pillow from her bed and tossed it accurately at her head.

Clarise grinned and rubbed the back of her head as she got in the last word. "Stick with Eric. He's more your kind of people."

Casey had only been in the pool a few minutes when Eric joined her. They swam a few laps together, then relaxed, floating at arms length from each other and staring at the bright evening sky.

"Hard to believe that there's a storm out there somewhere, just waiting to land," Eric finally commented. "This is the nicest weather we've had in weeks."

"That's why they used to be even more dangerous. They usually follow heat and low pressure areas. Before radar, people on the coast had no warning. The weather could go from a clear, hot, blue sky to rain and winds of fifty or even a hundred miles an hour in just a few hours. I just wish they could predict where it's going to land, but at least everyone knows that there's one out there and they can prepare for it. Thanks for working on the house today. I hope it wasn't necessary."

"I didn't think we would want to be worried about storm damage if we had to go vampire hunting unexpectedly. Speaking of vampires, it's almost dark. Don't you think we should get inside?"

"I thought you didn't believe in vampires?" She watched the first star appear overhead, and made a wish.

"I'm still looking for another explanation, but until I find one, I'll accept yours. And that includes taking care of you. We better get inside."

"Just a little while longer. I had a hard day. My muscles are still tight. Just a few more laps ought to do it. Besides, he or she can't bother us in water."

"Are you sure of that?" Eric asked wryly.

"No, but that's what all the legends say." She shook her head and he admired the drops that sparkled in those midnight waves. "And I'm willing to take the chance. Paul and Clarise

335

are within shouting distance. I think we're safe."

"I see you brought your own protection." He ran one finger under her necklace from her collarbone down between her breasts to the scalloped edges of the antique silver cross. "No bad feelings? No premonitions?"

She shrugged away from his touch, then cocked her head and considered him carefully. If he wasn't serious, he was a better actor than she gave him credit for. She relaxed in the water and tried to reach into her mind, to open it up to impressions. She floated for a few moments while Eric waited patiently. Finally, she lifted her shoulders and feet and submerged gracefully. She came up a few feet from him.

"No bad feelings. No premonitions. No vampires." She dove again, turned twice underwater, then burst to the surface, spraying him with cool droplets. He closed his eyes and carefully laced his fingers across his stomach as he floated. He heard her go under and waited, tensing his muscles in anticipation. The water rippled and he gulped air just as her hand pushed him under. He reached for her, but she slipped away easily. Sputtering to the surface, he started after her. She was faster in or under the water than he was, even after her illness, and she twisted and turned just beyond reach until he cornered her in the deep end. He ducked her once, then again, reveling in the cool, slippery feeling of her skin and the slick wetness of her hair.

She bounced back to the surface with her eyes laughing and drops clinging to her eyelashes. He let her up and braced his arms to either side of her. She tried once to sink straight down and escape, but he grabbed her gently by the hair and tugged until she surfaced. She gave up gracefully and rested her hands on his shoulders to steady herself. He watched her smile falter and her face grow solemn as he moved closer.

His head dipped to the right and he kissed her. His body pressed closer to hers, but her hands on his chest pushed him away until her back was against the rough concrete of the side.

"I think it's time to go now." Casey turned her head to the side to avoid his searching mouth. He kissed the curve of her cheek and the corner of her eye.

"Casey, Casey. I never knew how dear you were to me until

336

I almost lost you." His lips moved slowly, coaxingly to the swirl of her ear and down the line of her neck, then back up to her lips.

"We . . . better . . . go," Casey murmured, hearing an echo of Simon's words to her.

"You said it's safe." His head twisted slowly back and forth, and his tongue parted her lips. He fought with himself to be gentle; she was so fragile now that he was afraid of hurting her. One hand, of its own volition, left the side of the pool and brushed lightly against the soft fullness of her breast. His finger traced the hard tip of her nipple. It could not match the hardness throbbing between his legs. He pressed against her eagerly now, overwhelmed by his need for her.

She made a small sound of protest and tried to push him away. He was momentarily puzzled by the low growl that answered her. He could almost feel the glaze over his eyes as he opened them and looked at her. The low, menacing sound came again, and he made an effort to focus his gaze beyond Casey. He looked up, over her head and shoulders braced against the pool's edge.

A snarling mask of hate met his gaze. Black on black eyes were surrounded by silver and gray fur. A long, blunt muzzle lifted in a snarl to show sharp white fangs, dark red gums, and a blood-red tongue. Massive shoulders framed the sunken, outthrust head, and sharp claws scratched the concrete apron.

Casey tilted her head back, following Eric's gaze. She stared, upside down and nose to nose with the monstrous canine. Almost simultaneously, Eric brought his arm around in a flat-handed slap at the water. Casey screamed, and the wolf opened his mouth wide enough to show shark-sharp teeth ridging the jaw line. A bright red tongue rasped across her cheek like a file, as the wave of water hit his face. Teeth snapped shut an inch from her face. The wolf shook his head angrily and took a step back as Eric continued his motion and swept her away from the side. The wolf took another step back, snarled once again, then turned tail and bolted for the line of trees. Eric's push sent Casey into deep water in the middle of the pool. She used the breath she had drawn to scream for a more constructive purpose. She didn't even slow as the momentum died, but swam at breakneck speed for the far side of the pool. Eric followed and caught her as she was scrambling out of the water. His fingers touched her shoulder and she turned at bay, fighting like a wildcat. He realized his mistake instantly as she struck at his head and shoulders. He slipped easily underwater and came up a yard away, calling her name.

She leapt from the pool and crouched on the concrete. Her eyes darted this way and that as she searched for the wolf. He called her name again, softly and soothingly, and she jerked toward him with such force that she almost toppled back into the pool.

"Casey. Casey, it's gone. It's gone now. You're safe," he repeated the theme with variations until her eyes saw him again. She sat down abruptly, casting a final look around the area.

"Eric." The sound came out in a whoosh of air. "Where did it go? Can we get to the house?"

He pulled himself easily out of the water and reached for her. She came into his arms, shuddering and cold to his touch. He held on tightly for a long moment, then lifted her to her feet. He flung a towel over her shoulders, but at the gate he hesitated, looking left toward Casey's house, then right toward his own. Casey clung to him until he tried to turn right.

"No, I want to go home. I'll be safe there."

"We'd have to go through the trees and that's where it went. My house is closer." He didn't stop to argue but pulled her through the gate toward his house. She nodded and gradually drew away from him until, by the time they reached the house, she was running independently, only occasionally touching his arm for reassurance. They hurried in the side door and locked it after them.

"You're safe now." Eric put his arms around her, but she drew away. As soon as the words were said, he wondered. Vampires couldn't enter an occupied house without an invitation, but did that hold true for an unoccupied house? He left her in the living room while he checked the house. It was empty. Casey had fixed two drinks when he returned. He accepted his gratefully.

"Are you alright?" he asked sternly.

338

"Yeah. You?"

He nodded. "Was that your mighty vampire?" he asked derisively. Anger mingled with relief as he turned away from her. "You've got a hell of a warning system there, Cassandra. But don't worry. If all it takes to scare your vampire away is a splash of water, I really don't think that we've got much to worry about. Christ! He scared me!" The admission burst from him almost unwillingly. She smiled and nodded, then nodded again, vehemently.

"He. . . . terrified me." She choked the words out. "All I could think of was Estelle Wiltz and what he did to her. I couldn't stand that. I would . . ." Her words failed as she tried to imagine a way out of such a situation. She shuddered again as a chill went down her spine. He took one step toward her, then remembered her reaction the last time he had reached for her.

"I'm going to call Clarise and Paul. My van is at your house. They can drive over and pick us up." He moved to the phone, but she stopped him.

"They shouldn't go outside."

"Is that another one of your 'intuitions?' " he asked sarcastically.

"No," she admitted defiantly, "it's just good sense. He tried to get her once before, maybe it was her he's after. Maybe that's why he didn't attack us. Call and warn them, but tell them not to go outside."

"They could always carry a squirt gun," he said bitingly. "But you're right. There's no point in them picking us up. We can walk back." He made the call then turned back to Casey. "Or maybe you'd rather stay here. It might not be safe to go out," he said mildly. His hand wandered to her shoulder.

She looked at him incredulously. It didn't take a psychic to read his mind. "You mean the wolf out there is more dangerous than the one in here?"

"C'mon, Casey. You know you've liked me for a long time. Besides, any vampire that runs from a splash of water is nothing to be afraid of. I just meant we could stay here."

"I know exactly what you meant," she replied acerbically. "Simon will be over to pick me up soon. I'll wait for him."

"This is the same Simon who told you to trust your so-called psychic powers?"

"You can't blame him because I didn't sense anything wrong!" Her voice was getting louder.

"I blame him because he's leading you on. He's filling your head with crazy ideas. Just because I'm willing to concede that there may be vampires, doesn't mean that you're psychic just because he tells you you are." His anger made his aura glow red, and it was making her head hurt.

"Then how do you explain what I've seen?"

"You had some nightmares and a hunch. Maybe it was true and maybe you just thought it was afterwards. You sure didn't tell anybody about it before it happened."

"Are you saying I lied about it?" Her fists clenched as she tried to control her outrage.

"All I'm saying is you can't start depending on this power because it may not be there when you need it." His hands spread innocently.

"You don't believe me," she stated calmly. "What about what Clarise saw? And Simon?"

"Simon is just trying to use you," Eric said viciously.

"If I'm not really psychic, how can he use it?" she screamed with the illogic of his reasoning.

"He's not using it! He's using you! You've changed since he's been around. You're scared out of your mind. You think you're on some kind of holy mission. He's warping your mind." He grabbed her arm as she turned away from him.

"Maybe I like being used by him. It sure beats the hell out of being used by you. Before I lost weight, the only time you ever asked me out was when you wanted something, or you had nothing better to do!" She jerked out of his grasp and went to the door.

He shook his head in disbelief. "You won't go out there! Simon's got you terrified of your own shadow!" He finished off his drink and walked to the bar to pour another one as she hesitated by the door. "You've even got me scared. For all we know, that was just a big dog out there, and if we had stopped for a minute, we would have seen his collar."

"Dog? You think that was just a dog? Have you ever seen a

340

dog like that? Ever?" Casey demanded angrily. "Next you're going to be telling me that Bev's death was all a mistake."

"Bev's death? How do we know she's dead, much less a vampire. All I've got to go on . . ."

"Is my word," she shouted furiously. She opened the door and stared out into the darkness. She didn't want to go out there, but everything seemed to be pushing her. "And Clarise's word."

"Clarise? You've got her so scared that she wouldn't open the door to your best friend on a rainy night. She couldn't see whether there was something wrong with Bev. As for Simon, this is exactly what he wants. As long as you believe in vampires, you need him. When you come to your senses, you'll get rid of him. Besides, the only vampires anyone has seen have been scared off like Bev and the dog. If they can be scared off by a word from Simon or a splash of water, I don't think anyone needs to worry very much."

"Then I guess I won't worry," she said quietly, fighting the tears in her eyes as she slipped out the door.

Chapter Seventeen

Casey ran from the house, knowing that it was a stupid, foolish thing to do, but unable to face another infuriating minute alone with Eric. How could he be so blind? Not ten minutes ago, he had admitted that the wolf was not only a wolf but a vampire, and now he was trying to cover his fear by saying it was really just a dog. And Bev! It would serve him right if he kept thinking that way and Bev paid him a visit.

She heard the door open behind her and put on a burst of speed until she reached the edge of the trees that separated Eric's property from her own. She heard him call her name, but refused to acknowledge it. If there was no danger, then what was he so worried about? She stumbled over a bush, and realized that she had missed the trail. That was no problem. She had lived here most of her life. She knew these woods like the back of her hand. She turned right and weaved through the undergrowth. The light of the full moon was intermittent as the clouds raced by. The wind was picking up and felt cool on her bare skin. There was something about being out at night in the woods, in only her swimsuit, that made her feel particularly vulnerable. She blessed Eric's practicality as she realized that if he hadn't picked her shoes up at the pool, she'd be barefoot, and that would have been even worse. There was the rumble of thunder in the distance. It went on for a minute or longer, and she wondered if the hurricane had changed course again.

She could hear Eric calling, but fainter now, as if he were moving away from her. There was a glimmer of light in the distance and she headed for it in relief. It didn't look like a house light, more like a reflection, but if she could just figure out where she was, she could find her way home. She was about to push her way through the undergrowth, when she heard a movement in front of her. She stopped, not even breathing.

All of the night's terror came back in a rush. She tried to force the air through her lungs and was appalled at the noise she made. The woods were absolutely still. Why hadn't she noticed that before? And what did it remind her of? Her mind wandered as if thinking innocuous thoughts made her inconspicuous. Simon should be at the house by now. If she screamed, Clarise and Paul would hear her, but would they be able to help? Where had Eric gone? Was he at the house by now? When she got out of this, she'd never be able to confess to him that she had lost her way in this small stretch of trees. Forget that! If she got out of this alive, she wouldn't mind a little healthy ridicule. The light flickered and she strained her eyes through the darkness. It was the moon, she realized. The moon on the water. She was almost on the beach. She knew exactly where she was, and home was right . . .

The brush moved again, and she realized that she had been waiting for it, trying to distract herself with irrelevancies hadn't helped.

It was only a few yards in front of her. The rustle it made was louder than the noise of the wind. She put one foot behind her cautiously. It made no sound on the thick carpet of pine straw. She shifted her weight gently, then moved her other foot. Slowly, gently, she moved backwards while her eyes remained fixed on the small patch of brush. It was just high enough to hide a man . . . or a wolf. She remembered the gleaming eyes and savage snap of those powerful jaws. His cold breath had frozen her in terror.

She moved again, feeling the weakness of fear in her knees, and her foot slipped. A twig cracked loudly and she froze. Was that a shape moving in the darkness? A few yards farther and she would be out of the woods and on the beach. If she could make it to the water, she would be safe. He couldn't follow her in.

Something fluttered in the bushes. Her hand clutched her necklace and she bolted. She dodged a tree, leapt over a fallen log, and felt soft sand beneath her feet.

It was too late! He was ahead of her. She turned back to run again and felt his hand on her shoulder. She wrenched around and struck out with the cross. There was a brilliant flash of light and she screamed in rage and terror.

"Casey! Cassandra! Stop it. It's me . . . Simon. Stop it." He grabbed her and shook her by the shoulders, but she no longer needed it. She knew that voice, dark and smooth as fine wine. She threw herself into his arms.

"Thank God! I was so scared. I thought it was a vampire," she mumbled into his chest, then realized something and pulled back. "The cross. It flared when it hit you. You . . ."

His laugh cut her off and he pulled her back into his embrace. "As much psychic energy as you were throwing around, I'm surprised I didn't explode like that sheet of paper this morning. Are you okay?"

She nodded, but she wouldn't let go of him. "You?"

"Fine."

"Simon, there was a vampire. He's still here and I couldn't sense him . . ."

He lifted his hand for silence, and his concentration was obvious. "No, I'm sure there's no one around now."

"But he was there. It was the vampire."

"I don't doubt you, but he's long gone now. Let's get back to the house. Everyone is worried about you." He unobtrusively pulled down the sleeve on his right arm to cover the burn mark on his wrist, then buttoned it.

She told him about the wolf at the pool as they walked back to the house, but he didn't seem surprised or upset. The rest of the group met them at the door. The concern vanished from Eric's face as he saw them and he looked defensive. Before he could speak, Casey said, "It was my fault, Eric. I shouldn't have gone off like that." She held on tightly to Simon as they went in.

"We heard a scream and we were on our way to find you when Paul spotted Simon. Are you alright? Did you see the vampire?" Eric's voice trailed off uncertainly.

"You mean you admit it was a vampire?" Casey asked sarcastically.

"It was a wolf," Eric admitted. "I was wrong. It seems I've said that a lot lately. You just made me so damn mad." He finished antagonistically.

Casey grinned at him understandingly. He wouldn't be Eric if he gave in completely. She moved to a chair and sank down gratefully, her legs trembling with reaction and fatigue. Clarise handed her a drink, but Casey winced as her hand closed. She shifted the glass to her left hand and examined her right. She must have been clutching at the cross so hard that it had dug into her palm. Blood was still trickling from the small cut.

"It seems you damaged yourself more than you did me." Simon took her hand in his. "I think you'll live." He lifted it to his lips and kissed it slowly. His eyes never left hers. Her left hand stroked his damp hair as his tongue tickled her palm. She pressed her hand to his cheek and wondered if he could feel what she felt for him, and if he returned even a small part of it.

"Tell me about the wolf." Clarise broke the spell rudely. "Eric didn't make much sense when he found out you weren't here."

"There's nothing much to tell. He didn't attack, he just scared us. It was his eyes that were unusual. Eric frightened him away by splashing water on him. Or maybe it wasn't us he wanted."

"I have to admit it doesn't seem likely that you scared a vampire away that easily." Simon grinned at Casey and she felt her heart quicken.

"Even Eric admits it was a vampire," she protested.

"So," Paul commented. "First the vampire comes after Clarise. Then he attacks and kills Beverly. Then Beverly comes back and tries to get Clarise, or maybe Casey. Then a vampire comes to the pool, but he doesn't attack, even though he has the chance. It doesn't make sense."

"We don't know that it happened in that order," Casey pointed out. "Beverly was already having dreams when she came to see me. Maybe the attack was earlier and Bev was having nightmares about it. Maybe he came back more than once."

Simon looked up quickly. "So what?"

Paul looked sternly at Casey. "All the incidents can be connected to one person. Clarise knew Bev, but not the Wiltz family. Casey knew them all. Casey stopped the attack on Clarise and me. Casey was at the pool."

"But he didn't try to attack at the pool," Casey pointed out quickly. "So maybe he was after Reese again."

"Thanks a heap, cousin," Clarise muttered.

"Maybe," Paul conceded, "but Casey is the one who may be able to find the vampire. She's the one who foiled the attack on us, and maybe more."

She felt very small and vulnerable. "You mean he knows we're after him." They were all staring at her. She took a deep breath and said what they were all waiting to hear. "He knows I'm after him."

"Which brings up another problem," Eric said slowly. "When we finish with him, the main vampire, or master vampire, or whatever you want to call him, when we destroy him, what do we do about Bev?"

Simon's eyes never left Casey as she shook her head mutely. He finally spoke, "Why do we have to do anything about her?"

"If she's a vampire, she'll have to be destroyed," Eric spoke positively.

"Why?" Simon asked coolly.

"Isn't that why we're tracking the master vamp?" Paul asked.

"It is not why I am tracking the master vamp, as you so quaintly put it," Simon responded. "You must decide whether you are going to kill him because he is a vampire, or because he is a killer."

"It's the same thing," Eric said impatiently.

"I know what Simon's talking about," Clarise interrupted. "Maybe she doesn't have to kill to survive. Maybe she could just . . . just take some blood without killing the victim." As usual when she was the center of attention, she became shy and confused. "I mean, you don't die just because you lose a little blood. And he, I mean she, if Bev does just take a little blood, she wouldn't be killing people, would she? Then we really wouldn't have to kill her. I mean, could you drive a stake through her heart?" She looked at the group helplessly.

"She's still a vampire," Casey said, remembering the horror of watching that man change into a bat. "You don't understand. She's a monster now."

"And if we're right about Bev, and the vampire just took a little blood from her, how come she died anyway?" Paul objected. "Maybe anyone she drinks from eventually dies as well and turns into a vampire. We'd have to get rid of her."

Casey felt sick as she tried to envision driving a stake through her friend's heart. Could she do that to Bev? Could she do that to anyone? She remembered what she had seen in her dreams and decided she could. "It wouldn't really be Bev if she's a vampire now. It would just be a monster."

"Can you really believe that of your friend?" Simon spoke softly, directly to Casey. "Do you really think she has changed so much? When you first saw her on the porch, you couldn't even tell the difference. The line between life and death is so narrow. Wouldn't she still be your friend even if she has . . . changed? Could you pound in that stake and watch her life's blood flow away?"

"I guess that's the question we all have to answer," Casey said miserably.

"No. The question *you* have to answer is whether you are hunting vampires because they are killing people, or just because they exist."

"You were here when she tried to kill me," Casey pointed out sarcastically. "I don't think we can rely on Bev's friendship."

"But I also scared her off with a word. I think she was being driven, rather than acting on her own," Simon stated.

"Which brings us back full circle," Eric pointed out. "I think we better wait until we meet Bev again to decide what we're going to do about her. Our main concern has to be whether or not the master vamp is aware of what we're doing. How much protection do we have if he knows who we are, where we are, and what we're doing? And we don't know anything about him."

"Why is everyone looking at me?" Casey asked, even though she knew the answer. "I didn't even sense him when he

347

was a foot away. I don't think we better count on my talent. We can figure out another way to find him." She looked at them hopefully. "Can't we?"

"You've had a hard day," Simon interjected. "If you don't want to work tonight, I'll understand. But as for quitting, I don't think you have an option anymore. He's after you now, whether you're after him or not."

"I do want to work. I just don't think there's much point in it."

"Let me decide that. If you want to try, we're wasting time here."

"I've got to shower and change."

"Hurry."

When she came back downstairs she was wearing a white sundress. The sweeping lines and frail fabric outlined her body with swirls and curves, and in the back it fell to a wide vee. The lace scarf around her neck matched the narrow straps over her shoulders.

"Exquisite," Simon murmured. His fingers tingled as his arm went around her shoulders and his hand pressed lightly against her bare skin.

"I'm almost ready." She picked up her purse from the table. "Is it raining?"

"Off and on," Eric answered. "They just called Paul and the hurricane has stalled again. He's gone to work." His eyes drifted to Simon's arm around Casey's shoulders. "Maybe you should put this off until after the storm passes."

"I wish we could," Simon said gravely. "But if we can locate him tonight, we should be able to get to him before he moves after the storm. And it's the full moon."

"What does that have to do with it?" Eric's voice was antagonistic.

"It may be nothing. It may be everything. There is a ritual I read about last night. It's called the Circle of Death. If a Nosferatu, a master vampire, creates a circle of thirteen vampires on the night of the full moon, his power is increased thirteen fold. And whatever area he encompasses, he will control."

"Superstitious nonsense," Eric declared.

"Yeah," Casey said softly. "Like vampires."

Eric had the grace to look embarrassed, but it didn't stop him. "What time will you be back?"

"I don't know. I'll call you if we find anything."

"And I'll call Paul at work," Eric announced impatiently as Clarise entered the room. "Fine, but if you haven't finished by midnight, I'll pick you up."

"What are you talking about?" Casey reacted more with amusement than anger.

"There's a hurricane coming, in case you didn't hear me," Eric said loudly. "This house is practically surrounded by water and we may have to evacuate. The water level has already risen six or eight feet. At any time, the storm could come out of that stall and the front edge could be here in a couple of hours. We might not have much notice."

"Listen to the Damn Yankee!" Clarise said sarcastically. "He's telling us about hurricanes."

"My suitcase is in the car, and I've already taken care of emergency supplies. Clarise has the candles, flashlights, and hurricane lamps," Casey replied reasonably.

"And the extra water, canned food, charcoal, kerosene—"

"And we packed Paul's things, and we went over to your house and your suitcase is packed and in the car—"

"And what the hell do you think we did all day?" Casey asked belligerently, then spoiled it by grinning at Clarise, who smiled back briefly as she snapped at Eric.

"We can be out of here in five minutes flat. We can take one or two cars, and we've already picked a spot to go to. Paul will probably have to stay here and work during the storm, so if it's not too bad, I'll go to a shelter. It looks as if you're the only one who still has things to do. We didn't get your personal things from the house. You'll have to decide what you want to take."

"I plan to work until the last possible moment, too," Casey interrupted Clarise with a look of amused gratitude.

Eric looked from one to the other. "How long did you and Groucho practice this routine?" He smiled slowly at Casey. "If the hurricane starts in this direction, I'll pick you up within thirty minutes. We can expect heavy traffic."

"We aren't likely to play the radio while we're trying to concentrate," Casey said. "So call us if anything changes. We'll be

349

prepared to run."

"We all will be prepared to run," Eric agreed slowly. "Although I don't see how you expect to run in that dress." His gaze lingered on her and Simon bristled. He stepped in front of Casey, removing his arm from her shoulder and stretching to open the door.

"Simon, what happened to your arm?" Clarise exclaimed.

"Nothing. I burned it slightly this afternoon. It is nothing." He adroitly slid the cuff back down to cover his wrist and used his other hand to open the front door.

Eric followed them to the doorway and stood looking after her. He started to speak, but Casey caught his eye and shook her head.

"We've got to find him tonight. He may move as soon as the storm is over and we must be ready. We will find him tonight." She looked at him and he could see the fear in her eyes.

"Casey? What do you see?"

Simon held the door open for her, but she stopped and turned to face Eric. "That's just it, I've tried so hard, and I can't see anything. I'm blank." She walked quickly back to him and hugged him. "You be careful tonight, too, you hear? I don't think that wolf is still hanging around, but you be careful." Clarise came up beside them and Casey hugged her, too. "You don't take any chances, okay? Without you, who would keep me in line?" She felt a shiver go through her. A sudden gust of wind snatched the door from Simon's hands and slammed it against the entrance wall.

"You be careful, too." Clarise frowned at Simon and kissed Casey on the cheek.

"We'll keep in touch," Casey promised and started for the door.

Eric captured her neatly and pulled her against him. "You be careful, too." He kissed her briefly.

"I will," she replied. He felt solid and strong when she gave him a final quick hug and moved down through the door. A gust of wind hurled through the opening. It pulled like fingers at Simon's shirt and plucked at her skirt until it flared up and her legs shone in the light.

"Leave 'em laughing," Casey muttered as Eric grinned.

"Something's wrong there." Eric turned abruptly from the door as it closed behind Casey. He bumped into Clarise and gripped her arms tightly as he spoke, "I shouldn't have let her go."

"How could you stop her?" she asked, and winced as his grip tightened painfully. "Eric," she protested.

"Sorry," he muttered as his grip eased. His expression remained puzzled and irritated as he walked back to the living room and retrieved his drink.

"If you're that jealous, why didn't you tell her how you feel?" Clarise spoke sharply.

"I'm not jealous," he flashed back. "Casey and I are just good friends. I just hate to see her acting like a fool over that arrogant bastard."

"I thought he was your friend. You're the one who introduced them."

"My mistake," he said sourly. "Again." Then he looked at her closely. "You don't like him either."

"No," she said, and abruptly changed the subject. "Five minutes till the next weather bulletin. Is there anything you need from your house? We packed your clothes and things, but we figured you'd have time to get some personal things. I thought I'd watch the news while you're gone."

"Okay. No!" He corrected himself hastily. "We can't split up. You can watch the news at my place while I pack."

"Right. Don't forget your papers: insurance, the deed for the house, passport, stock certificates and anything else that might be difficult to replace. Also small valuables like jewelry, coins, or stamps." Clarise began ticking off points on her fingertips as she moved toward the door. Eric realized that part of his relief was because he wouldn't be alone right now.

They drove the short distance to his house. Already, the wind was gusting hard enough to feel the short, sharp tugs in the van. He turned on the headlights, then shut them off quickly. Twilight had ended, but the sky was bright with a sickly, yellow glow. The headlights were the wrong color; white emphasized the strange ugly shade just on the edge of vision. The drive was littered with twigs and leaves, pine needles still sticky with sap, and fat brown cones. The tires crunched over the debris with a sound heard even over the background noise of the wind. The trees on either side dipped their branches to brush the van.

As Eric opened the car door, he looked around cautiously. Any movement would be hidden by the tossing of trees and bushes, and any sound would be muffled and distorted by the wind. They would have to take their chances and hope that a vampire would not be hunting in such weather. With the key ready in his hand, he hustled Clarise out of the van and up the steps. Inside, they blinked tiny grains of sand from their eyes and wiped the grit from their faces. He went straight to the television and flipped the channels for news. They both sat and listened to the eight o'clock broadcast and heard the same thing that they had been hearing for five hours. The storm was stalled due south of Mobile, Alabama. Lady Di was gradually gaining strength and the central core, or eye, that had formed this morning was stable. All the low-lying islands had been evacuated and the shelters were filling fast. The storm had reduced in diameter from three hundred miles to a little more than two hundred, and the winds had increased from 125 to 140 miles per hour. The coast was marked in red from Pensacola to Cedar Key as the meteorologists tried to guess where the eye might touch land first. The most likely city was Apalachicola, but Panama City and Ft. Walton Beach were also prime candidates.

Eric turned from the live reports of breakers on the beach and wandered from room to room aimlessly. This was one of those things that one never quite accepted. After the storm was over and the house still stood, he would push this memory to the back of his mind and hide it in a dark closet. The next time he had to pack would be just as traumatic, just as confused. Each time he had to face the thought anew, "This may not be here tomorrow."

He tried to think strictly of things that were irreplaceable: the photo of his mother, a lighter given to him by a friend, the picture of his ex-wife, a thousand memories in a hundred different shapes and sizes. His mind wandered to the people and events behind each object. His hands touched things at random, until Clarise came looking for him.

"I thought you might have gotten bogged down. Mind if I sit in here while you pack?" She perched cross-legged on the bed while he began tossing things into his suitcase. She watched him sympathetically.

"I did this at my house today." She waited for a response but he just grunted. "I can go through all the rest and it doesn't bother me, but when it comes to packing, I just sort of freak out." He glanced at her and back to the baseball in his hand. He bounced the ball off his palm a few times. The suitcase wasn't even half full. He tossed it in, and looked vaguely around the room. What was irreplaceable? What would hurt the most if he never saw it again?

"Don't forget your insurance papers for the house. You may need them," she reminded him. He dashed from the bedroom to the office. The papers were all in separate folders. He started looking through them hurriedly, picking folders and setting them aside. He moved faster, flipping through titles and jerking the files out roughly. A sense of urgency grew within him.

He reentered the room with an armful of documents, and Clarise narrowed her eyes.

"Eric."

"Yeah?" he shoveled the papers into his suitcase and they spilled on to the bed.

"You don't need all those, do you?"

"Uh, no. But I didn't have time to sort them out."

"You have time. Just take the ones you need."

By the time they finished packing, it was almost 10:00 P.M. He had filled one suitcase three times and emptied it twice. He had checked the house a dozen times, unplugging electrical equipment and checking to see that there was extra ice in the freezer. Clarise watched him sympathetically, but stayed out of the way. They delayed taping the windows until after the ten o'clock newscast. No change. At 10:15 they started taping, making broad crosses on the glass.

Eric checked the house carefully one final time before he peered out the window cautiously. The trees were outlined against a bright lemon sky. Shadows danced and streaked out like whips from the double lights at the end of the driveway.

The bulletin had said, "No change," but the wind was bending the trees in an almost gentle arc to the west. As he watched, a gust hit the treetops and they tossed violently. The shadows danced again. There was no way to tell if anyone was hiding out there.

They would have to take their chances.

The door pushed against him as he unlatched it. He jumped violently back, ready to fight, but not even a mist blocked his path. She went out and he pulled the door closed and locked it. He gave the wooden frame a thoughtful pat as he turned to go. The door, the house, all might be gone tomorrow.

"Spooky," she said as he climbed in the van beside her.

"That's the word," he agreed. The sky was completely overcast, but the clouds themselves were visible in the eerie glow. They streaked across the sky as if driven. The trees were brightly outlined and the house lights seemed feeble by comparison. The scent of pine was strong, and if he listened carefully, he could hear the tiny, sharp, pitter-patter of the needles hitting the ground. Under it all was the sound of the wind, like the steady hum of distant traffic.

They drove back quietly, aware of the power of wind and water. They arrived too late for the 10:30 P.M. update. Clarise headed for the phone to call her husband and it rang before she touched it. She flashed a smile to Eric. "That's Paul, I bet."

She picked up the receiver and said hello.

A cultured voice spoke, "Cassandra?"

"She's not here right now. May I take a message?"

"When will she return?"

"I don't know," Clarise said impatiently. "Can I tell her who called?"

A dry chuckle echoed down the line. "Tell her it was Franz. If you see her before I do." As the chuckle came again, Clarise hung up.

"Who was that?" Eric asked.

"Franz." She mocked his accent. "You know a Franz?"

"No, I don't think so. What did he want?"

"Casey. Said he'd see her later." She turned to him and frowned fiercely. "She never mentioned a Franz to me. Not

354

once. I always thought she was lonely, but she's got men coming out of the woodwork." She turned back to the phone. "I wonder if Paul knows him."

It was almost 11:00 P.M. before Paul called her back. Eric turned on the news. It had been an hour since he had heard the weather, but his brief trip outside had convinced him that the storm had turned west.

He was right. At 11:15 P.M., the National Hurricane Center at Miami reported that Hurricane Diana was proceeding northwest at five miles per hour. Eric checked his tracking chart as they predicted landfall about 3:00 A.M. between Mobile and Biloxi. He let out his breath in a relieved sigh. It could have been worse. This area would get hard winds and rains and be battered for the next six or eight hours. But unless she turned east, the worst of the storm should miss them by fifty to a hundred miles, and they had plenty of time to prepare. Even the bad news seemed good.

He turned to Clarise and saw the relief on her face. She covered the receiver briefly. "Paul will get off at midnight if the forecast doesn't change."

His broad smile died as he thought of Casey. He would still pick her up, he decided. He would call soon and see if they had finished. Everything was going to be fine, just fine. He wandered to the doorway and stared down the hall.

"Simon? Do you trust me?" he had asked her the question so often in their hypnotic sessions, that it came easily to her mind. They sat side by side on the couch. The large fireplace was empty in front of them, and Simon had opened the window so that the house was scented with the night air. After a long silence, he replied softly, "More than I've trusted or loved anyone in cen . . . in a longtime."

She snuggled closer to him, needing the physical reassurance of his touch. "Then why don't you tell me what's on your mind?"

He was a blank to her. After daily contact with people who were open books, he was an enigma. Most people seemed to broadcast their emotions, as if they wanted the whole world to know what they were thinking and feeling. Eric was funny about that. He had always been so closed to her, so controlled and contained, but since her psychic senses had opened up, he was more like a raging forest fire. He sputtered and crackled and sparks flew.

Simon had the true control. He kept his emotions to himself, except when he was fighting with Eric. She never knew what Simon was thinking or feeling. Simon's fire was banked and contained. She could feel the heat and see the glow, and even catch a glimpse of the flames now and then, but the heart of the fire was hidden.

"Why don't you tell me what's on your mind?" she felt a twinge of anxiety, then relief. At least it would be out in the open.

"You mean yesterday? I really was tired, Cassandra. I . . . I do not function well during the day." He regarded her seriously as he paused. This was the opening he had been hoping for, but he wasn't sure how to use it. "Why are you going to kill this vampire?" he finally asked.

It certainly wasn't the subject she had been expecting, but she answered easily. "He's a monster. He's killing my friends and family and he'll kill me if I don't stop him. People have to protect the things they love, or they'll lose them."

"A monster? Would you do the same if he were an ordinary human?" Simon's voice was politely interested, but she caught an underlying current that ran deep and strong.

"If he were human, there would be people I could go to for protection, the cops or someone. If it came down to his life, or the life of someone I love, including mine, I'd kill him in a minute if I could. But he's not human, he's a monster. He's a bloodsucking creature who doesn't have the right to survive by stealing other people's lifeblood." She tried to keep her voice calm, but there was no doubt of her sincerity. "If you're having doubts about whether or not I can kill, if it's necessary, I will."

"I have no doubt of that. My experience has been that anyone can kill under the right circumstances," his voice was tinged with pain. "I want to know if you plan to kill him because he's a 'bloodsucking monster,' or because he's a killer." His tone was curtly angry and she watched him worriedly.

"It doesn't matter. He still has to die."

"It matters to me."

"Both, I guess," she shrugged.

"If he wasn't a vampire, you'd still be after him?" She nodded yes hesitantly. "I guess that's something," he didn't even try to hide his angry sarcasm. "What if he was a vampire, but not a killer? Would you hunt and kill him then?"

"You're contradicting yourself. If he wasn't a vampire, we wouldn't have this problem!" Why wouldn't he just say what was on his mind? Why were they arguing?

"You mean he's a ravenous monster because he's a vampire? What about Bev? Is she a monster? She was your friend. Are you going to pound a stake through her heart? She hasn't killed anyone," he added honestly, "that we know of."

"She's not Bev anymore! Bev is dead and he killed her! If I have to pound a stake through her heart to make her lie down and stay dead, then I will. It's only a matter of time before she kills someone. Bev wouldn't want to go on like that, killing people to live."

"How the hell do you know what she would want? Have you asked her?" he was pacing the floor and yelling at her. She wondered briefly why she had ever thought that he kept his emotions to himself.

"How am I supposed to ask her? Hold a damn seance? Bev is dead. What's still walking around is . . . is a travesty. A lying, killing monster that feeds on blood and attacks her friends. That's not Bev!" She screamed the words at him, rather than break down and cry. "I have to kill it to release her."

"What are you doing? Going on some kind of holy war to kill vampires?" He was yelling, too. She had never been so aware of someone else's anger. His aura was blood red and surrounded him in a bloody haze. Even his eyes looked different to her. The red glow reflected off their dark surfaces.

The room seemed to darken and shrink around her until she was looking through a long tunnel into his eyes. They were black now, except for the red flames that leapt hungrily. Her gaze was trapped and her body trembled.

"Answer me!" he roared. "After this one, are you going to kill Beverly?"

"Yes!" She screamed the word at him, glad that she was still able to scream. She fought to tear her eyes away.

"Then what? Alert the world? Go on a vampire hunt? How many of us are you going to kill, Cassandra?"

"Us?" She whispered the word, then screamed. "Nooo! Not you! *You can't be."* She twisted her head around, trying to pull her eyes from him, but he wouldn't release her. His image became larger as he strode down that tunnel toward her. She would have moved back, if she could.

"Well, Casey? How many will you kill?" His hands ripped his shirt as if it were made of cobwebs. "There, Casey! That's where you'll put the stake. But don't let your hand tremble. Make it a clean blow. One chance, Cassandra, that's all you'll get. Can you sneak up on me during the day while I'm asleep and kill me with one blow?" His eyes filled her universe. His voice sank to a whisper that chilled her blood. She felt the shock as he took her hand and placed it flat on his bare chest. "Because if you hesitate," he continued, "if your hand trembles or your eyes blink, I will stop you, my love."

He turned away suddenly, releasing her with a gesture. Her mind reeled as a dozen thoughts fought for her attention. Rage built in her as all the pieces dropped gently into place.

"You bastard!" Her voice was thick with loathing as she edged across the fireplace hearth to the door. "Vampire! Monster! You killed Beverly, didn't you!" Her hand groped toward the mantel.

"No, I—" he started, but she hadn't finished.

"It was you at Eric's pool. Your hair was still wet when we went inside." She grabbed the first thing that came to hand, the ancient jade dog, and flung it at him like a stone missile. His movements were too fast to follow as he whirled, caught the heavy carving with one hand and set it down gently on the table. "You listened to our plans. We trusted you while you laughed at us. All the time, you were playing with us!" Her hand found the ashtray on the mantel and she used both hands to hurl it straight at his face.

He lifted one hand, and midway between them the ashtray exploded into black slivers that sang through the air around her. She winced away from the sting on her cheek.

"Damnit, Casey! That's not . . ."

"Liar! Bloodsucking, lying bastard! You killed Bev! And those children! Those poor helpless kids." She took a quick step backward; then all movement and all thought stopped as his rage hit her.

"I did not!" he roared at her. "I would not! I do not feed on children." He strode toward her until he towered over her as he snarled. "And I don't torture women." He grabbed her chin in three fingers and tilted her head up. "But for you I might make an exception." He released his hold on her, physically and mentally, and watched as she swayed unsteadily.

"You already have. The man in her dreams. She tried to tell me, but I didn't really listen. That was you, wasn't it?" Her foot crept backward as he wheeled away from her.

"She was alive when I left her. She looked vaguely familiar, but I didn't realize she was your friend until later."

"Would that have made a difference?" she asked.

He followed as if stalking her, as she crept slowly backwards into the hall.

She waited, but he didn't answer. At last she continued her tirade. "Why did you kill her? She wanted you to come back. She was falling in love with you. Like I did," she said wretchedly as her hand touched the doorknob.

"I didn't kill her," he said sadly. He listened without moving as she eased the door open and ran headlong into the night.

Chapter Eighteen

Casey darted down the walkway, dodged the hedge, and sprinted across the driveway toward the car. His Jaguar was a dark shape twenty feet away. Her heart pounded as she risked a quick look behind her, expecting to see a wolf snapping at her heels, but the night was quiet. The driveway sloped up and she leapt up with it. At the last moment, she looked behind her again. The thin, fast moving clouds broke around the moon and sent shadows dancing across the empty lawn. She jerked her eyes back to the ground to keep from stumbling, then looked up at the car.

Simon was leaning casually against the driver's door. Her heart seemed to spasm in her chest as she jerked to a stop. Her hands clenched in impotent fury as he lifted one eyebrow and smiled at her.

"Damn you, you bloodsucking liar."

Her words wiped the smile off his face. There was a grimace of pain, then a terrible coldness settled over his features, but he didn't move as she dodged around him and ran headlong down the driveway. At the first turn, she darted into the trees, trying to cut cross-country to the main road. Branches snatched at her hair and face, brambles ripped across her legs, and the darkness was overwhelming. She pushed her way through the undergrowth, trying at the same time to see through the deep shadows. She tripped over an exposed root and grabbed the trunk before she could fall. She stumbled around the tree trunk, and he was there.

She screamed in rage and fear, pushed off from the trunk

and ran again. Her eyes were adjusting to the darkness, and it was only a few steps until she found a path. It was easier running, but her breath was starting to come in gasps, and she bent almost double as pain stitched through her side.

The trail made a sharp turn around a thicket of brambles. She rounded the curve and he was ahead of her again.

"Nooooo!" She screamed in frustration and fear. Her fist lashed out and caught him in the chest before she whirled and ran again.

She forced her way through the bushes, barely feeling the lash of the thorns on her bare legs. The driveway was just ahead, but the relief of smooth footing was offset by the fear of his next appearance. Her feet pounded the blacktop until she could see the stone gate a hundred yards away. Headlights flashed across the massive stone pillars and she slowed as she clutched her side with one hand to try to stop the cramping pain. She limped forward, placing one foot carefully in front of the other. Her head was pounding so hard that she wondered if the bullet could possibly still be in there. She slowed even more, wishing that there was time to stop and think.

He stepped out of the darkness in front of her. The moonlight poured down on his fair hair and made a halo around his head. His torn shirt hung open to his waist. He must have picked up his cape before he left the house, because now it hung behind him, curling in the wind.

This was Simon. The man she thought she knew, the one who had saved her life, the one who had believed in her and taught her to use her mind in ways she had never dreamed possible. *The man she loved.*

But he was more than a man. It was as if she had seen him before through a fog, slightly blurred and diminished. Now her pain and fear sharpened her vision, and he stood forth proudly: stronger, wiser, and fearless for good reason.

"Are you ready to listen yet, Cassandra?"

"To more lies?" she asked painfully. She felt his power, but he didn't try to command her now. She walked on.

"I saved your life." The bitter pride in his voice made her pause. "I could have taken you anytime, but I didn't. And I didn't kill those people."

She nodded slowly, unwillingly, numbly. "I saw the one who did. He was a vampire. Like you. I saw him change into a bat. Can you do that?"

"Bat, and other things." His head tilted arrogantly. "I have spent lifetimes honing my abilities. Do you expect me to be ashamed of them?"

The wolf at the pool. She thought the words but didn't say them. That instant of total panic at a moment when she had been trusting her new talents would never be forgotten. "Why didn't you change tonight?"

He didn't answer.

"Why do you want me to stay?" she asked.

The clouds moved suddenly and his face was in shadow again.

She took a step away and hesitated. The night was so still that she could hear the oak leaves scudding across the pavement, and high above, magnolia leaves rattled together like dry sticks. A lone mockingbird sang once, a liquid trill of warning, then was silent. She looked back at him, knowing that if she left, she would never see him again. His eyes glittered in the night, and behind him, the cape flapped and swooped like the wings of a bat.

She set her face to the road, and took another step.

He was in front of her, pulling her to him and wrapping his arms around her. His head bent over hers, light hair protectively over dark. Her lips were pressed against his chest, and he smelled of the night and the coming storm. Her hands went under the shreds of his shirt and she could feel the hard muscles of his back.

When his head bent, she lifted her face to his. His kiss was featherlight, teasing her flesh, and every place he touched came alive. His lips caressed her forehead, lightly touched her eyelid, and moved to her cheek. She felt a slight sting, and remembered the glass splinter cutting her skin. She went cold as she realized that he was tasting the blood on her cheek. She twisted in his arms and her hand went to his face to push him away. There was a hard ridge under his flesh. She felt the point of a tooth against her skin, and she realized in horror that his canine teeth were growing,

362

long and sharp, stretching the flesh.

Her fist shoved against his chest, but he didn't seem to notice. She twisted her head wildly, fighting to get away from those warm, searching lips. She tore at his arms until her fingernails broke, but he held her head between his hands and bent again to kiss her. All her rage and fear exploded inside her.

"No. Let me go, Simon." She struck at him but he didn't flinch. He held her lightly until her struggles were exhausted and she stood frozen in his arms. Then he released her and stepped out of her path.

She backed away slowly, an animal at bay, watching for any sudden move. She had only taken a few steps when he spoke.

"What are you running from, Casey?" His voice seemed to blend with the soft sough of the wind.

"You," she said tersely, not pausing in her retreat.

"You have captured my heart. Why should you be afraid of me?" He sounded amused and incredulous.

"You're a vampire. You hypnotized me . . ."

His eyes lightened suddenly and one corner of his mouth twitched. "No, Casey. I did not use my power to influence you. If you have any feelings for me, they are from your heart."

She wanted to rage at him, to throw things and call him a liar, but she knew in her heart that he was telling her the truth. She turned her head away and started for the huge, stone gates.

"There's no reason to be afraid of me." He stepped in front of her.

"No reason?" She fought to keep from screaming as her fury erupted. "No reason? I woke up a week ago to a world of vampires and monsters. I have nightmares where I watch people die. I watched something that used to be human shed his skin like a snake, then kill five people, and I couldn't stop him because I wasn't really there. If I just point my finger at a piece of paper, it will burst into flames. My best friend is dead, and now she's trying to kill me. The thing that made her that way is trying to kill me. You're a vampire, too. For all I know, you're trying to kill me. What possible reason would I have to be afraid of you?" she finished sarcastically and turned her back on him. The massive gates were open ahead of her and it would be a clear run to the road. She had gotten her breath back, but she had no illusions about her chances of getting away if he decided to stop her.

"You don't believe that," he sounded bored and impatient with her fear.

She shook her head, knowing that she didn't, really. It would have been too easy for him to kill her. "Let me go, Simon," she asked quietly.

She waited, but there was no answer. She took another step toward freedom.

"Casey."

There was a pause. She looked back at him and hoped he couldn't see the tears in her eyes.

She set her face resolutely ahead, and took another step.

"I love you." His voice drifted to her on the wind, but he still didn't move.

The words stopped her. She reached inside for the anger that had sparked and sustained her before, but it was gone. She tried to take a step back to him, but something churned in her stomach.

"I can't, Simon. I'm afraid." She dragged the words out, unwilling to admit or explain, but driven to it.

"I'll protect you."

"And who'll protect me from you?" she asked bitterly. Her anguish forced the words out as she continued. "I'm afraid of losing me! I'm afraid that when you're finished with me, I won't be me anymore."

His sigh reached out and touched her. "I would not change you, Cassandra, no more than you have already been changed. What has been done cannot he undone."

"What has been done?" she repeated blankly. "What have you done to me?"

"You were dying."

"No!" She shook her head. Her lips felt numb.

"Yes. The bullet hit the bone and sent the splinters into your brain. You were dying." He leaned forward urgently. "I could not let that happen."

"What did you do to me?" she whispered. The numbness was spreading, making the soft night feel cold on her skin.

"I had no choice!" His voice wailed with the wind as he took a step toward her, reaching out to her, striving to make her understand. "You were dying! I watched the life running out of you. I held my blood to your lips and you clung to my wrist, fighting to live. I thought only that you would die and come back to me, but you lived! You have the blood of a Nosferatu in your veins, yet you live!"

"Nosferatu?" Even her brain was numb with shock.

"A vampire king or queen. When you die, now or a hundred years from now, you will become a vampire. My vampire-lover."

"Yours?" Something clicked into place.

"Mine forever." His voice was a soft caress. The clouds scudded aside and the moon touched her hair. He clenched his fists to keep from running to her, from sweeping her off her feet, from burying his face in her hair and covering her face with kisses.

"You mean I'll be your slave." She lifted her face and the cold light turned her features into a sculpture made of ice. It merely reflected the coldness in her voice.

He hesitated, unwilling to lie to her, but afraid of losing her if he told her the truth. "I would never force you."

"But that's it, isn't it? You wouldn't have to force me. I would literally die to please you. I can feel the longing even now. I trust you. I love you," she admitted in anguish. "But I won't be your slave, Simon."

"I do not want you to be! If that was what I wanted, I could have taken you any time. You would have adored me. You would have served me and loved me through the ages, until I grew tired of you and tossed you aside. Can't you see that I didn't want that?"

She waited silently, watching him, knowing that something was missing.

"There may be another way," he finally admitted. "My own brother made me as I am. He was my Bloodmaster, yet there were limits that even he could not force me to cross. You have that same strength. Even before you tasted my blood, you had the power to turn away from me. In hypnosis, you refused to obey me." He paused thoughtfully, and through the darkness his eyes locked with hers. "I want you with me, Cassandra, now and forever. As my companion, my lover, my friend and my wife, but not as my slave. If you stay with the living, your talents and will power may grow even stronger with time. Enough that when you die, you will come to me of your own free will to be my equal, and not my slave."

"How can I . . . ?"

"I do not know. If it comes at all, such power comes with pain, adversity and danger. Your life may yet have a purpose that neither of us has even suspected." He took another step toward her, hoping that she would meet him halfway, but it was as if she had taken root. He mentally opened himself up to her and said, "I will make a promise to you, beloved Cassandra. I vow that the time will not be my choice. It may be yours, or fate's, or God's, but I will not take your life unless you give it to me. Because I love you."

I'm going to become a vampire. Sooner or later. The thought was ridiculous and terrifying. Nothing that happens now can change that. Did he love her enough to let her live? Could she trust him with her life . . . and after?

She believed that he could have taken her at anytime. He could have killed her, made her his slave, but instead he had courted and protected her, taught her and loved her. Was he telling the truth now?

She moved her head slightly, and felt the tightness of the scar across the back of her head. He was right: what had been done could not be undone. He wasn't the one who had shot her and he hadn't given her this strange talent which made her feel so helpless. That talent should be able to give her the answer now, but she was reluctant to use it, to trust it. She stared at the open gates and tried to swallow, but her throat was too dry.

There was no alternative. She took a deep breath, relaxed as he had taught her to do, and opened her mind.

The woods shifted subtly from black to dark shades of green. The scent of pine and honeysuckle was intoxicating, and the buzz of insects was deafening. She could feel the pull of the big storm in the Gulf. She concentrated, and realized that the leading edge was only a few miles off shore. The Princess had changed course again, and was coming this way.

She tried to swallow, but her throat was dry as she turned to face Simon. His aura was the color of blood, and why had she always dismissed it as merely energetic? It reeked of power. It radiated from him, not threatening her, but controlled, contained by his will. The color was incredibly pure, unstreaked by greed or hate or envy. Nothing was false or hidden.

And there was love in his eyes.

She tried to speak, but her mouth was parched. Dust clogged her throat and she choked as she watched the light become smaller and smaller above her head. Darkness settled around her and held her motionless. The air was suffocatingly still as she wished longingly for water.

"Casey? Cassandra?"

Her eyes jerked back to his and she could breathe again. She gasped and clung to him tightly, feeling his arms lock securely around her. He wrapped his cloak comfortingly around her shoulders and waited until she relaxed against him. Then he tilted her face up and searched her eyes for an answer. What he saw made him smile, and her heart lifted. He kissed her hungrily, then gathered her into his arms and strode into the forest. The trees seemed to part before them. As they came to a clearing, he set her on her feet, then gently pulled her closer.

The scent of her hair was mixed with that of pine and sea breezes. Her lips were soft under his. Her arms went around him, under cape and torn shirt, and he could feel her hands moving on his back. He kissed her again, and could almost feel her pain as his tooth pricked the inside of her lips. Then her blood turned to champagne in his mouth.

His lips followed his hands as he moved the straps off her shoulders, and her dress slid to the ground. His kisses turned her flesh to fire as he undressed her, and her warmth drew him like a beacon. Even her fingers burned against his chest as she untied the laces that secured his cape. It whipped in the wind as he spread it over a soft blanket of pine straw.

Her hands moved down, across his chest, then back and up

367

along his spine. She kissed the line of his jaw to his ear. He didn't need to see the glint of mischief as she bit it gently. He held his breath as he wondered if she would taste his blood of her own will, but she didn't even attempt to break the skin. Her lips retreated to his cheek as his hand stroked the long line of her thigh.

He turned his head away as his eyes started to change, but her palm on his cheek forced him to face her. She watched as his eyes grew darker and wilder. When the time came, and his lips kissed her throat, she held him fiercely and called his name as his eyes glittered blackly above her.

"What's wrong?" Clarise asked impatiently as Eric moved to the doorway for the tenth time in the last thirty minutes.

"That's what I've been trying to figure out," he said cryptically. "It's like one of those brain teasers. 'What is wrong with this picture?' "

"What are you talking about?"

"Something was wrong with the picture when Casey left. I've been trying to figure it out. I think I'll call her." He picked up the receiver, then jiggled the cradle disgustedly. "It's out again. Damn!"

"It's not that big a deal, Eric. Simon will bring her home when they're through."

"But why should the phones be out again?"

"You may not have noticed, but that pounding on the roof is not a vampire. It's Princess Diana knocking. Those are feeder storms breaking off from the outer edge of the hurricane. It's hitting us now. If you hadn't been staring at the door for the last half hour, you'd know that."

"I heard it, Clarise, but there's something else wrong."

"The vampire? You think he's here?" She looked around uneasily.

"When Casey and Simon left—"

"The door blew open." She completed his thought. "You think something could have come in then?"

"No," Eric's first reaction gave way to doubt. "I don't think so. We were all standing here. We would have noticed even a mist. I think. Simon would have. He's supposed to be the expert."

"I don't know if he was paying attention. I was asking him about that burn on his arm, and he pulled the sleeve down. It really looked painful."

"It was in the shape of a cross," Eric said slowly. "Why would Simon have a cross burned into his arm?"

Clarise looked as if he was speaking a foreign language. "Cross?"

"It was just about the same size as the one Casey was carrying."

"But he's been . . . I mean, he and Casey . . . Eric, he can't be. We would know. I mean, I just looked at Bev and I knew she was . . . there was something wrong with her. But Simon looks perfectly normal."

"Have you ever seen him during the day?"

"Well, no, but Casey has."

"True . . . I'm wrong. I've got to be."

"And she said that he was in a dark room and the light bothered his eyes. He got real sleepy, and asked her to leave." Their eyes met with mixed dread, fear, and horror.

"We've got to get over there. Now." Clarise grabbed her purse and raincoat as Eric searched for the umbrellas.

"All those people. He killed Bev and all those poor people. Do you have the stakes?"

"Yeah, for all the good it will do us. You really think he'll stand there and let us drive a stake through his heart?"

"Maybe these crosses will keep him still." Clarise held up two large crosses. "We made all those plans and he sat there and agreed with us. You think he was after Casey the whole time?"

"He must have been. Look, if we can get her away from him with no trouble, we won't let him know we know. Then we can go over there tomorrow, after the storm passes, and blame his death on the hurricane."

"That's good!" Clarise declared. "If we can just get her away from him. Shouldn't we call Paul?"

"The phones are out, as you just reminded me. Besides, we'd have to wait for him to call back. Reese, why don't you stay here —"

"Not a chance! I'm not staying here alone. Let's go."

Water was running in small streams and rivulets across the driveway and the wind-driven pine needles tapped furiously on the roof of the van. There was an unearthly glow in the clouds above. As they turned onto the main road, the full fury of the wind hit them and the van rocked and shook.

"You sure you know how to get there?" Clarise asked nervously.

"Yeah, she was showing me a map today. Look, why don't we just honk the horn when we get there. Maybe she'll come out and we can take her home and explain. I think she's going to need a lot of convincing."

"It's worth a try. Careful!"

A tree branch whipped across the windshield. There was a sharp report, and the glass cracked. Reese flung her arm across her eyes as she cowered back against Eric, but the windshield didn't shatter.

"I've never seen it like this before." She hugged her arms to her shoulders and wished that she and her husband were safe at home.

"I can't believe it's this bad!" Eric yelled back. "And it's just starting. How long before the worst of it hits?"

"Hours! Five, ten? No one knows what it will do now. Look out!"

Casey lay silently, stretched out sensuously beside Simon. Her fingers played idly in the golden hair of his smooth, muscular chest. She realized suddenly that he was watching her, staring at her, devouring her with his eyes. She looked sideways at him from under half-closed lids, and finally asked the question that was on her mind.

"What's it like to be a vampire?"

"Hmmmm." He didn't take the question lightly, but his eyes left hers to follow the racing clouds. "It is wonderful. And terrible. There is great pleasure, and sometimes the pain is beyond bearing. The exhilaration of flying and the pure power of feeding is indescribable, but the loneliness . . ." He shook his head wordlessly.

"What about . . . I mean . . . Will I get hungry, uh, crave . . ."

"If you're asking, will you get the bloodthirst? You are not yet Nosferatu. For some reason known only to God, you did not die when you were shot. I am only thankful that when you do die, then you will rise again and we will walk the night, together."

She laid her head on his breast, watching him. "And we'll be together forever?"

"Forever?" His voice was hollow and his arm tightened possessively around her as lightning flashed and thunder cracked above them. "Centuries, at least. Someday we will both die the true death. You know the legends, don't you? After you become Nosferatu, you must avoid sunlight. For you, it would be a slow and painful death; for me, because I have been undead for hundreds of years, my body would return to the dust it should have become. Wooden and metal objects can pierce the flesh and still the heart or destroy the brain. Fire can destroy us completely. Moving water cannot be crossed without special protection, and even a hard rain can steal your strength. A vampire can drown in less than a foot of water. We become disoriented, and cannot find the strength or the willpower to stand up." He paused thoughtfully. "I will feel it when you are near death, and I will come. It will take years to train you to use the talents and powers that you will gain." A sly grin touched his lips. "It will be a great sacrifice, but as your Bloodmaster, it will be my responsibility to guide and teach you."

She cocked her head thoughtfully. "And my psychic talents? Are they because of your blood?"

"No. They are yours alone. We vampires gain some similar powers, telepathy which is particularly strong between Bloodmaster and . . ."

"Slave."

"Apprentice. We can call to those who can hear us and make them come to us, or obey our commands; we can learn to move objects and start small fires, and the oldest and most powerful can partially control the weather, or change our shapes, but all these skills are learned over many years, even

371

hundreds of years for some. I can only wonder what will happen to your own talents when you change."

"Maybe I'll lose them."

"It's possible, but equally as possible that they will be strengthened, and that new ones will develop."

"Like what?"

"Well, perhaps . . ." There was no warning. The sky opened above them and the rain came down in solid sheets. Simon grabbed Casey's hand and pulled her to her feet. They bundled the clothes onto the cape and sprinted, naked, for the house.

The van splashed safely through a flooded street and Eric grinned with satisfaction.

"That was stupid. You had no way of knowing how deep that was, or what was under it," Clarise snapped.

"Well, it worked," Eric said, still enjoying the small victory. Sheets of rain billowed in front of the vehicle. At times he could see as far as two hundred feet ahead of him; at others, he could barely make out the glow of the headlights. Twice, they pulled over to the shoulder of the road and sat silently while the deafening rain thundered inches above their heads. Lightning flared across the sky and rolls of thunder lasted for minutes instead of seconds. It was a nightmare ride, but forty minutes later, when Eric turned the van into Simon's driveway, the feeder storm was moving on. At the front door, he blew the horn and waited.

It was only a minute before the outside light came on. Casey looked annoyed as she came running out, using Simon's cape as a raincoat. It snapped like a flag as she ran to the van. Clarise had moved to the middle seat and Casey took her place in front.

"Are you alright?" Clarise asked desperately.

"Of course I'm alright. Why shouldn't I be?" Casey pulled nervously at the scarf around her throat.

"No reason," Eric asserted before Clarise could answer. "You just look a little pale." He turned right out of the driveway and concentrated on his driving.

"Oh well, I talked Simon into going for a walk in the storm."

"In this weather? Are you crazy? I thought you were supposed to be working," Eric snapped, peering through the windshield.

"We worked when we got back. I just needed some fresh air, and it wasn't raining when we went out. When it started, we had to run for the house." There was a glint in her eyes as she glanced back at Clarise for help, but her friend didn't notice. Reese was sitting ramrod straight, her fists clenched so hard that her knuckles were white. "Reese? Is anything wrong?" Casey asked hesitantly, trying to ignore her feeling of dread.

"We'll talk about it when we get home," Eric ordered.

"Why can't we talk about it now?"

"I'm rather busy, if you hadn't noticed," Eric said sarcastically. He fought the weather for five miles before Casey again interrupted his concentration.

"What's going on?" she asked, and twisted restlessly to look out the side mirror.

"Nothing," Clarise answered quickly. Much too quickly.

"Don't give me that. If this was some sort of plot to get me away from Simon, it really wasn't necessary."

"Yes, it was. I told you he gave me the shivers. Casey, he's a vampire!"

"Reese!" Eric burst out, but it was too late.

"Are you crazy? What makes you think that?" Casey shook her head, denying it even to herself.

"The cross burned a mark into his arm," Eric stated.

"And he never comes out during the day. And have you ever seen him in a mirror?"

"No," she admitted, "but . . ."

"He was the wolf at the pool. His hair was still wet when he came in," Eric interrupted as he and Clarise verbally stumbled over each other to convince her. Casey listened until the reasons had degenerated to stammered repetitions.

"He saved my life. I don't care what or who he is, he saved my life, and . . . I love him," she admitted.

"You knew!" Clarise gasped in outrage. "You're not even surprised!"

"He told me tonight."

373

The van swerved to miss a trash can rolling down the middle of the street, and Eric was slow to bring it back in line.

"It isn't what you're thinking," she begged them to understand. "He's incredible. He controls his hunger. He doesn't have to kill. He just takes what he needs and they recover in just a little while. He can even teach Bev, if we can reach her. He told me everything and he didn't kill anyone, I swear. There's another vampire out there, Simon's enemy. He's trying to find him, too."

"You believe he'd kill one of his own kind?" Eric asked derisively.

"It's true. He didn't ask to become a vampire any more than Bev did. You'd kill a human if he was after you and your friends. Simon is just like us, only . . ."

"Only he has a little eating disorder? Is that what you're trying to tell us?"

"Reese, please."

"Is this what he told you? And you believed him?"

"He's telling the truth. He doesn't kill people. He doesn't need to kill to live. The donor doesn't even remember it. And they don't become vampires unless he keeps going back to the same person and they die from it."

"Like Bev?" Clarise sounded as if she were going to cry.

"He didn't do that to Bev. He just drank once, then the killer chose her. Simon thinks he followed her from my house. If you want to blame someone, blame me. If she hadn't been my friend, he never would have noticed her."

"That's why he tried to get me," Clarise's voice shook. "Paul was right. You really were the link."

"You sure know a lot about it all of a sudden." Eric swerved the van into the long driveway and stopped abruptly, slapping the overhead light switch at the same time.

"He told me," she protested.

He reached across to Casey and pulled her head and neck into the light.

"Stop that!" She tried to push away from him, but he tightened his grip. Clarise tugged at his arm half-heartedly and added her protest.

374

"I want to see your neck." Eric jerked at the frail scarf and she struck at him suddenly.

"Get your hands off me! You have no right!" She pushed away violently and the frail lace came away in his hand. He grabbed her chin and forced her neck to the light. On a clear expanse of soft, white skin there were two punctures. A drop of blood slowly formed on one.

"Oh, Casey." Eric pulled her to him and hugged her tightly. Clarise wailed from the back seat as Casey shoved him away.

"C'mon, you two. Give me a break," she said loudly. Her hand went to her neck and Clarise took the scarf from Eric and gave it back to her. Then she helped her friend automatically, as if hiding something shameful. "Didn't you hear anything I said? It takes more than one bite to make a vampire, and I'm still obviously alive or I wouldn't be —"

"He's got you. You'd believe white was black if he told you to."

"He has no reason to lie to me. I love him."

"You're brainwashed!" Eric shouted at her. "The only way now is to kill him before he comes back for you like he did for Bev."

"No, that's not true."

A sudden gust of wind rocked the car, and a branch above them slapped the roof.

"The hurricane is almost here. We can discuss this calmly at home. At least the electricity is still on. You can see the lights from here," Casey stated easily, trying to smile. She could feel the unresolved tension as Eric started the car.

"He hypnotized you. You admitted that," Eric continued as he drove.

"Give it a rest. Hypnosis can't make you do anything you don't want to do. And Simon wouldn't force me to do anything I didn't want to do. He's a good man."

"Man? He's not a man. He's a monster. Remember? That's what you called him before he bit you." He parked the van in the drive. The house lights were blazing.

"I was wrong. At least about Simon." Casey opened her door and started to slide out. The wind caught the door and flung it open while Clarise and Eric struggled to open their

375

doors against the push.

Casey's scream rose above the roar of the wind while they were still in the van. Eric's door fought him like a live thing. He put his shoulder against it and shoved until a sudden lull made it easy. He rounded the front of the van just as Clarise slid the side door open.

Casey was slung face down over a man's shoulder. She beat savagely on his back, but he ignored her efforts. Eric saw her hands reach to her throat and yank at her necklace. She pulled the cross off and clutched it tightly in her fist. Her clenched hand beat at his back and every stroke struck sparks.

"No!" Casey screamed as she fought to twist her body upwards. Her left hand clawed its way to his shoulder as her right stabbed his back with the cross.

Sparks flew, and caught in her hair, but she ignored them. She jerked upward. Her hand gripped his hair, then she swung her fist at his neck.

The light burst from her hand. His body convulsed and an unearthly wailing roar filled the night as he screamed. He staggered, stumbled, and she jerked her body to the left, trying to throw him off balance. She hit the ground rolling as he tumbled forward. She scrambled to her feet and crouched as the wind and rain hit her back. Looking up, she met his eyes.

He towered over her, his eyes glowing black and his cape snapping in the wind. He reached down and his fingertips brushed her cheek, slowly and possessively. For the first time she saw him in all his glory and power. She recognized him not only from her dreams of the coffin and the murders, from his beckoning presence behind the rainwashed windshield of Paul's car, but from the portrait in Simon's house. Her scream rivaled the howl of the wind.

Then his mind hit hers like a hammer, crushing her thoughts and will. She stared upward into bottomless pits and felt herself falling into his eyes. He motioned gracefully and she rose, following his hand. A sharp gesture, and the cross fell from her hand. She straightened up obediently. Her mind fought desperately, but her body refused to obey.

"Run!" Eric yelled at Casey as he plunged to the attack. His first blow was a powerful sidekick, but Franz was not off balance now. He blocked it with one casual arm, but it distracted his attention from Casey. She scooped up the cross as Franz turned on her friend. His hand gripped Eric's throat like a vise and lifted him.

Slowly, his fingers tightened until Eric's eyes began to bulge. His feet scrabbled to get a firm purchase, then kicked wildly at the vampire's legs as he was lifted from the ground. His fingers tore desperately at the hands choking the life out of him. He saw Casey creeping silently up behind Franz and he tried to scream at her to run, but no air would come. His lungs were burning, and red spots swam in and out of his vision.

Casey stabbed the cross into Franz's back.

He roared as the light hit him. Eric's head jerked as he was flung against the porch ten feet away. Franz turned on Casey, his eyes blazing. His slap sent her reeling. The impact was still ringing in her ears as she hit the wall. Stunned, she slid to her knees and watched in horror as her friends attacked.

Clarise had paused to pick up a fallen branch. She ran straight at the black-robed back, holding it like a lance. The green pine tree limb hit; slid, stuck, and bent; then snapped uselessly.

With a roar of rage, Franz turned.

Eric was up and searching for a weapon. He wrenched at the front porch and found a loose dowel. In the bright lights from the house, he could clearly see the hell pits of Franz's eyes and his gleaming white fangs. Still stunned, Casey crawled forward.

Clarise cringed as Franz turned those burning eyes on her. She took one step, trying to get away, but he picked her up from the ground by the nape of her neck. She was lifted by her neck and one leg. She struck out with her hands and her other leg, fighting frantically as she was lifted high over his head. She connected once, twice, but the blows bounced off ineffectually. One last deep breath and her head was forced backward. She took a last long look at a sky that was lit from within by an angry yellow glow. Her head snapped forward, then back, as she was jerked down and broken across his knee. The scream she would have given was cut off before it started. He tossed her aside like an old rag.

Eric was almost fast enough. Franz turned to face him as he swung the stake. Eric's wrist was caught in a viselike grip and he heard the bones snap. He screamed more in rage than in pain as his hand was twisted sideways and his body followed. His feet tangled under him and as he fell he stumbled over Casey. They tumbled on the slick wet grass and his broken wrist hit the ground. The bone tore his flesh and he screamed again. Casey's face loomed over him, and over her shoulder two stygian eyes looked back at him.

He let go of his throbbing left arm and grabbed Casey by the collar of the black raincoat. He flipped her over his body, thrusting with his shoulder and hip to ensure that she missed his hurt arm.

"Run," he shouted hoarsely. He rolled unsteadily to his feet and crouched between Casey and the vampire. "Get inside."

Casey cast one despairing glance at him and dashed toward the veranda. Mentally, she screamed Simon's name again and again, but her lungs were too busy to waste air on useless noise.

Franz brushed through Eric as if he were a paper doll, and backhanded him almost absently as he went by. Eric's head and back exploded against a tree trunk and he slid to the ground helplessly. He could feel the rough pine bark against his wet flesh, and he strained groggily to move his hands, his feet, anything. One foot jerked in reflex and his head sagged backward.

Casey had only covered half the distance when her hair was grabbed from behind. She slid to a painful stop and swung at him futilely. He laughed as he picked her up and squeezed her against his chest, her arm pinned tightly. An arm circled her shoulders and one swept under her knees. Franz turned to look at the bodies, then strode over to Eric. He prodded him with his foot, then kicked him lightly.

"Stupid bastard!" he said contemptuously. He walked easily toward the car.

Casey pushed hopelessly against his chest. Franz smiled at her and his fangs glinted darkly.

Princess Di had changed her mind and turned northeast, directly toward Ft. Walton Beach. Her heart was a calm eye, still one hundred fifty miles south of land, but her seventy mile an hour forward winds were giving the coast a small taste of the punishment still to come. The wall of air around her eye, pulled by the low pressure, was spinning down and around at a constant speed of 120 mph, with gusts up to 140. It spun counterclockwise, driving the air and water north and west. Her tremendous suction swirled the water like a giant broom. As she approached the coast, the floor of the Gulf slanted sharply, giving the water nowhere to go but up. The tides surged to five feet above normal, then ten and more and soon the island of Santa Rosa, long since evacuated, would be under water.

Santa Rosa Sound roared its fury as it swelled. It invaded the bayous and inlets, pushed upward through the rivers and creeks, and flooded the area in between. Torrential rain made breathing difficult for anything without gills, and added inches to the flood every hour. The rain moved inland in solid sheets, driven parallel to the earth by the force of the wind.

Oak and magnolia trees groaned under the beating, while pine trees bent and swayed. The roots of the smaller trees rocked back and forth underground, loosening their hold on mother earth. Pecan trees had already been stripped of their leaves, and soon any branch that would not bend, would be broken.

Tornadoes spun off to the north and east, adding to the destruction. One danced through a mile long brick wall, leaving twenty feet of untouched bricks, then twenty feet of empty space. It ran for half a mile, dodged to one side, and sucked up a car and half a house. It ripped them apart as it sent them spiralling upward. The vacuum cleaner funnel left the ground, jumped five miles, and found a supermarket. It playfully removed everything but the front wall and the sign. Before it died, the tornado destroyed two supermarkets, five cars, and a trailer park. During the next twelve hours, Princess Di would spawn more than fifty tornadoes.

Chapter Nineteen

The rain pounded Eric's face, washing the blood from the cut on his jaw. His eyes opened to a watery world and he tried to remember why he was outside in such a storm.

A lightning flash brought a memory of Clarise, outlined against the clouds as the vampire held her high. A sense of urgency grew in him as memories flooded back. The sight of her body, broken over Franz's knee, stirred him to action. His muscles tensed as he tried to get up. He changed his mind abruptly as spasms of pain started in his left wrist, moved up his arm, and stabbed into his side and back. The cramps pounded through his body as he gasped for breath. He lay very, very still until the gripping agony eased. His left hand throbbed to the beat of his heart.

He lay until the rain on his face made breathing difficult, then he tried to brush it away. His right hand came up easily and landed on his sore side. He grunted with the impact, but the spasms had relaxed so he tried again to turn over. The pain was immediate and intense. It started in his wrist, shot up like a streak of liquid flame, hit his shoulder and radiated through his chest. He gasped for breath, then slowly brought himself under control.

He forced his right hand up, across his body, and lifted his shoulder to turn left instead of right. He kept his left hand motionless, walking the fingers of his right to his left wrist and cradling it carefully. He could feel the muscles tremble, and only thoughts of Casey and Clarise kept him going. He moved slower, trying consciously to relax the muscles. He lifted his wrist gently. It moved as a unit and the pain was bearable as he cradled it on his chest.

He turned on his side and lurched up onto his elbow, then let out a sharp yelp as the pain hit. Gathering all his courage, he surged to his feet with what should have been a swift, smooth motion, but instead he screamed as he staggered like a drunken sailor in a high sea. He made it to Clarise's side by taking tiny little steps that tended to wander with every push of the wind. He released his arm long enough to feel the pulse in her throat. He called to her, but there was no reaction. When she didn't respond, he slid his raincoat off one arm and gingerly pulled it off the other, then he tucked it gently around her sodden form.

He staggered to his feet again, fighting the rain and wind to reach the porch. From there it was almost easy. With each movement, his muscles loosened and his brain cleared. He turned the doorknob and the wind opened the door for him. The phone was on a table in the living room and he lifted the receiver with an irrational moment of hope. Everything would be alright now. Modern technology would take care of everything. He would call Paul and Paul would get them an ambulance. The police would rescue Casey and Clarise would go to the hospital and she would be fine. Casey would come back and the doctors would fix his arm or cut it off or something to make it stop hurting. Anything to make it stop hurting.

There was no dial tone. He hugged his arm and looked around the room vaguely. There must be something he could do to help Clarise. His eye lit on the long oak coffee table. He had to get her out of the weather without hurting her more. Maybe he should drive to the hospital and send back help. He sighed regretfully as he realized that he couldn't leave her. He grabbed the coffee table and kicked the fragile wooden legs until they broke off. The top was awkward, but he dragged it out the front door. The wind caught it as he stepped outside and it banged painfully against his hurt arm. He laid it down next to her, then went back for strips of cloth to tie her on to it.

Tearing up a sheet was more than he could do one-handed, so he grabbed a knife from the kitchen. He was still sawing strenuously at the cloth when the headlights came over the hill.

Paul. He almost sobbed with relief. Paul would take care of everything. He sat down weakly next to the inert body and tried to shield her from the rain. He couldn't hear the sound of footsteps over the noise of the storm, but the hand that touched his shoulder was no surprise.

"I'm sorry," he gasped out. "The vampire, we tried to fight him off, but he got Casey and he hurt Clarise bad. We've got to get her to the hospital. I think it's her back. I—"

"Where's Casey?"

The knife seemed to leap into Eric's hand as he whirled to face Simon. "What are you doing here?" He held the knife at the ready, but Simon ignored it.

"I thought I heard Casey scream, then there was nothing. When did he take her? Where?" he demanded.

"We've got to get Clarise to the hospital. I think he broke her back. Help me get her on the board."

"Never mind that. Where is Casey? She told me that she showed you a map this afternoon. Where is it?"

"Map? Why? The phones are out and we—"

"She took a wrong turn. She said she showed you on the map. I think his hideout is there. He may have taken her there. Where is it?"

Eric's fogged brain began to clear. "Yeah. I know where the map is, but it can wait until we help Clarise. Put her on the stretcher. We can take my van and lay her flat in the back."

Simon's hand batted the knife aside as he grabbed the front of Eric's shirt and jerked him to his feet. His eyes glinted darkly as he whispered, "Where is she?"

"He took her," Eric answered dully. The pain in his dangling arm receded as he stared into Simon's eyes.

"How?"

"He was waiting for us. We tried to stop him, but . . . Clarise. He hurt Clarise." Eric tried to force his gaze to look at her, but his eyes would not obey. His right hand twitched with urgency.

382

"How did he take her? Did he carry her away? Did he drive?"

"He took Casey's car. Clarise . . ." He clenched his right fist, then tried to do the same with his left. The pain made him break into a cold sweat, but it helped his concentration. "We have to get her to the hospital."

Simon's eyes flashed and he winced from their glow. "Where is the map?"

"In the house. I—"

"Get it." Simon shoved him away. "I will phone for an ambulance from my car."

"Call the cops, too. Tell Paul to meet us at the hospital."

As Eric stumbled toward the house, Simon bent over Clarise. Her breathing was slow and labored, but her pulse was steady. He ripped the sodden sheet into strips and laid them crosswise under the board. She moaned faintly as he shifted her, but she didn't awaken. He tied the strips across her shoulders, waist, and hips, careful to keep her body straight. Then he went to the car to phone and to transfer some supplies to the van.

Eric opened the front door and hesitated. Where was the map? He remembered Casey tracing the route as they sat at a table, but had they been in the kitchen or the living room? Kitchen, he decided, and strode down the hall. He could not leave Clarise alone with that monster for long, and he had a lot to do in a very short time. While his mind was clear, he had to find protection before he faced him again.

He was right. The map was on the table in the kitchen. He stared at it for a moment, then picked up the pen next to it. He added two new routes, one east and one west, then folded it and slipped it into his jacket. He opened the refrigerator, grabbed two bulbs of garlic and put them in his pocket. He saw the wooden table legs from the hall doorway. One had splintered to a sharp point. He tucked it under his coat, then spotted the large cross above the doorway and added it to his collection. Simon was going to help Clarise whether he wanted to or not.

He burst out of the house in a fury, holding the cross in

front of him like a shield. Simon was bending over Clarise. Eric kept the cross in his hand as he jerked Simon around.

"Listen to me, you bloodsucking leech!" He thrust the cross in Simon's face and tried to avoid his eyes. "We're taking her to the hospital right now!"

Simon smiled contemptuously as he slowly reached out to grasp the cross. It burst into flames with such force that burning splinters peppered Eric's face and clothes. He snatched his hand back to brush away the sparks. His mouth dropped open and his eyes widened as he gaped at the flaming wood, still hanging motionless in midair.

Simon was still smiling as he gestured negligently at the burning cross. It flew through the air for a dozen feet before it hit the ground and sputtered in the wet grass.

"Religious symbols have only the power you give them, and your faith isn't strong enough, Eric," he explained almost kindly. "Do you have the map?"

Eric nodded numbly. Simon's eyes returned to normal and Eric faced him squarely, almost beyond fear now.

"Good. Can you drive?"

Eric started to nod, then changed his mind. "In this weather, I don't think I can handle the van alone . . ." His explanation trailed off as Simon's eyes narrowed suspiciously. At last the vampire nodded, then bent over Clarise and picked up the board, careful to keep it level.

"The ambulance would be delayed because of the storm and the number of emergency calls. So I told them we would bring her in, and left word for Paul to meet us at the hospital. Open the door."

Eric slid the side door of the van open and slapped the seats down to make a flat platform. They maneuvered her in and Eric stayed in the back to brace her.

The ride was a nightmare. Clarise moaned as the van rocked and swayed in the wind. Potholes, limbs, and debris were hidden by the running water, and speed was cut in half by the pouring rain. The radio announced evacuation procedures and shelter locations in between warnings to stay off the roads. Highway 98 was almost impassable. Eric yelled directions to get them away from the coast. When he looked out the passenger window, he could see the Santa Rosa Sound licking hungrily at houses that had been a hundred yards from the shore. Salt spray filmed the windshield and sand peppered the side of the car. Simon turned north on a side road to get a line of trees between them and the water. He could feel the tension grow as what was normally a fifteen minute drive dragged into half an hour and more as they had to reverse direction to avoid a power line that sputtered across the road.

The emergency lane at Seaside Hospital was the only clear area for several blocks. Cars filled the parking lot and overflowed into the streets as people streamed to the shelter. Simon threaded the van carefully to the emergency entrance. Paul and an orderly were waiting to help, but Simon carefully lifted the board out by himself.

"What happened? How is she?"

"Alive," Simon said briefly as the orderly wheeled the stretcher into the hospital. Paul went in with the stretcher, but when Eric took a step forward, Simon stopped him. "Give me the map."

"You won't need it. I'm going with you." Eric avoided looking into his eyes. His right arm cradled his aching left arm as he wondered if they had time for him to get a painkiller.

"Give me the map," Simon snarled. His fist closed on Eric's shirt and pushed him back against a wall. "I've lost enough time because of you."

Eric pulled the map from his pocket and silently handed it to Simon, then watched him unfold it.

"Which one is it?"

Eric shook his head. The hospital guard was watching them closely, and he began to move in their direction.

"That was a stupid thing to do! You will tell me which one is right! Where is she?" His eyes were black with rage, but Eric stared solidly at the approaching guard.

"It'll take ten minutes to put a temporary splint on this arm. You'd waste more time than that trying to find the best route. I'll check with Paul to find out which roads are still open. And unless you let me go right now, you're going to have to kill me,

385

that guard, and the security force he's already called. And you still won't know which route is real."

Simon ground his teeth impotently as he gave Eric a final shove into the wall. There were enough doctors on call for the emergency that Eric only missed his deadline by three minutes.

Chapter Twenty

Casey stopped fighting as Franz carried her to the car. He set her limp body on the passenger seat and she stared straight ahead, afraid to look at him. He ran his fingers through her tangled hair and she bent her head to keep from showing her revulsion. There was a tickling feeling, deep in her head, like an itch that couldn't be scratched. As it increased to a painful whine, she realized with horror that Franz was probing her mind. She let her defeat overwhelm her.

Satisfied, he patted her cheek once, closed the door, and circled the car to get to the driver's seat. She waited until he was on the other side of the car, then she flung the door open and bolted for the house. She took three quick strides, and he was ahead of her. She swerved, but one long arm reached out and he pulled her to him. Her fingers hooked into claws and she went for his eyes.

"No," he said quietly, and her hand stopped in midair. "Come with me."

Once again, she obeyed. He buckled her into the seat belt, then crushed the lock.

"I wouldn't want you to fall out." He smiled at her, tugged once more at the belt, then strolled slowly around the car. When his attention left her, she could move again, but it was too late. She stopped fighting as he climbed behind the wheel and reached for the keys. The ignition was empty. He looked at her and she shook her head wearily.

"I don't have them."

"No matter." His fingers snapped an inch away from the metal, and the engine roared to life. He backed the car easily and headed up the drive. Casey turned in the confining belt and gazed back at Clarise and Eric, searching for any sign of life. There was none.

She straightened in the seat and rubbed her face gently, smearing the blood and tears. Her cheek was sore and red, and his ring had torn a long gouge under her eye. She shifted carefully, testing her arms, legs, and neck. There were some sore spots, and her left side felt as if a train had hit it, but everything still worked. Unfortunately, the same could not be said of the seat belt release.

She stared out the window, fighting to get her emotions under control. When she remembered the white light that Simon had taught her to visualize, it seemed natural to use it for protection. She concentrated until she could almost see the radiant white light as a column in front of her, stretching upward to infinity. Then she stepped into it. It was a shock to her system, restoring and invigorating her. When she felt his hand touch her shoulder it was such an evil contrast that she shuddered uncontrollably. He seemed to enjoy that. As he forced her to face him, she tried hard to look at his lips and not his eyes.

"You'd better be worth this." His grip tightened slightly, just enough to remind her of his strength. "Are you?"

She shook her head, confused.

"Are you worth the trouble of taking you from Simon? Or should I simply twist your pretty neck and dump you on his doorstep!" His head lifted imperiously, and she felt a shock of recognition. She had seen an identical gesture before, but whose and where? "What can you do? Why should I keep you alive? What power do you have over him?"

She stared out the windshield blindly. What did he want from her? What could she tell him to keep him from killing her without helping him to hurt Simon? His hand crept slowly up her shoulder and she felt his cold fingers brush the nape of her neck. Her whole body shuddered

388

in revulsion. Her mind leaped at survival.

"I can see things sometimes."

He considered it calmly, as if weighing it against the inconvenience of her life. She glanced at his profile and his face was as blank as if he were playing poker. She decided to up the ante.

"You're a vampire," she whispered.

"No shit, Sherlock." His laughter roared through the car. Too loud and much too long, it had more than a hint of madness in it. "But vampire is such a small word for what I am. I am Nosferatu—the Undead. I am the Bloodmaster! I make vampires as slaves. I will be the ruler of all this rich, new country. I will take it away from him and leave him nothing!" Casey cringed against the far door, her fingers scrabbling at the seat belt.

"Stop squirming!" he ordered, irritated. "What else do you know?"

She choked out the words. "You arrived here more than a week ago. You floated to shore in a coffin or a crate. That young airman found you and you—"

"I sucked out every drop of his strong, sweet blood." His blue eyes flashed red as he glanced at her. "The crate," he mused softly.

She could feel the madness building in him. The hand on her neck tightened until a low moan was forced from her. He glanced over in surprise, then brutally squeezed again. His fingers released their grip and moved to caress her hair.

"You're like them. Scared, but still trying to act brave. Brave!" His fist clenched in her hair. "They were so brave that they couldn't even open the crate to look me in the eyes. They put a lock on it and then tossed me overboard to drift and starve. They hoped the crate would break open and the sea would do their dirty work for them. But I didn't drown. Cowardly fools."

"Three months ago," her whisper was in awe of a creature that could survive that horror. "A storm drove you back out before you could get help. It was the day I was shot."

389

"Simon was interested in you. Too interested to listen to my call. He ignored me. My own brother would have let me drown. I pleaded with him. I begged him to save me."

"Your brother." Her chest was so tight she could hardly breathe. She tried to break through the growing rage and insanity, but he was beyond reason. "He couldn't hear you. He knew it was a vampire, but he couldn't find you and —"

"He wouldn't listen! I made him! I gave him immortality. I took care of him for all those years when his squeamishness would have left us both hungry. I taught him to use his power and he would have let me die. But that wasn't enough for him. He started plotting against me. You think I didn't know? I heard him . . . and you!" He turned on her savagely, ignoring the erratic movements of the car. His open-handed slap sent her head against the window.

"He didn't know it was you. He thinks you're dead," she screamed the words as her fingernails scratched at his eyes. He laughed at her efforts as he brought the car back into line. She huddled against the door as he continued.

"He's a traitor to his own kind. He is using you. What did he tell you? That he loves you? That you'll have eternal life? That he'll love you forever if you just help him kill his crazy, worthless brother?"

"He doesn't know it's you," she said softly, then turned her head. His words were too close to the truth. She stared out the window as she tried to divert him. "We're going to the icehouse, aren't we?"

"You know about that? Have you told Simon? Does he know?"

She stared at the darkness in his eyes and didn't answer. His fist lifted from the steering wheel and his lips snarled. She waited until he was ready to strike before she answered, "I didn't tell him." His fist hit her shoulder with less force than she had expected.

"No, of course you didn't," he agreed easily. "If you had, he would have attacked by now. My brother is many things, but never a coward. Do you know what he plans to do? Has

390

he confided in you, his beloved?" he asked mockingly.

Carefully now, she cautioned herself. If I know nothing, I'm worthless. If I know too much, I'll be forced to tell too much. Is it better for him to be afraid of immediate attack, or to be too complacent? Complacent, she decided.

"He doesn't believe you can move around in this storm. He'll wait till it's over to look for you."

"Is that a prediction?"

She heard the suspicion in his voice, but there was more: a willingness to believe. "Yes," she lied easily.

"Good. That will give me time to deal with you."

Oh, God, she thought, more in prayer than blasphemy. I just outsmarted myself. Any contradiction now would make everything she said suspect.

"What . . ." Her voice faded and she tried again. "What are you going to do with me?"

He didn't bother to answer as he turned the car off the main road onto the deserted lane to the icehouse. The narrow ruts were filled with water and the grass on either side had turned to marsh. The concrete bridge made a hollow rumbling sound under the tires. He drove across the rutted parking lot to stop next to the loading dock. Walking around the car, he courteously opened her door. "Get out."

"I can't." She tugged at the seat belt helplessly.

He leaned down and yanked at the metal buckle. It gave an agonized screech and snapped apart. He herded her into the icehouse, then paused to let her look around.

There wasn't much to see. An empty, rectangular room with concrete floors and brick walls. Rows of concrete pillars sectioned the room into thirds. Twelve coffins filled the center space and the ornate thirteenth was set back on the raised platform. An old, warped wooden table had been pushed to the back. Candles lit the area and threw strange shadows on the cobwebbed walls.

A child sat and drummed her heels irreverently on one of the coffins.

"Is she for us?" Janie asked alertly. She hopped off the box

391

and Casey noticed that she had a baby tucked casually under her arm, like a rag doll.

"Janie?" Casey almost didn't recognize this alert, healthy looking child as the withdrawn, sickly youngster who refused to speak.

"Sure it's me, Miz Casey. Davey and me sure are glad you're here." Janie smiled up at her and took her hand. Casey smiled back into those huge brown eyes. She was aware of mental pressure, but she had no trouble keeping it behind the wall.

"Oh, Janie." She wanted to tell her how sorry she was, how responsible she felt, and how much she wished she could change the past, but no words came. The child seemed to understand.

"Don't you fret, Miz Casey. Davey an' me, we're a lot happier here than we ever were at home. Leastwise, if he hits us, it don't hurt like it used to when Daddy did it. 'Cept he can do other things, things to your head, that hurt even worse. Hey," the child's face brightened. "You were right about Daddy not being a vampire. But I fixed that. An' after Davey an' me killed Daddy, Master Franz, he said we belong to him now." She leaned forward and whispered confidentially. "He's not very nice, you know."

Franz stepped behind the children and jerked Janie around to face him. His slap lifted her feet from the floor and sent both child and babe hurtling against the wall. They hit with a thump, but made no other sound as they slid to the floor. Casey jumped in front of Franz to try to stop him, but Janie stood up immediately and walked over to pick up the baby.

"We're hungry," she whined. Franz raised his arm and took a threatening stride toward her.

Thought had nothing to do with Casey's reaction. A monster was threatening a child. No matter that the child was also a vampire, he had to be stopped. She stepped in front of him and grabbed his arm with both hands. Her scream was involuntary. "No! Don't!"

392

He flipped her aside casually, then turned to face her. "You have a lot to learn."

He walked to the children and swept his cape around them, then turned dramatically as if posing for a portrait. They would have made a striking one. His thick dark hair was swept back from a high forehead. His dark blue eyes, proud like Simon's yet so different in shade and expression, silently caressed her. His lips were finely molded and sensuous. His face was almost triangular, with high cheekbones and a narrow chin. His snowy white shirt emphasized his broad shoulders and slim waist. Black slacks clung to his long legs. His strong arms sheltered the children like a bird of prey with its young.

She felt a sudden longing to go to him, to surrender herself completely.

He smiled at her knowingly and broke the spell. Janie tugged at his cloak and he bent down to listen to her whisper. He nodded agreeably, then straightened up and looked toward the deeper shadows along the wall. "Don't be rude, my pet. Greet your old friend."

Casey turned with a start as one shadow detached itself from the wall and moved slowly into the light.

"Bev?" she whispered.

"Hi, Casey. I thought you'd join us. Why didn't you just come with me when I came to get you? I was awfully hungry that night." She looked almost normal. There was perhaps an extra grace that quickened her movements and an almost translucent quality to her dark skin. Franz's hand stroked Beverly's hair but his eyes never left Casey's. "I'm hungry now, too."

"Did you bring her for us?" A short, dark-haired man stepped forward. His tongue slipped slyly out and licked his lips.

"Bev, you can fight this. You don't have to give in to the hunger. Simon can—"

"Shut up!" Franz screamed at her. "Simon can do nothing! I am Master here. You will do as I say. Simon is nothing."

393

She flinched from his upraised hand, anticipating the blow, but her fear was enough to satisfy him for the moment. The others came closer, waiting, and Casey backed up nervously. Jerry Wiltz had moved to a position behind Casey. Suddenly, he grabbed her shoulders and snatched her back against his chest. She screamed as his fangs touched her throat, but they never had a chance to pierce her tender flesh. Franz quickly tore him off her and slapped him, open-handed. The percussion rang through the icehouse like a clap of thunder, followed by a rumble of noise as Jerry hit the wall, twenty feet away.

"Take the children out and check the area," he snapped at Jerry. "All of you, get out! Check and see what damage the storm is doing. I will deal with her." Franz smiled at her look of horror. His expression gave her the strength to control it, but she couldn't stop herself from appealing to her friend.

"Bev? Please?" Her eyes made an eloquent plea, but all Bev did was give her a sympathetic glance as she turned obediently and walked to the door with the children. The candles flickered and danced as the door opened ahead of them. Just as they passed beyond the light, Janie reached up trustingly to take hold of Bev's hand.

Casey watched, disbelieving, as vampires seemed to appear out of nowhere to follow Bev and the children. She counted ten before Jerry Wiltz sauntered casually toward the door. He turned at the last minute, ducked his head slyly to look back at her. "I got somethin' special planned for you."

He grinned, showing long, ivory fangs. Casey's head suddenly felt very light and airy. The room swayed, then steadied.

"Ha, ha, ha," Jerry laughed. "I thought you'd like that." He waved insolently as he left the room. Casey watched the door lock itself behind them and knew that only a vampire could open it again. She fought back her fear and her certainty of defeat as she sauntered casually past Franz to the other side of the largest coffin. She sat down gracefully, ignoring the chill that coursed through her.

"Well?" She forced an unconcerned smile.

"I can see why Simon saved you, my child." He seemed genuinely amused by her bravado. "He did save you, didn't he? What did he do to my little tool?" He glided silently across the floor to stand in front of her.

"He broke his neck, or so I was told. I'm sorry I wasn't awake to see it. In fact, I had quite a long nap after that. I have you to thank for waking me up, I think."

"It was a pleasure." His hand touched her cheek gently, trailed lightly down her neck, and stroked her shoulder. She closed her eyes to hide her loathing and felt his lips on her cheek.

She swung her legs to the top of the coffin and leaned away from him. "I must say, at least your looks have improved since that night." Her tone was cool and distant.

"You saw me?" His hand stopped in midair as he reached for her.

"I watched the whole thing. His name was Mike Boyd, if you care to know."

"Why should I want to know?" he asked, amused.

"He was in the shop that day. He was a nice guy who loved to read, but he had to sell his books because he needed the money. I watched you kill him."

He was fascinated. "And the family? You were there?"

Casey nodded. His fingers played in her hair.

"And later?"

"You chased Janie through the woods."

"But later, when I tracked Simon to your house, you didn't know I was there." His fingers traced the line of her jaw, then tilted her face to his. After the casual brutality she had seen, his tenderness surprised her. His lips were firm and cool on hers. When she thought it was safe, her hands flattened on his chest and she pushed him away.

"It seems your talents have limits, my dear."

"They're getting stronger every day. Simon said—"

"I don't like to hear his name on your lips." The whites of his eyes turned dark gray and Casey shivered.

395

"He'll come after you, you know." She swung her legs to the floor on the other side of the coffin and slid off the box.

"Your powers are getting stronger and he'll come after me." He smiled as he captured her wrist and kissed her hand. "Are you trying to scare me? You really think that you and my little brother can stand against me?" His voice rose and she could smell his madness in the air.

Brothers! Every time she thought about it, she wanted to scream, so she didn't dare think about it. She didn't dare look away from him either, as she backed up. He followed her, step by step.

"You said that I might be useful to you. Si . . . he said that if I became a vampire I would probably lose my powers." She talked as he came around the end of the coffin after her. It was like watching a hooded cobra: something so incredibly dangerous that its beauty fascinated and mesmerized the eyes.

Her words made him pause, and she stepped to the table. Her eyes searched the darkness for a weapon.

"I wouldn't dream of arguing with him. Or of changing you too fast. Tonight will just be a taste of what is to come." He turned his back to her and laid his hand on the coffin nearest to his own. "Your ultimate ecstasy will be when you taste my blood. That night you will die and I will lay you to rest in this sweet bed. The next day at sunset, you will rise, and your whole heart and being will belong to me. Once my blood is in you, you will become Nosferatu. And you will be mine. Forever."

She moved backwards along the wall but he blocked her with one long arm. Her hand scrabbled frantically behind her. She felt cold metal, then hot wax dripped on her hand. A candle in a short, heavy holder. She had a momentary image of herself cleverly setting fire to his cape. It made her smile quite genuinely as he reached for her.

"But I'm still weak from the coma." Her eyes met his. She had no need to try to look frail and wan. The dark smudges under her eyes and the tremor in her hands were proof enough. "If you take my blood now, I won't live through it." Her arms came up to hold him as he kissed her. The candlestick was heavy in her hand.

"Simon said?" he asked, amused. His hands rested on her waist.

"I say," she replied easily.

"You're giving me orders now?" His voice was gentle, but one hand slipped casually up to her throat.

"I didn't . . . I mean, I was just explaining the situation to you. I'm no good to you dead and . . ." She broke off at his full-throated laugh.

"But you are, my dear. You don't think I believed those stupid lies about you losing your powers when you change? They will increase, especially under my guidance. You will enjoy my guidance. And once you taste my blood, you will feel strong and healthy again. It is the one sure way to make a vampire Nosferatu: strong, intelligent, and obedient. Unless, of course, you have already tasted his blood. Have you, my dear?" He slipped one finger under the fragile lace around her throat and pulled it slowly down. His lips trailed lightly from her temple to her ear, while she stood, frozen. When his head bent to her throat, she struck.

She slammed the heavy candleholder into the side of his head and shoved with all her strength. It was enough to knock him off balance, and she raced to the door.

She didn't even see him move, but suddenly he was at the door, waiting for her with open arms and open mouth. She screamed and swerved, her eyes desperately searching for another way out. She took only two steps before he was in front of her again. She turned, fled, and felt a long, slow stroke on her back. She whirled, but there was no sign of him.

The door swung open. She knew it was a trap, but it was still her only hope. She caught a brief glimpse of him as she felt his lips on hers, but his speed was incredible. She kept going. Halfway there, she jerked sideways as she felt him caress her breast. Her arms hugged protectively around her

397

body as she stumbled blindly toward the door. He boxed her in slowly, toying with her like a cat with a mouse. Finally, when she was only a few feet from freedom, Jerry Wiltz stepped through the door, grinning at her. Her legs were too weak to hold her. She sank to her knees, defeated.

"Simon. Oh God, Simon! Why aren't you here?" She cried.

"Don't use that name in my presence!" Franz screamed. He towered over her as he shoved her brutally. Her head rang as it hit the floor and she lay still, dazed. His eyes glared hot fire as he put his foot on her throat and pushed until she choked. "Do you understand? Or I will give you to him." His head jerked toward Jerry near the door, who grinned with anticipation. "After I have finished with you, would you enjoy being his slave?"

Her hands futilely gripped his heel and toe as she tried to shake her head. Anything. She would do anything to keep him from losing his temper again. He read the surrender in her mind and eased the pressure. She tried to scrabble sideways to get away from him, but Franz stepped down hard on her throat. She choked and turned her head as he laughed, enjoying his power.

Casey broke.

"Why are you doing this to me?" she screamed. Her hands tore at his legs. "What do you want from me? What did I do to you?"

He took his foot off her throat and jerked her up to dangle from his hand. His eyes glared into hers and his insanity terrified her.

"You took him away from me," he whispered. "When I needed him, his mind was filled with you." His voice gradually grew louder. He opened his hand unexpectedly and she dropped to her feet. Her head bowed and she stared meekly at the floor until he turned away from her and began to pace.

Oblivious to her, Franz strode up and down the icehouse as he screamed insanely. The candles flared like torches with

398

his anger, casting strange shadows on his face.

"You stupid bitch! I called to him but he could only hear you! Your mind! Your thoughts! I was his Bloodmaster. I made him what he is. I gave him the power, eternal life, and youth. I gave him everything! But when I needed him, you were there." He was raving. She could see the madness in him. His aura was a twisted mass of colors: the red of anger twined with black from his heart. Yellow-green envy sprayed from his mouth, and curls of orange flared from his body like flames. She squeezed her eyes shut, but the insane words went on and on. "I *needed* him! But I was only a blank in his mind. He wouldn't hear me. I drifted for three months in that cursed sea because of you and him." He abruptly stopped pacing and strode over to her. "I gave him everything. I shared my blood with him and he turned his back on me because of you! I spent three months in hell, and you *will* pay."

He returned to grab her by the front of her blouse. He shook her until her head was flung back and his eyes glared into hers. They were twin wells of black hate and red rage and she felt herself falling into them. His mouth stretched open and his fangs hovered over her neck. She wanted to plead with him, to beg for her life and her soul, but she never had a chance.

He struck suddenly like a snake. His fangs sank deeply into her throat and she screamed horribly. Her flesh blistered and tore. The terrible suction seemed to pull bits of her soul from her body. Her body writhed in his grasp.

His head jerked back and she felt his fangs slide out of her neck, like a clumsy doctor withdrawing a needle. She caught a glimpse of his lips, blistered and peeling before he flung her away. He seemed as startled as she was.

"His blood is in you," he said thoughtfully, wiping the dead skin from his lips to reveal firm new flesh.

"Yes!" She flung the word at him as if it were a weapon, and he hit her so hard that she stumbled onto the platform and slammed against his coffin.

"Stupid slut! You think that will stop me? Your blood almost boiled when I tasted it, which only means that your pain will be much greater. You belong to him, but he didn't finish the job. Why didn't he kill you?"

"I don't know. I didn't know he . . ." Her words trailed off as she remembered. "He tried to save my life the only way he knew. Instead, he made me into something like you." Her stomach turned in revulsion, but her emotions were wrung dry.

"What are you talking about? You are not Nosferatu yet." He grabbed the neck of her blouse in his clenched fist, but she hardly noticed.

"You sent Billy to kill me. You thought if I was dead, Simon would hear you. But he wouldn't. He couldn't. He can't hear you and you can't control him. What happened? How did he escape you for so long?"

"He didn't escape! I endured his cowardly ways for hundreds of years until I could no longer tolerate them or him. During the last great war, we were in Berlin, and the house was bombed and burned. I let him think that I was dead and I left without him. I was glad to get rid of the weakling. It's only been fifty years. He could not have grown so fast."

"But he did. And he's not a coward. He's outgrown you now." She reached desperately for something that would help her. "And if you touch me, he'll kill you."

He threw his head back and howled with laughter until the icehouse rang with insane echoes. "Then I can use you against him!" he finally answered. "First, I must cleanse your blood of him. Unfortunately, it will be a painfully long process for you. I may as well start now." He smiled in anticipation as his hands closed around and he pulled her to him. With her arms pinned under his, she could do nothing.

"Boss, the rain has started and the water has cut us off. The bridge—" Jerry interrupted urgently.

"I told you that the flood will not reach here. This building will not be touched by the storm."

"The bridge is undefended. The thing you set under the

400

bridge has been swept away by the storm. There is nothing there to mark your territory and the other vampires are restless. They are talking about going across the bridge to find shelter. If your brother comes here tonight, he can come in uninvited." Jerry fairly danced with urgency. Casey stopped fighting and waited, hoping.

Franz lifted his head arrogantly. "I will come." He flung Casey to the floor in front of his coffin and she watched as Bev entered and shut the door behind her. She began relighting the candles that the wind had blown out. Franz opened his casket and ripped off a small swatch of the red satin lining, then dug out a handful of the graveyard dirt. He trickled a fistful of soil onto the cloth, then turned thoughtfully.

"I think this will keep him away until I am ready for him." He pulled off his signet ring and added it to the cloth.

"What are you doing?" Casey asked. She couldn't meet his eyes so she found herself staring at the lock on the coffin in front of her.

"This is not the home of a living person, my dear, but it is mine. If I mark it properly, not even my own brother can enter uninvited. Then, tomorrow night when the full moon rises, you will become the thirteenth vampire, the sacrifice which closes the Circle of Death around my beloved brother. Once it is complete, nothing and no one can defeat me. Tonight I will cleanse your blood of him. It will be very painful for you, and eventually you will die from it. Tomorrow you will become mine and no power in Heaven or Earth can ever take you away from me. Together we will drain Simon dry." His sane tone and demeanor were more terrifying than his most violent madness. "I will leave him totally bloodless, weak and helpless, then I'll let the cruel sun finish him."

He took her hand and lifted her to her feet. His blue eyes twinkled good-naturedly as he put his arm around her waist and pulled her gently forward. "I have something to show you."

It was only a few steps to the far side of the platform, but she didn't think she would live through them. Her head was shaking no and her legs were wooden. She hung back stubbornly, but he didn't even notice. His arm swept her down and into the center of the room.

"This will be your new home, my pet."

She closed her eyes and turned her head, but his hand on her neck forced her forward as he opened the lid.

"Look at it!" He roared.

Dark brown wood, sandy brown soil with no covering, nothing to soften the impact of seeing her own grave.

He allowed her to twist away, then he was ahead of her, pulling her back onto the platform. "Now, now, darling Cassandra. Don't be upset. You don't have to stay there tonight. It hasn't been prepared for a guest. Tomorrow morning will be soon enough."

She was rigid as he led her, her head tight against his chest. For a moment, there was hope, then he turned her to face his casket.

"No."

"You can sleep here until sunrise," he whispered into her ear.

"No."

"Then during the day, I will join you."

"NO! NO! NO! NO!"

He held her in an iron grip as he dragged her forward. "Don't make a fuss, Cassandra. It's really so tedious. I just can't trust you. You might wander off while I'm busy with other things. You should rest. Rest and forget that you will betray your lover. Rest and forget. I will need all your energy tomorrow night. After I drain every drop of blood from your body very, very slowly, your blood will accept me. Of course, it may sting a little. But nothing worthwhile comes easily."

"No, don't. I promise I won't try anything. Please don't put me in there. You don't have to do that." She hated herself for begging, but she would have done much worse to keep from being locked in there. She twisted from Franz to

Bev, who took a step forward, frowning. "Bev, please. Don't let him do this to me. Bev! Help me!"

Franz picked her up as he spoke to Beverly. "Outside. Now." Bev fled.

Casey's fists crashed into his face and shoulders, and her legs kicked wildly until she realized that he was enjoying her panic. She stopped fighting and she could feel her body grow rigid.

He laughed as he lowered her into his casket. He smoothed the red satin under her head and kissed her cold lips. "Rest well, my pet. I will be back . . . eventually."

He lowered the lid slowly, closing her world upon her until she broke.

"Oh God! Don't! For pity's sake, don't!" Her hands went up, pushing against the cold wood. He smiled as he forced it down even more slowly. When there was only an inch of space, she jerked her fingers away just as he slammed it shut. She took a deep breath of the stale air and screamed. She could hear his laughter.

The air became very still. She could smell the aroma of new satin through the freshly turned earth. For a long moment there was silence, then she heard the sharp rattle of the lock. The pressure changed as the box was sealed.

Silence.

She twisted her shoulders and heard the rustle of satin over bare earth. She pushed at the polished ebony above her.

Silence.

She ran her fingers around the rim, probing at the seal. She couldn't even fit her fingernail into the crack. Her hands scrabbled frantically in the darkness. She began to sob the stale air into her lungs.

There was a sharp rap on the lid. She screamed, begging him to reconsider and let her out. Then she pushed wildly at the top. She doubled her legs up and kicked. She stopped only when there was no more hope.

She heard a quiet chuckle, then soft footsteps receding. A

muffled thud echoed through the warehouse, then the door slammed shut.

Silence.

She was alone.

Chapter Twenty-one

The van rocked slightly as a gust of wind hit. The radio announced winds of eighty miles an hour and gusts over a hundred. Only a fool would try to drive in this weather. Simon snapped the radio off and forced his concentration back to Casey. There had been no sign from her since the mental scream, but he knew she was out there, somewhere. He laid the map across the steering wheel and stared at it blindly.

He narrowed his concentration until he could see an image of Casey in his mind. It was dull and lifeless. He imagined her voice and emptied his mind to listen. Nothing but the sound of the wind. Five minutes passed, then ten, but he was unaware of time until Eric opened the door.

He looks pale, Simon thought with a certain satisfaction and I haven't even touched him. *Yet.* He looked at the metal splint with a Velcro fastener that ran from Eric's fingers to his elbow. He gunned the engine as Eric noted his glance.

"I had to argue to get this instead of a cast, but it was faster." He looked out the window and shouted, "Wait!"

Simon slammed on the brakes, cursing. Before he could ask, there was a pounding at the sliding side door. He turned around as the door opened and Paul slipped in.

"She woke up," he announced quickly, waving for Simon to drive on.

"Get out," Simon ordered.

"No. I told you, she woke up. I told her what was happening and she told me to go. There's nothing I can do for her there."

"I don't care where you go, just get out," Simon snarled. "I don't need any humans along."

"Wha . . ." Paul looked at Eric.

"Yeah," Eric nodded. "We figured it out tonight. But he's not the one who hurt Clarise. And from what I found in that bag, he's dead serious about killing this one." He jerked slightly as Simon decided it was not worth the time it would take to throw Paul out and gunned the car into the street.

Paul kept one eye on Simon as he opened the bag and peeked in. His face lost all expression as he reached in and came out with a handful of short wooden arrows. "How many bows you got?"

Simon took his eyes off the road just long enough to glance in the rearview mirror. He could see Paul's face, but his own reflection didn't show. "Right or left at the light."

"Right," Eric answered automatically as he stared out at the storm. "How is she?"

"She couldn't feel her legs. I think her back is broken." Her husband announced bleakly. He leaned forward and tapped Eric unobtrusively on the shoulder. "She'll live, but they don't know if she'll ever walk again."

Eric reached up to take a small vial of clear fluid from Paul's hand. He nodded, then slipped it into his shirt pocket.

Simon glanced at Paul's face in the mirror. "She's alive. She's lucky to be alive. Six."

Paul looked up, realized he couldn't see Simon's reflection, and checked along the sides of the van. There were two long bundles wrapped in cloth. Without a word, he began unwrapping.

"Have you ever used one before?" Simon asked.

406

"They're not exactly standard police issue," Paul snapped.

"These were specially made, a very, very long time ago, for the same purpose for which we will use them tonight. They are vampire killers. You cock them with your thumb, like an old-fashioned revolver. The bolts load from the side, and six is a full load. Just pull the trigger to fire. Quick load and quick fire, but the enemy we fight is quicker. The vampire slaves he has made will be slower, but there may be as many as a dozen of them. If you want to practice, do it with an unloaded weapon, we can't afford to waste any bolts."

They drove east out of Ft. Walton Beach in a raging hurricane. Every gust of wind made the van shake and slide, until it was threatening to turn over. Simon had to brake suddenly and Eric thought wistfully of his seat belt as he braced his good arm against the dash. He flinched as a real estate For Sale sign was torn from a lawn and blown almost parallel to the van. Simon swerved and slowed as it changed course and cut across in front of them.

Simon wondered if Eric could feel the challenge. The wind was like a live thing, pushing them, urging them on faster and faster, daring them to race her. Small branches, leaves, and paper went zipping along, keeping pace with them, then dropping down and skittering away. Pine trees bent at a sharp angle. As the wind shifted, they whipped back and forth, sometimes lashing the ground with their topmost branches. Debris littered the road.

Simon drove cautiously. Even his extraordinary eyesight was limited by the rain and the wind that drove it in sheets against the car. They passed a bayou with a sandy beach, and could hear the sand as it pitted the paint. The wind and rain slapped at the top of the van and pulled it roughly in various directions. His speed was down to ten miles an hour.

"What will he do to Casey?" Eric finally asked.

"He will want to convert her . . . to make her a vampire, but he will soon discover that he has a problem. You see, my blood is already in her. It has been since the shooting. I thought she was going to die, and I wanted her to live. My blood gave her the strength to fight and live, so she did not become Nosferatu, the undead. It's the only reason she's alive now. When he tastes her blood, he will know she is mine. It will burn his lips and mouth like acid, and she will feel as if she is being ripped apart. He will have to drain most of her blood away, very, very slowly. It won't be easy for either one of them."

"Damnit! You did this to her!" Eric yelled. He had had his fill of Simon's clinical description. "You bastard, when we get out of this I'll—"

Paul grabbed his friend by the shoulder and shoved him back into the seat. "Shut up, Eric. We have to know what we'll face. Why does he have to drink it? Why can't he just drain her blood and replace it with his own? Is it possible that Casey will be on his side by the time we get there?"

"Not likely. He has to drink it because his own blood will make the antibodies to protect them both. When enough of it has been converted in his bloodstream, he will force her to drink his blood. She will die in agony, literally torn apart as the forces in her body battle each other. He will win, and she will belong to him, body and soul, forever."

"Is that any worse for her than belonging to you?" Eric asked sarcastically.

"I would not kill her," Simon protested. "My blood is already in her. Wherever and *whenever* she dies, she will return to me. It does not matter if she lives a hundred years, after she dies, she will become as young as she is now. I will wait for her natural death. Long life teaches patience, Mr. Tyler. And I have lived four hundred years."

"How long will the conversion take?" Paul asked.

"A night and a day, but if we do not rescue her tonight,

before he weakens her too much and gives her his blood to drink the first time, she . . ." His words faltered, and the lack of expression in his voice was countered by the bleak sorrow in his eyes. He shook his head, and finally said, "The final death would be a gift, in that case."

"Casey . . ." Eric gripped his crossbow firmly, then reached into the back and took another one. He hefted it gently, then asked. "Will she be able to fight?"

"No. He can take control of her mind and body."

"Even while he's fighting us?" Paul straightened slightly as he caught on. "I taught her to shoot. She's better than I am with a pistol and just as good with a rifle. She'll take one look to figure this contraption out, and take to it like a cotton mouth does to swamp water. And I just bet that other vampire won't expect that!"

A small smile lightened Simon's eyes. "No, he won't expect that. He may not have any idea of the trouble he kidnapped. Once his attention is distracted, she'll be free to act. Take her a bow. Take her two."

Casey kept her breathing shallow and steady as she tried to picture the brass clasp that kept her in. She had looked at it almost absently before, but now she brought back every detail. Brass, about six inches long and two inches wide. Metal wires snapped down to seal the coffin, and a hasp extended from the lid to cover a metal ring that had been bolted to the side. Anything that was slipped through the ring after the hasp was closed would effectively lock the hasp in place and seal the coffin. That had been the noise she had heard, she realized now, just before she had gone a little crazy.

She winced now at the memory. When she had known that she was alone, that he would not return to free her, she had screamed until her voice was hoarse. Her feet were bruised from kicking the stony wood. She had

409

pounded at the sides and lid with her fists until they were sore and swollen. Her nails were torn and broken from clawing at the seals.

Now she rested and planned, and wondered how long the air would last, and whether he had thought about that when he locked her in here. What would happen if she died now? Would she belong to Simon, or would his brother find some way to control her? What would it be like to die?

The thoughts were not appealing and she forced her mind to other things. She concentrated on a shiny brass lock and an old icehouse, stripped of fixtures and furnishings. The floor had even been swept, she remembered, and she wondered if Bev was still obsessively neat. What had Franz found to secure that hasp? And where?

Her hand wandered to the inside of the fitting and she tapped it thoughtfully. No give, no rattle, not even the slightest tick of metal on loose metal. If she knew what was in there, she might be able to get it out. Her arm drew back and she slammed her hand sharply against the wood, then held her breath and listened.

There was the slightest of rattles. Or was it wishful thinking?

She did it again, hard enough to bruise her hand. It sounded almost hollow.

Even if I get out of here, what about the icehouse door? Simon taught me that first impressions are very important to a psychic, and my first impression was that no one but a vampire could open that door. But what if I'm wrong? What if I could escape, and didn't bother to try?

That certainly won't be the problem, she decided. It won't be for lack of trying. But even if I figure some way to get out of the icehouse, how far do I have to get before he can't find me? Can I survive the hurricane out in the open?

She shuddered and brought her mind back to the lock.

One step at a time. Franz must have blocked the lock with something already in the building, or something he brought with him. Her fist beat slowly at the sides. The lock that the sailors had put on had dropped into the water while she watched. He would have had no reason to get another one. Would he? What would he have used? What would be near to hand?

Her thoughts raced until she realized that her breathing had quickened and her fist was beating a tattoo on the side of the casket. She pulled her hand back and ground her teeth impotently. She had seen objects moved by the power of a mind. Hadn't she caused a piece of paper to burst into flames? If they could do it, she could. And if she couldn't then what did she have to lose by trying? What else could keep her thoughts away from the closeness of that lid and the narrowness of those sides, and the way they seemed to move closer every time she took her hand away and put it back. Wasn't the air just a bit more stale? The utter lightlessness made everything seem closer, smaller, and more frightening.

She forced her thoughts back to the lock, then relaxed her muscles one by one, taking as much time as each one needed. Her mind became calm and clear. Methodically, she outlined plans in her mind until they were imprinted there. When she could see herself performing each action perfectly, she stopped her thoughts and let her mind drift.

In a moment or an hour, the lock appeared in her mind. She could see it perfectly. There was an L-shaped pipe stuck through the ring. For an instant, her concentration narrowed to the pipe. How could she possibly move that? It wavered in her mind and disappeared.

I can't move that, she thought, horrified. It's too big, too heavy. Maybe, in a couple of years, after I have had time to start slow and build up to it. I could start with a feather . . .

I've seen it done. Things can be moved that way, and

411

the size and weight don't matter. It's the fact that it can be done at all that matters. I've seen too many incredible things lately to balk at the idea of moving a metal pipe.

She blocked her thoughts again and stilled her mind. It was harder this time. Over and over she had to wipe out the expectancy, the small comment that one part of her brain made to another, that she would see what she wanted to see. When she finally let go, it came immediately, as if it had only waited for her mind to let it in. The pipe was there.

She tried to push it with her mind. She focused all her power and frustration, her pain and fear into grasping that bar and lifting it.

It didn't move.

She kept up her effort until her hands shook and her tears dampened her hair. When she finally gave up, her muscles cramped uncontrollably. She was gasping for air.

She started over again: controlling first her breathing, then her muscles, then her thoughts until her mind seemed to float comfortably over her body. When the bar appeared, she studied it as if she had never seen it before. It was old and worn. The bend of the ell was weak with rust. She probed it mentally and felt the brittleness. A little heat, a little pressure, and it would shatter like glass.

She held the image in her mind as she felt the power grow. Directing it into her hand was easy. It flowed through her body under her direction until her hand felt warm and incredibly sensitive. She felt detached, as if she was more of a conduit or a dam rather than the source of the power. It tingled through her body like an electric current. She gathered it in for a moment, then thought about releasing it through her hand into the lock. She heard the pipe shatter and two separate pieces hit the floor. Thunder announced her success.

Her concentration and her carefully made plans slipped away. She shoved at the lid, kicking at it when it didn't give, but the hasp was still tight. Then she wasted more time berating herself for her impatience.

"Concentrate, damnit!" she said aloud. The sound of her own voice was comforting. "Concentrate. See it. I just blew up an iron pipe. I won't be stopped by a stupid piece of metal that I can lift with one finger." The finger appeared in her mind and she looked for the lock. It was there. One finger wasn't strong enough, but her mental hand was. A hiss of air announced her release. Both physical hands hit the roof and she scrambled out.

The reaction came and she was shaking. She took one step toward the door and had to lean back against the black casket. Her legs had that peculiar liquid-rubber feeling that comes with narrow misses. Her breath sobbed in and out of her lungs in great gasps.

"Not now!" she told herself savagely. She wheeled around and forced herself to look into the coffin. Red satin and black wood and lumpy earth. A luxurious open grave.

It was enough. She raced toward the door. It was one of the old-fashioned kind. Like a barn door, it was split in the middle and each half could be rolled open.

Except they wouldn't. Her hands scrabbled at the wood until the few nails she had left were torn and bleeding. She barely noticed. Her fist hit the door in frustration, and she recoiled at the booming noise. Would he hear it over the hurricane?

She held her breath, but all she could hear was the storm. She finally turned, one finger thoughtfully in her mouth to try to stop the pain. She picked up a candle and went back, shielding it from the wind. A crack showed the crossbar, securely blocking the door from the outside, then the wind blew the candle out.

"Plan B," she announced firmly, and she turned back resolutely. Empty and bare, most of the icehouse was in darkness, but she searched it rapidly. The ring of candles illuminated one small section of the back wall, and she re-

413

lit hers as she went by. The concrete platform ran along the back, with the warped old table pushed to the side. There was a trash heap masquerading as a shadow in the far corner: scraps of paper, an old, broken pair of ice tongs, and pieces of rusted pipe. Nothing of wood.

She chose a two foot long section of pipe that was broken to a sharp point at one end. She ran past the coffin, trying hard not to look at it.

The table was wood, and two lengths had splintered away from the top. The nearest one was small, about ten inches from the wide end to the sharp tip. The other was longer and thicker. If she could break it off, it would be over three feet long and six inches at the base.

Too long or too short? A lance or a dagger?

She glanced nervously at the door and wondered if he was already on his way back. How long had he been gone?

She turned resolutely back to the table and reached inside herself for the power. The icehouse brightened suddenly as lightning sizzled outside. Thunder rumbled until she felt as if she were inside a brass drum, played by some insane giant. It overwhelmed the senses. She glanced back at the door before she placed her hands on the table.

Old, solid, impersonal. The impressions flooded in, but with them came the noise of wind, lightning, rain and thunder; all competing for her attention. Lightning cracked a warning and there was a noise like a cannon shot just outside. She held her breath and waited. A tree had broken, snapped like a twig in the wind, and now the only question was where it would fall.

She heard the rending crash and let out her breath. By the sound, it had taken another tree with it. She reached again for the power, feeling it build. Lightning cracked again and she finally caught on.

There must be something electrical about this psychic power, something that would attract lightning.

She grabbed the improvised prybar and attacked the

414

table. The long splinter was rock hard and all her pounding didn't break the stem. She finally wedged the bar under the wood, climbed onto the table, and kicked it viciously.

The long splinter didn't budge.

She moved to the other side of the table and used the same tactics on the smaller piece of wood. She pried at it twice, and it fell into her hand. She ripped a length from her dress and wrapped it around the thick end. It felt good to her hand. The "blade" was almost six inches long.

Casey looked at the casket, then at the door. She had to try one more time.

She didn't bother with a candle this time, but she kept the dagger clenched securely in her fist. At the door, she put her free hand flat against the old wood. The storm made it vibrate. With her eyes closed, she could almost see the wind and rain lashing the crossbar. She gathered her power, her neck arching unconsciously and her fingers tingling as she concentrated.

The lightning struck the parking lot, dancing on the surface of the water. Casey reeled backwards as the blast slammed into her. Both her body and mind felt singed at this assault on her overly sensitive faculties.

As she walked reluctantly back to the casket, she noticed the two pieces of iron pipe next to the lock, still warm from the break. She thought a moment and her hand went to her throat, but the lace scarf wasn't there. She found it under the table.

She bound the pieces together with the torn lace while she recited the Lord's Prayer, then added the Twenty-third Psalm for good measure. When she finished, she buried the cross in the dirt under the satin cover. Even if he killed her tonight, he would find no rest there.

She stepped back and looked at the ebony coffin. Before it had loomed over her, now it seemed pitifully small. She ran her hands over the dark wood, careful not to touch the

415

raised crest of arms. She could still feel a lingering trace of warmth as her hands went to the lid.

She peeked inside at satin the color of fresh blood. My blood is exactly that shade. My blood.

"No!" She slammed the lid down and turned away. "There's got to be another way." She rubbed her arms to relieve the chill. The rain drummed down, a constant, irritating reminder that time was passing. Her eyes searched the empty icehouse desperately, but there was no place to hide, and no way to get out. She ran across to the door and tried one more time, but it didn't move. Finally, she returned to the trash heap and replaced the rusty pipe she had used as a prybar for one that formed a rusty L. Her feet dragged as she walked back with it.

She lifted the lid cautiously. Such a tiny space inside for such a large box. It was claustrophobically small.

"I can't do it," she carefully explained to herself. "I didn't know it would be this bad. I just can't."

She looked around the room for an alternative, but there was none.

"I can't," she whispered. "I just can't." She tore her gaze from the coffin and glanced toward the door. How long? Was he out there now?

She leaned over the open box and began to tremble. Her hand opened nervelessly and the wooden dagger dropped onto the torn satin, point down and quivering.

"Am I supposed to kill him with a splinter? It's not fair! In the movies, they always carry an extra stake, or he falls on a wooden fence or something. Something long and sturdy. Not something so frail that even I can break it off. It's not fair!"

The temper tantrum made her feel better. She opened her clenched eyes and stared at the tiny space. Very carefully, she propped the pipe on the side of the casket, next to the lock. She picked up the dagger, then climbed in awkwardly and crouched there, shivering. The smell of the

416

dirt clogged her lungs and she sobbed for breath. She wiped the tears from her face with the back of her hand and stared at the dagger.

"I didn't know it would be this bad." She was fighting for control. Her hand clenched around the cloth grip and she watched every movement as she brought it up, over her shoulder, then plunged it down into the scarlet satin. Again and again, savagely she attacked her jail, until the beautiful cloth was in shreds. She lifted the dagger and stared at it. The point was not dulled. The ancient table had hardened before it split, until the splinter was almost like a sliver of stone. She had the feel of it now.

She was calm.

She reached over her head and fumbled with the hasp. If she slammed the lid down just right, and gave it just one extra little push with her mind, it should lock itself.

Her eyes were drawn to the door and she wondered if he were on the other side of it, just waiting for her to come out.

She closed her eyes tightly and leaned back. The walls were closing in and the lid was going to fall and crush her. She sat up, clutching the sides frantically.

Slowly, she brought her mind back under control. She steadied her breathing and calmed her thoughts. A few moments later, she felt detached and remote. She planned each separate movement. Her mind rehearsed it until it was like watching a movie. She just had to move thus, and her power would go there, and the hasp would fall over the metal ring. The pipe would be dislodged and fall. Another little push and the end of the pipe would go into the ring. When she finally moved, she did it spontaneously. Her movements followed her thoughts so closely that there was no space of time to slow her. Everything just happened.

Once again, she was locked in.

* * *

417

Simon hit the accelerator briefly to cross a dip in the road that had become a fast running stream. He felt the pull of the water even through the insulation provided by the van and the earth lined shoes he wore. They were through it quickly and his strength returned.

"How much farther?" he finally asked.

"A couple of miles. The rest isn't on the map, so look for an overgrown dirt road on the right. About two hundred feet in, there should be a concrete bridge over a deep drainage ditch." Eric studied the map and tried to make out shapes and signs through the darkness and the storm. The yellow glow of the sky had diminished and the darkness was growing. "I think the storm is gaining on us. What about the rain? Won't it weaken you?"

"He will be weakened the same amount," Simon nodded. His eyes searched for a break in the trees. It seemed longer than a mile, but when it came he knew there was no mistake. He turned the van, parked it heading out in case they came out running, then looked at Eric thoughtfully.

"If either of you," he included Paul with a glance, "get in my way!"

"We won't."

"If you do, I'll kill you."

"You'd enjoy that," Eric said.

"Not particularly," Simon responded thoughtfully. "Casey would mourn and you are not that important. In fifty or a hundred years, you will be dead and Cassandra will be with me."

"No!" Eric burst out. "I'll see you in hell first!"

"And I'll help him." Paul held one of the loaded crossbows at the ready, pointed at Simon.

"We're wasting time. Eric pulled the hood of his raincoat up. "We can worry about fighting each other after we get Casey out of there. He opened the door and the wind jerked it out of his hands. He heard the hinges groan as it

418

slammed open. Soaked before he got out of the van, the wind buffeted him from all sides as he shut the door. Paul took the lead with a flashlight, and Eric noticed that Simon walked in the center of the road, where the rivulets of water did not yet reach.

Their eyes were slitted against the wind and rain. They walked at an angle, braced against the storm. The winding trail cut up a hill. As Eric and Paul struggled for each slippery step, Simon glided surefootedly up the slope and over the top. They skidded down the far side and slid into Simon at the bottom, careful not to jab him with the unfamiliar weapons. It was like running into a wall; Simon didn't give an inch as he stood gazing at the concrete bridge over a freely running stream.

Simon stepped off the road and waded through a puddle of water parallel to the bank.

"What are you doing?" Eric asked, watching him.

"We can't pass the bridge. It is guarded. I think he must have circled the whole area, but there may be an opening."

"What do you mean 'guarded?' Mines and machines guns?" Eric asked sarcastically.

Simon wheeled on him viciously. "No! I mean . . ." his voice trailed off as he looked at them speculatively. "I mean," he continued quietly, "that the vampire who lives here has put something on the bridge that marks this place as inhabited. I can not enter an inhabited dwelling without an invitation. But you can. You can cross the bridge and bring me whatever he has placed there. It should be in a pouch of some kind. Bring it to me."

Paul and Eric walked halfway across and paused. There was no need to search. It waved like a red flag in the light. The cord had been tied to keep the bag out of sight by letting it hang under the span, but the wind had whipped it over the side and now it fluttered like a banner.

Eric caught it and started to open it.

"Bring it here."

He ignored the order and yelled back, "Shine the light this way." He put his hand in and felt cold metal in the mud. He fished out the ring gingerly. "This is what keeps you out?" he asked derisively.

"Give it to me," Simon growled.

He held it up to the light and Paul stared curiously. The rain washed the wolf's head until the ruby sparkled in the light.

"Let me see that." Simon tried to step on to the bridge, but his foot hesitated reluctantly. "I must see it."

Compelled by the urgency in his voice, Eric moved closer and held the ring out for him to examine.

Simon didn't try to touch it, but his eyes closed in pain. He felt the water drain his strength as it cascaded down his body, and his blood felt stale in his veins. "Throw it into the water. Throw it all into the water."

Paul studied him thoughtfully. "You recognize it."

Simon turned away and walked back down the path. He stopped under the partial protection of a tall pine tree and leaned against the trunk. The ring still glowed on Eric's palm. Simon moved his hand into the light and they stared at the ring there, then the one on Eric's palm. They were identical.

"I thought it looked familiar. Then you are in on this! What's the matter? Did your partner lock you out?"

Simon shook his head wearily and put his palm flat against the tree trunk. He could feel the living wood stretch on one side as the wind pulled the tree off balance. The opposite side felt compressed, as if it were trying to bend double. He felt the same way.

"He isn't my partner," he said to Paul. "He's my brother. I thought he was dead! Why isn't he dead?" His words were a cry of pain.

"We can fix that."

They ignored Eric's mutter as Simon continued. "He's insane. He was cruel before, but now he is completely

420

insane. I can't go in there. He's still my brother."

"Are you trying to tell me that your brother is here and you didn't know it? That he came after Casey and you didn't know who he was? You used her for bait! You were in on this." Eric came toward him with the pouch in his hand.

"No!" Simon roared at him. "He was dead. I thought he died the true death fifty years ago, but he must have disappeared deliberately. Now he's back, and he's after me."

"To hell with you! Casey is the one he's got. I'm going in." Eric flung the pouch in the stream and put the ring in his pocket. "You do what you have to. But if you try to stop us when we come out, I'll kill you. One way or another, I'll kill you."

"If you go in there without me, you won't be coming back. You fought him once tonight and lost. Now you are on his home ground. He will suck you dry."

Eric and Paul turned and walked into the darkness.

Chapter Twenty-two

Casey's mind was playing tricks on her. She heard the door slam a dozen times, and quiet footsteps echoed around her. Eyes floated in the darkness until she pricked her finger on the dagger to make them go away. Her throat was dry as the dust beneath her, and she licked her lips nervously. Every time the thunder rolled, she thought of the water pouring down outside.

A hundred times she imagined Franz opening the lid. She plunged the dagger into his heart, and yelled triumphantly. She tried not to let reality intrude, but the wooden splinter felt frail and weak in her hand. Was it long enough, strong enough to reach his heart? Was she quick enough?

"Will I kill him before he kills me? Dear God, give me strength," she prayed.

Scenes of the fight at her home flashed through her mind and she wondered if Eric and Clarise were alive. Were they still lying where he had left them on the grass with the storm battering their bodies? Maybe Paul had found them, but if the storm had arrived he wouldn't be able to leave work. He would call, but if the phones were out all over the area he wouldn't be surprised to get no answer.

What about Simon? Was he on his way? For just a moment, when she had screamed she had reached out to him, but even if he had heard her, even if he somehow managed to follow her, he could not get in. Franz had seen to that.

What would that monster do to her when he returned?

Her fingers scratched lightly at the ebony lid. He had

spent three months locked in this airless, lightless box, going insane. While she had been sleeping, examined by doctors, fed through tubes, massaged daily, pampered by friends and family, he had been in this tiny crate, conscious and starving. He had watched his body shrivel and his strength drain away. His hands had turned to claws as his flesh withered. And all the time, the deadly waves had rocked him, a constant reminder of death. How many storms had he weathered?

She didn't want to look at the picture her mind painted.

Her fingers lightly traced the wood over her head. There were deep grooves in the coffin lid. Had he tried to scratch his way out? He could have ripped it apart any time. It wasn't the lock that had kept him in, it was the fear. How many times had his control wavered? Had he screamed as his fingernails scored the hard wood? Had he trembled at the splash of the waves as she did now at the thought of his return? Had he cried as he forced his hands down to his sides? As she did now.

If injured, his body would heal itself almost instantaneously, but what about his mind? If he lived a thousand years, would it heal the horror of those three months?

Her neck burned where he had bitten her, and she wondered what it would be like to be the slave of such a thing. She remembered the way he had hit the children. Would she be able to defend herself any better? She touched her throat gingerly and felt the jagged edges of the wound, hot and swollen.

It would be better to die, she thought hopelessly, then realized that even that was a stupid idea. If I die, that's when it really starts. I have to kill him first, or . . . Her mind shied away from the thought.

"Simon," she whispered his name. "How did you live like that for hundreds of years? How long could I survive with someone who enjoyed hurting and degrading me? How could I block him out? How could I fight him? How did you fight your own brother?"

Locked in Franz's coffin, she could understand his fear and pain, she could empathize with his horror, but it took a certain kind of weak, twisted mind to survive that and take revenge on the whole of humanity. She could not, would not, fathom someone who would torture a helpless woman, or terrorize and kill children.

Her hand clutched the dagger and her mouth stretched in what could have been a smile, but wasn't. Maybe she would forgive Franz after she killed him, but it wasn't likely.

Where was he? What was keeping him?

Her eyes strained to pierce the darkness, and her ears magnified each sound. The smell of earth clogged her nostrils. Franz had spent three months in this stinking hellhole going insane. Three hours would do the same to her. She shifted restlessly and listened to the slither of satin over dirt.

He was stronger than she. He had controlled the urge to rip his way out, but the control had cost him. She could imagine those leathery claws gouging the wood in frustration. It had cost him his sanity.

She thought about Clarise and Eric, Bev, Pat, Mike Boyd and Estelle and the kids. And about Janie and Davey.

"C'mon, you bastard," she whispered when she ached to scream it aloud. She clutched the splinter in both hands. "Come and get it."

Franz opened the door, holding it easily against the wind. Bev, the children, Jerry, and the other vampires filed in silently and gathered around the coffin. He withdrew the pipe from the lock and opened the lid, smiling.

She screamed defiantly as she lunged at him out of the darkness, but he was fast, too fast. The blade barely penetrated his flesh before he jumped back. She was still coming when he swept the blade aside and grabbed her by the throat. He jerked her out of the casket and shook her.

"You bitch! You'll pay for that!" he roared at her. His mad eyes glared at her and she knew that when the rage passed he would be pleased to have an excuse to hurt her. He twisted her wrist to make her drop the wooden knife.

424

She closed her eyes and let the knife drop. Her left hand caught it and she brought it upwards, into his stomach. This time the blade went in two inches before he flung her away. Drops of blood splattered the floor.

Casey landed sprawling and a dozen vampires fell on her hungrily. She screamed hopelessly in rage and fear as she fought them, until Franz jerked her out of the melee.

She landed at his feet and stared up at him. He loomed over her, his black cape ruffled by an unseen wind. He plucked the splinter from his stomach with two fingers, and she watched the wound heal itself, leaving only a torn shirt, stained with blood.

He put the bloody dagger under her chin and lifted slowly. She scrambled obediently to her feet, then stood on tiptoe to relieve the pressure. Her eyes filled with dread as her head tilted back. The point pricked her throat. She felt blood trickle warmly down her throat and Franz licked his lips in anticipation. She tried to grasp his wrist and stop him, but there was no strength left in her arms.

She tried to wrench her eyes away from his. Her head trembled, but she couldn't move her eyes. He drew out every moment, enjoying her internal struggle. No! her mind screamed silently, but he controlled her body.

She caught a glimpse of movement from the corner of her eye, and her heart leapt.

Franz must have seen the hope in her eyes because he whirled and dropped the dagger just as Eric burst from the shadows with the crossbow raised and ready. The vampire turned to meet this new threat, and Paul glided silently through the door. Screaming with rage, Franz leapt twenty feet in one bound to knock the bow from Eric's hand. He grabbed Eric by the shirt and lifted him from the floor.

Casey dodged Beverly to get to the dagger, then charged back. Paul was trying to get a clear shot at Franz, without endangering Eric and Casey. Franz was like a man plagued by mosquitoes, unsure which to swat first. He backhanded Casey toward Bev while trying to keep Eric between him and the crossbow, but his grip on Eric loosened. Casey ducked, tripped, and turned it into a roll that landed her past Beverly.

Eric's undamaged hand sought his shirt pocket for the vial that Paul had given him, but Franz's arm was in the way. He tried to pry open the viselike grip, but his strength was nothing to the vampire's. He lifted his hurt arm and forced his swollen fingers into his pocket. The strain showed on his face as his hand clenched around the small glass tube that Paul had given him. He screamed as he wrenched his hand back and smashed the vial against Franz's forehead. Water trickled down Franz's face, burning the skin like acid. He screamed shrilly as he dropped Eric to scrub his hands against his eyes. The Holy Water had etched the skin with angry red burns that were already turning black. His beauty was gone, melted into his skull.

Paul fired as Franz stepped away from Eric, but even in pain, the vampire was much too fast. He ducked under the arrow and wheeled around to smash Paul against the wall before he could fire again. There was a scream from the middle of the room and Casey looked up to see a vampire in a security guard's uniform clutch at the bolt sticking out of his chest and collapse, blood streaming thickly from his chest and mouth.

Casey spotted Eric's bow on the floor, dodged Bev to pick it up, then fell heavily as Bev jumped on her back. Casey's arm cradled her head as Bev twined her fist in her long black hair and jerked upward. Her fangs glinted in the candlelight as Casey tried to roll to dislodge her.

Eric twisted around, trying to grab the extra bow strapped to his back, but the splint on his left arm was in the way. As the crowd of vampires rushed toward him he spotted Casey's dagger on the floor. He scooped it up and turned at bay.

Paul had bounced off the wall still clutching his weapon. He had Franz in his sights when the first two vampires reached Eric and his friend went down. Paul put the first

426

bolt into the back of a woman in a red evening gown, but the second went wild as Franz grabbed him by the throat and arm.

The vampire's eyes were wild as he opened his mouth to strike.

"Stop!" Simon's voice shook the air. Lightning and thunder announced his presence.

Franz dropped Paul and wheeled to face his brother. Everyone else was frozen as Simon strode forward into the flickering light of the candles.

"Get out, Franz! This territory is mine." His hair glittered with rain and his eyes were dark.

"What's yours is mine. Isn't that the way it's always been, brother? I'm your Bloodmaster. Or have you forgotten? Will I have to remind you?"

"That was fifty years ago. It was another world." Impatient with explanations, Simon's eyes briefly checked Casey, then swung watchfully back to Franz.

"You're still my brother," Franz's voice was soft and loving. Alarm bells rang in Casey's head as she listened to him try to seduce his brother. "We were together for over four hundred years. Remember our strength? No one could stand against us. We could be together again, like it was before. *Brothers.*"

"Brothers? Slave and Master, you mean," Simon said scornfully.

"And more than brothers," Franz continued obliviously. "We traveled the world. Kings and priests bowed to us. It could be that way again. We could rule this rich new land, Simon. I could forgive you for plotting against me, if you swore allegiance and tasted my blood again. I might even give you the girl."

Casey's breath stopped as she waited a long heartbeat for his answer.

It started with a chuckle and grew to a full-throated roar. Simon's laughter boomed through the icehouse, diminishing the storm's thunder to background noise. Bev didn't resist as

Casey shoved her aside and stood up.

"You can't give what you don't own, Franz." His laughter tapered off and he spoke gravely politely. "No, brother. I don't want to go back to being your slave. I don't want to rule this land. But more than that, I don't want you to rule it. Or to rule me."

"I order you!!" Franz spat the words. Shaking with rage, he stalked forward. "You will obey me. I made you what you are. You can't refuse me. I'm your Bloodmaster. Down on your knees to me!" His clenched fist rose as he screamed. "Kneel to your Master!"

The force of his will spread through the room. Casey, Paul, and Eric stumbled back as Bev, Jerry, and the other vampires dropped to their knees, covering their heads as they cowered before their Master. Only Simon stood proudly, facing his brother. Casey strained to keep her eyes on him, and gradually she straightened as the wave of fury broke and ebbed around them.

Simon still stood, but his eyes were sick with pain. His brother had finally gotten through to him.

"No."

The quiet word hung in the air between them.

Franz went mad. His fist crashed down on Simon's face and sent him reeling to the floor. Franz spun away, then charged back as a wolf, slashing at his brother's throat. Simon's hand hit the furry chest, just before the sharp fangs clicked shut. A thin red line opened on his neck, but Simon bounded up, on four feet.

The wolves circled, growling, then leapt to the attack. Fangs clashed as each sought the throat of the other. Then Franz, his muzzle still scarred from the Holy Water, dipped his head and snapped at the other's paw. Simon slashed at the exposed head and realized too late that it was a trap. Franz's muzzle twisted upward, under his brother's chin, and Simon felt the cruel fangs in his flesh.

The crossbow was in her hand, but as Casey watched the spinning wolves, she knew that any bolt was as likely to hit one as the other. The dagger was on the floor, only a step away. She scooped it up and hurled herself across the room with the wooden splinter held before her, while Bev raced in from the side. Franz's back was to her as Casey leapt forward with the dagger held high. Her fist came crashing down, just as Bev threw herself in front of her master. The wood pierced her breast and went all the way through. She fell on Franz, and he slashed at her angrily as his hold on Simon was broken.

Her body convulsed, flopping like a fish on a gaff. Spasms racked her muscles and twisted her head as she collapsed. Her eyes were curious, puzzled and remote as they stared at Casey. Her body curled around the protruding splinter and her hand gently touched the wood. Her soft brown eyes beseeched her friend to pull this terrible thing out of her, but she didn't speak.

Casey looked at her helplessly, frozen in horror.

"Bev?" She knelt by her friend as the spasms came again. She held her tightly and felt her pain as the muscles writhed and agony distorted Bev's aristocratic features. Casey rocked her, loving her fiercely.

And Bev was gone.

Casey sat, stunned, holding her lifeless body. Sorrow closed her throat and burned her eyes. Carefully, she placed the cold, cold flesh on the floor and straightened the arms.

Her fists clenched as she looked up.

There was an instant of silence, then the mighty growls of combat. The wolves leaped and spun, claws and fangs sought any advantage where there was none. They fought in a rapid series of slashing, writhing, growling encounters. The icehouse echoed with their screaming howls and the impact of furry bodies. Fangs tore flesh and crushed bone. The resulting wounds healed, rapidly at first, then more slowly as wound was laid on top of wound.

Eric and Paul ran toward Casey with their weapons raised, yelling something she couldn't hear over the sounds of combat. She tore her eyes from the wolves, and realized that the rest of the vampires were closing in on her.

Franz had intended to kill her, then use her as the thirteenth vampire to close the Circle. But now Franz was fighting Simon; and four other vampires, including Beverly, lay motionless on the cold concrete floor.

Seven vampires swarmed toward her, eager to make the kill. She cast one last regretful glance at Bev and grabbed the crossbow, then she hesitated. She had that awful feeling that she was forgetting something, something important. She stretched her hand out to Bev, then, acting on some impulse she didn't understand, she snatched the stake from Bev's chest and shoved it into her belt. Firing as she retreated, she backed toward Eric and Paul.

Both wolves drew back, heads down and panting. Casey spotted Franz by the slowly healing scars on his muzzle. She crouched as she ran across the platform, straight for him.

"You bastard!" she screamed. She swerved left, firing her bow as he looked up, and Simon moved in from the right.

Again, it was his incredible speed that she underestimated. It would have been a fatal mistake, if Simon hadn't ripped a furrow along his side, breaking ribs and crunching a hipbone in the process.

There was a tug at her calf as she plunged and rolled to the side. Before she hit the floor, Franz had whirled to meet his brother's attack. She didn't feel the pain until she tried to stand, then she looked down to see blood dripping from her leg.

The vampires saw it, too. Their howls filled the icehouse as Eric reached Casey and pulled her backwards toward the door. She fired again, saw the bolt tear into a woman's chest, then realized with a shock that she knew her.

"Pat!" she cried, but Patricia Shell was lost as the others rushed forward. With Eric on one side and Paul on the other, Casey turned to run, but the wolf fight was now in front of her. She stared in awe.

One moment, two wolves were snapping and growling, the next a bat flew at a wolf's eyes. He ripped the wolf's scalp

430

as it ducked. Blood spurted, then slowed as the wound worked to heal itself.

Casey dodged as it passed over her head, and then there were two. In and out of the light they streaked and darted. The second bat twisted upward, his wings a blur. His fangs clicked together on empty air as his brother sideslipped.

They were moving so fast that it was impossible to tell one from the other. Their only grace was in their attacks as long wings flapped over fat, furry bodies. Claws and fangs slashed new cuts until one black wing was shredded. Blood splattered the floor with every stroke. They dodged around pillars and pipes. One clawed his way up the back of the other, then was scraped off on a pipe.

Before Simon dropped two feet, sharp claws dug into his back and fangs stabbed into the back of his neck. He changed to a wolf in midair, and plunged against a pillar on the way down. The bat was left with two tiny clawed fistfuls of black fur as the wolf limped for the door. Overhead, the bat hit the tumultuous air and was tossed backwards into the room. Franz changed to a wolf, hit the floor in a giant leap, and streaked after his brother.

Casey turned to fire one more time as her limping run took her through the door and into the storm. Rain, hard as hail, hit her face in sheets. Her shoes were gone with the first step, and she ran free.

Lightning stabbed down, and she heard a tree die. She ran in a crouch through six inches of standing water in the parking lot. The pavement was broken and pitted, and she ran lightly, cautious of every step.

The darkness outside was only an illusion. Once she was out of the building, the sky was yellow, with a terrible brilliance. Trees along the flooded ditch were a dark line and the bridge was a lighter strip. Her eyes adjusted faster than Eric's or Paul's and she followed the wolves without hesitation, leaving the men to slam the door shut and shove the crossbar into place, locking the rest of the vampires in the icehouse. Then they followed at a more tentative pace.

431

They stumbled in the dark as she ran toward the bridge. Two dark figures struggled against a light background. One human, one wolf. Her eyes strained, but she couldn't identify who was which. She stumbled as her foot went into a hole and her torn muscles were wrenched. Her hands clutched at the wind as she kept her balance by lunging forward.

Lightning struck again and she flinched. The creaks and snaps of the trees could be heard even above the locomotive roar of the wind. The rumble of thunder made the ground vibrate. Her face and shoulders were battered by the rain. The constant overload left her senses reeling. She fought for each step.

Simon had stepped onto the bridge in human form. He was ready and waiting for Franz's attack, but it still took him by surprise. The wolf came out of the shadows behind him, and his fangs reached for the ropy muscle in Simon's thigh, trying to hamstring him. He felt the skin rip as the fangs snapped shut. He whirled and kicked, catching him in the head and stunning him. One leap took him to the wolf's back, and he locked his arm around the furry throat and lifted. Slowly he strained back. His knee was braced against his brother's spine as he sought to break it.

Lightning lanced down, striking the old tree he had leaned against earlier. The sap had retreated to the surface roots. Liquid boiled to gas in an instant. Explosions like land mines peppered the area. Shredded bark and clumps of mud flew up and out until the wind caught them and flung them at the bridge. It rocked Simon for an instant, and Franz was gone, twisting away with a slash that caught his brother across the collar bone. The rain drove the blood down his chest, robbing him of strength.

Eric and Paul caught up with Casey as she fought the storm. Her leg was seeping blood as she limped forward.

"Go back!" Eric yelled in her ear.

She shook her head stubbornly. The crossbow was in her hand as she pointed. The struggling figures were blurred by

432

the rain. There was no way to tell if Simon was the one being bent over the railing, or the one with his hands around his brother's throat. Casey increased her limp to a run.

Eric passed her and stayed ahead until they were only a few steps from the bridge, then his foot sank out of sight and he fell sprawling. Casey ran on.

Franz hit Simon as he turned, a tremendous blow. His fists were a blur, battering at Simon's face and body. Cuts opened, bled for a moment and stopped, but didn't heal. Simon lashed back with feet and fists, catching him once in the solar plexus and doubling him over.

Then he kicked up, aiming at Franz's chin, but he dodged just in time and Simon was hit from behind as he spun. He hit the rail and bounced, right into Franz's hands. They forced him back over the rail, while his own fists beat at Franz's face. The flesh bruised and tore, but Franz's grip didn't loosen.

Just as Casey stepped onto the bridge, Franz gave a triumphant yell, and she stopped. Even through the storm, she could hear the creak of tortured metal as the railing gave way. Casey sprinted on the sure footing, her hands outstretched to Simon, but she knew it was too late.

Simon looked for something to grab on to, but Franz gave him a brutal shove. Casey stretched, trying to reach him, but she was still six feet away when his blond hair disappeared over the side. She screamed in rage, and reached the gap in the rail just as Franz turned around. She jerked the wooden dagger from her belt.

She didn't hesitate. She could see his satisfied smile change to a grimace of pain as she shoved the stake in with both hands. His heart's blood spurted, drenching her hands in darkness. Franz looked down in disbelief. His right hand clutched weakly at the stake, but he couldn't tug it out. Before she could step away, he had grabbed her. Her fists beat at him in panic as he opened his mouth and pulled her closer.

She slipped on the wet concrete and his teeth clicked together an inch from her throat.

"Take it out!" His words roared in her mind, but his lips barely whispered. She pushed at him futilely as his hand gripped her neck and forced her to look at him. "Take it out."

Her hands touched the stake as she fought his mental command. She had never felt so helpless. She raged inwardly, but her fingers curled around the wood, slippery with his blood, and tugged tentatively as Franz's hand clenched in her hair.

A light flashed in his face, blinding them both.

"Casey! Get away from him!" Paul's voice ordered.

Relief poured over Casey as Franz was distracted, and she hammered the stake in with both hands.

Franz wrenched away. One hand groped for the protruding wood as he staggered back. His heel hit the edge and he gaped at her, his eyes burning with hate.

She tried to jerk back, but his hand was still tangled in her hair. He pulled at it eagerly, trying to catch his balance, but she wasn't strong enough to hold him. Her head was wrenched forward. Her hand grabbed for the rail, but the weight of his falling body jerked her in after him.

Her hair pulled out in clumps as the water, four feet deep and swirling dizzily, sucked her away from him. She tumbled and rolled, struggling to get her feet under her.

Eric reached the rail as Paul shone the light on the gap. He barely hesitated as just beneath him, Casey bobbed to the surface, then was swept downstream by the fierce current. Eric stepped over the side, feet first.

Paul yelled helplessly, then bypassed the bridge and ran along the bank. His feet sank into the soft mud and the tall weeds hid the uneven ground. Paul focused the light on the black, tossing water. There were hundreds of shapes moving in the stream. He saw the pointing finger of a broken tree limb flipped end to end in the current. His light followed it far downstream until the branch crashed into an enormous tree lying across the stream.

If Casey, Simon, or Eric hit that tree, he knew they

434

wouldn't come out alive. If they weren't impaled by the branches, they would be swept under and pinned down by the flood. Shining the light ahead, he saw a bend in the stream where the water eddied. He sprinted across the edge of the parking lot and down the bank to the water.

Hurricane Diana hurled herself against the land, and it killed her.

Santa Rosa Sound roared its fury as it swelled. It invaded the bayous and inlets, pushed upward through the rivers and creeks, and flooded the areas in between. Torrential rains made breathing difficult for anything without gills, and added inches to the flood every hour. The rain moved inland in solid sheets driven parallel to the earth by the force of the wind.

As the floor of the Gulf slanted up, the displaced water was caught by the low barometric pressure of 27.92 inches and sucked even farther up. A plateau of water formed, thirty feet high at the coast. It smashed inward, a dirty, salty, swirling wall of force that crushed everything in its path into splinters, then added the splinters to its mass.

The lightning and thunder was continuous, a deadly rolling cacophony punctuated by the cannon shot crack of trees breaking. The wind turned every loose object, natural or man-made, into a deadly projectile, destroying everything in its path.

Lady Di hurled the 110 mile an hour core winds and driving rain and tidal surges at the coast, and it killed her . . . and everything in her path.

Casey hit the water with a shock. Her feet were jerked forward by the flood and she landed flat on her back in the raging turmoil. Her head was twisted, then jerked as her hair was ripped out by the roots because Franz would not release it. Her hands and feet desperately sought something, anything stable to hang on to. Something hard hit her hand and she grabbed wildly at a small thin piece of wood. It held for a moment, then there was a jerk and she was left with only a splinter. She dropped the useless end as the water tumbled her wildly.

It was a maelstrom. She felt as if she had been dropped into a tornado. The water spun and twisted her wildly, until she couldn't discern up from down. One leg was jerked forward and she felt rather than heard the crack as the other was wrenched to the side. While she fought to keep from being split apart, her face broke the surface. She gulped air, but in an instant, she was thrown to the bottom of the ditch and tumbled by tons of rushing water. Her arms and back were wrenched and twisted in different directions.

Intellectually, she knew what to do: align herself with the current and try to work her way to one side of the stream. But physically it was impossible. She couldn't even tell up from down, much less where the shore might be. She managed to pull her arms to her sides and clutched them around her body, hoping for the slightest break in the turbulence.

If she could just fight the disorientation of being jerked, thrown, crushed, tumbled and rolled; if she could keep her desperate, burning lungs from inhaling, and still cling to consciousness; if she could avoid being impaled by a broken branch, or smashed by the tumultuous tons of water, or pinned under the debris from a house or car or tree. And if, just maybe *if* she was very lucky and the water pushed her against something solid without crushing her, then maybe she could push her way to the surface and *breathe* again.

And then she'd . . . what? Start it all over again?

It didn't matter. Nothing mattered except air. Only an act of will kept her throat closed while her chest heaved and her muscles spasmed. Her eyes were opened wide, straining to see any glimmer of light, when one foot broke the surface.

Instantly, she jackknifed, folding her body at the waist and reaching frantically for the open air. Sweet, dry, wonderful, breathable air! She gasped it in desperately, fighting

436

the demanding vortex for one last sweet breath before it sucked her under again.

That final precious breath renewed her strength and hope. This time when the currents whirled her to the bottom, she doubled her legs up and tried to push off, but the mud was too slippery, and already the water was too deep.

She was still fighting weakly, when something hard hit her in the chest and all the air was driven from her lungs.

This is it, she thought regretfully. I want to live! But at least the mission was accomplished. The dirty, churning whirlpool was too strong, and the constant battering had overwhelmed her senses. The pain of twisted muscles and wrenched limbs seemed very far away. With her first watery breath, she could feel her soul begin to separate from her body.

It was so peaceful. As if she had suddenly awakened from a violent nightmare to the security of her own home. There was a single tiny spot of light, high above, and she drifted weightlessly toward it. She could feel pressure around her chest, but her arms and legs were numb, and there was no more pain. She was grateful for that.

The water dropped out from under her and there was a sudden rush of incredible speed. She was surging forward on a wave of dirty, swirling force. Free of the water, she skimmed lightly just above the terrible maelstrom. If she was dead, why did it still have the power to scare her?

The rush seemed to last forever, but when the end came, it was swift and violent.

The water vomited her up, onto the shore and into what was left of the bushes. She lay dazed and broken, her lungs paralyzed.

Something dark and huge loomed over her, then fell forward, trying to crush her. Her only thought was that it really needn't bother. She was already crushed. Her head flopped to the side and she closed her eyes, unwilling to see. She tried to lift a single finger, but it was too late.

It hit her in the chest, and water spewed out of her mouth.

437

Again and she coughed harshly as pain shot through her. Again, and she forced the last of the water out of her abused lungs, and gasped in pure, sweet air.

"Casey. Casey," Eric's familiar voice sounded harsh.

"I'm still alive?" she whispered. The pain in her chest was a sharp knife and she couldn't stop coughing.

"You are! You are!" he laughed, wiping the rain from her face as he leaned over to shield her from the storm.

"Eriiic! Caaaseeey!"

It was hard to hear him over the rumble of thunder and the roar of the wind, but when Paul shone the flashlight on them, Eric lifted one arm weakly, then gradually slid back.

"Eric? Casey? Are you alright? Anything broken?"

"My leg," Casey said apologetically, remembering the crack she had heard earlier.

"My arm. But we're alive. We're alive." Eric's voice was filled with wonder.

"Great! Let's keep it that way. We've got to get to shelter. The icehouse is over there!" Paul grabbed Eric's good arm and helped him to his feet. The wind raged around them, trying to push them back down, but it only made them stagger. They both lifted Casey until her feet barely touched the ground. Her arms went around their shoulders and she was grateful for the rain because they couldn't tell she was crying. Pain and shock mingled with relief had left her weak as they crossed the field to the parking lot. She kept telling herself that compared to the tidal surge she had just survived, this was a walk in the park.

The lightning was almost constant, and so explosively close that she couldn't help wincing every time the sky lit up. The wind howled insanely, buffeting them from every direction, making each step a victory won. The air was thick with rain, and every time she inhaled, she coughed up more water. Despite the sheets of rain, when the lightning flashed she could see the squat bulk of the icehouse in the distance. They were going to make it — and without Franz. She wasn't really worried about the other vampires. Everything was go-

438

ing to be okay.

So why couldn't she stop crying?

Lightning cracked down ahead of them, so close that she felt the hair on her arms writhe. She jerked violently to her right, throwing Eric off balance. If it weren't for that, she would never have seen the body. It was crumpled in a heap on the slope leading up to the parking lot. The wave must have hurled it there, far above the bend in the stream where they had landed.

"Simon . . ." A shock went through her and once again it was hard to breathe.

"Simon!" she screamed, jerking at Eric's arm and pointing. "We've got to help him."

"I'll get him!" Paul screamed. "Are you sure it's Simon?"

Simon? Of course it was Simon . . . it had to be . . .

"No!" She yelled back. "Be careful."

She and Eric followed at a slower pace as Paul ran ahead. The light bobbed brightly through the gloom, then focused on the back of the head. The hair was thickly matted with mud.

"Is it Simon?" Casey cried as she limped up the slope.

Lightning flashed as Paul turned the body over, face up. Simon's eyes were lifeless and staring, dark holes in a dead white face.

"Simon . . ." She stumbled as she let go of Eric and tried to rush forward. She fell heavily, biting her lip to keep from screaming as her broken leg collapsed. She didn't even notice Eric as he tried, one-handed, to help her up. She crawled the few steps to Simon's side and fell on top of him. A trickle of water escaped his lips. "Simon, Simon, get up. You can't die! You can't . . . die."

"Casey . . ." Paul tried to lift her from the corpse. "He knew the water could kill him. He told us in the van."

"Shit!" Eric burst out. "He's been dead four hundred years. It's time he was buried! Leave him here. We've got to get to shelter." He grabbed Casey by the arm and pulled her toward the icehouse.

439

She shook off his grasp and leaned over Simon. Shaking him by the shoulders, she searched for any sign of movement or returning consciousness. Nothing. Finally, she leaned over him, trying to shield him from the storm as she appealed to Paul and Eric. "Help me get him inside. Maybe, out of the rain—"

"Are you forgetting that if he lives, he'll own you? Throw him back in the river. This is your chance, Casey. He told us his blood is in you, and when you die, you'll become like him. You'll be his slave. Is that what you want?"

She looked from one to the other. "No, but—"

"The only way you can ever be free is to leave him to die," Eric yelled over the storm.

"We've got to get out of here, now!"

Her hand wandered to Simon's face. She pressed her palm against his cold cheek, then gently, so very gently closed his eyelids over those deep, dark wells. She sat back, unwilling to leave, watching the drops of rain driven across his pearly white skin by the wind.

Now is the time, Cassandra. You must choose.

Her whole body jerked in shock. She had been watching his face. His lips had not moved, and she realized that she had not heard the words. She must have imagined them in his voice, in her mind.

It didn't matter. Her decision had been made in the dark, airless confines of a coffin, but she hadn't foreseen this. The blood trickled from her bottom lip where she had bitten it as she leaned over and kissed him. "I love you, Simon."

In that storm, her whisper couldn't have carried more than a few inches from her lips, but his eyes slowly blinked open and his lips twisted. His tongue eased out to taste her blood, then he coughed painfully, spewing out water.

"Simon! Oh, Simon! Thank God!" She clasped him to her, sobbing.

"Casey? I looked back and saw you fall . . . I thought . . . Cassandra, my beloved Cassandra." He pulled her to him, tucking her head under his chin and cradling her in his strong arms.

Simon recovered quickly. It was only a few minutes before he rose easily to his feet, pulling Casey up with him. He nodded as Paul pointed wordlessly to the icehouse, then watched as Paul helped her take one painful step.

"You help Eric," he yelled as he effortlessly picked Casey up.

She clung to him against the darkness and the storm and it was like clinging to a rock. The trip back was endless. Her senses were filled with the darkness and the wind and rain. The storm howled angrily. Lightning and thunder boomed around her, counterpointed by the crack of trees breaking. The rain pelted her face and shoulders, stinging the bare flesh. The water formed a moving tide on the parking lot, tugging Simon's feet into holes and trying to make him stumble. The utter lightlessness was only emphasized by the small circle of Paul's flashlight. The darkness invaded her eyes and made her want to wave her hands in front of her face. She prayed that Simon knew where they were going.

He did. After an eternity, there was suddenly shelter. Simon lifted her up the steps. The door was open and the crossbar was lying on the steps in three pieces. Simon checked inside before he helped Casey in, then closed the door after Eric and Paul were safely inside.

After the storm's pandemonium, the icehouse was blessedly quiet. Paul began lighting the candles.

Casey limped painfully to the platform and sank down wearily as Eric cradled his arm against his chest and leaned against a coffin. She tried twice to speak before the words came out.

"It's over and we're still alive."

"Speak for yourself." Simon grinned as he tore what was left of his shirt into strips, and knelt down to bandage her leg. His own wounds were already healing, except for the sign of a cross, burned into his forearm. Casey touched it curiously. "It will heal, eventually. You must have great faith to have marked me so."

441

"The vampires, uh, excuse me!" Eric interrupted sarcastically. "The other vampires are all gone."

"Not all." Simon nodded toward the shadows. Janie was dragging her feet as she stepped into the candlelight. David followed closely, one hand clutching her slacks.

"They broke down the door and went into the storm," Janie said breathlessly. "They wanted us to come with them, but—"

Casey hugged her, cutting off the useless explanation. She understood. They all did. "He's dead," she said harshly.

"I've thought that before," Simon commented dryly. "I think your leg is broken." He stood up and looked around, then spotted the old warped table with the split board.

"He's dead," Casey repeated. "I stabbed him in the heart before he fell into the flood, and not even Franz could survive that. He's dead." She waited, wondering how Simon would react.

"If you're expecting me to disapprove, you may have to wait a few hundred years," Simon said sarcastically. He used one hand to rip off the long splinter that Casey had worked so hard trying to separate. Picking up the heavy table, he walked toward her, then laid the table down on its side so she could brace her back. Then he began to fit the small piece of wood to her leg. "This is going to hurt," he said casually as he began to splint her broken leg. "I'm more likely to give you a medal for killing Franz. The older brother I loved was gone long before he became a vampire. What was left was . . . not pleasant to be indebted to. I'm not sorry he's dead."

"And we're alive."

The storm raged around the icehouse, and the relative quiet that had been so appreciated before, was now full of sound. Trees snapped with echoes that circled the room, and the wind howled insanely outside, while inside it rushed past with a whisper.

The vampires' bodies had been moved to the far wall, but

Casey couldn't take her eyes off Bev. She lay sprawled on the floor, one hand curled, as if beckoning. Eric had covered her with his coat, but the arm kept slipping out.

Their stories had been exchanged in short bursts, in between listening to Lady Di's power break against the land. They should all have been exhausted, but there was something in the storm that filled them with energy; not fear, but excitement, and a kind of nervous edge that kept them all awake and alert. There was an expectant feeling, as if at each moment the world could end.

They were in awe of the storm.

Physical contact was comforting, but nerves were strung too tightly to stay still for long. Janie had been huddled under Casey's arm, holding the baby protectively, but now she moved restlessly. When she took David over to play next to the black coffin, Casey was almost relieved. Despite the pain in her leg, she stood and stretched, then took a few steps, testing out the splint. She limped quietly, stopping to listen to the dying storm.

It had been a long time since anyone had spoken, then Janie shifted Davey behind her and the movement drew Casey's attention.

"What are we . . ." Casey stopped next to Eric, cleared her throat and tried again. "What about them?"

"They're just kids!" Eric said, horrified. He turned away shaking his head. Janie watched him alertly. She grasped her brother's hand and shielded him with her body.

"Look at her. They're terrified of us," Casey murmured. Her heart ached for them. "What . . ."

Eric wheeled back suddenly. "I can't! I don't care if they are vampires. They're still just *kids!* I can't hurt a child."

"That's terribly kind of you," Simon drawled aristocratically, while Paul hid a smile. "In your present condition, you wouldn't even make a good snack to them."

Eric shrugged ruefully. "You're probably right."

He was a mess. Paul had replaced the splint on his arm, but the sling had been lost in the flood. Now, purple and

443

swollen, his arm stuck out from a scrap of his shirt. His face and chest were splotchy with scrapes and bruises. One eye was closed with a rainbow of colors and the part of his face not covered with scratches was white from pain and shock. His grin was lopsided.

"I'll take the children," Simon decided, and surprised himself by grinning back at Eric. It was a rare moment of truce.

"You?" Eric looked at him in disbelief. "You don't seem like the fatherly type!"

"You know nothing of my 'type.'" Simon snapped, and the smile disappeared as the truce ended. He turned his back on them both and went to the kids. Leaning casually on the coffin, he smiled as he ruffled Janie's hair, then tickled the baby.

Casey sat back down and leaned against the table. Her leg throbbed with every beat of her heart, but either she was getting used to the pain, or she was just so tired it no longer mattered. She blinked heavily, her eyes felt gritty and sore. Her muscles were loose and relaxed and her head nodded unsteadily. She had never been so totally exhausted before.

The night was dying, along with the storm. The wind no longer sounded like a freight train bearing down on them, but one far in the distance, with only an occasional lonely whistle as a reminder. The thunder was a tired grumble and it had been a long time since she had heard the sharp crack of a tree trunk breaking.

The sound of a child's laughter broke her reverie and she smiled, wondering what Simon had said to make that sad child giggle like that. She didn't hear his footsteps, but suddenly she knew he was there in front of her. She opened her eyes slowly, smiling as he stretched out his hand to her and drew her to her feet.

"Let me show you, beloved, what our life will be like, together." His fingertips delicately touched her forehead, and she was lost in his dream.

Casey was flying.

She hardly realized it at first, it seemed so natural and

right. Her arms were the thinnest, most sensitive of membranes, able to discern the slightest change of temperature. She could feel the wind on every inch of her body as she soared high above the trees where the air was sharp and cold. She looked down at an enchanted landscape.

Sharp mountain peaks, covered with snow, tall spears of evergreens that ended abruptly halfway up the mountains, the creeping white glaze of an ancient glacier leading to a small sapphire blue lake, black and white Swiss chalets perched on steep hillsides; all created a dizzying kaleidoscope beneath her. It was more beautiful than she ever could have dreamed.

She felt like some ancient goddess surveying her domain, then wondered what it would be like in the sunlight, when every separate snowflake would glitter and sparkle. Her flight was effortless, as if she had conquered gravity. Her wings were motionless as she glided high above the frozen landscape. She tried to picture it with the sun shining brightly down on the white glacier, and red geraniums in the window boxes of the tall, majestic chalet.

She realized suddenly that she had become so enthralled watching the landscape, that she had neglected her altitude. The snow rushed toward her as she dove toward the ground.

No problem. She snapped her wings out, feeling the crisp, clean air fill the membranes until they stretched like a balloon, then she was soaring again, reveling in the glory of flight.

The rush of air above her startled her, and her triangular, flat-nosed head whipped around, teeth bared.

Simon hovered above her, grinning. His velvet black wings, twice the size of her own, beat in perfect concert with hers. Love and adoration shone in his great black eyes as he turned slightly and swooped to one side, glancing back in invitation. She followed without time or need for thought.

Their flight became an aerial ballet, a pas de deux, as he led the dance. His wings beat too fast for her eyes to follow as he skimmed the top of a mountain, then darted down the opposite side. She circled curiously, only to find him a dozen yards below her, hovering in midair. She flitted toward him, but he slid backwards, staying just ahead of her.

His movements were graceful and bewitching as he darted and swung, swooped and soared, always leading her on. The first time she turned to go a different way, his wingtips brushed hers, coaxing her gently. The fiercest of predators had become the most graceful, most tender of lovers, and he had completely captivated her.

She joined the mating dance coyly. Twisting away at the last moment, teasing him, she darted forward and back, under and then above him. He could have caught her in an instant, but he chased her with restraint, following as she spun around the top of a huge evergreen, then dropping a few hundred feet to skim the shoreline of the lake.

He glided above her, his wings caressing her back with every stroke. His touches were electric. She had never imagined how sensitive skin could be with fur on it. It seemed that her nerves extended outward an inch or more from her skin and every touch raised her to new heights.

She could feel his warm breath on her neck. Her eyes closed as his moist tongue reached out to lick her furry little ear. Every stroke became more intimate and insistent, and she was barely aware that he was guiding her up the side of a mountain to the chateau. They touched down simultaneously onto the balcony, and changed.

Her love for him was bursting inside of her as he swept her into his arms. It felt the same as flying. Weightless, exciting, effervescent rapture bubbled up inside of her until she was laughing with the sheer joy of her love for him.

Her hands combed his hair, shining whitely in the moonlight. As he kissed her, she gripped him fiercely, wanting to pull him so close that they would merge into one spirit. He smiled possessively as he carried her into the chateau and down the hall to their inner chamber. For a moment, she lost her smile. Things seemed strange to her, and she was almost afraid to look. But Simon kissed her as he set her gently on

446

their bed, and she remembered that they had no need to sleep in a coffin. The mattress was filled with soil and the silk sheets rustled comfortingly as he lay down beside her.

Their lovemaking was a passionate dream of soft, intimate touches and gentle, searching kisses. Everything was familiar, yet mysteriously strange. Each taste and smell aroused her to new heights of ecstasy and she wished that it would never end.

But it did, and as she melted in his arms, she smiled . . . and slowly opened her eyes.

Simon's fingertips withdrew from her forehead, and she swayed slightly, disoriented. His arms went around her to hold and support her. When he spoke again, it was like the echo of her dream. "You think you would be my slave, but you have owned my heart from the first time our eyes met." She filled her eyes with him as his dark velvet voice reverberated eerily in her mind.

"Now is the time, Cassandra. You must choose."

"Slave?" The beautiful dream was over. She lifted her head from his shoulder to gaze steadily at him. "You mean I'm not strong enough yet to come to you as your equal."

"No," he said simply.

"Is that what you want, Simon?" A single tear escaped and trickled slowly down her cheek.

There was a long silence.

"No." The sadness in his voice wrenched at her heart, but his gaze was clear and direct.

She waited silently, her love and faith in him shining in her eyes.

"I will wait for you, my beloved Cassandra. If you ever need me, I will be there. When your time is near, I will know. We will live and love for a thousand years."

His voice whispered in her mind as he kissed her.